Endorsements

I traveled back with Violet to a place of simpler times filled with love, faith, and triumph. I was unable to leave this place for only moments at a time. Reading this novel I found myself feeling as though I, too, lived in the little cabin with Granny, Sally, and this amazing girl/woman, Violet.

Based on a true story, this book changed my perspective on life, touched my soul, and deepened my faith.

Thank you, Sue Skeen, for an amazing novel. My only disappointment is in wanting more.

> Angela Timm, owner, Cottage Garden Collections;
> distributor, Sue Skeen Art-Poetry
> Bainbridge, Indiana

Since reading this book, A Violet of Faith, I have pondered on how Sue Skeen introduced the precious people, wove their lives together, and wrapped them in a package that seemed just right for each of them.

I experienced every emotion they felt as I read the novel and was so sorry when it ended. Sue, you have left me hanging, and I hope you will let me be first to read the sequel!

> Lois McCarty McGinnis, owner,
> Cedar Springs Christian Bookstore
> Knoxville, Tennessee

After reading the first nine pages, I called the author and told her I wanted to endorse this book!

Doris Morgan,
published artist, writer
Atlanta, Georgia

The inspirational writing of Sue Skeen set the pace for gift products sold all over the nation that effectively express words of love and gratitude for important relationships. Now Sue tells the story of one of the most important influences on her life in this poignant novel based on the life of her maternal grandmother—a woman of courage, conviction, and deep faith.

Janie Seltzer
licensing agent and author of
Spa Treatments for Your Body and Soul

A Violet of Faith

SUE SKEEN

A Violet of Faith

TATE PUBLISHING & Enterprises

Published by Tate Publishing & Enterprises, LLC
127 E. Trade Center Terrace | Mustang, Oklahoma 73064 USA
1.888.361.9473 | www.tatepublishing.com

Tate Publishing is committed to excellence in the publishing industry. The company reflects the philosophy established by the founders, based on Psalm 68:11,
"The Lord gave the word and great was the company of those who published it."

Book design copyright © 2008 by Tate Publishing, LLC. All rights reserved.
Cover & Interior design by Joey Garrett

Published in the United States of America

ISBN: 978-1-60604-686-9
1. Fiction / Religious
2. Fiction / Romance / Historical
08.12.02

Dedication

For Gary, my husband, biblical and historical advisor
Thanks for carrying the weight of all of us on your shoulders—
But mostly for being my best friend

Acknowledgments

I would like to thank Richard Tate as well as everyone at Tate Publishing for your time, consideration, and support of my work.

You inspire me not only with your beautiful statement of faith in Jesus Christ but with your boldness to confess His name before men. Philippians 1:3–6 is from me to you.

Table of Contents

Introduction

Dear Reader:

This book, *A Violet of Faith* is based on the first twenty years of my maternal grandmother's life, her fascinating love story, and the mysterious adventures she experienced and eventually shared, speaking in her distinct Appalachian dialect (which has all but disappeared today). A lot of her life story came from discussions between her and my mother as I played at their feet, hanging on to every word.

How I regret the innocence and insensitive attitude I had as a young child that kept me from asking her, as well as many others who came before me, the mountain of questions I now long to have answered.

Since Vy is now with her beloved heavenly Father, and not around for me to query, this is not a biography of her life. Because it is impossible to know each and every thing that took place a century and a half ago, there is a bit of fiction woven in here and there, and I have made a few name changes as well. However, the story is accurate in the big picture.

Vy lived an exciting but hard life in 1800s Appalachia—so different from our world today. Her lighting was provided by the sun or a kerosene lamp. She was warmed by wood from a tree that had to be cut down, chopped up, split, carried inside, and then burned in a fireplace. Her food had to be planted, tended, and raised by hand in one's own plowed-up plot of land, ultimately harvested, prepared, then cooked over an open fireplace, or if one could afford it, a wood cook stove.

Harvesting and preserving foods consisted of many grueling hours of picking, peeling, scalding, canning, curing, smoking, or "putting-up"(as Vy called it) meats, vegetables, and fruits for sustenance throughout the cold winters.

Milk, butter, and cheese were derived from the family cow, which had to be milked every morning and fed and tended as well.

Perishable foods were stored and kept in what was called a "spring house" (a little dwelling built over the cold spring waters) where you could keep them chilled and safe from hungry wild animals.

Fresh water came from a well, and it had to be pumped, drawn, and carried to the house, and heated on the stove if you desired it to be hot.

There was no indoor plumbing, and Violet's bathroom was an outhouse, a little dwelling out back that could sometimes be a cold and dreaded place to visit.

Violet's mode of transportation was on the back of a horse or mule (which had to be fed, watered, and tended as well), and a family was considered rich if they owned a coach or buggy for the animal to pull. Most families only owned a wagon to haul supplies such as flour, sugar, meal, or other staples from the local mill or mercantile. Bartering, or the practice or system of exchanging goods and services for other goods or services, was commonly practiced, thereby relieving citizens of having to deal with limited cash. Clothing and household linens were bolts of cloth either woven by hand or bought from the mercantile and sewed into needed garments at home. These garments were cleaned by beating them on rocks down in a cold spring or river, using homemade soap made from animal fat and lye.

If one grew up in Maynard's Valley during the 1800s, one enjoyed no electricity, indoor plumbing, cars, airplanes, radios, TVs, or telephones, and your rural doctor, if indeed there was one, was rare and miles away.

Although Vy grew up in that world where today's populace would have a tough time adapting, it was not these hard times that made her life difficult. It was those personal tragedies and events she was forced to face as a young girl, as well as others throughout her lifetime that could have turned her into a bitter and angry soul.

Instead, Violet found a faith in God that allowed her to overcome personal difficulty and molded her into the beautiful lady who spent her life walking hand in hand with Jesus.

I can truthfully say that I never saw her act in an unforgiving way or heard her speak a word of despair or anger to anyone. My memories of her consist of her open arms to me, her warm smile, her sense of humor, her positive words of encouragement, and her love for the Lord and His Word, which she almost constantly read.

In my attempt to introduce you to my precious grandmother and mentor, and one who motivated my Christian walk greatly, I pray that her love for God and His Word, as well as her unfaltering faith in Him, comes through in this book, not only to entertain and inspire you, but to give glory to our Lord Jesus Christ, which is exactly what she would have wanted.

Sue Skeen

The White Horse

"Git y'self over here to me, Violet Louise Vittoye, in'steada'wanderin'off in this here darkness. They ain't no tellin' what's on yon side of that barn there!" Sally Vittoye spoke sharply in an Appalachian dialect (a derivative from Scotch-Irish, Welsh, and German immigrants) to her six-year-old daughter and called the little girl by her full name like she always did when she was harried. She clutched her limp and whimpering two-year-old even tighter with her left hand as she hoisted him a bit higher on her hip. With her right hand, Sally pushed and turned the creaky well handle with all the strength her slight ninety-eight pound body could muster and drew the old wooden pail of cold water up from the deep well.

In the last rays of twilight, Vy peered through an unredeemable tangle of auburn curls, straining to see her mama, and reluctantly let one little frog go that struggled to slide out of her chubby hands, then reached in her coat pocket to free the other.

Most times, long before dark, the water pail had been filled, drawn, and carried up the hill, sitting on the bread board beside the big black wood stove where meals were prepared and heat was provided for Sally, Vy, Baby, and Granny Vittoye. The long walk down and up the hill was crucial that night, for Baby was sick. Baby had been crouping badly for the past two days. Sally had administered the usual drop of turpentine on brown sugar to her son, rubbed his chest with Granny's strong homemade menthol salve prior to swaddling him with outing flannel blankets in an effort to loosen his congestion. Baby's condition had only worsened, and tonight more cold water was needed to bathe the little one's burning fever down.

"Y'd best leave that youngin here and not trek him down that hill with you'uns!" Granny shrieked. "Else he'll be a whole lot sicker come morning.'" Gran, with hands on hips, stood yelling beside her bed, clad in nightcap, nightgown, and bare feet as her daughter started out the cabin door, hipping Baby.

"I know what I'm a doin,' Ma," retorted Sally. "The night air helps a youngin's croup." Sally defiantly tossed the long mane of chestnut hair out of her face, grabbed the black wool cape hanging on the peg, threw it over her shoulders, slammed the cabin door, and started the traipse down the hill, with Vy trailing in her footsteps.

There was no man on the place, and there had not been any for the past six years since William Vittoye passed on. It appeared Will had not a fault; nary a soul could find one unless you'd count taking a little homemade whisky now and then—and of course for medicinal purposes only. For over twenty-five years, that dear man took good care of his wife and daughter. No, siree, n'er a woman would be carryin' water if Will Vittoye were alive, for he saw to all the hard chores. Although he never complained about a thing, it could very well have been pure labor that killed the old soul, if the truth be known. Paw, as his family called him, avowed that "hard work never hurt a body," and he lived it. The old soul had known nothing except grueling times since he was knee high to a grasshopper, and as Rebecca, his wife of forty years, would say, "That blessed man didn't stop a workin' till he lay right down in this here bed and died." On this particular night, there was no Paw to help Sally, and there was no neighbor either.

As a usual thing when children were sick, folks would call Maudie Ellis. Maudie and Clyve Ellis, their sons, Calvin, Amos, Arly, and daughter, Sadie, were the Vittoyes' neighbors. The Ellis clan had lived over the hill in the next farm for years. They were good people who would readily drop anything to come help a friend in need.

Maudie had a heart big as gold, and she had that special gift of healing to boot. Adept in using the Appalachian mountain remedies that had been handed down for generations, she used the cherry and slippery elm bark to make her miracle cough syrup. She could splint up a youngin's or old one's broken limb to heal back good as new, and folks came from miles around to purchase her black drawing salve.

Maudie planted and cultivated a host of plants and herbs to use as ingredients in her preparations for the treating of various and sundry ailments. She was knowledgeable in a world of folk cures and believed God had bestowed upon her this strange and mysterious ability. For that reason, she was tireless when it came to her doctoring.

The Ellises had watched Sally Vittoye grow up, running in and out of their old farm house with Calvin, the oldest of their sons, and had grown to love the girl as one of the family. They'd come to love Sally's children, too.

Maudie and Clyve had been especially attentive to the Vittoyes since Paw had passed, helping the lone trio of women to tend their farm.

Sally had not contacted her neighbor with this crisis, for she had learned that Maudie's youngest boy, Arly, had been near critical for a week or more with the dreaded influenza that had spread itself all around Maynard's Valley. She had been sure her neighbor was worn out from taking care of her own boy, as well as other sick families in the valley, and was probably well in the bed by now. Sally decided she would try to make it through the night with the little one on her own and only call Maudie in the morning if he was no better.

Squinting her eyes in the thickening darkness for a glimpse of her mama's figure, Vy answered, "I'm right here, Mama. I'm a comin,' Mama!" As the last rays of daylight sunk deep into the indigo sky, Vy ran up and almost knocked Sally off balance as she bounded round her mama's long skirts.

Years later Violet would say she could not remember any other sound that night. Only Sally's godforsaken scream that seemed to originate from the pits of hell as it split the darkness of Maynard's Valley and echoed inside her own six-year-old ears.

As the thundering white horse's hooves cut deep into the mournful sounds of her mama's heartbroken wail and faded far into the distance, something told Vy that she would never see her baby brother again.

Lanky and tall eleven-year-old Theo Taylor choked back tears, swung his knickered legs, and kicked the ground with his dusty toes as he perched there in the darkness atop that rough cemetery headstone outside the old Ailor Springs Church. I'd rather take a beating from Pa as to go back in that church house tonight where preacher Edmonds don't have the good sense to know how or when to end a prayer meetin,' he thought.

Theo was yearning to be frog gigging down at the pond with Sam Watson or Will Graves and pondered for the hundredth time why in the world anybody had to go to church on a Wednesday night.

"Call it prayer meetin,' do they?" he muttered to himself. "Can't people just stay home and pray—seems like it's a whole lot more preachin' than prayin—and why did Pa get so annoyed tonight? I only talked to Bertha McVaye for a minute."

Theo could still hear his pa's admonition and feel the humiliation of Pa's stinging hand on his backside.

"Ye'll sit right out here, boy, till ye cn' learn how t' act in church! How many times you gonna embarrass your ma and pa 'fore you learn th' manners that we've tried to teach you?"

Asbury Taylor, or "Pa" as his children called him, did not allow that God's house was any place for Theo's, or anyone else's, talking or foolishness. He had always been quick to discipline any one of his four children when it was called for, although he did love them all dearly. Theo's disrespect and non-attentive attitude had landed him outside the church house again and again with many a stern warning or strong swat on his backside from Asbury Taylor, Theo's dad and Ailor Springs Church's head deacon.

Theo was a manipulative and stubborn child but in spite of it was charming and had a strong appeal to other young people. Unusually handsome with tanned skin, ebony hair, and steel gray eyes, friends surrounded Theo by the droves. Young girls were especially taken with his wit, and boys tried to imitate his every move.

The only thing was Theo could not stay free of trouble. It was as though he was drawn to it from birth. He also seemed to pull those who were near him into trouble as well.

The scene down at the creek last fall when he was found swimming with another friend proved especially distressing to the Taylor family. All the boys in the county were used to swimming naked, or "jaybird" as it was called, but not with the opposite sex. Most dismissed the incident as "normal, simple childhood curiosity," but Asbury and Delia Taylor believed that the whole incident was in fact Theo's doing, which had eventually caused the young girl and her parents such embarrassment that they had long since sold their place, leaving Maynard's Valley.

It had crossed Asbury and his wife Delia's mind from Theo's early childhood that this boy, their middle son, might possibly be their nemesis.

Although sitting in the cemetery was absolutely nothing new for Theo, he did admit to himself that the darkness made it somewhat unnerving. As he looked around and meditated on just how weird and spooky it was there in the old graveyard, suddenly from over the mountain there came a hysterical wail. The boy comforted himself.

"Aw, that's probably just a coyote or an old catawampus..."

Theo hopped down off the old tombstone and ran back toward the church door as fast as his skinny legs would carry him.

Secrets and Sunsets

The day was warm as Vy gathered up her petticoats, ran down toward the well, and then decided to take a sharp right and head on over the hill. The honeysuckle and magnolia blossoms made her feel delightfully exhilarated and somewhat heady. It almost took the edge off having to look for Granny Vittoye, who had disappeared this morning after breakfast as Vy and Sally cleared the table, making ready to hoe weeds from the garden.

In the last few months, Granny had begun to take spells of wandering all over the valley. Last time she was gone for a whole day and overnight before neighbors found her all the way down by Miller's Creek bleeding, half naked, and murmuring unknown sounds.

"It's just old age seizures that's a getting' her. I think she will be fine in a few days." Maudie Ellis gave Sally her diagnosis as she poured a thick yellow tonic down Granny, and it was true that Gran did seem to be much better in a few weeks. Only thing was that after they got Granny back home that first time, it took Sally and Vy weeks applying the liniment and black drawing salve just to heal up the cuts and bruises on her legs and arms.

Good grief, where do I start a lookin'? Vy pondered. Please just let me find Granny soon and let her be okay and not be hurt or gone crazy in the head or anything this time.

As Vy reached the bottom of the hill and rounded the creek's path, sure enough, there was Granny squatting down at the bank, gathering armfuls of daisies and Queen Ann's Lace from the tall spring growth.

"Granny, come on here to me and drop them old weeds. They's chiggers and poison ivy both in them wild flowers, and you'll be an awful itchy sight by mornin.'" Granny lowered her head and kept right on adding to the lacy bouquet that was forming in her arms. "Girl, you hold yer horses now, fer I'm a pickin' some of these here flowers fer my blue vase, and I ain't through yet. Come over here n' help yore ole Granny git a big bunch of these here violets.

"You know that's where yore name come from, Vy—t'was one of these here purple violets. I seen them purty thangs rite here on th' creek bank, n' I told Sally that she orta name that baby she's a carryin' Violet. Violet Louise, I told her. Ya know, she listened to me that one time in her life. Probably was th' only time she ever did. Back then she was so wild n' crazy a runnin' after that old—oh, shoot, never mind about all that ancient history anyways. Help git yore Gran up from here, and aid me in carryin' these purty flowers back t' th' cabin, honey."

Vy held out her hand, grabbed Gran's, and slowly but surely pulled the tiny and fragile old woman to her feet while supporting her arm.

"Okay, Granny, come on now, and thank goodness y' ain't hurt like you was th' last time. I declare I don't know why you want to run off and scare me and Mama half to death like this. Don't y' know you could stumble, fall, and break y' neck on these rocks down here?" The words came out with a bit more agitation in them than Vy had meant them to have, and Gran's eyes met Vy's with a hurt look.

"Just hold on there, now. I ain't crazy, darlin.' I might be old and forgetful, but there is some things I just have t' do ever now an' agin by myself, ye know? Summer's here, n' I needed t' git out a that ole dreary cabin. I wanted to come down here to this old spring branch like I did years ago and gather some of these wildflowers to take inside the house while they's a bloomin' good. Why, when you was real little, h'it pleased you no end t' come with yore Gran n' gather these purty bouquets, don't'cha remember that, hon?

"Look here, Vy, I found some cresses yonder for a salad tonight, an they're good fresh uns!"

"I'm sorry, dear—of course they are, and I do remember gatherin' bouquets with y,' Gran. And it's okay if y' needed to gather some of these purty flowers. They really are nice, and to be sure I know how Mama loves the watercresses…"

And thanks be to glory y' ain't hurt this time and I found y' as quick as I did…

After leading Granny back to the cabin and settling her inside to washing the watercress, Vy rinsed out the blue and pink crystal vases with a dipper of water and dried them to a fine shine with a soft rag. With Granny all settled in tending first to the salad greens and then plans to arrange her bouquets of flowers, Vy could go ahead with her own plan to gather the mushrooms Mama said she had a craving for today. Matter of fact, Vy jumped at the chance to go roaming about in the fragrant woods looking for mushrooms. It gave her a chance to steal some precious moments alone, simply dreaming or skimming the creek stones. Filling her mushroom basket to the brim then dangling her bare feet in the cold spring water surely did beat hoeing garden weeds in the hot summer sun.

Vy studied her mama's face hoping she appeared to be in a good mood. "Mama, y' okay workin' the garden by y'self this morning? Y' sure y' don't need my help?"

Sally didn't even look up. "I'm fine, Vy. Go on about your gatherin.'"

Vy was so delighted she skipped all the way over the hill and down into the hollow without a pause. Then she started to fill her basket with the special edible field mushrooms that were plentiful in the dark damp woods. When the little basket was full to the brim with the plump umbrella-shaped goodies, she kicked off her sandals, put her basket down, and stepped into the cool creek where she would play and dream until supper time.

After supper was finished, the dishes washed, rinsed, and stacked, Vy and Gran drug their woven straight-back chairs outside so they could enjoy the cool of the day under the big oak and maple trees that shaded their little cabin. Many nights, the three Vittoye females would just sit out after dark staring up at the glorious expanse of sky beyond Maynard's Valley's mountains. The trio chatted, relaxed, and watched the crimson sky in awe each time the hills swallowed up the golden ball as daylight faded into darkness. "Look at that sunset, Granny—ain't it purty, Mama?" Gazing into the clear night sky was one of Vy's favorite things to do. As the stars made their appearance, she would grow more and more enchanted and enthralled with the wonder of the universe. Her mind was so full of questions.

Hello moon—hello first stars—where did y'all come from? Did y' come from God?

If y' are there in the stars, God, why don't you show y' self—or say something t' me?

Do you live up there? Is that heaven? Gran used to go to church—did my mama go too?

There are a lot of things Mama n' Gran won't tell me about—like that big silver box I found of Granny's today—th' one with the pretty things inside it. Why did Mama get so mad when I opened it? She said it was hers—not for me. I don't even know what's in that box—why couldn't I see? I thought it was Granny's, not Mama's.

Why won't Mama tell me about my daddy? Everybody has a daddy. Why is Mama so sick or somethin' all the time? And why is Granny so upset with Mama all the time? Hey there, you stars, do you have any answers—for me?

In the twilight the rider startled Vy, Gran, and Sally as he rode up on his horse and dismounted.

"Howdy do, Mrs. Vittoye, Sally, and Violet." The tall figure bent over slightly and tipped his hat. "How y'all a doin' this evenin'? Jest thought I'd ride by here and offer y' some o' this here meat if y' can use it. They ain't no charge fer it nor nothin.' I butchered a big old sow last fall at hog killin' time and ended up a having a right smart more smoked meat than my family will be able to eat. My wife's been sick; she can't cook none, nor she shore don't eat much neither. Since you ladies don't have no man on the place now t' take care of th' butcherin' and smokin,' I thought you might enjoy this here cured ham—it's a good 'un."

It wasn't the first time this man had considered her family when he had something extra to share. Many was the time he had come bearing a fine cured ham, some salt pork, and nice gifts, and it seemed peculiar to Vy since he was only a passing acquaintance.

She forced herself to stand up and welcome the neighbor with

Mama and Granny. She recognized him as a Mr. Seth Seaton, had seen him around town at times, and it always struck her somehow that he looked a little sad.

Granny offered her gaunt little hand to the man in appreciation but cocked her head to one side, answering in a defensive tone, "Thank ya, Mr. Seaton, we'uns do appreciate your kindness a thinking of a widow woman and her youngins, aye, but we do right well a takin' care of ourselves a workin' our own garden, put up our own food n all. Y' know, we three barter linens that we sew t' buy our firewood 'n have our own animal's fer milk and transportation.

"I might add, sir, I think we three females have done right well since my husband up and died over twelve year ago."

"No offense a'tall to y,' Mrs. Vittoye. Like I said, we just got a lot more meat than we can eat, and they'll be more hogs t' kill come fall. If you'uns can use it, you'd do us a right smart favor by takin' this here ham."

Vy stared at the man but did not offer a word and mused, We ain't hardly any charity case yet, but a cured ham would sure be good eatin.' Mama might tell you to go away and leave us be—Mama might not accept this gift—"Mama!"

Vy looked around for Sally, but she had disappeared into the cabin. Where is she? This is kind of rude. Why, it isn't like Mama to be so unfriendly to a neighbor. He does seem like a nice neighbor, though we don't need no handouts.

In spite of her pride and mild antagonism, Vy smiled, exemplified her Granny, and held out her small hand to the man as well. Vy studied the man's weathered face and smiled up at his sad eyes. You're the man I overheard Mrs. Oliver and Miss Price talkin' about when Mama and me was pickin' up supplies at the Skene's Mill. They was talkin' about Seaton's Store—the store you own, and about your nice wife and little girl. They declared that your wife was lucky to catch a fine man like you—like Mr. Seth Seaton—for a husband.

As Gran calmed down and determined the man meant no offense, she offered him her thanks. "It's nice of ya to be a thinkin' of us, and yes, we will help ye out and take the ham off your hands, but only if you are sure it will help you'uns out. Wouldn't want to be a takin' one that you yourself or somebody more needy than us could use."

"Well, I'm shore glad you could use the ham, ladies, and I best be a getting on home now. I reckon it'll be dark in a bit. I do wish y' all a good night."

"Thank y' again, sir, and we do hope y' wife's health improves and that she feels a heap better real soon."

As the sun sank below a crimson cloud, Vy watched Mr. Seaton mount his horse, tip his hat one more time, and ride away while Gran accepted the gift ham and lugged the heavy cut of cured meat inside to hang on the cabin's rafter.

Night was coming down quickly in Maynard's Valley. A myriad of stars were beginning to sparkle high in the deep velvet sky.

Vy's mind wandered. Up among those stars would be a beautiful place for God to live—if indeed there really is one. It's so beautiful and so cool—wish I could sleep right out here. She followed her mama in the cabin, yawned, rubbed her eyes, and crawled in the bed beside Gran, who was already there and snoring.

She was almost asleep herself when she heard the cabin door open, shut softly, and a wagon drive away. Vy's heart sank.

I won't sleep a wink till Mama comes home.

As they gathered vegetables from the garden next morning, Vy began to get excited thinking about the fancy meal they would sit down to that night. "How long has it been since we have had some good country ham, Mama? Tonight I'll fix red eye gravy with leftover coffee like Granny showed me how, and you can fix your mouth watering biscuits. I'll make some tea cakes too if you'd like." Vy watched closely for a reaction from her Mama but Sally kept hoeing the weeds stone faced.

"T'was awfully nice of that Mr. Seaton t' share a big country ham like that with us wasn't it Mama?"

"We don't need any handouts Violet. You remember that young lady—we don't need any handouts!"

"I know we don't, but we will have a—a fine supper tonight, won't we, Mama—kinda' like a party?

Vy dared to hope that a good supper might just get her mother to talking and laughing a little with she and Granny—just like she remembered the three of them doing before Baby had been taken. The festive occasion might possibly keep Sally home tonight. She reminded herself that it was a good thing she had learned to cook before her Mama got sick and Granny had started going crazy. If she hadn't they might never have a fine feast such as the one tonight. Why, maybe after such a fine feast, Mama might even play her mandolin and sing.

It had been six years since the fateful night of Baby's kidnapping, and tending the garden sometimes seemed like the only thing twelve-year-old Vy and her mother had in common. Working side by side in that rich soil was about the only time Sally would converse with her daughter or anyone else for that matter.

After that horrendous night five years ago, Sally had taken to her bed crying day and night for her lost baby. She lost weight, so she looked like a skeleton in such distress that everyone who saw her expected she would die; everyone except Granny and Vy, who tended her daily, forcing her to drink soups and strong broth, simply willing her to stay alive.

Some still small nagging deep inside her made Vy wonder if Sally might know something about the fatal kidnapping of Baby than she let on but could get no answers from her.

The county sheriff had got no more from Sally either. Old Sheriff Butcher put his arm on Sally's shoulders and chided her in a grandfatherly way, "Sally, now you've a gonna have to come clean with me and tell me who you think it was that snatched that baby from y' if y' have any idea about it, do y' hear me? If I ain't got a clue to go on, such as what th' horse looked like, what th' rider looked like, smelled like, or felt like, y' baby is probably just gone forever, and y' can put that down in yer book. I must have a lot more information than what ye have a given' me if I'm to help find y' youngin." Tears welled up in Sally's eyes, and she swore once again that she didn't know who it was or why they had taken Baby.

Vy did get up nerve enough to ask her mama plain out if the kidnapper was somebody she knew, but Sally just hushed her up. Many were the nights that Sally would take to her bed, crying herself to sleep. Even under the loft and over Granny's snoring, Vy could still hear those mournful sobs. Tossing this way and that she would flip over and over in misery until her mama's weeping stopped.

Then there was that mystery looming in Vy's mind concerning the "stranger" that Mama left with at night. It became a quest for her to find out the identity of the loathsome stranger who drove by and took her mother off somewhere and why it was so secretive. However, as long as Sally made it safely home, Vy didn't even mind the musky scent of something that permeated the whole cabin when she would finally stumble in. She could only relax as long as her mother was safe inside the cabin with her and Gran, although her mind was filled with questions.

I will find out someday who the person is who causes Gran and me such worry and torture—and I will stop him.

Vy's soul was weighed down with issues concerning her mama. She couldn't for the life of her imagine how the answers she sought could be so bad that it would send her mother into a bad state of depression, or worse yet a fit of anger. All she wanted to know was what her mama did at night and who her daddy was. The truth was what she needed. Was that so much to ask for, she reasoned—the simple truth?

Vy pled with Granny time and again, "Why won't Mama tell me who my daddy is?—and who she takes off with, and what does she do so late at night? Do you know who comes by and picks her up in that wagon?"

Gran would answer her the same way every time. "Even if I should know, Vy, it ain't for me to say, and I rather think you would do well t' let it all go. Sally ain't listened to me once in her life, and she ain't goin' t' listen to you either. I learned a long time ago my daughter's got a stubborn streak in her and is bound t' do whatever she wants. What's more, all th' cryin and naggin' you do ain't gonna change her. That there would take a much higher power than you or me, child!"

"I will tell y' this, though. Y' mama is really sick in some ways and has been for a long time. I do know Sally loves you, Violet, even though she don't show it much. Y think y' could try to remember that?"

Violet refused to accept Granny's reasoning. She had felt brave that day. Sassy, insolent almost, pushing harder and harder, pressing her mother for answers. Vy thought that her mama would break down and give her some answers if she could just make her understand how these questions tortured her brain. Little did she know that Sally would break down, all right—have a fit and go berserk was more like it.

"If my daddy really is dead, Mama, then where's he buried? You should tell me about my daddy, Mama. I have a right to know!"

Sally's eyes narrowed. Her cheeks and neck turned red as she swirled round to face her daughter then raised her hand to strike. Screaming hysterically Sally cried, "Y' daddy's dead, Vy! And y'll not speak of the subject again t' me—do y' hear?"

Violet was horrified at the dreadful look on Sally's face and ducked quickly, heading toward the door, feeling the rush of air as her mother's hand missed her face by inches. As she scrambled outside and climbed high in the oak tree, she realized that this time she had probably gone too far.

Sally's voice took on a high-pitched shriek as she bellowed through the screen door after her, "Ye insolent girl! Y' have a right to know nothing! Y' have a right to know what I decide, missy! Y' will shut y'r mouth driving me crazy with th' insane questions and leave well enough alone! Leave me alone! Do y' hear what I say, girl? Do ye?"

Vy stayed settled into her hiding place after her mother lost it that morning. She climbed up and cowered in that big old oak tree for some time. She could hear Granny talking to Sally in a low, controlled voice. Gran was, of course, trying to calm her daughter's temper just like she always did when Sally flew into one of her fits.

In the days following that episode, tension filled the cabin, making it very uncomfortable between mother and daughter. Sally's sharp tongue never ceased to wound Vy in their every conversation for what seemed like many days after the incident, and Vy blamed herself for every conflict.

Gran continued trying her best to ease the tension between Violet and Sally with genuine love and concern for both of them, and it was usually her wonderful sense of humor, a funny story or bright wisecrack, that would eventually cause the trio to abandon anger and break out in hilarity.

Sally's smile was welcome to Granny, but it was so much more than that to twelve-year-old Violet. The sound of her mama's simple laughter was a magical resonance that dissolved Vy's anxiety. That delightful sound literally filled a little girl's soul with joy and happiness.

Everything is good now—Mama ain't mad at me no more.

Existence and Endurance

Mountain people cherished the summer mornings. Maynard's Valley was deep in the heart of the beautiful southern Appalachian chain that reveled in abundant flora and majestic hardwood trees. Flowering bushes such as forsythia and baby's breath covered the hills with the dawning of spring. Day lilies, jonquils, wygelia, wild roses, and honeysuckle burst with bloom in May and June, filling both the mountains and valleys with spectacular beauty and fragrance. Apple and cherry blossoms, dogwood, laurel, and magnolia blooms permeated the sweet mountain air with perfume. Deep rivers and mountain creeks had provided the Cherokee Indians, who resided there long before the white settlers came, with abundant fresh fish and game. A long growing season as well as rich soil, warm, sunny days, and good rainfall deposits added to the fall bounty, which farmers in the Maynard's Valley area harvested.

The valley ladies knew how to cure meat with salt, sugar, and smoke and put up fruits and vegetables in glass jars by the hundreds. This allowed the country families to have a good supply of meats, vegetables, and fruits on hand to last through the mountain winters, which could be harsh and long. Many people still used the old time bartering system, thereby exchanging goods and services for other supplies instead of using cash. For example, cattle or chickens could be bartered for such supplies as milk, meats, eggs, butter, flour, cornmeal, and even piece goods.

Some people are born with a penchant or green thumb for growing things, and that was one of Violet Vittoye's gifts.

Granny and Sally had included Vy in the gardening, putting up, and daily cooking of food since she was a mere tot. It was necessary for mountain women to pass these gifts down to their daughters and granddaughters for survival.

Vy could ride and care for a horse and milk the old cow, too, but actually it was Gran who got up before daybreak every morning to do it.

Vy had washed and brushed Sable, the horse, till she shone. Feeling a little smug, she cocked her head and with a mischievous grin looked at Granny.

"I can take care of my horse n' the cow, too. Mama showed me how. Bet I can get more milk n' you can from Bessie 'cause she likes the way I milk her."

"Well, Vy, y' just git on up at th' crack o dawn to gather that milk Bessie gives us, an I won't be a arguing' who gits th' most in the pail. Yore a whole lot more able to do it than I am, y' know."

Goodness knows I ought to be a doin that for you, Gran—but why ain't you a sayin' that Sally your own daughter orta be a helping with milkin,' too? Truth be known it's cause you know she ain't never gonna do it, and that ain't gonna happen long as Mama stays out all night.

Gran and Sally were both skilled dressmakers, earning the occasional dollar by sewing for ladies in town, and they had not failed to pass their dressmaking abilities on to Vy as well. The young girl did love to sew and had a natural flare for it. Gifted as she was by the age of eight, Vy had begun to make her own clothes and could quilt and make many other household linens. She excelled in dress pattern design and was talented in the tatting of lace. She often, without the aid of Gran or Mama, fashioned the delicate trims to decorate the gowns that Sally tailored for the ladies of the town.

Jessie May Mynatt's eyes widened, for she couldn't hide her delight.

"Oh, Sally Vittoye, I do declare, you will make my Mary the belle of

Whitesville society with this pretty frock. I had no idea it would turn out so lovely, or that you were so capable of fancy quality. Why, this is even nicer than the ones we ordered from the catalogue last spring. Look how it fits her perfectly. Of course, she does have the ideal little figure now, doesn't she? Turn around, darlin,' and let us see the back of the dress, Mary."

Thirteen-year-old Mary shifted awkwardly, scratched at the lace on the high neck of the garment, and turned around. Her eyes met Vy's, quickly flashed to her mother, then dropped to the floor.

Mary's long black hair, dark deep-set fringed eyes, pink cheeks, and rosy lips fascinated Vy. As she sat quietly, sizing up the two women she reasoned she had never seen a girl as beautiful as Mary and was quite pleased to think a dress she had fashioned would be worn by such a lovely person. It was apparent to Vy, however, that Mary was terribly uncomfortable since she had not uttered one word since entering the cabin.

Jessie Mae gushed, "You can be sure to get more of my business, and I am going to let all my friends know about your superb dressmaking ability. They will every one be a coming over here to get their sewing' done."

"Thank y' fer th' kind words, Mrs. Mynatt. That one does look purty on Mary there. She's about my Vy's age, ain't she? Vy's twelve years now, and she tatted and sewed in all those rows of lace on the front there without any help from Gran or me, y' know?"

Jessie Mae glanced at Violet but did not reply.

"Well, come along, Mary dear. Here's some money, Sally. I'm sure it's enough." The woman shoved a quarter into Sally's hand and started toward the door. "We must be getting on home now. And Sally, I have some beautiful green silk I would like a dress for myself made of, and I will bring it here later. You do have my measurements, of course, and since I must have it right away, you will need to get to it quickly. Do you hear?"

Sally nodded in agreement, and Gran just stared in complete disdain at the woman.

Jessie May Mynatt grabbed Mary's hands and nervously rushed her daughter out of the cabin and into the carriage, snapped the horse's reins, and started flying back down the winding dirt road toward town.

Jessie Mae clicked her tongue, shook her head, then addressed her daughter sternly.

"Now listen to me, Mary Mynatt! If you ever tell anyone that we have come over here to those trashy Vittoye women's house, you will have me to answer to. Child! Are you listening? Do you understand me? And never ever tell anyone where we get our dresses. Do you hear me? If you run into any of those women in town, you just turn your head, pretend you don't know them, and keep right on going. I would die if any of our friends knew that we had anything to do with them. Birds of a feather flock together, and that's a known fact."

Jessie May continued to preach and clicked her tongue again.

"Tsk, tsk! It's shameful what those Vittoye women are." Her voice took on a low whisper. "Mmmm... I could tell you a lot about them, but your ears are simply too young. Do you hear what I am saying, Mary?"

Mary wondered what could be so shameful about those three women who could sew up such a beautiful garment as her dress. They seemed like perfectly nice people to her, but she had learned a long time ago to do as her mother asked, even when she questioned her demands. Mary listened quietly to her mother rail about keeping their little shopping trip a secret all the way home in their bumpy old carriage, and she had endured quite enough.

Okay! Please! Enough! Be quiet, Mother. I wish you would just shut up before I scream. I hear you! I hear you, and my head hurts.

But she only answered, "Yes, Mother, I will remember."

Clyve Ellis was faithful to bring his mule team to turn the garden soil under in the fall long before spring planting time was thought about. The women gathered and saved their valuable seeds from year to year, drying them in the top rafters of the barn. Sally was a stickler for perfection when it came to gardening. She sowed neat and straight rows of seeds in the food-bearing patch, and she expected the same from her daughter. Tending the vegetables was a special time for Vy and her mama, even though it was hard back-breaking work. There they were, side by side, mother and daughter, sweating, hoeing, and pulling weeds, trying hard to give every food-bearing plant the greatest chance possible to produce the best. Rows were planted tenderly with corn, cabbage, mustard, collard and turnip greens. There were red and yellow tomatoes and Irish as well as sweet potatoes. Okra was especially prized, and the cucumber, pumpkin, and watermelon vines had to be tended daily and kept at a good distance to keep them from running over everything else.

Vy had a little patch all her own for strawberries. She constantly battled with the birds over the juicy red fruit, taking scraps of straw and cloth to make scarecrows donning various and sundry outfits. Sometimes the scarecrows seemed useful in deterring hungry predators and other times did not.

Usually Sally was up before daybreak chopping the garden weeds with a vengeance. It sometimes seemed she expelled the futility of her sadness with her trusty hoe. When Gran said Sally was in one of her moods, Vy never ventured too close to her mother. She learned to garden on her side of the plot, weeding and coddling her own little food-bearing plants. At times she would crack a silly joke to her mother, hoping for a laugh or a comment, and if she got one would feel a major accomplishment.

When the noonday sun sapped the entire energy mother and daughter could muster, the ladies would retreat into the dark cabin for a rest then sew on linens or garments till dark fell. Hot "soup beans" and cornbread with buttermilk or mush with honey and milk were usually served up by Granny for their noon meal, and the leftovers sufficed for supper. This evening, however, there was a feast to be prepared. Sally had already stirred the flour into dough and started to cut out round biscuits for the oven.

"Vy, loose that ham from the rafter, cut off two fairly good slices, and get it going," she ordered. "Y're going to need that pot of leftover coffee as well—that is, if y' intend to make gravy. I think there is plenty enough t' make it with." Vy held out the two slices of ham for her mama's approval then plopped it in the hot iron skillet to fry.

She was stirring the red eye gravy when Gran wiped her hands and interrupted.

"I just brought in enough leafy greens for the killed lettuce salad and done chopped up the green onions, so I don't need any more. Careful, child, don't scald yoreself on that skillet of bacon I got fryin' thar t' top this salad. Now, where'd you'uns put my cider vinegar?"

Vy handed Gran the vinegar and, while the gravy was boiling, peeled and sliced two plump red tomatoes and arranged the slices in the little crystal dish that was used especially for chow chow and other relishes. Gran bent over the open oven door and took out a pan of hot fluffy biscuits.

"Th' biscuits are done, girlies. Let's eat!"

Vy scanned the feast, inhaling the aroma of creamed potatoes and crispy browned fried okra. The platter of ham looked luscious and tender beside the bowl of redeye gravy. How good it all looked. Granny's savory killed lettuce salad made a body's mouth water and was sure to whet anyone's taste buds. Then there were hot buttered biscuits and honey for dessert, if you could manage to hold it. Suddenly Vy realized she was starved.

What a meal. Eating put-up foods in the winter is something to be glad about, but a supper fresh from the garden, like tonight's, is a celebration.

The three ladies sat down to the fine meal that was set on their best handmade, lace-trimmed tablecloth. The day had been lengthy and tiring, and for a while the three ate quietly, just savoring the moment.

Vy was the first to break the silence.

"Ain't this a fine meal, Mama?"

"Mmmm—it's very nice, Vy. You just finish up now and help me clear th' dishes, cause Gran's legs is a gonna give out on her."

Vy looked up and reached across the table. "Well, may I please finish, Mama? I'd like just a wee bit more of that gravy on another biscuit if it's okay with you."

Granny swallowed a mouth full and laughed. "More killed lettuce for me."

The two continued to eat until they were stuffed to the brim, but Sally left food on her plate mid-meal and ambled on outside. This made Vy uneasy until she heard the lilt of music drift in the cabin door.

> Ooo—Ye'll tak' th' high road, and I'll tak' the low road, an' I'll be
> in Scotland afore ye;
> But me and my true love—will never meet a'gin …
> On th' bonnie, bonnie banks 'o Lock Lomon'

Where little Violets do spring an' th' wee birdies sing and in sun-
shine th' waters are sleepin'
But th' broken heart it kens nae second spring again
Though resigned we may be while we're greetin'

"Glory be! Gran, leave them dishes. Let's go out and sing with
Mama."

Clouds and Violets

"Look, Mama, there's Mrs. Mynatt and her daughter."

Vy and Sally had just come out of the mercantile in town and were starting down the boardwalk on Maynard's Pike carrying piece goods, thread, and some other supplies that Gran had declared she needed when they spotted the lady and her daughter walking straight toward them. Vy raised her hand in greeting and stepped up her pace, eager to speak hello to the beautiful girl with the long black hair who was looking her way. Suddenly, Jessie May Mynatt jerked Mary by the arm as the two turned their heads to the other side of the road.

"That girl and her mama turned their heads away. They a doin' that a' purpose, ya reckon? I swear they were lookin' right at us, Mama. Maybe they just didn't see us. They're a crossin' to th' other side of th' road. Do you think they don't remember us makin' those dresses fer 'em?"

"Of course they remember. They just don't want anybody else t' know they mix with th' likes of us."

"Are y' sayin' they're avoidin' us on purpose? Why in the world would they do that? We made all those pretty dresses for them, didn't we? They said they liked our work. Why wouldn't they like us? Is it because we're poor—huh, is it? Yep, that's it, ain't it, Mama—they are crossin' over t' the other side so they won't have to speak t' us—because we're poor!"

"I said for you to hush now, child, and leave it be. Do you hear what I say, Vy?"

Vy pressed Granny for an answer later on.

"What's wrong with that Mrs. Mynatt, Granny? You know that she and her daughter, Mary, and that old Mrs. Hein, too, are just real friendly when they come to our cabin and want us to sew them a frock or two, but when they see us in town, I swear they turn their heads and cross the street to avoid speakin' or runnin' into us. It happened today— Mama saw it, too. Didn't y,' Mama? Ain't we made at least ten dresses or jackets total for those women, Granny?"

Gran's face began to turn red as she twisted and narrowed her eyes, looking straight at Vy.

"Let me tell you somethin,' girlie. Old women like that ain't worth y'r givin' it a minute's thought. Her own evil and more will come home to haunt old Jessie May Mynatt one o' these days. Y' just hold yore head up and fergit all 'bout such as her. What it amounts to is they just think they're better'n we'uns—t' tell the truth, they think they're better'n a whole lot of people in Maynard's Valley, but I assure y' they ain't!" Gran's jaw clenched. "There's a name fer people like Jessie Mae Mynatt, Vy, though I'm too much of a lady to say it. They cn do whatever they want or say anything t' me, but I can't take it when anybody insults ye or y' mama though. I just believe I might have t' go an put that lady in her place, I will."

Vy was not accustomed to seeing Gran get upset like that, and the purplish red color her face took on worried the girl. She put her arm around Gran's shoulders, trying to calm her down.

"Oh, Gran, y' just forget I gave it a minute's thought. Why, it don't really bother me none—and don't you worry about it no more either. Okay?"

What do I care about them old women anyway? she thought. We have plenty other friends. We're just fine. We have each other—yeah we do.

There's Granny, Mama, and me.

Violet took a deep breath as she walked outside, heading for the well and another pail of water. She passed the now dormant garden plot, meandered on across the yard and down by the pumpkin patch, where the fully ripened squash lay in all their orange-carroty glory. Stopping to inspect the perfect skin of an oversized pumpkin, she rose up, stretching her arms toward the sun as if to gather in the wonder of it all. It was harvest season in Appalachia, and joyful thoughts raced through her mind. What a beautiful morning, she thought. I love fall. October has to be my favorite month of the year. M—mm, well, maybe second to May.

The garden vegetables had been gathered in and put up. Clyve Ellis had already turned part of the soil under with his mule team.

There was a crisp feel to the afternoon with its slight breeze and a clear sky of deep azure that seemed to start nowhere and end forever. The red of the dogwood and sumac blended with the yellow of the poplar and the sienna of the oaks. The maples had to be the most magnificent sight, though, as they swayed to and fro, reflecting the glittering sunshine on their bright gold and wine-colored leaves. Evergreen pines and cedars completed the beautiful backdrop for this wonderful fall season. The beauty of it made a body just want to lie down on a soft mossy bed and drink in the beauty.

After fetching the water and depositing it on the breadboard for Gran, Vy scrambled down the cellar stairs to bring up some canned peaches because her mama mentioned she had a hankering for a cobbler.

Vy felt a burst of pride in Gran's, Mama's, and her own labor as she scanned the bounty that now lined the cellar shelves. There was one whole shelf of canned tomatoes for soups and sauces, and another one that held thirty-five quarts of blackberries ready for jam or pies. Big green cucumbers had been stuffed into the blue jars by Granny with brine and dill weed for pickles, and the smaller cucumbers Sally and Vy had sliced up for sweeter fare. The three women worked consistently every day, picking, cleaning, and snapping green beans, peeling peaches and pears, as well as coring, slicing, and preparing apples to be laid out on the roof. Dried apples were cherished to be used for savory fried pies and stack cakes.

Gran rinsed out a pan and dried it well. She washed her hands in lye soap and scrubbed them where the sticky okra had cut her flesh.

"Wish there was a way to preserve good ole okra fer fryin' in the winter, but it'll just have t' be canned for use in our soups and stews. I'll go ahead and fry up this last batch for supper tonight. I reckon it'll not be too tough. They was some that was purty hard t' cut though."

Vy glanced back at Granny as she went out the door. She longed to relax and feel the sun on her face once again, not ready to think about seeing to food right this minute.

"It's okay, Gran. Just let it be right now. I'll come back in a bit and help you with supper. I'll fry that okra up for y.'"

Vy walked out of the cabin, adjusted her straight back chair, and tilted it back against the big old oak tree. *Ohhh, that sun feels so good—and that wonderful fall breeze. I believe I could fall asleep right here.*

A familiar voice stirred Vy from her daydreams, and she jumped a little at the sudden sound of the horse and carriage.

"Hey there, Vy Vittoye. Brought you'uns a pack of some beef jerky we made up and another jar of this here drawing salve. How's yore mama and Gran a doin, honey? I hope they's well 'n all."

Vy turned around to see the two familiar faces of Maudie and Sadie Ellis smiling ear to ear.

"Me' n Sadie's a ridin' over t' Skene's fer meal and flour. Y' want t' come with us and save a trip over?"

Vy gathered her wits, stood up, and waved her hand in welcome. "Well howdy, neighbors. How's y'uns been? And thanks a heap. Mmmm, I love y'r jerky—and how'd y'all know we are out of that salve o' yours? Granny will shore be glad to get it.

"Can y' wait just a minute while I ask Mama if she wants me to ride over with y'? She was just sayin' yesterday she hoped we could get good bit of credit at Skene's fer th' quilt we just finished. We was aimin' t' take it over tomorrow and see how much they'd give us. We're in need of cornmeal and flour, too."

Vy ran in the door, yelling to her mama, and just as quickly reappeared with the handwork.

As Vy climbed in the carriage, Sally stuck her head out the door and waved.

"Howdy, Maudie, Sadie—glad y' are headed over t' th' mill, and thanks a heap fir thinkin' t' take Vy with y.' Y'are really savin' me a trip there n' back."

Truth was that, although they had always been real nice and friendly to her, Vy felt quite uneasy trading with the hands over at Skene's because they were all men. Since the older men were somewhat intimidating to the young girl, she felt more secure to go bartering in the company of the Ellis women, especially the deeply-respected Maudie Ellis, well-known folk doctor and midwife who had taken part in the healing or birthing process of almost everyone in Maynard's Valley. Maudie was and had been the Vittoyes' longtime friend, close as family almost, and Vy knew the woman would aid her in getting the highest price for her quilt—yes, as if she were her own daughter.

Vy adjusted her skirts as Maudie and Sadie oohed and ahhed over the beautiful wedding ring quilt that Vy spread out on her lap. Sadie's eyes widened, and she lifted a pretty hand to her mouth in wonder.

"Oh, Vy, you have to make a coverlet like this fer me someday. I will pay you fer it—it's the most pleasing one I have ever seen. Did you quilt it all by y'self?"

Vy shook her head from side to side and laughed out loud. "Goodness no, Sadie, it was all three of us a workin' hard as we could on that thing. Tell ya th' truth, I'm sick a lookin' at th' thing, but I'm glad yore eyes find it pleasin.' I just hope somebody over t' Skene's Mill thinks it's that purty, n' maybe they'll give us a good amount of credit fer it."

"Well, they certainly should! I declare, it's a work of art."

It was a long old road over to the Skene's Mill at Clayton's, and Vy was relieved and happy to have the Ellis ladies to ride over with. She was especially glad to see and talk to Sadie again. Sadie was barely three years older than Vy, and the girls had grown up and played together from the time they were very young.

"I haven't seen hide nor hair of you, Sadie. Why, ever time I come by y' house, you're off with that Campbell boy."

Sadie blushed. "You mean 'man,' don't you, Vy?"

Vy pondered seeing the two together in town and had thought to herself,

Winfield Campbell must be was at least fifteen years older than Sadie. And she was right.

The trip with Maudie and Sadie Ellis turned out to be a great time for girl talk and to catch up on the latest gossip of the valley. Maudie had a constant laugh in her voice, and since she traveled around doctoring the whole county, she was eager to share the news of everybody and everything that was going on.

"Guess y' hadn't heard that the Bakers have twin girls, have y,' Vy? Everybody's doing fine, too. I helped deliver those precious babies and, why, they must be about two weeks old today. Lord knows time passes so quickly. And, Vy ... did you know that Sadie, well, have y' heard—heard about Sadie and Winfield? Y' know Winfield Campbell, don't y,' Vy?"

Sadie lifted and held out her left hand, showing off a delicate white gold band on her finger. The tiny diamond gleamed and sparkled and rose from the delicate setting in the center as she twisted and turned her arm. She cocked her head, pursed her pretty red mouth, and declared, "Mama, Vy knows Winfield. She met him when we ran into her one day in town. Now let me tell Vy all about it, will y,' Mama? Y' tell everybody 'fore I can say a word—I declare!"

Vy sucked in her breath and whispered, "Ohhh, how beautiful, Sadie. I never saw a diamond before. That's what it is, ain't it, Sadie—a real diamond ring?"

Sadie giggled, nodded, and impulsively hugged Vy. "I want you to be in my weddin,' Vy."

"Oh my gosh, you're not a gettin' married! I can't believe it! To that Mr. Winfield Campbell! I heard his family is terribly well-off, Sadie—rich even! Where ... how ... did y' ... when? Oh, tell me all of it!"

Sadie put her hands over her mouth, stifling an excited giggle, and nodded her head affirmatively. "Well, I don't know if you could say they are rich, but most everybody knows that Win, uh, well, his father has done right well here in th' Valley. My Granny says I am awfully lucky to be a marryin' a boy like Winfield Campbell. And that brings me t' one of th' reasons why we come by for y' today, Vy.

"Y' are my good friend, and I want y' as a bridesmaid. Of course, Bertha will have to be my maid of honor cause she's my cousin n' all, but y' are going to be one of my two bridesmaids. The other one will be Ivy Taylor—that's Winfield's cousin. Do you know Ivy, Vy?"

Vy shook her head.

"Oh, y'll love her—she's a sweet thing—and, oh yes, th' other thing we needed to ask you was, will you and y' mama sew the dresses for my weddin'? Please. Please, Vy, can y' do it? Th' only other good dressmaker is my grandma, and she can't sew worth nothin' anymore 'cause her eyes are a goin'.

"Our weddin' is gonna be way over cross th' county at Ailor Springs Church where the Campbell family and Ivy Taylor are members. Matter of fact, my cousin, Bertha, is a member there, and since we will be living right there close to the Campbells after we are married, I'll join that church, too. Win says that we must live close by his family's farm in order for him to help his daddy manage the tenant laborers. Their farm is the largest in the county Vy, and Winfield's the only child the Campbell's have, you know."

The ride to the Skene Mill and back was a treasured visit with friends, and Vy savored all the gossip she had heard so she could repeat the valley news to Gran and Mama. By the time the Ellis ladies drove up to the Vittoye farm, it was getting very late in the day, and long shadows were forming over the front yard of the cabin. The women thanked Vy when she invited them to come inside, but they replied they'd better be headin' on home before the dark clouds that had just appeared started pouring rain. Vy thanked the Ellises one more time and pulled the big cloth bags she had brought home from the mill down off the wagon.

Even before Vy could haul the cornmeal and flour bags inside the cabin, the savory aroma of pinto beans wafted out the door to meet her. Mouth-watering cornbread sat on the breadboard, and a blackberry pie perched right beside it. A pitcher of sweet tea was waiting on the table, as well as a dish of tender scallions.

Vy sat down to supper between Gran and Mama and tried hard to repeat every single detail of the gossip she had gleaned that day from the Ellis women. She especially enjoyed elaborating about Sadie Ellis and Winfield Campbell's wedding plans.

Between big bites of soup beans and buttered cornbread she excitedly declared, "Guess what, Mama, Sadie and Maudie want us to make the wedding dresses! Ain't that wonderful, Mama?"

Sally looked away and put a stack of dishes on the shelf, speaking in a sharp tone.

"Don't seem so wonderful to me. Last time I sewed weddin' dresses, the lady fussed n' fumed about everything. I'd just as soon not go through that again."

Vy's spirits fell with Sally's pessimistic retort, and Granny quickly intervened. Her eyes glared with scorn at her daughter's discouraging words.

"Sally girl," Gran scolded, "you ort' be 'shamed o' yore self fer such a negative attitude t' y' daughter. In th' first place, we couldn't do enough for Maudie Ellis as good as her family is t' us, and besides that, it will be a fine prospect t' bring in a little extra money. We can always use the cash that much dressmakin' would bring in, and with all three of us a sewin' every day, we could get Sadie's dresses ready in no time. Tell y' th' truth, I think it's an opportunity t' be thankful for, Sally."

Trying to soothe Vy's feelings, Gran queried, "What about the weddin' gown fer Sadie, Vy? Did Maudie want us t' make it as well? Do they have the piece goods n' patterns yet?" Granny rose and walked over to Vy's chair, rubbed her shoulders, smiled, bent down, and hugged her tightly. "Y' bet y'r boots we'll do this, hon, and Sally, you don't hav t' even help us if y' don't want to. Me 'n Vy cn do it every bit, can't we, darlin'? Don't y' worry none about it, child, Granny will help ye."

With weariness in her voice, Gran rose from the table, looking straight at Sally and Vy. "Now y' girls try to git along tonight without too much fuss and wash these here dishes. I'm a goin' t' have to go lie down now." Gran wrinkled her brow and frowned. "I'm awful tired. The rheumatism in this here arm is actin' up, and I got an old headache fer some reason—must be th' rain movin' in."

With supper dishes washed and stacked, Vy worked on her laces in the light of the coal oil lamp while Sally took a book up in her loft bed to read. *Maybe Mama ain't goin anywhere tonight.*

The old clock struck eleven-thirty, and Violet began to get sleepy. At the first yawn, she decided to put away her handwork and turn in. Putting out the kerosene lamp, she crept softly down in the bed alongside Granny, who had been there for some time now.

W-what? Is that Gran talking in her sleep? What's she saying—is she praying?

"Y' ... help, Lord ... t'find ... r ... p ... aw ... atisfy r'm ... nd. Do'yer will ... 'n help ... Sally. Fr'giv ... us. ... me. . fer. ... evr thing ... take care ... help ... "

Vy turned over, rose up on her elbows, and peered closely at and spoke softly to her grandmother.

"I do wish I could make out what you are saying, Granny." But she simply covered her ears with the quilt so as not to hear the old one and drifted off to sleep.

The sun peeped through the little cabin window on the east side, played down through the oak tree, and landed across the patchwork quilt that covered Vy Vittoye. It seemed later than usual, and she thought it strange that Gran was still in bed since she was usually up every morning before daybreak and out milking the cow. Vy turned over and pulled back the quilt to reveal the still, small, unresponsive, and unmoving woman whose face was perfectly at peace.

"Gran? Granny, wake up! Granny? Granny!"

A cold sweat suddenly covered Vy as fear gripped her heart and soul.

"No…n…n…n…no! No! Oh, dear heavens! Mama! It's Granny, Mama! There's something wrong with Granny! Mama!"

Sally slammed the coffee pot down, sloshing the hot brew across one of her hands, and ran to the bed where Gran lay still. She climbed up on the bed and shook Gran's shoulders gently, then harder.

"Ma! What's wrong? Please, please, wake up, Ma!"

As her mama's face went ashen, Vy felt as though her own heart had stopped.

Sally turned to her daughter and spoke slowly and deliberately.

"Violet, ride quickly to the Ellises' house. Bring Maudie as fast as you can."

Vy saddled the horse and set to riding. She dodged trees and jumped logs and creeks without a thought, pushing the horse to its full limit as she silently pleaded and begged someone, somewhere, to spare Gran.

Please. Please don't let my Granny be dead. She just can't be dead. She will be all right. She must! Please. Please.

It was the fastest trip Vy had ever made to the Ellises.' Before the girl could even spit out all that was wrong, Maudie Ellis, without a pause, had mounted her horse and was on her way to the Vittoyes' cabin. Vy followed closely. She had never made it to the Ellis house and back in that record time, but it felt like the longest trip of all. Maudie, an expert rider as well, spared no time getting to the Vittoye home.

Stumbling as she dismounted, Vy ran into the cabin right behind her neighbor. The two of them stopped abruptly, however, at the grim sight of Sally sitting on the chair by the bed, slowly brushing out Granny's hair. Tears streamed down her face as she carefully plaited the long gray mane, winding it up into the familiar bun that Granny always wore. Vy had never seen her mother look so old—so tired and worn. Looking up slowly, Sally shook her head.

"It's too late, Maudie. My mama's gone."

Maudie gently moved Sally aside and began to examine the old woman. She felt for a pulse and laid her head to Gran's chest to see if there was any sign of a heartbeat. She tried motioning Vy out of the cabin, but Vy stubbornly refused. Maudie then proceeded to examine Gran's body thoroughly before speaking to Sally.

"If'n it's a comfort t' you and Violet, I don't believe the poor soul suffered any. Seems like t' me she's just gone on real peacefully in her sleep. It was probably another one of them old strokes, y' know, like she's had in the past, only this one was much worse. Tell y' the truth, I'm surprised she ain't had another one 'afore now, Sally. One thing's a blessing, though. Y'uns can be proud she went on th' way she always told me she aimed to. Y' know, Granny always told me she prayed to go in her sleep, 'n that's exactly what she did."

Vy and Sally stood motionless, numb—unsure of what to do next. Maudie understood and simply took charge. She reached into the bag that was always with her, extracted the chamomile, and set a pot to boiling. "This here tea will help to calm both of y,' for yore gonna to need y' strength until we can see this dear old one has a proper burial."

"Now Sally, I'm a gonna send one a my boys fer old Doc Haun to come and pronounce Mrs. Vittoye. Could do it myself, but y' know how th' men in town like to get a genuine doctor's report for th' courthouse records.

"You don't have to worry 'bout the service nor nothing, honey. I'll get Clyve and my boys, and, let's see … oh, yes, Jake McKenzie. They'll be proud to bear Gran's pall t' the wagon for the trip up the hill where you'll be a layin' her. Right thar beside William's grave—that's right, ain't it? I'll get Parson McKinley from my church to hold the services at the grave, Sally. He's a man of God and real nice—preaches good, too. Is that all right with you and Violet, honey? Would you uns want anything else? Singin' or somethin'?"

"No, er, yes—oh, I don't know… Singin' would be nice—but we don't have to have any—but thank y,' Maudie. What would we do without you. Thank y' so much."

Maudie put her arms about Sally as Sally's tears began to flow again.

Later on, all of the Ellis family, as well as Jake McKenzie's wife and kinfolk and even many people Vy did not know, came bearing food for Granny's wake. They loaded down the table in the cabin until it could bear no more and then filled up the breadboard as well.

Vy felt sick, as though she were going to faint. It is so hot in here. These people are all talking and laughing. Vy wanted to scream, to stop it all, to wake up.

Why are they doing this? My Gran is dead.

Why is everyone bringin' all this food in here? How in the name of heaven could anyone eat? There she lays—right in our bed where she told me goodnight and not to worry. Last thing she said was, "Vy, don't worry, don't worry."

How did all these people find out about my granny?

Vy did not yet understand that was just the way of good people in the valley.

Maudie washed and prepared Granny's body for the burial, and Sally wept aloud as the two women raised up her body to dress her. They chose Gran's favorite purple dress with pearl buttons and a lace inset at the neck that Vy herself had tatted.

At the point of her mother's loud sobs, Vy held her hands over both ears, dashed out of the house, and ran all the way down the hill to the creek. I have to get out—out of here. She felt frantic, out of control.

Weak and weary, she dropped down on a mossy stone, burying her head in her hands. Her throat ached, and her stomach churned as her eyes came to focus on a rag she was twisting in her hand. Where did this rag come from?

As a mockingbird started to sing above her head, Vy lifted her eyes and gazed toward Oak Mountain. Clyve Ellis and his boys are up there on the hill right about now, digging a six-foot-deep hole where I will have to leave my dearest friend. How can I leave Granny up there? How can I live without my Gran—the one who gave me so much.

Vy slumped to the ground, beating the dirt with her fists. Heart wrenching sobs blotted out all sounds of nature around her. In a guttural voice, she cried as a flood of tears burst forth. "Granny, oh, Granny, please come back to me. I want to be with you. Just let me die, too."

Exhausted and heartbroken, the little girl's swollen tear-dimmed eyes opened, coming to rest on a cluster of tiny flowers miraculously blooming out of season.

Violets! She named me…

It seemed as though she would come walking right through the door any minute with orders to start supper. Everywhere you looked inside the cabin and out, you could see her—hear her. The wicker seats she had just finished re-weaving in the straight-back chairs, her zinnia bed, the big yellow rose bush. Even the patch she had just finished sewing on Vy's cape that had gotten torn.

It was much quieter around the Vittoye cabin these days due to Vy and Sally simply attending their chores instinctively, each one living within their own thoughts.

"Mama, y' goin' out tonight?"

"No, Vy. I ain't a leavin' y' here by y'self tonight."

"Thank y,' Mama. I'm glad you ain't goin' nowhere."

Maybe Mama does care some about me. Not as much as Granny did—but she cares some. She hasn't been out as much with that stranger since Gran passed on.

Thank y,' Mama. I do not like to be here in this cabin alone. It ain't that I'm afraid. I just miss Gran too much when I am by myself. *Mama misses Gran, too.*

Maybe Mama won't go out at night no more, but she seems awfully sad. There's something wrong with my Mama.

Holy Days and Birthdays

Vy scratched her head with a thimbled finger and narrowed her eyes, trying to focus through the little window pane. Is there some white stuff mixed with that rain?

She shifted in her rocker and tried to see through the icy window again. Shivering, she pulled her woolen cape tighter around her shoulders as the wind made a howling sound, circled around the corner of the little cabin, wound it's way up the logs, caught the black smoke from the chimney, and lost it again in the darkened sky. A cold rain was drizzling from the sky and was threatening worse.

"Glory be, I'm glad we got plenty of firewood, ain't y,' Mama?"

"Well, I'm glad they's plenty outside, but it might be wise t' git some more in here fore it comes a bad snow storm. Y' want more soup 'fore I wash these dishes?"

"No, Mama, I ain't hungry. I was just thinkin' about the Holy Days a comin' up. Y' thought any about them, Mama?"

Sally ignored Vy and did not answer.

Today is December 21. Christmas is coming. How can we have Christmas without you, Granny? So many wonderful memories—and all of them with you.

For as long as Vy could remember, Gran had been there at Christmas, singing carols and baking oatmeal cookies and gingerbread men. There had never been much in the way of presents or such, but Gran, being partial to Christmas, never forgot to sew Vy a little button-eyed rag doll complete with yellow yarn hair, an outing flannel nightgown with slippers to match, and a bright colored scarf or new petticoat for Sally. Granny would carefully wrap the gifts in flour sack cloths and tie them up with red strings. The gifts were necessities, of course—except for the rag dolls—and then they were lovingly laid beneath a small cedar tree that the girls had decorated with popcorn strings, gingerbread men, and handmade braids of colored yarn. Early on Christmas Eve night, little candles were attached carefully to a few branches of the little tree and the coal oil lamps were put out as they were lit for a few moments.

Vy's eyes misted. *How can I go out and cut a Christmas tree without her? Maybe Mama will help. She ain't never been interested in a tree, though. I hear Granny plain as day—"Get y' boots on, Vy. It's Christmas tree time"*

Vy and Gran would pull on their old boots, traipse through the snow to Huckleberry Woods on Christmas Eve, and chop down the perfect tree with Paw's old axe. After letting three, four, and five-year-old Vy chop until her arms grew weary, Gran would take the axe.

"Let Gran git it fer ye now, Violet." With a couple of Granny's hard licks, the prize evergreen would give way, plummeting to the ground, causing Gran to lose balance and plunge headlong in the snow with tree and Violet right on top of her. The comical scene would bring on enough laughter between the pair to cause their stomachs to ache.

After dragging their prized cedar home, a little criss-cross stand was fashioned by Gran with Vy's help, nailed onto the bottom, and up the tree stood with shouts from the Vittoyes, including Sally.

Vy smiled, lost in her precious memories of those special Holy Days that were gone forever. *Gran always watched me lie down in the snow and make snow angels. She said I was her snow angel.*

Will Mama like the apron I made her from the leftover scraps of Sadie's bridesmaid dresses?

With some ham and green beans and some sweet taters, we could have a right good Christmas Eve supper.

The apple stack cake ought to be just right to eat by then. We'll never eat the whole thing—maybe Mama would ride over t' Sadie's with me—take some of it to them. They have those boys who eat everything. Mmm um, they would like that...

Sally looked up, rubbed her eyes, put down her glasses, and broke the silence.

"It's not th' work that's getting t' me on these here gowns, Vy. It's th' fact that between these here dark clouds and disappearing daylight, it's a takin' all th' coal oil lanterns we own plus this here fireplace t' give my old eyes enough light t' sew by."

"Y' eyes ain't old, Mama. Y' don't even have to wear your specs all the time."

"Y' just try n' tell that t' these old peepers right now, child."

"It appears that bad weather's a comin.' I'm a telling y' again, Violet, y'd better git a heap more logs in here 'fore it comes a bad storm. Y' don't want t' wait till y' can't get out there t' the wood shed."

Several of the dresses for Sadie's wedding were coming along, nearing completion, even though Ivy Taylor had never been able to attend a fitting. The girls were compelled to sew Ivy's gown by written measurements alone, which could mean a lot of ripping out and redoing if her dress did not fit right. Vy turned the garment over in her hands and calculated the remaining bits and pieces that would need to be done.

Sally spoke sharply. "Violet! Did y' hear me?"

"Hmm? Oh, I'm sorry, Mama. I'm goin' out and bring some firewood in right this minute."

Vy bit her thread in two, carefully knotted it, put the needle through the dress to mark her spot, and folded and placed the dress in her basket. Throwing on her woolen cape, she pulled the hood around her head, tying it securely under her chin.

As she started outside, the door flew open with the wind's power, hitting her on the shoulder. Vy put her head down, pushing her way outside as the door slammed shut behind her, and bent over to maintain balance. The wind shot stinging pellets of sleet onto her skin as she fought her way to the wood pile. The cold and sheer force of it was overpowering, freezing Vy's hands and causing her to drop a log smack on the end of her toe. "Oh! Ouch—dag nab it, that hurt!" Vy grabbed at her foot, hopping up and down on the other. Between the howling wind noise and the confusion of a hurt toe, Vy barely heard the sound of a carriage that drove up behind her. Her arms finally loaded down with fire logs, Violet turned around, both surprised and overjoyed to behold the smiling face of Sadie Ellis.

Sadie pulled on the horse's reins, yelling "Whoa there, boy!" then quickly tightened her coat around her body.

Sally was already yelling out the door before Sadie could dismount, but you could hardly hear her for the howling wind. "Get yerselves inside here, you two!" she shouted. "Violet! Please hurry up and get back in here!"

Sadie, in an effort to help, grabbed some of the wood from Vy and bounded toward the door as the wind picked up her long blonde hair and spitefully smacked her in the face. Her plaid woolen cape whirled up and down about her body and acted like an umbrella that didn't know whether to rise or fall.

Sadie banged the wet boots on the stoop, peeled off dripping cape and bonnet, and threw them over the straight back chair by the blazing fireplace. Vy tramped in behind her and dropped the heavy logs on the hearth."

"Boy, I'm sure glad y' all are home 'cause the trip over here has 'bout turned me into a big icicle!"

Sally lifted a ladle from the steaming pot, poured soup into a mug for Sadie, and placed it in her hands. "Drink this now, child, and get y'erself over here by the fire to thaw out a little bit."

Heat from the hot cup felt good to Sadie's frozen hands, and the soup tasted yummy. The girl sipped the brew then rolled the cup back and forth, extracting every bit of warmth from it that was possible.

Sally stood nearby shaking her head in disdain at the sight of the girl and asked bluntly, "What in th' world are you a doin' out drivin' in this winter weather all alone, child? Don't you know you'll catch yer death o' cold?"

Sadie backed up to the fire, shivered, and answered timidly, "Y' know what, Miss Sally? It didn't even look bad when I left home. It was real cloudy, but that was all. This bad weather just came on like lightnin'! Me and Momma got to thinkin' about a askin' y' and Vy to come over and stay the Holy Days with us—with our whole family, Miss Sally. We've really missed seein' y' here lately, and there'll just be th' two of y' here by y'selves fer Christmas. Momma says tell y' she ain't gonna take no fer an answer, so you'd just be a packin' yer things up so we cn git back over the mountain t' our farm fore the weather gets worse—and 'fore it gets dark. But I mean it, you'd better bundle up with plenty of clothes 'cause that wind's a whippin' it t' beat th' band out there, and it's beginning t' drizzle an awful icy mist."

Vy squealed in delight, jumped up, and clapped her hands with joy. "Ohhh, Mama, oh, how wonderful! Ain't that the finest thing? Can we go, Mama? We're almost finished with the bridesmaid dresses, and we could finish the rest of the sewin' on Sadie's gown right there at the Ellises' and have her close at hand for fittins. I bet we could get all th' gowns done in no time, Mama, and wouldn't that be pleasin' to Mrs. Ellis and Sadie!"

Sally's look was terribly pensive, at best. She glowered at the idea of this arrangement. It was evident to all that she did not like anything about this idea, especially with bad weather threatening, but she didn't see a quick or easy way out of the situation.

She felt pressure at being placed in a circumstance that she did not ask for—not to mention that she had no desire to spend the holidays with a large group of people.

She pondered the situation. Here was Sadie, who had driven all the way to the cabin with a friendly invitation to spend the Holy Days with the Ellis family and would have to drive back alone in the bad weather if Sally refused to participate. Sally frowned at Vy and Sadie with a marked clinch in her jaw. She simply wanted no part of this nonsense.

"This ought not be, girls! The weather is just too bad fer a body t' start out in. Tell y' th truth, Sadie, I'm surprised Clyve and Maudie Ellis let you drive that coach all the way over here alone on a bad day like this. That just ain't like them."

Vy crossed her fingers behind her back and avoided her mother's displeased expression as Sadie pled.

"Oh, Ms. Sally, I beg ya please t' come back with me. If y' don't, I'll have t' drive back alone, and what if I was t' git snowbound or somethin'? Daddy'll be plumb mad at me if I hafta drive back alone. I never told him I was a comin'over here all by myself."

Sally rubbed the back of her neck with an irritable jerk, realizing there was no way out of this and that she, indeed, would have to accompany these girls to the Ellises.' She threw down her sewing and agreed to go with a stern warning.

"Violet, I'm going only b'cause Sadie here ought not drive back alone, but I'm hitchin' up and a follow'n you girls in our carriage so we'll have it t' get back home in or just in case we should need it fer somethin' another while we're over there. Sadie and y'self will ride on ahead of me in her carriage. Now hurry up and pack a few o' y' things so we can get going—quickly—th' weather's turnin' bad now. Do y' hear me, Violet?"

The girls hugged, screamed, and jumped up and down all at once. "Whoopee! Thank y.' Thank y,' Mama!"

"Yes, yes, thank y,' Ms. Sally! Oh, Sadie, we're gonna have such a wonderful Holy Day—a Holy Day with best friends!"

Vy and Sadie hurriedly folded, wrapped, and secured the wedding dresses and piece goods, along with sewing supplies, and loaded them inside the carriage box. Sally put out the fire and grabbed her gown, some extra underwear, and the basket of fragrant soaps and dried spices she had prepared especially for Maudie's Christmas gift.

Vy climbed up to the loft and brought down the new wedding ring coverlet, already wrapped in brown paper, that had been quilted especially as a present for Sadie, and the gift she had wrapped for her mama. After the girls packed the canned berries and sweet relish for the rest of the Ellis family, Sadie helped Vy fold underwear, a nightgown, two more skirts, and her best shirtwaist to pack in the velvet brocade grip that had belonged to Gran. The coach was sufficiently loaded, but the girls were shaking from cold and dampness, so they came back inside the cabin, changed into dry clothing of Vy's, added another pair of socks, pulled on their overcapes, and tightened the hoods securely under their chins.

The girls boarded Sadie's carriage and huddled side by side as she snapped the horse's reins. The cruel wind whistled, blowing hard from the west, as an icy mist slapped against their faces. Vy was glad for the extra woolen stockings she was wearing under her boots and the pile of quilts Sally had given them that swaddled their bodies.

I hope we make it to Sadie's before it gets dark. This is bad.

The girls had no more got on their way than the rain turned to huge snowflakes and layers of white started building higher on the frigid ground. They rode for a long while, enjoying chatter and gossip, oblivious to the weather because of their obvious excitement.

Vy gazed down the snowy path in front of them.

"Mama was right, Sadie, we are in a snowstorm."

"Hang on, Vy. It just can't be too much farther now. We've been on the road for at least an hour. Can you see your mama behind us?"

"I-I think so—barely."

The old horse was slowing now, laboring against the blowing wind but dutifully plotting on as the little coach's wheels made deep ruts in the snow that were filling up just as quickly as they rode on. The ground and trees had turned totally white, and the sky was filled.

Sadie's voice trembled. "I can hardly see the road, Vy. Can you?"

"No, I can't see it eith—" Vy's words were interrupted by a loud cracking noise as the earth went askew. The carriage tilted, stalled, and suddenly lunged over sideways, spilling the girls and all the contents that had been so carefully packed.

Vy felt a jolt as she tumbled over, hitting the ground. The fall stunned her, but the soft snow on top of leaves definitely broke a landing that could have been much worse.

Shakily, she looked up from her position from the cold snowy surface to see Sadie's now unrestrained horse galloping down the snowy trail, dragging its reins behind.

She looked around for Sadie, who was lying a few feet away, seemingly in a daze.

Sadie—Sadie's hurt. "Sadie! Sadie, are you okay?"

"I-I don't know. My head ... "

The girl sat up, feeling for the area of a bulging bump on her forehead that was beginning to grow.

Vy crawled through the thick snow on her hands and knees to get a better look. "Oh, you got a terrible whack on your head. It almost knocked you out didn't it, Sadie."

Sadie rubbed her head. "What happened? It hurts right here."

The arriving sound of Sally's carriage was the most wonderful sound the two girls had ever heard.

Vy uttered a sigh of relief. Thank heavens Mama insisted on following us.

Fear gripped Sally's heart as she came upon the wreckage through the thick falling snow, and she barely stopped the horse before jumping off—dashing to see to the two bewildered and snow-covered girls while screaming, "What in the world happened? Vy? Sadie? Are y' okay?"

"I am, Mama, but Sadie here, she hit her head."

"Good Lord in heaven, help us all. This is the very thing I was afraid of."

Sadie smiled and looked up sheepishly. "I'm sorry, Miss Sally. I'm so very sorry."

"Never mind that now. We've got to get both o' y' in my carriage first, and then I'm going to see what I can salvage from this here spilled stuff." There were a couple of jars of foodstuffs that were broken, but most of what had been packed had stayed secure in boxes and grips, though it was half buried and snow-covered. Sally gathered as much as she could as quickly as possible after settling the two girls inside her carriage under dry blankets. Her gloves were now soaked and her hands and face frozen. She wasted no time, working very fast, for the snow was coming down even harder now, blowing sideways and making it very difficult to see.

Sally clicked the reins, and the horse started in forward motion once more. The little party had come too far to turn back now.

Sadie peered out the little carriage window and rubbed the bump on her head. "Sure hope we don't go trailing off in another hole."

Vy held Sadie's hand, huddling close while trying to comfort her. "D-don't worry, dear. Right about here y' can tell where the road is by those cedar trees, and my mama has made this trip a million times or more. My mama will take care of us."

"We can't be far from the cabin now. Are you okay, Vy?"

"I'm cold, Sadie, but not shivering like ye are."

Sadie uttered a pensive laugh.

"I always shake when I'm nervous, but we're almost there. Look, Vy! Thank God! There it is! I can see our cabin right yonder in the distance."

The cabin lights shone brightly against the dark and snow-filled night sky with light from a host of coal oil lanterns that Maudie had lit to welcome the trio.

The little Christmas tree that had been placed jauntily in a front cabin window was the happiest sight Vy had seen in many a day.

Vy sighed. "We made it, Sadie. I told y' my mama would get us here."

Sally breathed a sigh of relief and pulled her carriage in front of the house as Clyve Ellis excitedly ran out to meet the girls and took the horse's reins.

"My heavens! We been worried t' death about y'all, Sally! I'm s' thankful t' see y' an' these here girls. I was just saddlin' up to head out t'wards your house and see if I could find y'all. What in the world happened t' our carriage? The old horse came on back without it."

"It's turned over in a ditch about a mile back, Clyve. The girls were drivin' an' ran off to the side and hit a hole r' somethin.' I'm just glad they wasn't hurt too bad. Sadie got a bump on her head. Maudie will need to look at it, but I think they're both okay. I don't know about y' coach, though."

Forgetting the close call they had had only moments ago, Vy and Sadie were already chatting and smiling as they hopped out of Sally's carriage and ran into the cabin.

Maudie Ellis was waiting anxiously with her sons for sight of the girls and had them ready to help unload their things. She quickly examined Sadie's head injury, applying some unknown remedy to help take the swelling down. She then ushered the girls inside to the fireplace where she helped pull off their wet clothes, wrapping them with dry quilts and serving bowls of steaming soup with thick slices of warm salt-risen bread.

Vy hugged the quilts around her and looked around the room in awe, for there in every direction she looked were beautiful signs of Christmas. Pretty fat cookies of all shapes and sizes, including sassy gingerbread men with raisin eyes and candy buttons, lay smiling as though they were going to jump up and say hello at any minute. The jaunty little cedar tree decorated with apple rings, popcorn, crescent cookies, and handmade ornaments already had tiny little candles attached for lighting on Christmas Eve. Maudie's own mistletoe garlands, fragrant woven pine boughs, and wreaths draped both mantle and doorway. Vy's eyes darted around the room first to one thing and then another. She sucked in her breath and put her hands over her mouth in wonder.

"Oh, Maudie, I've never seen a more cheerful or pleasin' sight in all my born days. Y' are really ready for Christmas!"

Clyve Ellis unhitched Sally's horse, securing him inside the barn with food and water while Maudie met Sally at the door with a big hug and an apology. "I'm s' sorry t' have caused ya' t' be out in this, honey. It was my entire fault, but I sure am grateful y' followed Sadie back home. Now y' come on in here by this fire and let me help y' take off your wet things. Sit here in this rocker, Sally, and here's y' a blanket and a nice cup of coffee t' help y' get warmed up. Cream and sugar, hon?"

Sally, still annoyed at the unexpected direction the whole day had taken, started to soften a little. Maudie's friendly smile, her delicious coffee, warm blanket, and roaring fire were going a long way to relieve her raw nerves.

Clyve snuffed out his lantern, stomping the snow off his big boots. He bent down slightly to keep from hitting his towering head on the little entrance and shut and bolted the cabin door, addressing his wife sternly.

"Hit's an awful blizzard out there, Maudie! I'm afraid we're in fer a bad one this time. I could hardly see my hand in front of my face gettin' from th' barn back to th' cabin it's a comin' down so hard! Thank God these women made it home safely. I'd a never approved Sadie a drivin' out by herself with the likes o' this storm movin' in. No, siree, I would not have, and I don't ever want her out in such as this a-gin, and that ain't even takin' a mention of th' coach she's done went and wrecked!"

Maudie helped Clyve pull off his wet things and motioned him to his rocking chair with a cup of hot brewed coffee.

"It'll be okay, Clyve. I'm sure that old coach ain't in such bad shape that you can't fix it up again, husband!"

Sally sat her steaming cup back in its saucer. Her face turned red as she shifted uneasily.

"I want y' t' know I didn't think we should a come, Clyve. N' I tried and tried t' tell th' girls. This trip wasn't necessary a' tall, n' I'm awful sorry for a causin' you un Maudie any worry. I was afraid fer Sadie t' light out n' come home by herself, though. I should a kept them both at home with me and waited this storm out before we ever started across that hill."

Clyve held up his hand, shaking his head, supposing he had said the wrong thing.

"I thank th' Good Lord y' was with th' girls when they wrecked that wagon, Sally. If Sadie had been by herself, she's liable to died fore she got on back. Nothin' ain't y' fault, Sally. Y' might have saved m' daughter's life tonight, n' we're most grateful. Me n' Maudie's more n' glad t' have y' uns fer th Holy Day n' all, especially since you uns don't have nobody else. I'm just upset that Sadie went off by herself that way. Why, I'd a been glad t' drive her there t' pick you girls up if she'd just a asked me!"

Maudie rubbed Clyve's shoulders and broke in. "T'was all my fault, Clyve. They was no way t' know bad weather was a comin' earlier today when Sadie struck out o' here, and there's no need to second guess now. Let's just be so thankful that y' are all safe n' sound now an' we're all gonna enjoy this here Holy Day celebration together."

Maudie turned her attention toward Sally. "We are awfully glad you 'n Violet are here fer the Christmas celebrations, Sally. The more the merrier, we always say. Don't we, Clyve?"

Maudie's voice was almost drowned out as the wind howled louder, and the cabin creaked and groaned with its mighty force. The snow thickened and piled high against the doors and windows of the Ellis cabin, but all was cozy and warm inside.

The girls had a full tummy and warm hands and toes by now and had taken their leave of the adults to climb up into the loft and sit together on Sadie's bed, laughing and talking. After a while Clyve's head begin to nod. He shook it off, poked the fire, added more logs, and watched as the blaze flamed higher. Warmth had thawed his tired body, and sleep was taking over. The big man looked at Sallie and Maude.

"I declare, ladies, I'm awful tired and believe I'm a goin' t' have t' say goodnight to y.'" The giant of a man excused himself to his little room off the kitchen where he lay down across the bed he shared with Maudie and started a deep snore that would last through the night. Clyve had split wood since before dawn, along with two of his sons, as well as repairing the old broken plow. The worry over Sadie had certainly not helped to soothe his or anybody else's nerves either, so rest was most welcome.

Maudie and Clyve's two sons stretched their arms over their heads, yawned, and announced they were tired, too. They bade goodnight to all and bedded down in the little side room Clyve had added to the house years ago before they were born, lying side by side on cots homemade by their father.

At first, Sally felt ill at ease after the unsettling events that had taken place, but she soon warmed up to Maudie, who was always easy to talk to and was trying really hard to make her feel welcome and at home. The two ladies sat by the fire in creaky old rocking chairs, chatting and sewing on wedding dresses until almost midnight. Then Maudie settled Sadie down in a little bed on the east end of the loft secured by a heavy drape that had been hung for her privacy.

On the west end of the loft, under a pile of quilts so heavy they could hardly breathe, Sadie and Vy giggled and whispered low until the wee hours of the morning, discussing Sadie's coming wedding.

"Oh, Vy, I am so excited and scared at the same time. Do y' know what I mean? I mean, I will be sleeping right in the same bed with a man—right next to Winfield. I think about it all the time now as the days get closer to our weddin.' I hope I can be a good wife. Oh, I know all about cookin' and cleanin' and sewin' and those things, but there's the other thing—y' know—that I'm not sure about. Y' know what I mean, don't y,' Vy? Do you think I will be a good wife to Winfield, Vy?"

Vy stiffened up. She could only imagine what Sadie was talking about but dared not answer. Don't ask me about bein' a wife, Sadie. What do I know?

Sadie continued talking, as if to herself. "Winfield's a wonderful person, Vy. And y' will think so, too—when you get to know him. I know he's much older than I, but I believe he's the right husband fer me, n' Mama and Pa think so, too. With his daddy a owning all that land and farmin' big n' all, we ought t' be well off someday."

With a far off look in her sleepy eyes, Sadie yawned and said, "Did I tell y' he's a buildin' us a real purty house? Y'll have to drive over there with me and Win to see it, Vy."

Sadie's eyes closed as she turned over on her side and yawned. It was very late.

Vy studied Sadie's profile. Sadie was beautiful with all that yellow hair and those blue eyes. Vy wished she could be beautiful too. Then she quickly reminded herself that she would not like to be marrying an old man like Sadie was going to do. But it sure felt good to be here with friends. Friends were almost as good as a family—because they cared for her, this Ellis family. What's more, with Mama safely asleep across the loft, she would not be going off anywhere tonight.

The laughter and friendly chat had relaxed Violet. This was the first real happiness she had felt in a long time. *I'll have sweet dreams tonight.*

Christmas Eve came with all its enchantment and beauty. Tiny hand-dipped candles had been attached securely to the Christmas tree limbs and were lit as the house lanterns were snuffed out. The tree glowed in the darkness as the little ornaments dangled and sparkled while the Ellis family, along with Sally Vittoye, sang "Joy to the World." Vy did not know all the words but hummed along as best she could. The Ellis family went to church regularly and knew all the Christmas songs. Carols was what they called them.

Why does Mama know all these songs—how does she?

Maudie excused herself to the kitchen where she was finishing some baking. She invited Sally to help her, but she declined. The rest of the Ellis family's eyes suddenly turned to Sadie and, in expectation, watched as the girl lifted her head upward, closed her eyes, and began to sing with a voice so sweet it could make a body cry!

Angels we have heard on high, sweetly singing o'er the plains,

> And the shepherds in reply, echo back their glorious strains,
> Glo—oo—oo—oo—oo—oria
> In excelsis D—ee—eo ...

When Sadie was finished with her song, the boys and Clyve put their heads together, their voices in beautiful harmony to "Silent Night" then "Joy to the World." Vy did not know all the words, but she hummed along.

Maudie placed her cocoa cake in the oven to bake then returned as Clyve motioned for everyone to bow their heads. Vy was astonished to see her mama bow her head and close her eyes.

She could not take her eyes off the mesmerizing sight of this family bowing before God—this family praying together.

Clyve Ellis opened his mouth and talked to the Lord in a loud but sincere voice.

"Oh, God, our Father, We uns just thank ye a whole heap for a comin' into this here world and a sacrificin' y' life for us sinners so we could be forgiven and come t' live with ye in heaven someday. Help us t' celebrate y' birth, Lord Jesus, by a bein' the people y'd want us t' be. Help us t' glorify you, Lord, to all them that don't know ye. We pray fer their souls, dear Father, and we ask all this in Jesus' precious name. Happy Birthday and Merry Christmas to y,' Lord. Amen."

Vy felt the need to bow her head and close her eyes as the prayer was lifted, but she could not keep from staring at the sight of her mama's bowed head and closed eyes. The sight confused her and bombarded her head with more questions. Did her mama know this nice God Mr. Ellis was talkin' to? What about the times she had seen Granny pray—times when Sally was not around. She suddenly remembered that Gran had even taught her a little prayer to repeat before she went to sleep at night, though it had been long forgotten. She concluded that her mama's bowed head and closed eyes were only in politeness to Maudie Ellis and her family.

Sadie shouted, "Presents everyone!" She and her brothers passed out gifts to all among shouts of joy and laughter. Amos bought Clyve a new shotgun and gave Arly a jar of hard candies. Arly reciprocated Amos with a new axe because his was broken.

Clyve presented Maudie with some pretty pink silk for a dress that he had saved all year for. Maudie declared it was too expensive and would probably inquire down at the mercantile if she could swap it for three lengths of some more practical cotton calico. Clyve was not happy with her reaction and sank back in his chair, polishing his new shotgun.

Maudie presented Sally with a pretty waist that had been hers—one that she had never worn, and one she knew would fit Sally to a tee.

Sally tried not to act too overjoyed with the fancy lace tunic but could hardly hide her pleasure in the gift. She then opened the apron that Violet had fashioned from the bridesmaid dress scraps. She smiled at Vy and dutifully thanked her. Vy told herself, Well, at least she didn't hate it.

Maudie then handed Sadie a small box tied with red string. The tag read:

"To Sadie, from Mom." Sadie opened the little box to discover a beautiful strand of antique pearls. Sadie sucked in her breath, and her eyes began to mist. "Oh, Mom, how beautiful. I can't take these. They are your treasured pearls. Look how beautiful they are, Vy."

"Oooh, Sadie, it's the prettiest necklace I ever saw."

Maudie went on. "I want you to have them, Sadie. They're to wear on y' wedding day. They belonged to your grandmother and y' great grandmother before they were mine. Now they are yours, and y' can hand them down to y' own daughter someday."

Sadie ran to the tree and brought out a square present all wrapped in yellow and tied with red string. She handed it to Vy, who nervously tore off the paper and opened up the box. Inside was a small, leather bound book with My Diary printed right on the front.

"Oh, Sadie, thank y.' I have always wanted one of these. I promise to write my very deepest thoughts in here every day and confess them to no one but you."

Sadie laughed. "A diary is for all y' secrets, Vy, and y' don't have to confess your private thoughts to me or anyone, but I'm glad y' like it!"

Vy grabbed the big package wrapped in brown paper marked "To Sadie: from Sally and Vy" and shoved it in her friend's lap. "Here. Open this one, Sadie!"

Sadie smiled, eyed Vy impishly, and hugged the big package. "Thanks, Miss Sally and Vy! Mmmmm, I hope this here's what I think it is!" Sadie's eyes widened and then misted up once more as she tore the paper off, catching a glimpse of the lovely hand done quilt. "Oh, Violet, Miss Sally, how could I ever thank y'? This is just like th' other one y' made—no, it's even purtier than th' other one! It's the most beautiful bedcover I've ever seen. Look here, Mama. Just you look what they made f'r me?" Maudie put on glasses and lovingly ran her fingers over the fine stitches, marveling at the perfectly beautiful double wedding ring pattern.

"I declare, Sally, I think you two have gone and outdone y'selves on this one."

"Shucks, Maudie. Tis th' least we could do as much as you and your family's done fer us. There's nothin' too fine for you or Sadie."

"Well, that's bout th' purtiest n' I've ever seen y' uns make! Such beautiful work"

Sadie hugged first Sally and then Vy. "I- I don't know what to say. You've made me so happy. I'm so glad you came for th' Holy Days. This is the best Christmas we ever had." Everyone agreed wholeheartedly.

It is a good Christmas. Yes, it is, but oh, Granny, I miss you so much. Christmas ain't never gonna be th' same for me.

A special Holy Day dinner was almost ready to be set on the table as word came from a next door neighbor that Calvin, the Ellises' oldest son, and his wife, Lucinda, would be arriving shortly. They had spent Christmas Eve with Lucinda's parents and were planning to have their Christmas Day meal and the exchanging of presents with Calvin's family.

Vy did not know Calvin Ellis very well, Maudie and Clyve Ellises' oldest son, but now recalled Mrs. Lucinda Ellis, his wife, was a teacher at Rose Hill School in Maynard's Valley. As a matter of fact, Vy had met Mrs. Lucinda the day she had accompanied Jessie Mae Mynatt to their cabin to pick up a dress Gran and she had tailored. *Hmmm … I remember Lucinda Ellis, all right. She wouldn't even come in our cabin with Jessie Mae Mynatt that day. Acted hoity toity, if you ask me. Guess she's afraid I'll give her cooties or somethin.' Me and Mama will have to be nice to her, though, since she's the Ellises' kin.*

The girls busied themselves, picking up the sheets of paper that had wrapped all the gifts and folded the ones not torn to save for future use.

Afterward, Sadie spread her quilt on her loft bed to get a closer look at the beautiful gift. Vy settled into a corner by the fireplace and started writing the first page in her diary.

Dear Diary,

This is the first Christmas I ever had without Granny. I do miss her so much. Me and Mama have had a nice Christmas here with all the Ellises and especially with Sadie. Mama gave me my own real sewing box. It has a brand new pair of scissors and a new thimble that fits my finger. I was so surprised. She told me it was from Granny and her. I hope Gran knows I love it.

Mama said she liked the apron I made her. I hope she did.

I loved all the Christmas carols the Ellises sang and the prayer Mr. Ellis said. I wish me and Mama could have a real family like Sadie's. If only I could find my daddy, Dear Diary, maybe we could.

Maudie called up to the loft, "Sadie, will you and Vy please come down and set this here table fer me?"

Sadie handed Vy the stack of plates from the shelf and grabbed the silverware and cloth napkins from the pine hutch's drawer. Vy began to count as she started laying plates around Maudie's big table.

Let's see now ... there will be Clyve, Maudie, and Sadie, Amos, Arly, Calvin, Lucinda, Mama, and me. That'll be nine people—hmmm ... I only have eight plates, and there will be nine of us eatin' dinner, Sadie."

Maudie broke in. "Oh, I'm sorry, I forgot t' tell y,' honey—there'll only be eight here fer th' meal. Y' Mama done left a little while ago. She told me t' tell y' that she had t' go home fer somethin' a'nother she just remembered."

"What? Mama left already? She left me? Why? Where'd she go?"

Maudie knew Vy would be upset and was ready to try and calm her. "H'it's okay, darlin.' Sally said she has something' er other real impor- tant that she had t' see about back at yore cabin. You n' Sadie don't mind any o' that none. Just enjoy y' stay here fer these here Holy Days, n' one of us will see y' back home. We wanted you n' yore Ma both to stay till th' New Year come in. I asked her if it was all right fer you t' stay, n' she said t'was fine. Now try not t' be too upset, child. I'm sure she'll be on back over here soon—said she'd be right back soon as she took care o' some things."

Vy was not so sure. What in the world does Mama have to take care of at home? Why would she leave me here by myself? I ain't never! Yeah, Mama might come back, but she might not!

The Ellises' Christmas dinner table was lovely and laden with suc- culent roast ham, roast turkey, cornbread stuffing, gravy, and cranberry sauce. Luscious creamed potatoes swam in fresh churned butter next to stuffed cabbages, green beans, and creamed corn. Pecan pie, apple stack cake, bread pudding topped with whipped cream, and assorted Christmas cookies served to fulfill the dessert menu, if there was room in a body's stomach after the main course was finished.

Steaming mugs of coffee with thick cream and sugar, or homemade eggnog if you preferred it, was then served on a tray by the fireplace while Arly strummed his guitar and the family sang more Christmas carols and folk melodies.

Calvin and Lucinda opened their gifts from Maudie and Clyve. Vy was enjoying herself so much that she almost forgot that Sally had gone off and left her. She felt comfortable and right at home with the Ellis family.

After all the presents were opened, the family settled together around the fireplace to talk and relax, but it became evident that Calvin, the oldest Ellis son, could not calm down. He shifted several times then finally rose from his chair and pulled on his heavy coat and boots while ignoring his wife's glaring eyes and growing irritation.

Lucinda Ellis turned her head away from Calvin, at first trying not to speak, hesitating to start something in front of the family, but resentment got the best of her and she addressed her husband with a pleading tone that quickly turned to anger.

"I wish y' wouldn't go out Calvin. It's getting dark now. Anybody knows y' can't see to do a single thing out there. Good grief! Can't you spend one blessed single minute here with your family and your wife on a Christmas day?"

Calvin turned toward Lucinda, looking straight into her face with narrow and menacing eyes. After casting a long and ominous stare toward his wife, he retorted deliberately, "Lucinda, you would do well t' keep yore' mouth shut and mind y' own business. Do you hear me? Don't you go tryin' t' start somethin' right here in front of my family. I'm headed out to take a ride and look over this here farm. And I've told you before not to interfere with my intentions when I decide I'm goin' out. You know better than that, woman!" Lucinda did not move, but tears filled her eyes.

As Lucinda's countenance fell, everyone in the room immediately became uncomfortable feeling the harm Calvin had just imposed upon his wife. Maudie broke in quickly, trying to soothe the awkward situation.

"Now Lucy, dear, it'll be okay. Cal just has got to get out of this old hot cabin a minute t' clear his head. Why, he was always like that as a boy. Y' come right over here by me, hon. I want t' show y' Sadie's beautiful gown. It's almost finished. Violet there has done such a good job on it."

Lucinda's jaw was set, and she made no reply to Maudie and never cast a glance at the beautiful dress she held or toward Vy.

Lucinda Lou Beeler had fallen hopelessly in love with Calvin Ellis from their very first date. She had learned early on that Calvin Ellis had some emotional problems, was really an unstable soul, but had hoped against hope that her adoration of him would change the boy into a considerate and loving person. She had married Calvin strictly against her best judgment, since she, as well as everybody else in the valley, was aware of his reputation as a shiftless, eccentric soul leaning toward the weird. In fact, most days Calvin could be spotted roaming about in the woods feigning work at what he called a "woodcutting business."

Through the years Lucinda had used almost all her teacher's pay to indulge Calvin's every whim since he worked so little. His so-called "business" earned him practically nothing, but Lucinda's salary from the Rose Hill School sufficed to keep the two comfortable since they had no children.

Maudie walked to the door with Calvin as he left and rubbed his shoulder. "Now you be careful out there, Son. Do your bidding and come on back soon. Remember that your family who loves you waits at home, Calvin. Just get some fresh air and come on back now, you hear me? Lucy is upset, Son."

Calvin was heard muttering something under his breath. Maudie ignored it, shaking her head in disappointment.

Calvin never returned to his parents home that Christmas night.

Next morning Clyve hitched his horse to the old sleigh and drove a tearful Lucinda Ellis back to her home alone.

Maudie, Sadie, and Violet worked hard the week between Christmas and New Year's getting the wedding dresses to a finished point. The last fitting to be done was Ivy Taylor's, who lived across the valley in Ailor Springs, and all that was needed to complete her dress was to make some adjustments at that fitting and put in the hem.

Sadie had been invited to spend some time at Winfield Campbell's home in order to become better acquainted with his family and planned to take the dress along for Ivy's older sister, Neppia, to finish; she was an accomplished seamstress as well. The Campbells and the Taylors lived in close proximity and were longtime friends.

Morning light peeped in the tiny loft window of the Ellises' cabin. Vy opened her eyes, crept out of bed, wrapped a blanket around herself, and crawled over beside the little opening where there was enough light to see. She opened her diary and began to catalog her thoughts.

Dear Diary,

It is New Year's Eve. It's my birthday, and I'm thirteen years old today. I don't know where Mama is. She left me here at the Ellises' on Christmas day. Why? Who knows? I sure don't.

I'm leavin' here day after tomorrow, which is New Year's Day. I just got all my things packed. Winfield Campbell is comin' to get Sadie in his new carriage on Monday and take her over to spend some time with his family. They are goin' to drive me home on their way over there. I wonder what I'll find when I get home. I dread goin' home. I wouldn't if Granny was goin' t' be there, but she ain't.

Gran never forgot my birthday. She always baked me a chocolate puddin' cake and put a candle on it fer me t' blow out.

It ain't that I cared about no cake nor nothing, though. I just hate that Mama left me here and didn't tell me where she went or why she left.

I ain't met Winfield Campbell yet. I guess he's the right person for Sadie—at least she says he is. She says he's real nice.

I hope Sadie does not change and that she will still be my friend after she gets married.

I hope Mama's okay. Yeah, she's probably okay. She's just out doin' somethin' she don't want me to know about, and I think that's why she's left me. When I ain't there, she don't have t' stay home nights with me. Yep, that's why she left me here at the Ellises.' She wanted to go out every night with that old stranger.

She's completely forgot about my birthday, and I ain't tellin' nobody but you, Dear Diary. I don't want any of 'em t' know that Mama forgot me.

No, she didn't forget. She just don't care.

Interaction between Vy and Sally had gone well enough throughout those first winter months after Gran had passed away even though Sally had, in fact, gone out a few times. It was always very late and after she thought Vy was sound asleep. There was no sleeping for Vy, however, who had been a light sleeper since she was a baby and never missed that certain sound of the stranger's wagon. She actually still had no idea where or with whom her mother spent those nights, or where the blood came from that was on her clothes.

It was one cold February morning when Vy first discovered it. She was doing laundry down by the creek, beating out the dirt as she usually did, with a smooth stone, from Sally's as well as her own clothes when she noticed the sticky dark red stains all over Sally's skirt and waist. It was blood, all right, and came out of the clothing quick enough with the cold creek water, lye soap, and some hard scrubbing.

Vy had cut up a chicken enough times to recognize the stains were blood but had never seen that much of it before.

Then there was also that strange and repugnant, although very indistinguishable, odor coming from her mama's garments, and even though she had smelled it many times, Vy still couldn't figure out what it was. It would do no good to question Mama about anything; it never had.

Beginnings

Spring descended on Maynard's Valley like a lovely green bird. Granny's blue iris and golden daffodil opened, following the little purple crocus. Robins built nests and sang in the trees that were bursting with tender green leaves. The air was pungent with lilac and fruit tree blossoms. Sadie and Winfield's wedding day was only one day away.

Vy could hardly wait. She had looked forward to the day almost as much as Sadie. It would be so much fun to take part in a wedding and meet new people. Final plans were all made. Dresses were hanging from the rafters, having been pressed by heavy sad irons in hopes they would remain unwrinkled.

Sadie had requested that Vy assist her with the church's decorations as well as her other attendant's last minute dress and hairstyles.

Winfield arrived promptly, picked up Sadie then Vy in his new carriage, and deposited them both, along with a world of wedding paraphernalia, at Ailor Springs Church. The activity of making ready for the Ellis-Campbell wedding had begun.

The decorating was almost completed, and Vy was set on securing the last of the window candles in their holders. Everyone had worked feverishly, adorning the church with blossoms and candles from head to toe. All of the girls, with the exception of Vy, had headed for the side prayer room to get dressed. As Vy backed up to get a better look at the little church, the double doors flew open, hitting her in the back and nearly knocking her down.

"Oops, pretty one, I'm sorry there." Theo Taylor caught Vy's arm and helped her regain her balance. "Please excuse me! I didn't see you for this armload of flowers. Almost ran you over, didn't I? Are you the decoratin' committee?"

Vy turned to see the most striking man she had ever seen in her life. He was handsome in a black tuxedo and white tucked shirt, even though his tie was slightly askew. He was statuesque as a soldier, towering over Vy's five feet two inches, and she guessed him to be at least six foot two or three inches tall. His ebony hair and tawny skin framed a pair of deeply set steel gray eyes that peered deeply into hers, making her feel quite uneasy.

Vy instinctively cleared her throat as she straightened her blouse and skirt.

"Well, I've almost finished with the window tapers but can't seem to find the rest of them. They aren't where Sadie said they'd be. I thought she said they would be right here on this stage."

"Look! Here they are behind the parson's pulpit." Theo scanned Vy from head to toe, marveling at the lovely combination of curly auburn hair and bright blue eyes as he handed her the tapers. He mused that although the girl was young, she was strikingly beautiful.

Sensing the intent look coming from this attractive young man made Vy want to run. Blushing, she almost dropped the wax tapers as she accepted the box from Theo. His gaze was making her terribly uncomfortable.

"Do you know that you have the most beautiful auburn hair that I have ever seen on a girl? Does everyone tell you that?"

Vy dropped her eyes, and turned away uneasily.

Theo continued his interest without hesitation and extended his hand.

"I am Theo, Theo Taylor. May I ask your name? Y'—you're in Winfield's wedding?"

"Mmm hmmm. I'm Vy. Violet Louise Vittoye." *Oh, m'gosh, now why did I say that?* I—"I'm one of Sadie's bridesmaids." Vy tried to continue the conversation politely with a question. "Did y' say your last name is Taylor? Are y' any kin to Ivy Taylor."

"Yep, Ivy's my baby sister."

"Really? I just met her. I really liked Ivy. She's very nice."

"Ummm, yeah, she is. Course I'd think so since she's my baby sister. And just how are you acquainted with Sadie Ellis, Miss Violet Louise Vittoye?"

Vy blushed. "Please just call me Vy. And, well, I reckon I've known Sadie all my life. She lives right cross the mountain from me n' my mama. Our family has always been friends with th' Ellises far back as I can remember. They are like family to us. I, well, me n' my mama, we sewed all th' weddin' dresses, includin' Sadie's bridal gown. Maudie n' Sadie helped some with th' hemmin',' but mostly it was just me n' Mama. How do y' know Sadie and Winfield, Theo?"

Theo secured his last candle in a tall window, turned, and took long strides over to where Vy was working. He perched himself on a church bench and continued.

"Well, pretty, I only know Sadie through Winfield, but Win, and all the Campbells, well, my family and their family have been friends since long before I was born. Their farm adjoins our land. Since there were hundreds of acres between the two houses, Theo gave a short laugh at the thought. "They are our next-door neighbors. The Campbells and the Taylors have always gone t' church together and are all charter members of Ailor Springs Church."

Vy scanned the little sanctuary. Blossoms and ivy fronds decorated every corner. With its stone pillars and stained glass windows, the little chapel resembled a beautiful medieval garden. There was only one window left that needed a candle. It was the far back one located very high on the wall. Vy walked back to it and attempted to place her candle in its holder. She stretched her arms, stood on tiptoe, and reached up as high as she could, but her fingers faltered, causing the candle to tumble and fall down to the floor as Theo rushed to her aid.

"Here, let me help you, pretty one." As Theo reached for the candle, Vy thought she felt his hand purposely linger on hers. Vy caught her breath at the spicy aroma surrounding him that reminded her of something—someone. She felt she should get out of there, away from this beautiful boy, but her legs felt paralyzed.

The awkward position Vy found herself in had her body wedged next to Theo between the end of the church pew and the window. Trapped here with a young man's body so close to hers, Vy could not decide whether she felt discomfort or pleasure. The candle slid into the holder just fine, and still Theo did not move away. Instead, the handsome young man who towered over her small frame looked down into her face, his steel gray eyes studying every inch of her features.

Vy was caught in a trance. She had never been this close to anyone other than Gran or Mama, much less a gentleman. His face was only inches away from hers.

Those eyes. He's the most beautiful person I have ever seen.

At that very second, the double doors of the church flew open and a loud voice stormed in the quiet sanctuary. The enchanting moment between the couple was over as quickly as it had begun.

"Hey, you two. Gettin' to know each other?" Winfield Campbell sauntered up the aisle and sat down. Close behind him was Will Graves.

"Eh, yes, we have met, Winfield. Vy, you know Winfield, of course, but this goofy guy here's Will Graves. Have you met him? Will, old buddy, this here is Miss Violet Louise Vittoye." Vy could feel her face flush as Theo extended his hand to lead her from the cramped place where they were standing out to the main aisle.

"No, I don't think I have met y,' Mr. Graves, and please just call me Vy."

"Heavens, girl! Don't y' call me mister anything. Will is just fine."

There I go again. Oh, m' gosh, now why did I call him that? I am so stupid. "I'm sorry, Will, it's still nice t' meet you."

Theo turned to Win, motioning to the decorations all around the church. "I think we're finished with the window candles in here. Anything else you want us to do, Win? Looks as though everything's about ready, doesn't it? Y' ready to tie the knot? What ya' think, pal?"

Win eyed the beautifully decorated sanctuary with pride, and in his most humble voice spoke to Theo and Violet. "Yes, everything looks real nice. Me n' Sadie do appreciate all of you pitchin' in to make our day so special."

Theo chose to ignore his friend's serious tone, moved away from Vy, slapped Winfield on the back, and changed the subject.

"Hope you know what you're a doin', old boy! Marriage! Wow! Can't believe you're really doin' this. Nothin' against Sadie, o' course. She's a good gal, all right. Just can't believe you want t' get married n' stay on th' farm. I always saw you leavin' this one horse town someday with me, Win. Marriage ain't fer me, and farmin' ain't either. No, siree. I got deals and plans for m'self as well, but it ain't marriage or farmin.' No, brother!"

"Soon's I get my hands on enough cash, I'm gone from here. I'm leavin' this town and probably headin' west. I'd sure like t' have a business of some kind in one o' those gold rush towns. I just believe I would be likely to make it prospectin' f'r gold."

Winfield Campbell put his hand on Theo's shoulder and spoke earnestly. "Well, Theo, old pal, y' go right on and prospect for gold out west somewhere. My little pot of gold is all wrapped up in a sweet little girl named Sadie Ellis. All I ask the Lord for in this life, Theo, is a decent living from my farm, Sadie for my wife, and a couple of sweet little youngins."

Theo shook his head at his friend in mock pity.

The back doors opened one more time and Theo recognized the familiar feminine voice of his sister Neppia. "Theo, what you doin' in here, boy? You need to let me fix your tie properly before you go escortin' anybody down that aisle. Just look at you now. You have flower petals all over your trousers."

"Hey there, Sis, I want y' t' meet Miss Violet Vittoye. Vy, this is another one of my beautiful sisters. May I present Miss Penelope Taylor, but you may call her Neppi!"

It was apparent that Neppia was amazed at the young girl. "Hello there, Violet, dear. It's very nice to meet you. Are you the very talented young lady who has produced the beautiful gowns for this wedding?"

Vy nodded in affirmation.

"I simply can't believe you have done such a wonderful job tailoring all those gowns, you being only thirteen years old."

At his sister's statement Theo jerked around abruptly, taking a long hard look at Violet. The shock on his face was evident as he mused, *Glory be, the pretty one is only a kid!*

Neppia continued talking to Vy as her nimble fingers retied and straightened Theo's tie. "There, that's better now, dear. Since I'm a seamstress myself, I am quite appreciative of all the hard work you and your mother have put into the beautiful dresses. They are certainly exquisite, and the laces you fashioned are magnificent. Y' know, Vy, I've been sewing for a long time, but I was never so adept at tailoring when I was as young as you are."

"Thank you kindly, Miss Neppi. And I'm glad t' meet ya, as well. I'd also like to thank y' fer finishin' Miss Ivy's dress for Mama and me since we could never get together for that last fittin.'"

"Shucks, t'was nothin,' dear. I was glad to do it." Neppia turned and motioned to the older couple who had come in with her and were now admiring the decorations. "Ma! Pa! Come up here n' meet this little girl who sewed all the beautiful gowns fer this here weddin.'"

Theo met the couple halfway, cocked his head to one side, and ushered his parents the length of the church to meet his new friend. With a sly grin, he proclaimed, "Vy, may I present the famous Mr. and Mrs. Jacob Asbury Taylor. You may call them Ma and Pa, Jacob and Cordelia, or just Jake and Delia like everybody else does."

Delia shook her head in disdain at Theo then looked at the girl and smiled. "Don't pay my son no mind, dear. We are very glad t' meet y,' Violet, and are very impressed with the wedding attire ye' and y' mama have produced. Y' sure ought t' be very proud of y'selves."

"How d' ya do, Vy?" Jacob Taylor extended his hand, smiled, and nodded his head in agreement.

The church bells began to ring out, inviting the crowds to come on inside and take their seats.

"O m' gosh, I don't have my bridesmaid dress on yet."

Neppi patted Vy on the shoulder. "That bell means we only have a few more minutes before this here church is filled up with people. Better git on down t' the little prayer room, dear, n' change into your dress, hadn't ya, hon? Winfield Campbell, you'd better go on and find your place with the parson, or y' goin' t' be late fer y' own weddin.' Go on along with th' boy now, Theodore. Don't you let Win be late."

The Ailor Springs Church was packed to the gills and would have been stuffy and suffocating inside had the windows not been opened at the top, allowing the cool evening breeze to give a cross draft. Even so, at the front of the church the old parson kept wiping perspiration from his bald head with a red kerchief, but Winfield looked calm and cool standing beside him, waiting for the music to begin.

The bride's family and friends were seated on the left side of the aisle, and the groom's on the right side facing the podium. The Ellis family, including Maudie, Clyve, Amos, Arly, Lucinda, and Calvin, two grandparents, a myriad of aunts and uncles, as well as some cousins took up most of the bride's side, and good friends finished it out.

The groom's family was not quite as large as Sadie's, but the wedding being held at Win's home church, it was full of well-wishing friends and curious church members who pressed in until there was not another seat in the little sanctuary to be had. A standing crowd lined the sides and back of the sanctuary as well, spilling out the open doors of the church onto the lawn.

The organist started to play the wedding march. The ushers looked perfectly handsome in their black tuxedos as they escorted the couple's parents to their special reserved front seat places. Two adorable little flower girls toddled in, tossing daisy petals all down the church aisle that had been draped in white.

A little ring bearer who followed stumbled and fell but quickly jumped up on chubby legs, recovered the pillow as well as the gold rings, and obediently found his place at the front.

Following the ring bearer, Ivy Taylor, Theo's sister strolled down the aisle.

Behind Ivy walked Violet, then came Bertha McVae, Sadie's cousin and maid of honor. The three young girls looked like a breath of spring-time completely multihued in their soft coral, yellow, and blue voile dresses.

They carried bouquets of daisies and baby's breath tied with white satin ribbons, which had also been wound into the braids of their upswept hair.

The pump organ boomed louder as the wedding march announced the arrival of the bride standing at the back entrance, and the whole congregation stood to their feet in unison, turning to face the lovely young girl walking down the aisle on the arm of her father. Vy gasped as thoughts raced through her mind. Oh, Sadie—you look like an angel! I wonder if you really love Winfield—if he really loves you? Will I ever walk down the aisle to someone—someone who loves me?

Vy's thoughts quickly snapped back into the present by the parson's words.

"Who gives this woman in marriage?"

"I do, Reverend." Clyve Ellis somberly placed Sadie's hand in Win's. Vy observed the whole service intently, caught up in wonder as Winfield Campbell and Sadie Ellis pledged their troths one to another. After the couple's vows were given, the parson turned to the congregation and finally announced, "Let no man put asunder what God hath joined together. I now present to you Mr. and Mrs. Winfield Campbell."

The reception party was held outside, for there were no facilities inside the church. Long wooden tables had been draped in embroidered white linen tablecloths on which were centered tall vases of pink apple blossoms arranged together with shrouds of dainty baby's breath, all tied with pastel ribbons.

The wedding cake on the center table stood five tiers high and was bedecked with hundreds of tiny icing rosebuds. There was ample food for the crowd, and everyone eagerly lined up for the feast.

There was a special table decorated for the bride and groom and their parents, with a good many others scattered around the grounds for the sit-down meal, but not nearly enough for all present.

Friends and relations were finding shade on the ground under the huge oak trees, sitting picnic style all around the grassy churchyard. Fiddlers played lively music, and some guests had chosen partners for singing folk and gospel songs. Conversation, shouts of laughter, happy children running to and fro, congratulations, hearty handshakes for the groom, and kisses for the bride abounded.

One table was piled high with wrapped wedding gifts. Vy had never seen or been to a festive occasion such as this, and she was quite taken by it all.

Ivy Taylor bounced up and grabbed her by the arm. "Come on, new friend, let's us have some vittles. I'm starving. How 'bout you?" The food line had shortened some, and the pair walked up and approached a group of girls known to Ivy.

"Hey, everybody, wan'cha' t' meet my new friend, Violet Vittoye. Vy, this here's Mindia Seaton, Mary Mynatt, and y' already know Bertha, Sadie's cousin."

Vy recognized the girl with the long black hair immediately. Her eyes narrowed and her jaw tightened, along with a growing knot in the pit of her stomach. *Yeah, I know who you are, Mary Mynatt. Matter of fact, I helped make that dress you have on, but I guess you will turn your back and cross the street to get away or maybe just spit on me right about now...*

Ready to rebuff any rude thing the girl might do or say, Vy forced a smile, replying sweetly, "Hello, Mindia, it's nice t' meet y.' Hey, Bertha. Hello again, Mary."

Mindia bubbled, "You look so pretty in that bridesmaid's dress. Yellow is your color, all right. It just sets off your auburn hair and blue eyes. Myself, I can't wear it at all. Makes me look all washed out or something."

Mary smiled, met Vy's eyes boldly, agreeing, "You do look beautiful in yellow, Violet, or should we call you Vy? It's been awhile since I've seen you. Do you remember me? I want you to know I have sure loved wearing this dress I have on." Mary turned, speaking to the other girls. "Did you all know that Vy and her mother made the dress I'm wearing? As a matter of fact, they have made several for my mother and me. Haven't you, Vy?"

The nice comment from Mary Mynatt took Vy completely by surprise. Her face took on a bright blush, and she started to stammer but nodded instead in affirmation.

Mindia perked up. "Oh, Vy, I can't believe you can sew so well. Those weddin' dresses you sewed are gorgeous! Wish y' would make me a dress. I get so tired of wearing the same old things to church. Could y' sew something for me, Vy? Y' think you might be able to? See, I don't really take t' sewin.' It's just not me, I guess."

Mary interrupted Mindia's chatter. "You really are very talented. Do you realize that, Vy?"

Vy looked down, taken aback. She was simply not prepared for Mary Mynatt's friendliness. "Oh, sewin things is nothin' t' me. I been doin' it with Mama and my gran since I was a tot, I guess."

The girls lined up and walked both sides of the tables, piling their plates high with goodies, then headed to the big flat rock under the shade of an old oak tree where they could sit and eat comfortably. Mary chose to perch between Vy and Ivy. Mindia sat on the other side of Ivy, and Bertha chose to sit on the very end."

Ivy swallowed a big mouthful of cake, looked curiously toward her newfound friend, and queried, "Where do you live, Vy? Do you have a big family?"

"Well, you go through town and over the hill a good long ways to our cabin and, no, it's just me n' my mama now. We, well, my granny did live with us and before that my papaw too, but Papaw and Gran Vittoye are both gone on now."

Bertha gave Vy a questioning look. "So you live with your daddy's people, do y,' Violet? I mean, y' last name being Vittoye and theirs, too."

Vy flushed. She had never been asked that question before. There was an awkward silence as she pondered her answer.

Ivy was staid on Bertha and Vy's conversation as she turned to pick up her iced tea. In doing so, the close proximity of the girls caused her elbow to bump against Vy's arm, which made her hand ricochet and strike the top of the iced tea glass. At that instant, tea, ice, and glass soared about and landed smack into Mindia's plate of food, which toppled over as well, shattering and splattering all over the bottoms of dresses and shoes. The girls screamed first then jumped up, shaking off skirts, petticoats, and shoes now strewn with potato salad, crumbled sandwiches, coleslaw, and fried chicken, along with a mass of crushed and crumbled wedding cake.

Shrieks and screams of laughter erupted as the girls fell all over each other trying to dodge and avoid the mess. The girls were giggling, talking, shaking off spilled food, tea, and glass shards when Jessie Mae Mynatt cast a glance toward the crowd. Perceiving that Violet was one of the girls with whom Mary was having such a merry time, the woman moved close enough to catch Mary's attention, gave her a threatening look, and frantically waved for her to come there at once.

As Mary caught her mother's eye, she muttered under her breath, "Oh, good grief. Not again!" Turning, she spoke to the group apologetically. "I'm sorry, girls, looks like I have to go now."

"Don't go, Mary," Mindia said. "We'll get all of this mess cleaned up in a minute, n' then we can' talk some more."

"I'm sorry, Mindia. Mother calls!" Mary gathered up her dishes and shrugged her shoulders with a remorseful look to Vy as she walked away toward her mother.

Vy watched Mary catch up to her mother. Assessing the whole the situation, she concluded that Jessie Mae Mynatt was the real snob—not Mary. She silently promised herself that although she would try to honor Granny's previous warning to overlook the snobbery and rudeness of women such as Jessie Mae Mynatt, she would certainly not be sewing dresses for her—ever again.

Girl chatter was suddenly interrupted by male voices.

"Well, what is this? Just look what we've found! The fairest of Maynard's Valley right here under an oak tree at the Ailor Springs Church."

Two very tall and handsome young men strolled closer to the lovely feminine assemblage. Ivy waved them away.

"Oh, get on out of here, you two boys; we're having a girl party."

"And just what are you discussing that our ears can't hear, little sister? Nope, I think we will just stick around and learn all the latest from you ladies." Theo perched himself on the rock beside Bertha. Bertha moved closer toward him and wedged herself in between the tall, handsome Theo and Will Graves, who settled on the other side of her. Theo slid his arm around Bertha's waist as Will questioned her.

"Who was that ray of sunshine that I just saw leave here?"

"Oh, that's just Mary Mynatt. Why y' want to know that, Will?"

"Hmmm, I was just askin,' Berthie."

Bertha promptly slid her hand into the crook of both the young men's arms and smiled coyly up into first Will's eyes and then Theo's. "Well, Mary is gone, but I might have a secret or two, boys."

"Think you could tell us something that we don't already know, Miss McVae?"

Without the bat of an eye, Bertha answered, "I could tell you boys a lot of things that you don't know."

Sadie approached the group of young people hurriedly, her gown and lacy veil blowing in the breeze.

"Violet, would you come help me get my gown off and into my travel clothing? I need to get this dress packed away. It's a good two hours to Whitesville, and Winfield wants to be leaving soon before it gets too dark."

Ivy interrupted, appearing with fresh glasses of tea and another plate of food. She put her arm around Vy's shoulders in protest and begged, "Please don't take our new friend away, Sadie. We're having our own girl party here."

"Oh, dear, I'm really sorry t' take Vy away, Ivy, but I must have some help with this here dress and gettin' ready to leave. You'll forgive me, won't y'? Hey, listen! After Win and I get settled in our own home, right near here, well, I promise you, dear, that I'll plan a nice girls only party for all of us. How's that sound?"

Vy rose to take leave and help her friend, stating, "It's okay, Ivy. I'm finished anyway."

Sadie and Vy headed back inside the church to the prayer room where they had dressed and prepared for the ceremony.

The little room was littered with skirts, waists, shoes, hair brushes, hairpins, lip rouge, and other girlie paraphernalia, as well as Sadie's trunk full of clothing, among other things for her wedding trip.

Vy helped Sadie undo the myriad of buttons on the gown and pull the long and cumbersome dress over her head. She was about to hang it up when Sadie took it from her. "Here, Violet dear, I will take care of this. I forgot to tell Win where I was goin,' so could you please go and tell him what I'm doin' and that I'll be out soon's I get changed. And, oh, yes, tell him I said he better find someone who will help him load my trunk and things into our carriage."

"Our carriage." It's Sadie's carriage, too. Wonder if I'll ever have my own carriage.

"Sure, Sadie. I'll go tell him." Vy ran outside, found Winfield, and quickly delivered Sadie's message then headed back inside the church to see if there was anything else she could do for her good friend.

Upon entering the side door of the little church, there were voices coming from the back of the sanctuary. Vy could only make out two figures in the darkened church because her eyes had adjusted to the bright sunshine outside.

Although the silhouettes looked like a man and a woman, it was impossible for Vy to see clearly. The voices, somewhat familiar, sounded harsh and irritated. Vy did not want to eavesdrop on the couple's conversation and turned to make her way to the prayer room, but before she could get away, she could not help overhearing some of what the two were saying, even though only a few words here and there were distinct.

"Please...no! Please...don't...will hurt...not...I don't...please... know—we...Worry...don't try to...fer you...try...derstand...please... quiet...hush...shhhh...someone's there."

Talking ceased as the mystery couple became aware that someone else had entered the church.

The two figures hurriedly made their way toward the double doors in the back for a quick exit. The small female figure rushed through the doors and disappeared, but the male figure in haste glanced back over his shoulder as he opened the door. In doing so, the late afternoon sun caught and rested on his profile so that Vy recognized him immediately as Seth Seaton. She instantly remembered someone saying Mr. Seaton's wife was sick and would not be able to attend today's festivities, and recalled that because she had been curious to see who this kind and generous man was married to. Wasn't that girl's name Mindia Seaton?—the one Ivy Taylor had just introduced to her? I'd bet Mindia is kin to that man, very likely his daughter. I wonder what he's a doin' in the back of this dark church sneakin' around with some woman? I took him for a real nice man bringin' our family gifts like he always has.

The girls gathered up and packed their things for the journey back home.

"Goodbye, Vy," Mindia said. "This was such fun! Let's hold Sadie to her promise and all get together at her house someday soon. I would sure love to see all of you again sometime." Then came hugs and good-byes as the girls went out the door and headed for their rides.

Vy had planned to ride home with Maudie and Clyve since she had been carried over that morning with Winfield Campbell and Sadie. She gathered her dress and grip together, looked forlornly around the empty room, then went outside. I've got to find the Ellises and see when we're leavin.' She spotted Clyve and the boys pacing nervously near their carriage.

"Hey, Mr. Ellis! It still okay if me n' Mama rides home with you'uns, ain't it?"

"Of course it's fine, Vy. Me n' th boys is ready t' light out of here when everybody, well, when Maudie says she's ready. I reckon she's still a talkin' t' that Campbell woman like she has been fer th' last hour r' so. We are all ready t' go whenever she says."

Vy surveyed the clearing churchyard. What had been a magical festivity only hours ago was now looking deserted and barren. The musicians had packed their instruments and taken leave. The once white banquet tables had already been stripped, reverting back to old, worn wooden tables once more. The pretty dishes had been gathered, washed, and stored. The floral décor and ivy fronds that had bedecked the church so beautifully were now wilting in a heap that had been thrown near the edge of the woods. The rice trail that had been flung upon the newly-weds was being swept up by some ladies, and the newlyweds themselves were well on their way to their honeymoon destination.

Sadie's enchanted wedding day was over. It was time to go home.

From where she was standing, it looked as though Maudie Ellis was indeed getting up and bidding her goodbyes to the Campbell family.

Clyve interrupted Vy's thoughts. "You see our carriage yonder, don't you, Violet? It's right over there."

As Vy turned to see the Ellis carriage, something caught her eye. *Who is that Theo Taylor is getting in the carriage with? It's Bertha— Bertha McVae. I bet he's courting her. He's so nice—*"Theodore." *Ivy said he thinks I am pretty. Lucky Bertha.*

At that moment, Maudie and Lucinda Ellis appeared with their announcement. "Let's head on home, Clyve."

It was plain to Vy from the look on Clyve Ellis's face that this wedding had not been an enjoyable occasion for him. Besides stating plain out that Sadie was too young to marry a man so much older than her, Clyve did not take much to social events. Or as Maudie would say, "It nearly takes an earthquake to get Clyve off the farm." Vy reasoned the man was in a nervous state, ready to start the journey home, and she was right.

Amos Ellis had walked down the hill and pulled the carriage up closer to the church so the ladies would not have so far to walk in the rocks. Maudie and Lucinda held up their fancy skirts as Clyve grabbed each of their outstretched hands, fairly lifting his wife and daughter-in-law aboard the carriage. Arly took Vy's brocade grip as well as her bridesmaid dress and some other things, then settled them on the top of the carriage trunk where they could easily be found upon reaching her cabin.

Vy stretched on tiptoe so she could see better, scanning the grounds.

"Maudie, have you seen my mama?"

"Oh, yes, Vy. I forgot to tell y,' dear. Sally came around a while earlier, about an hour ago, and asked me t' tell y' she was going on ahead of us. Said she was not feeling well a'tall and for us t' bring y' home."

"Do you know how she got home, Maudie? Who she went on with?"

"She didn't tell me, darlin', but I'm sure she aims t' answer all that later when y' see her. Tell you the truth, Sally looked pale to me, like she was going to be sick or something had upset her. I hope she ain't comin' down with an old cold or th' flu that's going around, but don't y' worry though, Vy. I'll go inside with y' and check on y'r mama when we get y' home."

Vy extended her hand to Clyve, who helped her in the carriage. Amos was driving with his dad beside him. Clyve Ellis was ready to get started. His patience was wearing thin. "Maudie, do all of you uns have everything now? This is the last call!" Amos snapped the reins and called, "Giddy up, mule."

It was completely dark when the Ellis carriage pulled up to the Vittoye cabin. During the trip home, Maudie had leaned her head over to one side and fallen asleep. Arly found Vy's valise, dismounted, and helped her to the ground. As he picked up her things and walked her to the door, he spoke with concern. "Don't look like anybody's home, Violet, and it's awful dark in your cabin. I'll wake up Maw to look in on your mama, see if she's okay."

"Mmmm, no thanks. She, I mean, yore maw's already sound asleep, Arly. As much as she's gone through today, I'm not going to disturb her. Besides, I promised Maudie that if Ma is sick in the morning, I will ride over and let her know." Vy gave a weak laugh. "I think we ought t' let y' maw and mine rest."

Vy opened the door and lit a lantern before Arly returned to the carriage. "We will be fine now. You-uns don't have t' worry bout us. I really do appreciate you a bringin' me home, though."

Arly bade Vy goodbye, joined his family, and the Ellises' carriage drove on off toward home.

Vy shut the door and called up toward the loft. "Mama! Mama, are y' there?" There was no answer or no sign of anyone. The beds were empty and made up exactly as they had been left.

Mama, why do you always do this to me? What a wonderful day this has been for me, only to end up like this—worrying about you. Why should I be surprised? I ought t' know what t' expect from y' by now.

Vy sat up until eleven thirty waiting for Sally and then finally fell down across the bed, dozing on and off. She was weary but could not relax.

Someone let Sally out of a carriage at a little past 3:00 a.m.

Vy feigned sleep as her mama opened the door, climbed the loft stairs, and peered over to look at her.

Maybe I can finally rest now. Vy shivered and reached for another quilt as Sally turned down the lantern and fell into her own bed.

Who have you been with since early afternoon, Mama? What did you do from two in the afternoon until three in the morning? Who did you leave the wedding with? Was it the stranger who picks you up at night? Have mercy! The stranger was at Sadie's wedding.

Ventures and Adventures

The Taylor family farm was near the Graves's farm, so the two boys had attended school and played together from early childhood. Will Graves was a happy-go-lucky kind of fellow, very adventuresome—leaning toward the mischievous—and since this scenario also described Theo Taylor, the pair had found much in common during their nineteen years of life. As the boys grew up, playing hooky from school and various other mild but foolhardy antics had gotten both of them licks on their backsides from the headmaster of Ailor Springs school, as well as from their parents, which actually served to make them good friends. One other thing the two young men had in common was the fact both of them had sworn from childhood to get out, or leave Maynard's Valley at the first chance. Theo and Will charted out their plans together at a young age and decided early on that if they discovered some prospect that offered any chance of fortune (of course, not requiring a whole lot of capital investment), then it would be considered.

Recently, Will had set aside a small but adequate sum from selling off a house that his late aunt Emma Claiborne had bequeathed him. Although he had no intention of investing the whole of his cash or taking off somewhere alone, he had decided it was time to seriously seek an opportunity for his old friend Theo and himself, or at least try to make a childhood dream come true. Will had only to mention his thoughts to his friend, who immediately was in favor and excited with the whole idea. The two began their search in the local newspaper ads for a break, or some wonderful opportunity.

In the September 4, 1884, Whitesville Journal classified advertisements. the following appeared:

Bargain! For Sale!
Health Springs Resort Hotel
Little Moon, Ark.
Rare opportunity
for Young Ambitious Men
No experience necessary
Small capital investment

The boys had actually dreamed of going out west—Texas was the place that came to their minds—to prospect for gold, manage a hotel, run some sort of business on their own. The kind of business did not matter to the boys if it served to free them from Maynard's Valley and offer them a chance to make some real money—to become a big success.

And right here it was! Here in the morning paper. Will Graves assured himself that he had just discovered a grand opportunity.

The newspaper ad told of a hotel near some warm spring waters in an Arkansas resort town called Little Moon. Will had heard of these mineral water health spas before , and how the rich and famous clamored to them for cures of their various maladies. It was said that if you bathed in those mineral springs enough, you could come out cured of the quinsy, rheumatism, neuritis, neuralgia, and even palsy—and it was rumored that the baths would not only give you skin like a baby, it could regrow hair on a balding head.

Will was convinced this was the opportunity he and his friend had been waiting for, but he had to talk to Theo—to run it by his old friend to see if he was still in and whether he thought they could financially swing the deal.

"Theo, how'd y' like to be the owner of a hotel in a resort area?" It didn't take a whole lot to get Theo's attention. The boy's interest peaked immediately. The newspaper ad was read, reread, and pored over by the two in great anticipation. This was surely the grand venture they had been looking for. It had all the prospects of wealth besides the bonus of getting the heck out of Maynard's Valley. How could they possibly lose if their hotel was in an area where people were flocking to seek cures for various and sundry physical ailments?

There was only one problem at hand, and that, of course, was cash! Will had his part all ready and was eager to go, but Theo did not. That did not mean, however, that he did not have a plan. On the contrary, he had been thinking on it for some time now. Only drawback was his plan included approaching his parents and asking them for an early share of his inheritance. He would suggest selling off a small portion of the family farm, which might possibly be hard to convince them to do, but it was his only option.

Theo reasoned. What could it hurt? Ma and Pa own far more land than they will ever use.

Asbury kicked a dirt clod, spit the wad of tobacco out, and shook his head side to side.

"Y' got to let me think about this, Son. I have to talk to your ma. I just don't know."

When Cordelia Taylor learned of Theo's plan the next morning, she shook her head in dread and wagged her finger at the boy. "Will Graves! I might have known he was in on this. He just got his hands on a little cash and has stirred up some harebrained idea in your head about leavin' here and runnin' off out west to God knows where! You ain't interested in no business, Theo. Y' nineteen years old and interested in a scurryin' away from home and family just quick as y' can!"

"Is that it, Son? Y' just want out of Maynard's Valley?"

"No, Pa. It ain't that a' tall!"

"It was that Will Graves givin' y' such a hair-brained idea sure as th' world," Cordelia broke in.

"No, Ma. It wasn't. We both been lookin' a long time for an opportunity like this. Here, Ma. Just read this ad."

Cordelia turned her back, shook her head, and started rinsing out dishes in her bowl of lye soap water.

"Ma, it ain't no silly idea to leave home and try to make my own way in th' world. I hate caring for livestock and raisin' corn 'n beans. Y' know I hate all that goes with this backward country life! I just wish y' both could understand that I need to do this." Theo sat across the table and earnestly searched his father's face. "Listen, Pa, just give me half a chance. I aim t' pay you and Ma every penny you loan me, plus interest..." Theo's pale gray eyes would have melted the heart of any stranger, no doubt so a bewildered mother and father.

Theo turned his pleas to Cordelia with a beseeching look. "Have some faith in y' son, won't you, Ma? I aim t' work very hard at this opportunity. Y' know I ain't cut out for farmin' like you and Pa."

Asbury Taylor slowly chewed a mouthful of bacon and eggs, buttered another biscuit, and raised his coffee cup. He looked at Cordelia, who was near tears. "Cordie, I know y' don't want me to give in to Theo here on this here, and, yes, I admit I'm real uneasy about the whole thing, too, but th' boy does have t' learn to depend on himself someday. Leavin' home may just be the thing he needs t' come t' that."

Asbury turned to Theo. "Son, away from y' home and family, yore gonna find that life ain't no bed of roses. They'll be nobody out there ready t' hand you somethin' just 'cause you want it. Runnin' out t' Arkansas or anywhere else and undertakin' a big responsibility like this is going t' be more hard work than y' ever faced in y' life. I guess y' have made up y' mind and there's no way for y' t' learn unless y' go ahead and try it. Some hard work might even erase that 'get rich quick' dream out of y' head, Son. Th' Lord Himself knows I ain't been able to do it."

Theo knew he had won. Smiling from ear to ear, he hugged Ma first, then Pa, and shouted over his shoulder to them both as he ran outside where Will sat waiting. "You ain't gonna regret this, Pa. I love y,' Ma!"

Cordelia lifted the hot pot with care and filled Asbury's cup with the strong brew one more time. She sat down close beside her husband of thirty years and studied his lined face as tears welled up in her eyes.

"I'm just afraid we'll never see him again, Asbury. Those two youngins ain't never been nothin' but trouble together. And y' know it ain't th' farmland I care about, Az, but I shore don't want th' other kids t' hear about us a givin' Theo his share of this farm early on."

Even though both the Taylors and the Graves family were brokenhearted with the boys' plan, Asbury Taylor contacted Simpson Waller, who lived on the western adjoining farm, and agreed to sell him a plot of land that he had been wanting to purchase for some time.

It was early on a September morning when Asbury finally called to his son.

"I may be crazy, but it is done, boy. Theo, I have wired the first compensation for y' hotel to Mr. Arnold Zayle at the address out there in Arkansas. Here's th' receipt, Son. You keep it in a safe place. The balance of y' money is in an account I've established fer you. Y' just need to sign and return these papers to Mr. McNeely down at th' Valley bank and it's finished."

With a feeling of exultation, Theo all but shouted, "Whoopee! Oh, th-thank y' so much, Pa! Y' won't be sorry. I promise y.'" Involuntarily, Theo hugged Asbury's neck and dashed off to fetch ink and pen.

I'm on my way! This is my big chance.

When the big day arrived, Zachary and Will Graves set off first to pick up Theo and Asbury Taylor in their wagon then head for the depot. Asbury was full of last minute words of wisdom for his son as they waited outside for the Graves to arrive.

"This here undertakin' is a solemn responsibility, Theodore, and I hope y' realize that your mother and me are doing this again' our own better judgment. Just hope we ain't bought y' a pig in a poke! Promise me, Son, that when y' get there, y'll write and let us know if the place is all you expected. Promise me?"

Theo nodded in affirmation.

"And there's another thing, Theo. Y' must keep this transaction to y'self and don't breathe a word to y' sisters or E.E. what I have gone on and given y' ahead of them. Y' hear me, do y'? The lot of them would be awfully upset if they found out I sold part of the farm for y,' Son."

"They ain't never gonna find out, Pa, and I promise, y' won't be sorry y' did this."

Theo's heart beat wild with anticipation when he spotted the Graves's wagon coming down the dirt road.

"There they are, Pa!" Will and Mr. Graves rolled to a stop in front of the Taylor house.

Delia Taylor shed another tear and watched from her kitchen window as her men climbed aboard the wagon to depart. She and Liza Graves had both chosen to kiss their sons goodbye at home rather than accompany them to the railway station, airing a sad and teary farewell in public. Cordelia watched until the wagon topped the distant hill, made a turn in the road, and was gone.

The depot was all abuzz with activity as the Graves's wagon neared. The sight of hurry scurry passengers, mail bags, parcels, luggage, and especially of the big steam engine being prepared for the trip to the west, held Will and Theo spellbound so they could hardly speak.

Will looked first at Asbury and then at his son before admonishing both young men. "Boys, now I hope to see y' use good business sense, diversify, and not use every dime of y' money on this one venture. I'll be a prayin' for the both of y' that God go with you and that y' make wise decisions in this here undertakin.'"

Asbury's eyes watered. His voice broke, but he cleared his throat, regaining his composure. "I will only add y' remember this, my boys,

> Trust in the Lord with all thine heart;
> and lean not unto thine own understanding.
> In all thy ways acknowledge him, and he shall direct thy paths
>
> Proverbs 3:5–6

"Now, Son, don't y' fr'get now, if things don't work out, y' just come on back home."

"Things gonna work out, Pa. Don't y' be worryin' now."

"Goodbye, Pa ... Mr. Graves."

"Goodbye, Paw ... Mr. Taylor."

The four men shook hands. "Goodbye, boys. God bless y' both."

The conductor shouted "All abooard" as the boys wound down the aisles past other passengers and found their places. Wiping the moisture off the window, Theo peered out. *Pa looks so small and sad standing there beside Mr. Graves. I guess he will miss me a whole lot, like Ma and th' whole family will. Pa believes in me. He knows I will be a success. I'm sure of it.*

The whistle blew as the train started to roll slowly down the track, bellowing and puffing clouds of black smoke. The depot grew smaller and smaller. Finally, Theo could not see his father and Mr. Graves. His excitement mounted as the train gathered speed.

Asbury Taylor and Zachary Graves stood and watched the train disappear in silence. The red caboose finally went round a curve and rolled out of sight. Only a curl of black smoke from the engine was now visible.

Asbury was the first to speak. "How long y' give 'em, Zach?"

"Six months, a year at the most. How about you, Az?"

"Th' same as you, if that long."

Theo's hopes were sky high riding the train that first day on the long journey to Little Moon, Arkansas. He could scarcely hide his enthusiasm from his friend as they discussed the adventure lying before them and watching the picturesque countryside roll by.

"I just can't believe it, Will, ole buddy. We're actually doin' it! We have cut th' family tie, th' old apron cord. Yep, we've cut it from our birth place—rinky dink old Maynard's Valley. The two of us are headin' for a real town, where we will live like kings. Why, I don't know why we haven't done this before now, do you?" Theo stretched his long legs, reared back in the dark green velvet coach seat again, took out a long brown cigarette, lit it slowly, and exhaled the smoke out in perfect little rings.

Will accepted a cigarette from Theo, lit it, coughed, turned a bit red, and then nodded his head in agreement. After gaining his composure, he replied thoughtfully, "Besides owning a thriving hotel business, Theo, old friend, with plenty of money comin' our way, we will run our own restaurant. Just imagine fancy chefs and waiters serving up thick steaks, roasted potatoes, and fat rolls."

Theo chuckled, looked off into the distance with an impious smile that fit him so perfectly, and added, "Not to mention another plus, Will.

The best thing is, we are going to come into contact with new people—new and interesting business men and good lookin' women."

"Yeah, women, not immature country girls from Maynard's Valley, but intelligent, sophisticated, mature females."

"Yeah, bona fide women," Will said and laughed. As quickly as the words were out of his mouth, the young man's thoughts bounded back to Maynard's Valley. *Could any girl ever be as lovely as the one I'm leaving behind?*

The train ride turned out to be a long and tiring one. It took more than a week to get to Arkansas, what with stops for the loading and unloading of freight and the boarding and departing of passengers in cities along the way. The young men enjoyed their rich meals on the train, and the scenery was pleasing enough, but as the days wore on, with stops growing more frequent, they both grew tired and impatient to arrive and get on with their new and wonderful lifestyle.

On arrival, it certainly appeared to be a tourist town. The main street in Little Moon, Arkansas, was lined with hotels and the like. The boys hailed down and boarded a coach after they departed the train but could have walked to their destination had they known how close they were. The driver simply turned a corner, drove about a block, then quickly pointed out a building, or boarding house to be more accurate, on which hung a slightly crooked sign that read:

Health Springs Resort Inn
21 So. Main Street
Little Moon, Arkansas

"There she is, boys," the driver said and pointed to a large dwelling that was crying maintenance as loud as it could cry.

"What in the world, Theo? Would you look there? Heavens t' Betsy, that ain't it, is it, Will?"

"Lord help us, I reckon it is."

Located at 21 South Main Street in Little Moon, Arkansas, and for which Asbury Taylor had already wired a considerable down payment, stood an old building—a rooming house, maybe, but certainly no hotel. It was a frame house that sagged slightly, reaching three stories high in a Federal style. Its once white paint was now gray and peeling, and its green shutters were loose and hanging crooked.

The old structure was two bays deep with double chimneys on each gable end, and both were in dire need of masonry work. Although it may have been impressive in its day, it was evident that a lot of money would be needed to repair what was obvious, let alone that which was hidden.

The shock of the sight was taking a toll on Theo and Will's nerves, to say the least, but they dismounted the carriage and lugged down their trunks and gear in spite of obvious disappointment.

The front steps creaked and sagged as the boys walked up on the porch, and since no one answered after knocking for several minutes, the boys pulled open the screen and stepped inside the front door.

The furnishings looked to be a mix of period antiques, and Theo judged them to have been fine quality when they were new. On the stairway's handrail leading up from the lobby, one could still see what had once been elaborate carvings and embellishments though now chipped and in bad need of lacquer. The carpets were imported wool in what had been a gold and crimson design, but were now worn slick with soil and faded in strategic places. Several big ceramic spittoons sat here and there, as well as a couple of yellowing and neglected potted ferns.

An ample dining room sat to the right of the entrance and held a long mahogany dining table with fluted legs that terminated in casters. The table itself had an extending mechanism that allowed it to seat at least fifty. At present the table was stretched out to its maximum length, but there were only about twelve side chairs pulled up around it. The chairs were handsome ones made of solid carved mahogany, and a good number of the same style were stacked at the back of the dining room, looking as though they hadn't been used lately. Some pieces looked in fair shape even though a few were sagging in the seat area.

Theo could see through swinging double doors that the kitchen area adjoined the dining room at the back, but he could not spot a single soul in either room.

Will pointed to a sign hanging over the desk in the lobby that read:

Private Rooms (One bed)—$1.00 a day
Shared Rooms
Whole bed . . . . 50 cents
1/2 Bed . . . . 30 cents
1/3 Bed . . . . 20 cents
Meals 25cents
Including bread & coffee or tea
Two towels per occupant
Extra towels. . . . . . . 01 cents ea.
Hot water (first bowl). . . Free
(Extra bowls) . . . . . . 01cents ea.
Bottled Mineral Water
Jug 25

Two more signs were posted just outside the dining room and adjoining bar.

Meals . . . . 25 cents
Includes bread and coffee or tea
Breakfast . . . . served from 5:30 to 7:30
Dinner . . . . served 11:30 to 1:30
Supper . . . . Served 6:30 to 8:30
BAR OPEN 4:30 PM to 11:00 PM
Spirits. . . . . 10 cents
Sarsaparilla . . . . 05 cents

Another sign on a door down the hall from the entrance toward the back read:

OFFICE
"Private Keep Out!"

Suddenly, out of that door and leaning heavily on a cane, tottered a short, round male figure. Theo guessed him to be in his fifties or sixties. Squinting his two little eyes that were almost covered by his scraggly eyebrows, the old man grinned, peering over a pair of wire spectacles at Theo and Will. He wore a wrinkled white collared shirt with red suspenders and a pair of baggy pants that were trying their best to keep from popping open atop a huge belly. His thinning mouse brown hair just sort of stuck out harum-scarum over his huge ears in a brush-like fashion, leaving the top of his head slick and bald.

"Come in, come in!" the man spoke in a rather high and squeaky voice. "And what can I do for you young men, now? You wanting a room for the night?" With a depraved smile, he added, "And maybe some right nice female companionship as well?"

Will looked at Theo, relinquishing the right to answer.

Theo extended his hand to the man. "Uh, no, sir. We boys, er, men, I mean, this here's Will Graves, and I'm Theo Taylor, sir. We're the ones who wired you the down payment on this here hotel, uh, place, sir."

"Well, well, well ... So you two are the new owners of Health Springs Inn!"

The old man let go of his cane and shook Theo's hand. "Arnold Zayle, here. Well now, welcome boys. Of course, I mean men!" Zayle motioned for Theo and Will to follow him into the little dingy and cluttered room that bore the sign "Office" over the "Private Keep Out" sign.

"Let's take a look at these books now. I see that, that you have sent a down payment of five hundred dollars—meaning you owe me a balance on this property of one thousand dollars, including interest, and it will need to be paid in full in the next ten months. Now, I'll need you gentlemen to write me a check for one hundred dollars today and continue with payments of the same amount every month until the balance is complete. I warn you, don't be late with your settlements, either. That will put us both in a mess and just end up costing you over charges."

Theo, being good at numbers, knew instantly that he was looking at hard times and rough going ahead unless he and Will could get a lot of customers in, and very soon. The payments and repairs to be made would quickly eat up what cash they had left between them.

Theo pulled out the stack of checks his father had given him and began to write. "Here is my half of the hundred dollar payment for the month, sir." He turned to Will, who was busy looking at the cracked plaster on the facing wall.

"Will, where's your half?"

"Huh? Oh, Theo, just go on and write a check for the whole hundred. My checkbook is in the bottom of my grip. I'll reimburse you tonight when we unpack."

Theo voided the check and tore out another one, which he wrote for the full hundred dollars. Arnold Zayle folded the check and put it in a fat black wallet. "There, young men. Your first payment is made. You two should be able to manage this inn just fine and make a handsome profit, besides. Well, if you watch your expenditures and advertise a bit with some signs around the depot and the Springs.

With a mischievous wink, he nodded toward a desk drawer with his bald head.

"Let me tell you, boys, be sure to put out plenty of these." At that point, Arnold Zayle reached inside the desk and pulled up a pre-printed sign that read:

Female Companionship Available
Ladies—Ladies—Ladies

"I'd like you both to meet Miss Mandy Rose Nichols." Zayle's beady eyes narrowed even more with an evil grin as he gestured to an eye-catching girl who had just walked up behind him. The young woman stuck out a white gloved hand to the boys as Zayle continued. "Mandy Rose will be happy to accommodate any of your patrons who desire the company of a lovely young lady for the night."

Theo and Will had already taken a good long look at the pretty girl who had just followed Arnold Zayle out the door. She was a petite thing, less than five feet tall with a billow of upswept yellow hair that reminded Theo of spun cotton. Mandy Rose's eyes were large, round, and copper in color. Her long lashes were blackened, curled tightly, and batted up and down, almost touching perfectly arched brows.

She was clad in a costume of black transparent fabric with a hint of lace peeping out here and there. A blouse hugged her body from a ruffled collar in the back, rounding to a low-cut bodice in the front, revealing ample cleavage. Mandy's tiny waist was cinched with a silver belt, leading to perfectly rounded hips, which swayed with her every move. A satin skirt flirted and flipped up with every step she took in shiny high-heeled boots.

She spoke demurely. "Theo. Is that short for Theodore?" The girl's bright red lips opened to expose a soft sweet voice.

Theo tried hard not to blush, but he could feel the red creeping up his neck, burning his cheeks and forehead. Stammering, he replied, "Um—yes'm—it is—nice t' meet ya, ma'am."

Mandy continued. "And Will, of course, is for William."

Will shuffled his feet and stared at the floorboards. "Yes'm. Yes it is."

"Welcome to Little Moon, you two. And there's no need to call me ma'am. Mandy will do just fine."

Arnold Zayle's small beady eyes narrowed even more as he explained, "Mandy Rose lives next door there, and you boys should be a seeing quite a lot of her, I think."

The unkempt old man chuckled and continued talking. "Or at least you better hope you do. Mandy Rose works right here at the hotel from time to time, you see. Her escort services and all those the girls next door provide to our customers are of the highest quality. You boys should enjoy a real nice working arrangement with Mandy and the others over there at Cora Bell's."

Theo rubbed his chin and thought, Escort services, my foot. There are a lot of things that describe me, but stupid is not one of them. I know what goes on in a hotel, Mister Arnold Zayle. And I know what kind of work Mandy Rose provides.

Theo's conscience instantly told him that he should flee from this scene. He had been raised attending church and had learned more than enough of God's Word to conclude right from wrong. Pa's word of warning echoed loud in his ears, or was it Mrs. McVae, his church school teacher who had just talked about it a few Sundays ago—or maybe he was hearing the apostle Paul, himself.

> Flee fornication. Every sin that a man doeth is without the body; but he that committeth fornication sinneth against his own body. What? know ye not that that your body is the temple of the Holy Ghost which is in you, which ye have of God, and ye are not your own?
>
> For ye are bought with a price: therefore glorify God in your body, and in your spirit, which are God's.
>
> 1 Corinthians 6:18–20

Theo pushed the words of Scripture to the back of his mind. Far, far to the back he pushed them, attempting to reassure himself.

I am already in Arkansas now. I have to make this business I've gotten myself into work—somehow. I don't have to participate in whatever is going on here. Even if, indeed, it is actually what I suspect, it won't affect me. I will not let this stop me from having my success. It may be entirely possible that Mandy Rose and her friends are only ladies who provide friendship—companionship—yes, to the customers of this establishment. Don't hardworking men deserve that? Who am I to judge them? Mandy Rose is a sweet, beautiful, yes, and truly sophisticated woman. I'm sure she is a very nice lady.

Mandy interrupted Theo's thoughts as she started out the door. The striking girl waved a lace handkerchief as she took leave, calling over her shoulder, "Goodbye, boys. It was so nice to meet you, both of you. Be sure to call for me if you need me—for anything. You hear?"

Will stood staring at the girl in a paralyzed state, while Theo tore his eyes away from hers, raising his hand to say goodbye.

Arnold Zayle watched the two young men in amusement and chuckled in a sly way, gesturing toward the stairs. "Mr. Taylor, Mr. Graves, right this way. Let old Arnold show you just what you boys have bought."

Zayle led the two up the creaky winding stairway to view the rooms and the apartment where they would eventually reside—one that he promised to be vacating very shortly.

The boys followed the pudgy man as he wobbled down the hall, stopping in front of the only entrance painted dark green, chose a special key from the huge key ring that hung from his belt, and unlocked the door.

Theo and Will entered the room hesitantly, eyeing the area in dread of what they would find. Enough disappointment had ensued since arriving at Health Springs, Arkansas, and they were fearful to say the least. To their amazement, the boys found a sufficiently furnished, though small, apartment that had two bedrooms, a real indoor privy, and one small kitchen that appeared complete with icebox, table, chairs, cabinets filled with silverware, dishes, pots, and pans. There was a fireplace standing on one side directly across the room from two windows that faced Miss Cora Bell's Rooming House. There was a single bed in each bedroom and chests in both of them, as well as dry sinks and small desks. The main parlor sported a brown leather settee, old rocking chair, a dinette suite, and a large writing desk openly displaying cluttered receipts, worn ledger book, ink, ink pens, and various other papers.

Arnold Zayle removed Theo's check from his wallet and slid it into a leather pouch lying on the desk. He then turned his attention to his ledger and excused the two boys to continue on with their inspection of the inn. It was obvious by the open trunks and other unpacked trappings lying about that it would take Arnold Zayle another few days to finish packing and get completely moved out.

As the boys made their exit, Theo turned to take one last look at Arnold Zayle sitting there in his big swivel chair. For an instant, a great wall of pride washed over every problem nagging his brain and almost caused them to disappear.

I will fit very nicely back there behind that big old desk. Mmm hmm, I sure will!

Before inspecting the inn, Theo and Will deposited their luggage in the two single temporary rooms they would occupy until Zayle vacated their apartment. During the inspection, it did not take long for the boys to conclude that there had been a lot of heavy use to the rooms in this inn. The furnishings were sparse and most were badly faded and worn. Each room held one iron bedstead, complete with sagging mattress, which was made up with graying bed linens and three worn out pillows lying across the top.

There sat a small bureau or desk at one end of each room and a dry sink complete with ceramic pitcher, bowl, chamber pots, and towels at the other. At the very least, the rooms would require a good deal of sweeping, polishing, airing of mattresses, beating of rugs, and the purchase of new linens. The boys deemed that much could easily be accomplished. As the assessment wore on, the boys discovered a fire escape stairway from the second and third stories that led down a back way to the line of outdoor privies.

Suddenly Theo was exhausted. The long train ride and overwhelming responsibilities of this deteriorating building he had just purchased had put his brain into overload.

"I'm going up to our room to rest, Will."

"I'm going to the bar, Theo."

"You are? Well, maybe I'll just go, too—for a sarsaparilla, of course."

Dreams and Nightmares

Vy had a nagging feeling that something was amiss, and the question kept nagging at her brain. What is going on with Mama?

For the past week, Sally had been acting stranger than usual. The nightly jaunts had been lasting longer, and one night she didn't come home at all. It was the next day and almost noon before she showed up withdrawn, kind of sickly, and avoiding Vy at every turn. Where has she been? What is wrong? Maybe she is coming down with something, but what?

Vy pressed her gently, not wanting to upset and alienate her more than she already seemed.   "Is there somethin' th' matter with y,' Mama?"

"Ain't nothing' wrong with me, Vy."

Vy had always been good about reading her mother's moods and had caught Sally's eyes following her several times during the past week as she worked. She was sure there was some difference in her, but what? There was that weird look in her mama's eyes last evening when she told her goodnight. Vy assured herself that it was temporary and would eventually pass. Heaven knows I'm the only sane one in this household. Mama would perish if it wasn't for me. It was about noon one golden day when Vy learned that wasn't so.

The September sun was beginning to set, but Vy was still in the garden when Seth Seaton drove up in his carriage and pulled the horses to a stop right behind her.

Vy had been looking over the smooth orange pumpkins, which were round and fat and ready for gathering. She was reasoning to herself that the whole lot of them was somewhat worthless, since every homestead in Maynard's Valley and surrounding counties raised their own squash and pumpkin. However, cleaned, cut up, and cooked pumpkins could be canned for pies and custards. Wasn't to say they were any favorite of Vy's, but the punkin pies had once been a favorite of Gran, so Sally and Vy still saved and sowed pumpkin seeds.

Mr. Seaton dismounted the carriage and tipped his worn brown hat, addressing the girl in a neighborly tone.

"Howdy, Miss Violet. How y' a doin' today? Y' mama home?"

At the instant he spoke, Sally appeared in the cabin doorway, eyeing Vy nervously before she bolted toward the Seaton's coach. She suddenly stopped short and motioned her daughter to come near. "Come right here, child," she began. "I've got somethin' t' tell y.'" Sally's voice broke, and her hands started to shake.

"What is it, Mama? For goodness sakes, what's wrong?"

"Nothin'—nothin' is wr-ong, Vy. I mean, what I—y'—we got to do is for the best, darlin. It-it's the best for—y,' Vy."

Vy was already bewildered and now concerned. *Sakes alive! Mama ain't ever called me darlin' in her life. What in the world's goin' on here?* With an anxious expression on her face, she asked in a trembling voice, "W-what in th' world is th' best fer me? Whatever are y' talkin' about?"

"Now, Vy, just calm down and listen here. I need to tell y,' and y' need to try t' understand what I'm about t' tell y.' Please, please don't go and get so upset at y' mama." Sally apologetically went on. "I know I should have told you 'bout this 'afore now. I really meant to. I tried to. It's just that..."

Then Sally dropped a bombshell on Vy's thirteen-year-old shoulders. She could not even look her daughter in the face, staring straight at the ground the whole time she tried to explain.

"Anyhow, Vy, what I mean to say is, you know that you are old enough and smart enough to hold a job now, and this here nice man—y' know Mr. Seaton, our neighbor—well, he wants t' take y' home t' live at his house. Y' know you're old enough t' hire y' out for room and board, so what y' have t' do, Vy, is go with Mr. Seaton. He needs y' to come and help him and his wife with their baby, with chores, with their whole family, Vy. Y'll live with th' Seatons, but I will still be right here—right here at home, and y' can always come see me."

Vy sucked her breath in and gasped, turning weak at her mama's words. Her knees felt like jelly as her stomach churned and told her she was going to vomit.

Heaving, she ran as fast as her legs would carry her out behind the old barn and threw up. Sally followed her, still talking as fast as a crazy person, hysterical to make her understand. Vy ran back into the cabin, flinging herself down on the bed with her mama right behind. Closing the cabin door, Sally walked over and sat down on the bed beside Vy. Attempting a tender gesture, Sally tried to push back the tangle of auburn curls that were falling down in Vy's tearstained face, only to have Vy push her hand away violently.

Sally was beginning to see it was to no avail. She knew she had to make this girl see reason, and it was becoming much more difficult than she had anticipated. The right words were elusive. How could she make a child understand so much in such a small amount of time? All Vy was feeling right now was rejection, and all Sally was feeling was pressure and impatience.

Sally tried again. "It will be okay, Violet. I know y' don't understand this now, but this here is something that has to be, something that I can't help, and it is the best thing for you and the best thing for me, I promise y.'"

Vy did not easily show such emotion, but deep choking moans emanated from her throat, as the tears ran down her cheeks with pleas of reason.

"We've done okay, Mama. Ain't we? I don't need anything. I help out. Y' know I do my part and more, Mama … We have all we need … What have I done t' make y' hate me? Just tell me, Mama. And tell me how leavin' their own home could be the best thing for anyone?"

As Vy began to lose control of her emotions, the pleading turned to fury. "You are crazy, Mama! I always knew y' was crazy. You have really gone insane, sendin' me off with some old man. What kind of mama don't love their own child? Y' ain't no mama t' me, and y' ain't never been! Granny's the only person who ever loved me."

In spite of Vy's stinging words, Sally steeled herself, shook her head in finality, picked up things she had packed, took her daughter's hand, and led her like a calf to slaughter right out to Seth Seaton, who literally lifted the small girl into the carriage driver's seat beside him.

Vy was weary and broken by this time. Her sobs were simply falling on deaf ears that changed to empty echoes as the Seaton carriage turned, rolling over the hill toward town.

The velvet grip with Vy's stockings, hand sewn underwear, lace trimmed nightgown, extra waists, and skirts that Sally Vittoye had packed for her sat between Vy's feet as she rode in the carriage, but she could feel nothing. Numb from her head to her toes, Vy's mind raced. *I was in my garden looking at pumpkins just a moment ago, and all was well.*

What has happened to me? What is happening? Tears streamed down her cheeks, but the sobbing had ended. *Where are we going? I could just throw myself off this seat and onto them there rocks. Maybe it would kill me. No, with my luck it would just break my legs or arms.*

"I realize this is awfully hard on y,' Violet dear, but I need y' and want y' a whole lot—and we will be real good t' ya', dear. Our family all need y' and want y' t' come stay with us really bad." Seth, as he had instructed Vy to call him, was talking in a monotone voice.

Why is this evil man talking to me? I don't care about anything he is saying. I don't care, and I wish he would shut up.

Seth went on trying to explain. He told Vy that his wife was not a strong woman and had lately been through a hard childbirth. Their baby was only a few months old, and Lotia, his wife, needed help so badly. Vy didn't return any words to Seth Seaton, but her thoughts flung out the insults. *Old man, I allow you could have found someone else to help your old wife, someone who needed the work and was a heap more willing to go live away from home than me—someone who might not even have a home. Why me? Why me?* There had to be many a girl who needed a job—would love to hire out for room and board. *My life is over, ended. I know I can't stand living in a strange place with strange people.*

The trees moved slowly by and birds sang as the horse's hooves clip-clip-clopped along in a rhythmic pattern on the dirt road. Noises and sights all sounded ethereal. The carriage made twists and turns on the dirt road, the bumps jolting both passengers, but Vy could not feel a thing.

Where in the world am I going—and what will Mama do without me?

Maybe this is not happening. It's not real. It's a nightmare, yes, a horrid dream where I will soon wake up with the sun streaming in my very own cabin, falling onto my very own quilt, and I will hop out of bed and pour water in the black kettle for coffee and help Mama with breakfast biscuits. Yes, please let this be a dream.

It was true that Vy had never felt complete love or security from Sally, but she just considered that it was because her mama had been so grief-stricken and inconsolable over the kidnapping of Baby. But Mama knew how much Violet loved home—their little cabin was all she had ever known, where she belonged. Never in her worst nightmare did she dream that her mother would abandon her—give her away! Anger filled her soul once more. *Hire me out? The almighty gall of her! Why didn't she hire herself out? Same reason she never got up to milk the cow, I guess. She has to be free to run around with who knows where at nights. I don't understand. Didn't I do more'n my part? What is wrong with me that my own mama would send me away to live with someone else? She does hate me—t-that's it. She wishes I had been kidnapped instead of Baby.*

Rage took over as Vy thought of all the meals she had helped to cook, all the sewing she had done, and how many times she had sweated and hoed weeds in the garden beside her mama when she was no more than a kid, herself. Vy's mind raced, jumping from one angry thought to another. Gran would never have let this happen. *Granny loved me—only person who ever did.*

Vy glanced over at the man driving the carriage and sat silently beside her. *What kind of man is this Seth Seaton? How cruel could a person be to drag a young girl away from her home and mama? He is foul and wicked. I despise this evil, this malevolent old man. It's his entire fault.*

No, it ain't all his fault. It's Mama's fault. Visit her? Sure hope she doesn't count on that. I don't ever want to see her again. I ain't ever goin' to forgive or speak to her as long as I live. Mama hates me and, yes, I hate Mama. I hate this hateful old man right here beside me, and I hate my own mama. I wish they both were dead.

100 Elm Street

Mindia searched Nanny's face and asked earnestly, "Nanny, do y' think Violet will like it here? Will she like me? She was terribly sweet and fun at Sadie's wedding, but I can't imagine being forced to go to someone else's house to live, can you?"

"No, dear, I can't, but we are going to try our best to make her feel at home. And, to answer your question, I am sure she will like you, and I hope she will like the whole family and eventually like living here. She will probably have many reservations at first about coming here with us—with strangers. That kind of change is bound to be hard for anyone, especially a child."

"Nanny, I still can't comprehend her having to do this—come here to live."

"You know it was your pa's idea, Mindia, and I can tell you this much, he has prayed about the matter for some time now and is convinced that God wants him to do this—wants us to take this young girl in. We will all just have to respect Seth and support his decision."

"Well, Nanny, if that girl, Violet, needs another home, I am glad she's coming to ours. Even if I can't understand it, it will be nice t' have a friend my age living with me."

"Let me warn you, darlin,' don't expect her to warm t' our family too quickly. As I said, this will be a big adjustment for her. I expect we will have to give her lots of time t' become our friend and all such as that."

Nancy Selvidge laughed and changed the subject. "Y' room looks so pretty, Mindia. Y' have done well rearranging th' furniture. I think y' are a very creative girl and have the gift of decoration. Y' big bed looks pretty on that side."

"Do y' like the little café curtains me and Mama hung up, Nanny? I really love the blue and aqua rickrack Mama added to the ruffles. Don't you? They match the cornflowers in my new quilt now—or I should say 'our' quilt, shouldn't I—mine and Violet's. Y' know, when I met Violet I really liked her, Nanny. I just hope she likes me. Y' think she will become my best friend?"

Nanny hugged Mindia and squeezed her hard. "You already asked me that, darlin,' just a minute ago. How could anybody not love you, Min? But you are gonna have to remember what I said about giving her time and, oh, honey, how proud I am of y' for being so ready and willing to share."

Lotia was feeding the baby when she spotted Seth's carriage turn onto Elm Street and pull in front of the Seaton's house, but she finished quickly and went in the other room to put Dale down in her cradle. There had been at least a year's discussion between she and Seth about this arrangement, and Lotia had not looked forward to this afternoon's meeting. Having no idea what to expect, however, she had agreed to follow her husband's wishes. She yelled for Mindia and Nanny to go ahead into the parlor and try to make the young girl feel welcome while she checked supper cooking on the stove.

Seth unloaded the carriage and carried in Vy's grip and other belongings, taking them straight to Mindia's room and depositing everything on her big bed. He turned and headed back out to the coach where Vy still sat mute, limp, and refusing to move. Seth simply reached up, lifted the small girl off the coach, and deposited her to the ground.

Vy's legs were without a doubt weak but surprised her as they took first one step then another toward the pretty white frame house with the big front porch. The white wicker chairs and jaunty little ferns on the freshly painted porch appeared to say welcome along with white lace curtains and a delicious aroma wafting from the open windows. Roasted chicken and cornbread dressing...hot rolls...ugh! I'll have none of it!

Vy stepped inside the house and involuntarily sucked in her breath as fascination overtook disdain. Her eyes beheld brightly polished furniture and soft carpets, which accentuated the beautiful upright piano sitting in the hall foyer by the front door. In the parlor to the left were two facing settees and two identical rocking chairs expertly upholstered with needlepoint backs and seats. Pictures of family members were grouped here and there on the neatly papered walls. On one side of the room stood a curio cabinet holding lovely antique dishes, and on the facing wall a big fireplace lined with marble sides and hearth almost took up one whole wall. Painted floors gleamed and appeared as though they had been scrubbed and spit shined.

The beauty of the place made Vy feel forlorn and stupid. *I ain't never helped out in a place like this. I won't know what to do. I can't make a floor shiny as this one. All I can do is cook and sew.*

Vy looked around, sensing Mindia and Nanny standing there, and quickly recognized Mindia. *I know you, Mindia. Mindia Seaton—yeah, y're Seth Seaton's daughter. I remember now. I guess I have to be your maid! They want me for Mindia Seaton's maid.*

Mindia smiled as she slowly approached Vy, speaking very carefully, almost shyly. "Hello, Violet," she started, extending her hand. "Won't y' please come in and sit down? Is it Violet you prefer to be called, or is it Vy? Y' remember me, don't y'? I'm Mindia, Mindia Seaton. We met at Sadie Ellis's wedding. Y' recollect that day, Vy?"

Vy glared at Mindia's pretty face sizing her up. Mindia had long brown hair that hung in thick braids and was dressed in a dark blue skirt and pink shirtwaist complete with fancy tucks and round pearly buttons down the front.

Just look at the fancy store-bought dress—humph! Spoiled rotten! Like the whole lot of this rich bunch.

"I remember y.'" Vy's words came out reluctantly, flatly, and instead of accepting Mindia's extended hand, she turned and walked away. She had no idea where she was headed or what she was going to do.

I will find a way to make these people miserable, then they will let me go home.

Vy scanned the room quickly and spotted a rocking chair by the fireplace. She boldly walked over to it, allowing her weak knees to give way, her trembling body to fall into the cushions. She sank back in its pillowed seat, hoping she could disappear. Past crying now, she felt completely lost, confused, and forsaken. The shock of the day's occurrence had taken a great toll on Vy, and she had no intention of carrying on a conversation with anyone. Exhausted, she would simply refuse to talk.

Lotia came in, stood beside Nanny, and took control of the awkward situation. She did not wait for Violet to speak. "Hello, Violet, and welcome to our home." She put her arm out and gestured first to Nanny. "This here's Nanny, Vy. She is Seth's mama, and she lives here with us." She then turned and nodded toward Mindia. "Mindia tells me that she's met y' already—that the two of you met and ate a picnic lunch together at th' Ellis and Campbell wedding. Well, what I want to say is, Violet, we, well, all of us hope you are goin' to be happy here, and we all realize it will take a good deal of adjustment for all of us and especially for you. But we want y' to know we are here for you and want to make y' as comfortable and happy as we can. You will share a room with Mindia for the time bein.'

"Seth is havin' another wing built onto the north side of the house where y' will eventually have y' own room. We know y're quite talented in dressmaking, and we intend to put a sewing machine in there for y.' There are other things to discuss with y,' like school and chores, but all of that can wait 'til later after y've had time to get used to everything— to get used to all of us."

Lotia cleared her throat and coughed with a nervous laugh. She was beginning to get impatient and uncomfortable within Vy's cold hard stare. "In the meantime, dear, y'll just relax and get to know this family. It's important that you understand now that I, that we, that all of us, welcome you and are very glad y're here.

"Right now, supper is ready, and it'll be cold if we don't eat soon. So come on now, everybody. Follow me to the dinin' room."

Nanny had allowed Lotia and Mindia to do all the talking, but at this point she walked over and tucked her hand under Vy's elbow, gently urging her to come along. "Come on now, dear, you need nourishment after that long ride, and even if you ain't very hungry, you can take some broth, or maybe some hot bread and tea."

What does Mrs. Seaton mean? School and chores, a sewing machine, my own room? What is going on?

Seth Seaton bowed his head, and everyone followed suit, that is, except Vy. She sat motionless as Seth asked the blessing on the food.

Vy could not eat a bite, and no one insisted that she do so. The tea tasted sweet and cool and did relieve her parched tongue and throat a bit. The Seaton family tried to engage in pleasant chatter at the supper table, though it was extremely awkward since Vy sat mute.

When everyone was finished eating, Seth took the family Bible— yellowing and worn from years of use—off the sideboard. The family listened reverently as he opened the book and read from Psalms.

> The Lord is my shepherd; I shall not want. He maketh me lie down in green pastures: he leadeth me beside the still waters. He restoreth my soul: he leadeth me in the paths of righteousness forhis name's sake. Yea, though I walk through the valley of the shadow of death, I will fear no evil: for thou art with me; thy rod and thy staff they comfort me. Thou preparest a table before me in the presence of mine enemies: Thou anointest my head with oil; My cup runneth over. Surely goodness and mercy shall follow me all the days of my life: And I will dwell in the house of the Lord forever.
>
> Psalm 23:1–6

When Seth was finished, everyone bowed in prayer—all except Vy.

> "Dear Heavenly Father,
> Oh, Lord our God, Y' know all things
> We know they's some of us a hurtin' tonight
> Oh, Lord—please take the hurtin' away
> Help me, Lord—help this family right here
> We all just pray Y' will be done as always with us
> And we thank Y' fer all th' blessins Y' give us every day.
> In Jesus' Holy name,
> Amen."

Someone a hurtin? Oh, Mr. Seth Seaton, don't you be a prayin' fer me, you evil old man. Hypocrite! I remember seeing you at Sadie's weddin' with another woman. I did.

Right in the back of that dark church, you were. The valley of the shadow of death ...

Yeah, that's exactly what I'm in—the valley of death—and it's your fault, Seth Seaton!

Mindia rose from her chair at the table and took Vy by the hand, leading her to their room. She chattered on, trying to evoke memories and encourage Vy to join in with her small talk about Sadie's wedding but, drawing no response from Vy, finally got tired of trying and began to clear the bed of the things Seth had set there.

Vy dropped on the edge of the bed, turned her back to Mindia, and began to weep softly. Mindia reached over and patted Vy on the back in an effort to help.

"I know this has to be hard for you, Violet. I wish I could make you feel better."

Surprisingly, Vy did not recoil at Min's touch and neither moved nor replied. Min busied herself and tried not to look at the little girl anymore. Just listening to the heart wrenching sobs was hard enough. As the crying started to subside, Mindia pondered the trauma that her father had brought into this girl's life and her own family's as well. She knew that Nanny's words were right and that she should not expect a girl going through such trauma to immediately become her friend. She would begin this very night praying God's comfort on Violet and patience for herself.

Vy finally lay down on Mindia's bed, allowing the comfortable feather bed to soothe her body. It seemed to embrace her tired and worn out soul. She did not expect to, but finally drifted off into a fitful sleep.

Mindia eased into the bed quietly, trying not to disturb Vy, and studied the sleeping girl's tear-stained face. Questions crowded her mind as she waited for sleep herself. *I don't know why Daddy has brought you here, Violet, but I really hope it doesn't take you very long to feel at home with us, to like being here. It would be really special if we could be friends. I remember how nice you were that day at Sadie's wedding. I hate seeing anyone so unhappy like you have been tonight. Maybe if we all treat you really good like Nanny said, you will come to like our family—and maybe you will like me, too.*

Living in the Seaton house that first night was one Vy would remember in years to come as a time she felt most abandoned and alone yet totally unaware of the gigantic turn her life had just taken. Those first weeks were undeniably awkward and uncomfortable for all concerned. Vy had set her mind on being unhappy and let everyone know it.

She would catch Seth Seaton looking her way from time to time but was pleased to ignore him forever. Seth, Mindia, Lotia, and Nanny, however, tried their best to be friendly and caring to her, and if they were intimidated by Vy's silent hostility, it never showed.

The days went by slowly for Violet, and she was completely confused as to her role in the household. It appeared to her that Lotia was not sick at all, going about her work proficiently and caring for baby Dale as any good mother would. Nanny did most of the cooking, and Mindia always completed her own chores as well as attended Rose Hill School three days each week. Vy had been advised by Lotia that she would be enrolled in school with Mindia when the next term began. Vy pondered this fact daily, with curiosity as well as disdain. Who in the name of heaven sends a maid to school? I ain't never gone to no school before. I will probably just make a fool of myself. All I can do is read. What do they do in school?

Vy knew she was expected to assist in certain light chores such as picking up her clothing and keeping her personal things straight. She did help Lotia wash and hang clothes on the line to dry and folded diapers for baby Dale and carried water in for the family.   Seth   had told the child that she was welcome to use his well-stocked library shelf as she wished. Since one of her favorite things to do was read, the various and sundry books at her disposal, including the Bible, delighted her no end, though she was determined not to show it. Early in the day, Vy would see to and finish every chore she was asked to do. Then she would rush into Mindia's room, close the door, bury herself in a book, write in her diary, or lie on the bed dreaming away the hours, brooding about her plight and her future.

Nanny and Lotia left Vy to her dreaming and held down the heavy chores of tending the baby, gardening, milking, caring for the farm animals, cleaning, and cooking three meals a day while Seth was in town minding the family's store.

Seaton's Grocery and Supply was opened up early every morning by Seth. Vy had been present a few times when he had driven over to pick up supplies at the railway station then deposit them at the store. Seth and Lotia had told Vy from the first that she could take any personal items she needed, but to be sure and let them know so they could keep up with the inventory. Though she had never dared ask for a single thing, just looking at the lemon drops and licorice whips under the front counter made her mouth water.

It had been over a month since Vy had come to live at the Seaton house when Nanny announced she was in need of a few things and suggested that Vy take a ride over to the family store to fetch her a bag of sugar, a container of lye, half a pound of tallow, and a pound of pekoe tea. Lotia thought it was a great idea as well.

Jumping at an opportunity to get out of the house, Vy saddled up the horse and rode on over to Seaton's Grocery, repeating to Seth the needed provisions. Seth selected, wrapped up the packages, secured them in the saddle bags, and then searched the young girl's face carefully before he spoke. Up to now he had been ill at ease talking with her, so he avoided doing it unless it was totally necessary. Violet realized that and took a certain perverse pleasure in seeing Seth uncomfortable.

"I, uh, am glad to see you helping Lotia and Nanny out, Vy. Here, y' deserve a treat for y'self." Seth then handed her a paper bag that had been filled to the brim with lemon drops and licorice whips. Being the first bag of candy the girl had ever owned, it almost rendered her speechless. She managed to utter, "Uh, thank y,' Mr. Seth." At that moment, a pang of guilt about her hostile attitude toward this man nagged at Vy's innermost being. She turned away to avoid the eyes that seemed to penetrate hers. It was she who was uncomfortable now.

Vy grabbed the bag of candy, hurried out the door and down the steps, mounted the horse, and started riding away as fast as she could.

Although it was a cool fall morning, bright sun streamed through the trees. What a day for a ride! Vy sighed deeply, pondering the beautiful countryside as she sucked on a lemon drop. *I could be home in such a short time, and nobody would know. What if I were to ride over there*

right now? I will do it. I will ride to Mama's and tell her how much I despise her. I will tell her how miserable she has made my life. She will be the one who is miserable before I leave there. She will know that I hate what she has done to me, and that I hate the people she has sent me to live with. I will make her tell me why she has done this horrid thing to me. I will find out today.

The trip to the Vittoye cabin included up and down hill climbs, but it didn't daunt Vy one bit, being the skilled rider she was. Taking the fast way, "as the crow flies" straight through the woods, the breeze whipped her curly red hair high as she fairly flew across the mountains and down into the valley. After riding for more than an hour or so, she spotted the little cabin in the distance. The familiarity of home made her heart leap. *Maybe it hasn't changed at all. It is still my little cabin, my home!*

Drawing closer, however, Vy began to feel a bit unnerved. The place looked quieter, abandoned almost. She wasn't expecting to find home exactly the same, but she certainly didn't expect it to look deserted, empty. There was no sign of a horse or cow in the pasture. Weeds had overgrown the garden. Things looked strange and forlorn, and there was no sign of Mama.

After dismounting and tying up her horse, Vy tried the front door but to her disappointment, found it bolted. *There's no way to get in here. Mama has locked me out.*

Vy was ready to abandon her plan and turn back when she happened to think of the back window. *That window out back—the one with a broken bolt. I wonder if it could be pried up if I push on it.* She had crawled in it a thousand times as a little girl—just for fun to scare Granny. Vy walked around to the back of the cabin and found the dirty web covered opening. After a couple of very hard pushes on the bottom of the board, the little opening gave way and rose enough for her to climb inside the dark cabin. Her body began to tremble with excitement. *I'm home! I may never go back to the Seaton's—what can they do? Nobody could make me stay with them if I refuse to—nobody!*

Vy expected, even counted on feeling relief, some solace, or wellbeing as she climbed inside the haven of home, but the scene she encountered upon entering the cabin was anything but comforting. The beds were rumpled, dirty, and unmade. Grimy dishes with disgusting fungi growing on them were piled on the bread board, spilling over into the dry sink. A mouse scuttled across the floor and ran behind the greasy stove where half-empty cooking vessels lay. The cabin gave off a foul and repulsive odor. There was a strange looking bottle sitting beside the bed that still had a trace of red liquid in it, and a group of burned down candles sitting on the floor in some sort of weird pattern. Someone's old boots lay in the corner near a pile of soiled clothes on the floor. There was a ragged shirt hanging on the back of the door, which looked like a man's. It seemed familiar somehow. Have I seen that shirt before? Who does it belong to?

Vy looked outside, realizing the sun was already in the western sky. It would be starting to set soon, and Vy knew it would take more than an hour if she was going to return. The Seatons would be anxious, maybe even sending someone out to look for her. They would be angry, and she could admit that she did not want them to be, though she had no idea herself why she cared.

The decision was not hard to make. There was simply no choice. She knew she had to go back. Finding a piece of paper and a small stub of a pencil, Violet started to write a note.

Dear Mama,

I came over here to see you, but you wasn't here. How are you, Mama? Where are you? Whose shirt and boots is these? What kind of medicine is this here? Are you sick, Mama? What's wrong here? I ain't never seen our cabin like this. It ain't clean. You know I'll help you clean this place up real good, Mama. I go to school now and do real good. I go to church, too. I don't have to do much at the Seatons.' They really don't need me to help them out. I don't even have as many chores as Mindia, their daughter, does. The Seatons are okay, but I don't make any money for us, Mama. They just give me everything I need. I don't understand this. Why did you send me there? Can you explain things to me? I miss you, Mama.
Can I come on home now?
Please let me know.

Love, Vy

As Vy galloped the horse back toward the Seatons,' she was sure he had never been pushed that fast. The sun was going down now, and it was beginning to get dark as she neared their place. Even so, she could still make out a group of people standing outside in the yard.

Mindia started jumping up and down when she spotted Vy riding the horse and called out, "Everybody, look who's coming here. There she is! It's Vy! She's okay and she's back!"

Maynard Valley's sheriff was waiting in the Seatons' front yard with the family and was quick to make his pronouncement. "Well, it appears as though th' girl is okay now, Seth. I'll just be gettin' on my way unless they's something else y' need me fer."

"Sorry to have bothered you, Sheriff. We was really worried, that's all."

"Not a 'tall. That's what I'm for. Well, good night to all of y.'"

Vy slowed the horse to a stop, and before she had completely dismounted, Lotia rushed over and encircled the girl with both arms, giving her a big hug. "Oh, Vy, we have been sick with worry over you. Where in the world have you been?"

Vy, surprised at the look of relief on the family's face, stammered, "I'm sorry, Lotia, I just wanted to see my mama, that's all."

Lotia spoke earnestly. "Oh, honey, of course you may see your mama anytime. But you simply must let us know where you are going, please." When Lotia released her hold on Vy, Seth gathered her in his arms and spoke above her head. "Violet, don't you ever do this to us again."

Vy caught a glimpse of Nanny before she turned and entered the house. It looked as though she had been crying.

Dear Diary,

Today I rode back home to see Mama. I can't figure her out. Our cabin was a wreck. What has happened to my mama? She always made us keep our house clean. I am so worried about her.
The Seatons had called the sheriff because they were worried about me. It is nice to be worried about, but it is even better to be hugged.
I hate to admit this, but it is true.

The beautiful golden autumn days swept by with all things new to Vy, and not all of them unpleasant. Two new experiences especially enjoyable for the girl were attending Rose Hill school three days a week and going to Rose Hill church on Sundays with the Seatons. Vy surprised even herself on how she excelled in her studies since her previous schooling was from Granny and Mama, who had long since taught her reading, writing, and arithmetic. She adored books, reading everything she could get her hands on, and that fact had served her well. She excelled in geography, history, and more advanced arithmetic, as well as other new subjects.

Mrs. Lucinda Ellis was surprised with her new pupil's knowledge and the fact that she rated the highest marks in her class of twelve sixth graders. Vy did, however, pick up on a hostile attitude directed toward her from her new teacher, but she did not worry on this fact too much since Mindia assured her that Mrs. Lucinda was an embittered soul in general.

Vy loved attending church as well. She was fascinated by the little Rose Hill chapel, its friendly parishioners, the beautiful stained glass windows, and the sermons of soft spoken Preacher Daniel Poe from her first visit.

Nevertheless, more recently Vy had begun to dread attending services. There was something that had begun to happen during each service that had become disquieting to her. The feelings of distress always happened at the end of the pastor's sermon when he gave an invitation to all present—to those who did not know Jesus—to come down to the altar, repent, and accept Him as their Lord and Savior.

Vy knew who Jesus was, and she certainly wanted to go to heaven, but she had real difficulty believing that becoming a Christian was so simple. She would concentrate on the pretty stained glass windows and block out the words that tugged at her heart, her conscience—the words that made her feel very uncomfortable, even guilty.

Vy could not shake the conviction of God's call, though, so it put her in a very defensive mood. She found herself more agitated than usual and became more and more perplexed, mulling the situation over and over in her mind.

What is wrong with me? she would ask herself. Violet finally decided her feelings were nothing more than the dissatisfaction of having to live with the Seatons—a house full of strangers. My perpetual bad mood is Mama's fault for sending me here, just like everything else is.

Chores and homework kept Mindia and Vy busy most afternoons. Vy would hurriedly finish the few chores she was assigned and then spend the rest of the afternoon reading or writing in her diary. She was determined to be unresponsive to the family's friendliness, but it was getting more difficult each day.

A bright spot in her life three days a week was the fact that Mary Mynatt's table was located right beside hers in school.

"Hello there, Vy. Remember me?"

From Mary's question that first day, the two girls had become good friends. Since both were dealing with personal problems at home, it became natural to begin confiding in one another.

At first, Vy was unaware that she was offending Mindia by excluding her as she and Mary began to take their sack lunches and recess breaks together, swapping secrets and sharing private talks. When she finally realized it, she simply soothed her guilty conscience.

It serves Mindia right. She's not the one who had to leave her home and mama.

Mindia never once countered Violet's bad behavior, however, treating her as kind as ever in her own perpetually friendly puppy way. At times that was very hard for the young girl, but she kept remembering how Nanny had urged her to have patience with Vy, who was going through a terribly difficult transition. She was also still holding on to the hope that Vy might in time become her friend.

Mindia's kind ways in the face of her aloof actions mystified Vy. She was sure Mindia would get fed up with her hateful attitude one day soon, and then she would have a right to set the girl straight.

I will let the brat know that it will take more than a phony sugary sweet manner to make me her friend.

Dear Diary,

Why am I living with this family? When am I going to start all the work? Cleaning and cooking and waiting on them hand and foot—be their maid? I thought I was hired out so I could make money for Mama. They have given me a sewing machine and pretty material to make nice clothes. I have more to eat than I ever had. I have books to read, and Mindia has more chores than I do—it's for sure I ain't nobody's maid. She is so nice to me, and I don't know why. I ain't nice to any of them. Nanny always mops the floors and cooks. Lotia seldom asks me to take care of baby Dale. Does she think I am incapable?

Well, I'm not. I do better than Mindia and Mary in my schoolwork.

One late November evening, after Vy had been living with the Seatons about two months, Nanny approached her.

"Would you like to help me in the kitchen, Violet dear? I figured you might be bored with not a lot to do, and, well, here's the menu for supper tonight. Fried pork chops, gravy, field peas, and creamed potatoes." How's that sound to you? It's all Lotia can handle with the baby teething, and I sure could use your help since my back is in a cramp. Mindia is busy trying to learn some literary work or other. Oh, I'm sorry, dear. I guess you have to memorize that thing she's working on, too, don't you?"

"No, I've already done it."

"Well, good for you, Vy! I suspected you were a fast learner, just like Mindia is. Mmm ... well, maybe even faster! Come on out here to th' kitchen with me, dear, and don't you be shy. I know you are a wonderful cook. I heard that from others."

Since she was bored, Vy followed Nanny into the kitchen, silently admitting to herself, Why not? I do love to cook. Vy already knew where the pots and pans were by watching Nanny and Lotia work. The fire had been started and was going good in the enormous range when Vy placed the iron skillet on the largest front eye and spooned in just enough lard. She dipped each chop in beaten eggs and then dredged them in flour like she had done many times before at home. When the right amount of grease was scalding, she seared each chop to a golden brown, turning first on one side and then another. She covered the pan and moved it to a smaller eye so the meat would cook through and get tender. When it was done, she would use its drippings to make succulent brown gravy. Vy's paring knife fairly flew around the potatoes, and soon they were boiling in a pot next to the chops.

Surprisingly, it felt good to do something, to be useful. It was almost like being home again. All of a sudden, Vy looked around. Nanny was seated on a stool watching her and smiling as she rolled out some dough for an apple crumb pie.

"Is this okay, Nanny? Am I doing what you wanted me to do?"

"You are doing wonderful, dear, and everything will be delicious because you are cooking supper." Nanny walked over to Vy and patted her shoulder. "I, well, all of us want you to feel at home, Vy, because you are."

That night was the beginning of a very special relationship.

Angels and Jesus

Seth had stopped by and picked up the girls from school. The headmaster had dismissed school early, for it was a frigid day and threatening snow. Vy was in her newly completed room. She had adjusted somewhat to the order of the Seaton household and was beginning to warm to the people in it, much to her dismay. Lotia was taking a much needed nap and was asleep beside baby Dale. Nanny was busy in the kitchen.

Mindia bounded in Vy's room, excitement exuding from every ounce of her.

"Vy! Come on with me, but put on your coat, boots, and gloves, too. We, well, Daddy and me, we have a surprise for you."

"What? What are you talking about, Mindia? I don't want to go anywhere just now. I'm reading this new book, and it's just getting interesting."

Mindia tossed her heavy boots across the room. "Oh, pooh, you can read later! Now come on, Daddy's waiting for us." She drug out Vy's wool cape and hat, took her hands, and fairly drug her to her feet. "Hurry up, now, we're going to go chop a tree down."

Although Vy was a little put off, her curiosity was peaking. "Chop a tree down?"

"Yeah, our Christmas tree, silly!"

Seth had hitched up the horse and was already waiting in the wagon. The girls hopped aboard, and the three set out for Sharp's Mountain and soon arrived in a thick grove of evergreens. The winter air smelled clean, and the trees gave off their fresh pungent smell of resin.

Memories of Christmas past and cutting a Christmas tree with

Gran flooded Vy's mind. Mindia was beside herself with excitement, and it was infectious.

Seth drew the horses to a halt and posed a question. "What y' girls think about stoppin' right here?" The pair hopped down off the wagon as Seth pointed to a scrawny, half dead cedar bush. "Hey, girlies, look yonder at that beautiful one. Y' reckon it's okay?" Grinning sheepishly, Seth eyed the girls and chuckled as they broke out in laughter.

"We think not, Daddy. Y' know it's ugly and skinny."

"Hey, look over there, Vy." As Vy scanned the lush evergreen forest, her heart began to beat faster. It was too late. She was swept up in Holy Day excitement. There were millions of beautiful evergreens, a whole mountain of Christmas trees! Oh, it would be soooooo hard to choose only one!

The girls looked round about and wandered for a while in different directions, calling out, "There's one, there's one!"

Vy could not believe her eyes. The tree was about ten or twelve feet in height with perfectly shaped limbs. Running quickly to it, she lovingly fingered its green branches, walking in a circle all around to see it better. Not sure of herself, she called excitedly to Mindia.

"Mindia! Come right over here. "What do you think about this one? I think it's beautiful, don't you?"

Min heard Vy's call from over the hill. "Where are you?" she shouted then ran up the hill, caught sight of Violet, and quickly joined her.

It didn't take Min long to share her opinion. Covering her mouth with both hands, she burst out, "Ooooh, yes, Violet! Daddy, come look at this one, the tree Vy has found! Ain't it beautiful?"

Seth smiled, nodding his head.

"Is, is it too big for the house, Mr. Seth. Is it too tall?"

"Nope, dear, it's not too big a'tall! Looks t' me like you have found the perfect tree for us, Vy. Here's the axe, girlies. You go on and cut it down. Have at it!"

Excited and giggling, the girls took the axe from Seth and took turns chopping with intermittent laughter. Vy chopped the first few swings, and then Mindia tried her luck. Soon they were laughing so hard they nearly fell over each other trying to chop down their beautiful tree. After a few swings with the axe, the girls looked at Seth, recognizing they indeed needed his help since their efforts had only made a small dent in its trunk. Seth grinned and took his saw from the wagon since he aimed for a good clean cut. It was no time before he had the tree toppling. After Seth gathered up his tools, he turned to see Mindia and Vy talking, laughing, and dragging their beautiful tree back to the wagon. The sight of the girls enjoying themselves together warmed Seth's heart. Seth carefully lifted the treasured tree onto the wagon, settling Mindia and Vy on either side to secure and keep it safe on the bumpy ride home.

When they arrived home, Seth nailed a little criss cross stand on the bottom before setting it up in the parlor as Vy watched intently.

"It's just like the one Gran and me used to cut," she said.

"Did you cut down a Christmas tree with your grandmother, Vy?"

"Every year."

"Those must be wonderful memories for you."

Vy nodded. "Yes they are."

Nanny stuck her head out the door and called out, "Does anyone want hot chocolate?" The trio rushed in and draped their frozen clothes by the fire, warming their hands by the tall mugs of creamy chocolate that had perky marshmallows melting on top. The girls and Seth commenced to devour a tray of hot soup, cheese, and thick slices of freshly made bread.

Lotia walked in with a big box of ornaments that were ready to hang, as well as a box holding scissors, glue, trims, scraps, and materials so the girls could make more decorations.

As each family member placed a favorite ornament on their tree, everyone agreed the family had attained a sure masterpiece, their prettiest tree ever, not forgetting to mention several times that it was Vy who had discovered it.

After supper, the two girls sat in the floor with their materials and set in to creating their own perfect ornament. Mindia decided she would fashion a little snowman and used some leftover white woolen from a baby blanket that Nanny had sewed for Dale. She stuffed it real fat with cotton and set about sewing on eyes, nose, and mouth of shiny black buttons that she dug out of Lotia's big button jar.

"He's ugly, isn't he, Vy? Isn't he the ugliest snowman you have ever seen?"

"I think he is darling, Min. Just look at that little smile on his face."

The kind words surprised even Vy herself, and she felt pleased with them. She got started on her ornament slower than Mindia, deciding just what she was going to create. At first, Vy cut out two figures of a little girl from some pink cotton quilt squares. With her nimble fingers, she sewed the pieces together and had the little figure stuffed in no time, knowing just what she wanted to do now. She then cut out something that looked like a butterfly to Mindia, who had already finished her own, and was intent on watching.

"What is it gonna be, Vy?"

"You'll see." Vy chose white satin for the butterfly-looking thing and stitched without a word until Mindia realized she was making wings.

"I know what you are making now! You're making an angel!"

"Hmmm ... I'm trying to, Mindia, but I'm not sure if it will look like one!"

Vy laid the wings aside while she made a white robe from the same material to go on the little figure. She put the robe on the little pink girl and attached the wings. Long yellow yarn was then cut to fit and stitched carefully on her head. At last, Vy sewed a tiny halo of silk shiny thread all around the little angel's head. Her ornament was done.

Lotia had just finished putting Dale down for the night and came in the room to inspect the girls' crafts.

"Let's see what you girls have created," she said.

"Mine is hanging right there on that limb, Mom."

"Oh, how adorable, Min. What a cute little snowman. He looks perfect right there in the front of the tree."

"He's kind of ugly, Mom."

"No, Min, I think he's quite animated and adorable."

"Now let's see yours, Violet. Ohhhh! You've made an angel for our tree!" Lottie took the little angel and turned it over and over, inspecting the lovely work of art. "What a precious ornament!"

Seth looked up. "I think the handiwork of these two girls deserves special places on our tree. Don't you, Lottie?"

"Absolutely!" Lottie replied, and Nanny agreed.

Mindia took the little angel from her mama and lifted it high over her head, speaking excitedly.

"Vy's angel, it should go right on top of the tree. Could you perch her right on the very tip-top, Daddy?"

It was not a difficult task for Seth, who stood over six feet tall, to reach up and tie the little angel to the very top limb of the tree where she overlooked the whole room.

The Seaton family had given Vy's little angel a place of honor, which made her feel very humble and thankful.

Dear Diary,

I can't believe the wonderful day I've had. Seth took Mindia and I in his wagon to cut down a Christmas tree exactly like Gran and me used to do. It was the most fun I ever had since I came here. Lotia had hot chocolate to warm us up when we got back. Everybody hung up ornaments and decorated the little tree. We made some more ornaments from scraps Lotia found.
Mindia made a snowman, and I made an angel. The family hung my angel on the top of the tree.
I have to say the Seatons are good to me, but I still miss my mama and granny so much—especially at Christmas.

It was Friday and there was no school. Lotia had excused the girls from their outside chores because it was so cold. A frigid blanket hovered over Maynard's Valley, wrapping it in sleet and ice. Lotia pulled back the lace curtain and looked out the front window.

"Look, girls, that isn't rain anymore; it's snowing. We're going to have a white Christmas after all. It is coming down hard now—looks like a couple inches already. If it keeps this up, we will have a big snow like we did year before last. Ya' remember, Nanny?"

Nanny didn't answer. Her attention was on Vy, who was engrossed in reading a book by the fireplace and had not looked up.

"Violet, dear, would you come with me for a moment?" Nanny spoke in a gentle voice. "There's something I want to talk with you about."

Mindia, puzzled, gave her mama a questioning look. Lotia answered her puzzled look with a request.

"Min, uh, will you come into the kitchen for a moment? There's something I need help with, dear." Mindia was curious, knowing that being called away just now had to do with giving Vy and Nanny some privacy, but she complied, trotting after Lotia to the kitchen.

Vy looked up from her reading and obediently followed Nanny into her small but cozy bedroom where a fire glowed warmly in the tiny marble-lined fireplace. The cozy room was adorned with papered walls of tiny flowers and vines and completed with all kinds of family photographs. Nanny's room was exactly large enough for a mahogany half bed, complete with very tall headboard; a dresser, which had been painted so many times it was nearly black; a small nightstand to match; and a big rocking chair. The bed was made up neatly with a colorful patchwork quilt. Snow fell quietly on the window pane as Nanny gently closed the door.

Vy had always felt comfortable in the room with Nanny but was quite curious this morning as to what the elderly woman wanted. Nanny sat down in her rocker and patted the bed, motioning for Vy to sit beside her. Knowing the girl was confused, Nanny did not delay her intentions and began by saying, "I have been praying for you some time now, Violet."

"Praying for me? Why?"

"I want to know if you know the Lord, Vy. What I mean is, have you ever asked Jesus to come into your heart—to be your Savior?"

"No, I guess I have not, Nanny. I know who Jesus was."

"Not who Jesus was, Violet. Who Jesus is.

"Way back in the beginning when God created the first man and woman, He placed them in a garden where they had everything they needed and more. He did give them a rule, though. He told them not to eat the fruit from one special tree. All Adam and Eve had to do was obey that one simple rule. Satan tempted Eve, telling her that the forbidden fruit was good to eat and that it would make her like God, so she chose to disobey God. She then offered the fruit to Adam, who also ate it. That one sin of disobedience separated all mankind from the Father forever and brought about the curse of suffering and eternal death. At that point, there was no forgiveness of sin except through blood sacrifices.

"Thank God that is not the end of the story, Violet." Nanny lifted her Bible from off the table and held it up. "The wonderful news is right here in this book—God's Holy Word." It tells us that God loves us so much that He gave His one and only perfect Son, Jesus Christ, who took our guilt—all our sins—past, present, and future ones—upon Himself, suffered death on the cross, and bought our forgiveness, or rather "paid the price" for our sin with His life—His blood.

"The Bible also tells us, Vy, that all those who believe in Jesus and accept His perfect sacrifice of love and forgiveness are reunited with God and will live forever with Him. The fact is, my dear, that Jesus loves Violet Louise Vittoye and wants you to live for Him. He wants to come into your life and be your Savior. You can ask Him to do this at any time because He is ready and waiting for you."

Vy felt excited and scared at the same time. "Oh, Nanny, I do want Jesus to forgive me and take me to heaven someday. I want Him to be my Savior, but I'm afraid I don't know how or what to do."

"Simply tell Him what you told me just now, Violet. How you want Him to forgive you, to take any sin and hate away that you have in your heart, then merely ask Jesus to be your Savior, and He will do it. It is just that easy, darlin.'"

The tears started to stream down Vy's face. Her trembling hands reached for Nanny's wrinkled ones, and they both fell on their knees. Nanny held the little girl's shaking shoulders as she cried out to her Heavenly Father.

"Oh, Jesus, will you save me? I am so sorry. Will you please take away all of my sins? I want you to be my Savior. Please come into my heart. I want to live my life for you and go to heaven to live with you someday."

> Likewise, I say unto you,
> there is joy in the presence of the angels of God
> over one sinner that repenteth!
>
> Luke 15:10

Vy looked up and spoke through broken sobs, "Oh, Nanny, will you forgive me? I have treated y' so badly and y've been s' good to me."

Nanny put her arms around the humbled girl and kissed her on the forehead. "Y' did nothin' to me. I love y,' my little one."

The door opened softly as Seth, Lotia, and Mindia walked in. Violet's radiant face moved the whole family to tears, though they were tears of rejoicing.

Seth addressed Vy. "We have something for y,' dear. It's from all of us who love y' and prayed for y' and will pray for y' in yore daily walk with th' Lord." Then Lotia handed her a beautiful new black leather Bible. Vy got control of her sobs and opened the book. On the inside front page, it read, "To Violet: from Seth, Lotia, Nanny, Mindia, and Dale with love and prayers from your family."

Vy turned to face them all. "Can y' ever forgive me for treating all of y' so shameful? I don't deserve y' forgiveness, but will you?"

The family just smiled with joy and replied, "There is nothing to forgive."

Hugs, kisses, and tears were plentiful for Vy as the Seatons welcomed a brand new Christian into the family of God.

December 22, 1885

Dear Diary,

Something wonderful happened to me today. I gave my life to Jesus Christ. He forgave me of my sins and saved me, and now I am a Christian. I am born again...a child of the king. I feel so wonderful, like a weight has been taken off me. I don't hate nobody now.

Late that night, Vy knelt beside her bed and silently prayed:

Dear Jesus,

I pray for my mama—I love her, and I don't know whether she's a Christian or not.
I want to tell her about you, Lord—I want her to know you. Help me to help her, Father.
And thank y' for hearin' me, for forgiving me, and bein' my friend. Amen.

December 24. It was finally Christmas Eve and time for evening church. Since it was below freezing and snow piled up more than a foot high,

the family bundled up in coats and blankets then boarded Seth's sleigh, which he had hitched up to the old horse.

As they started down the snowy road, Nanny started to sing "Jingle Bells," and the family joined in. They had finished stanzas of "Joy to the World," "O Little Town of Bethlehem," and "Silent Night" before they arrived at the church.

I know almost all the pretty Christmas carols now. They are so beautiful.

The world resembled fairyland that night with every tree and house covered in glistening snow. The whole family was in a jolly mood, and Vy was feeling happy. Since the Seaton dwelling was only a few blocks from their church, it came into view quickly. In the distance, a glow from inside the building shone through the beautiful stained glass windows depicting Jesus' life on earth, making pretty reflections on the snow covered ground. Two blazing fireplaces warmed the little sanctuary of Rose Hill Church, and it was soft and welcoming as the Seaton family entered.

The ladies' missionary group had decorated around the pulpit and windows with fragrant pine boughs, scarlet velvet ribbons, and soft ivory candles. There were already several members seated in the pews waiting for the service to start, and everyone smiled with Christmas greetings as the Seaton family entered.

Nanny wanted so much for Vy to understand everything about Christmas. She pointed to the pretty decorations.

"Look, Vy, the red ribbons and red berries signify Jesus' gift to mankind, His death on the cross, the blood He shed for you and me. The evergreen boughs signify life. Jesus called Himself the way, the truth, and the life. All those who belong to Him have eternal life in heaven." Even as Nanny spoke, the parson stood behind the pulpit and asked the congregation to bow in prayer.

Vy prayed a prayer of her own.

> Thank y,' Lord Jesus, for this wonderful family y' have brought me to live with, for y' savin' grace, and for this church. Please take care of my mama. She's alone this Holy Day time. I know y' know all things, Lord, and if it's y' will, let me find out who my daddy is and whatever happened to him and my little brother.

The parson began.

"Tonight we will celebrate the Lord's Supper."

Nanny whispered to Violet, "Don't you remember reading about this the other night after dinner? At Jesus' last supper with His disciples, he commanded that all believers drink of the cup and eat the bread in remembrance of Him."

The organ music softly started to play. Vy's hands shook ever so slightly as the plate of broken unleavened bread was passed around and offered to all believers.

After praying, the parson opened the Bible and read from the book of Matthew:

> And as they were eating, Jesus took bread, and blessed it, and brake it, and gave it to the disciples, and said, 'Take, eat; this is my body.
>
> Matthew 26:26

And the people ate the bread. Then the cups were passed around. The pastor gave thanks then read again from the gospel of Matthew:

> And He took the cup, and gave thanks, and gave it to them saying, Drink ye all of it; For this is my blood of the new testament, which is shed for many for the remission of sins.
>
> Matthew 26:27–28

Exemplary of Jesus' disciples, the congregation drank of the cup, sang a hymn, then silently found their way outside to their carriages and homes.

The Seaton family huddled together under blankets against the cold wind and the drifting snow as the horse pulled the sleigh toward home that night. It was cold, that's true, but hearts were warm with Christmas cheer. Seth slowed the horse to a halt, got out of the sleigh, and lit a lantern so everyone could see making their way into the house.

Lotia, who was carrying baby Dale, was first on the porch. She almost stepped on a little package lying in the doorway.

"What's this?" she asked.

Mindia picked it up and read the label.

"It's a package for you, Violet."

"Is it for me? It's not for me."

"It has your name on it—right here."

Lotia handed Vy a little box wrapped up in brown paper and tied with red string.

Vy had seen many packages done like that before. She knew immediately who had left it.

"Glory be! It's from Mama."

Opening the door, Vy walked to the fireplace so she could see. Tears clouded her eyes as she opened the little box to behold that beautiful and familiar carved piece of jewelry that brought back sweet memories of her early life.

It had been Gran's favorite piece, given to her by her husband and one that she never failed to wear.

Oh, Mama, you remembered how I loved this cameo and would sit on Gran's knee and question her about the pretty lady on it. When did you leave it here for me? Why couldn't you stay n' see me, Mama? I wish you could come here for Christmas and be with me and this dear family. I have someone I want to tell you about.

Turning to the little group silently standing there, waiting for answers, Vy held out the beautiful brooch.

"Look, it's from Mama. It's the pin, the cameo that belonged to my Gran. She always wore it, and I loved it so much."

Lotia uttered a soft cry, "Ohhh! Vy, that's so pretty!"

"What a wonderful Christmas surprise," exclaimed Mindia.

Nanny held out her hands. "Here, Min, let me see."

"Look Nanny, this is one of the loveliest ones I've ever seen. The carving of the lady is so delicate."

Nanny turned the piece over and over, examining the beautiful cameo. "Oh, it is very beautiful, Vy. What a treasure for you. I can't think of a nicer gift from your mama, dear. Wasn't that thoughtful of her?"

Seth Seaton studied the situation, shook his head in silence, then turned and went to his room without a word.

Vy did not notice.

Treasure on Earth

Health Springs Resort Inn
Little Moon, Arkansas
June 12, 1886

Dear Ma and Pa,

I have been so stranded out on so many affairs here that I simply had to put off answering your letter.

Will a leavin' me and a comin' home sure put me in a bad way. He did send part of the lease money for that first year, and that helped, but he still owes me some.

The business has grown so that it is hard for me to look after it properly. Sometimes I think I just can't keep going this way.

I have about decided to sell this hotel and buy a larger one that will bring me in more profit. Selling this one should clear me at least $4,000, and that should be enough to where it would justify me turning the new one over to my manager, Mr. Page. Mr. Page is a good man and has had forty years in the investment business. I guess that is enough to qualify him. The one I am thinking of taking over has 100 rooms and is a first class place.

The one reason I hate to sell is because of the lady I've written you about before. Miss Nichols, the one who lives here now, has become my partner. She makes a good living for herself, and she has helped me out a lot, getting customers in here.

Mandy has been very sick, though, and has not been able to contribute much the past two months. I have been paying all her medical expenses and doctor bills. It seems to me the doctors don't know what they are doing sometimes, though. Hopefully she will get better soon, but the last report from her doctor was not very good. She bathes in the Health Springs as much as she can, but she has grown so weak it is hard to get her over there.

You know that I am speculating on some land closer to the Health Springs. There are droves of people still coming to bathe in the warm waters and receive healing for their various and sundry ailments.

Besides all of this, I have borrowed cash on the hotel for interest in a gold mine in Colorado, and I may end up living out there if all goes well. The stock went up from one cent to $1.00 in one day, and I have already been offered $10,000 cash for my interest. I would have taken it, but the other fellows, Mr. Page and Arnold Zayle, advised I hold tight to it, so I guess I will for a while longer.

You can see from my letter that I have been so busy I hardly know where to turn. I do expect some return in a short time from this gold mine deal.

When it comes through, I will send you all some money.

Tell the family I said hello and that I hope all of you are well in the Valley. I am as usual ...

Your son,
Theo

Theo sealed the letter with wax, addressed it, stamped it, and walked a block up the way where he dropped it in the mailbox next to the US Post Office.

After dispatching his post, Theo crossed the street, headed directly for the saloon a few doors down, and sat down at the bar.

"What'll you have today, Theo?"

"Let me have a pint of that Kentucky sippin' whisky and a bottle of Sarsaparilla to take home, would you, Franklin?"

From behind the counter, the old gray haired man in a white apron twirled his handle bar moustache as he selected an unopened bottle of Vogt Applegate whisky—his very best. He then picked up a big bottle of sarsaparilla and proceeded to wrap the two flagons securely, placing them carefully in a brown paper bag. Smiling, he handed the package to Theo and remarked slyly, "Have a great night, sir."

Theo grunted at the old man and then made his way to Old Doctor Payne's quarters, which were located one flight of stairs up and over the post office. Theo had one more thing he had to pick up before returned to his room with his purchases. It was a little something the doctor had waiting. His thoughts were dismal as he walked out of that office while reading what was written on the small bottle.

I surely hope this will help her. Why have I gotten myself into this mess? Sometimes I feel I am at the end of my rope. I've never faced anything like this before. What do I do? What would she do if I wasn't here?

Theo walked down the street to the inn, through the lobby, then directly up to his apartment. The establishment was about half full of guests at the present, and it was nearing 4:30 p.m., but there was no aroma of supper cooking. What is that lame brain cook doing? I should never have hired that loser. He hasn't cooked a decent meal on time since I hired him.

The apartment door was ajar. Theo pushed it open and walked over and sat down on the bed beside her. He uncorked the little blue bottle with instructions written in the doctor's own hand:

```
M. Willet Payne M.D.
# 719 Rx Carefully Follow dosage directions
Treatment for:
Mandy Rose Nichols
Contents: Mercurious Corrosivus
Directions: Take drops as directed with water
or other drinks two times daily
```

Theo opened the little blue bottle then took down a glass. He poured a generous amount of sarsaparilla in a small glass, added the drops of mercury as instructed, stirred the mix, then walked over and shook the bed. "Here, dear. You have to drink this."

"Wha—What is it, Theo?"

"It's your medicine, Mandy. The doctor prescribed it for you. I mixed sarsaparilla with it."

"It will taste awful, won't it?"

"You never mind that, dear. It will help you. Take it now."

The petite girl sat up and reached for the drink, almost spilling it because the sores on her palms were so tender that it was hard for her to grasp. She frowned as she gulped hard and swallowed the mix.

"Where's the other bottle? I need a drink now, Theo!"

"The liquor is beside the bed, right there."

She grabbed up the bottle and swigged down some gulps without a wince.

"I'm hungry, Theo. Please ... "

Mandy was still exceptionally beautiful, though the lesions on her hands and feet were grotesque, and the swelling of lymph nodes was apparent in her neck. Theo was alarmed but had little doubt which ailment Mandy was suffering from, and the doctor had confirmed his fears. He was just praying that he had not contracted it from her. He knew he might not know for some time.

Supper. I almost forgot. I need to go and see what's going on in that kitchen.

I bet I'll end up firing that incapable chap.

"Theo ... "

"I know, I know. You're hungry, dear. I'll have someone bring you a tray. Just try to rest. I will be back with some food in a minute. Please just try to go back to sleep, okay?"

"I'll try, Theo, but I'm hungry ... "

"I'm going down to get you something. I'll hurry back. Try to rest, Mandy. Just try to rest."

He did not see the unopened letter addressed to Theo Taylor lying on the front desk in the lobby.

Detours and Disappointments

The train pulled into the little station at high noon. Theo jumped off the passenger coach and down onto the rocks. He threw his suit coat over his shoulder and looked toward home. His head ached, and sweat rolled down the back of his starched high-collared shirt as he headed east toward Maynard's Valley.

Theo paid little attention to the carriages and wagons running to and fro until he heard a familiar voice call out, "Hey, Theo. You goin' home, boy? Git in this here wagon, son, and I'll carry y' by your place. Whur you been so long? Ain't seen y' in a month a Sunday's. Just how long is it that y've been gone, Theo?"

"Three years this past fall, Mr. Campbell. Thank you, sir," Theo answered politely. "Well, it's a good thing I had to pick up some freight here at the depot or I wouldn't be here t 'give y' a ride. I should think y'd get quite warm a walkin' out here in this heat." Theo agreed, taking out a monogrammed handkerchief and mopping his forehead and neck. It has to be ninety or more degrees today—August in the valley. My nerves don't help it any either.

Theo climbed up to Mr. Campbell's wagon seat as the horses began to trot. I'm home. The mountainous terrain and lush green pastures full of livestock danced by as the bumpy wagon jolted down the familiar old road he had traveled many times before. The green hills sparkled in the glory of summertime, and the distant mountains shone blue as the sky. The young man took in the surrounding beauty and admitted that there was no prettier place than east Tennessee, and in some ways it was good to be among the old stomping grounds again. However, he knew his longing for the social pleasantries and modern ways that came with city living was far from over.

It was for sure he was not anxious to face family or friends the way he felt right now—eighty instead of twenty-two. For the hundredth time he began to reprimand himself for not requiring enough information about the gold mine he had sunk money into, and for trusting the crooks who had swindled him. Things had been going good. How could it have happened? Good grief, how will I ever explain it to Pa? He will never have any faith in me now. Don't mean I'm going to go in business with EE, though—and sure doesn't change the fact that I refuse to be a farmer and kill myself like Pa has for his rocky two hundred acres of land.

Theo reminded himself he must forget, to look ahead and not backward, but his mind kept wandering back. His thoughts returned to Mandy Rose. He could still hear her crying as he told her goodbye. Poor little Mandy. I feel so bad having to leave her. Who will take care of her? Cora Bell will just have to do it. There's just nobody else.

Theo had, in fact, heeded his father's warning about righteous living when he first came to the Health Springs Resort. At first he had resisted Mandy Rose with all his might, that beautiful little creature of the night. But after a while her magnetism, allure, and availability became too great a temptation. Like a moth to a flame, he succumbed to her charms. Theo could admit that he had never really loved the girl, but she was beautiful, warm, and supportive, and he felt a sort of empathy for her having to do the work she did. After Will Graves had decided to return to Maynard's Valley, Mandy kept Theo from being lonely. She was in Theo's room so much that her presence seemed perfectly natural, and so she gradually began to stay nights as well.

Theo's conscience had constantly nagged him about his adulterous actions, so that he had never been able to feel comfortable with the arrangement. He had actually been pondering on asking Mandy to move out of his quarters before she got sick, but when she started feeling so bad, he simply couldn't bring himself to do it. Nobody deserves that awful curse Mandy has—and thank heavens she didn't pass it to me. It's a wonder she didn't, though. What will happen to Mandy? What's going to happen to me?

Mr. Campbell interrupted Theo's thoughts. "Did y' just miss home too much, Theo? Decided to come on back fer a visit? Did y,' son? Bet you enjoy a seein' all that countryside out west there, don't ya? Sure would like to travel some out west sometime, myself. Don't guess I'll ever get to, though. Maybe we'll just come t' visit you out there where you're a livin' now. Where do y' live again? Is it Arkansas? Is that right, son?"

"Sure, that's right, Mr. Campbell."

I ain't goin' into the whole story with old Mr. Campbell here. He'll hear it all soon enough, I guess. The whole town will. Maybe I can get another deal going and get on out of Maynard's Valley before the whole county hears of my failure—yeah, right!

Every time he considered the whole regretful mess—and it was hard to keep from reflecting on it—Theo burned inside with anger at his own gullibility and naiveté. He still could not believe he hadn't realized that Mr. Page and Arnold Zayle were crooked right from the beginning. He could see very plainly now that every thing they had told him was a blatant lie. His blind trust in the two swindlers had forced him to sell the inn back to them in order to pay off the loan for the mine. He silently promised himself that he would never make the same mistake again and the shysters who caused his downfall would not have the last laugh. No sir! Even though Little Moon Arkansas was behind him, there would be another opportunity and he would find it!

Theo could find blame for almost anyone except himself in the whole matter though. He swore that worrying about Mandy's condition had put him under so much pressure that he hadn't been able to think straight. Then there were all the bills and responsibilities of the inn plus the disrepair on it that he had not been advised of. Add to that his best friend Will running out and owing him money. He reasoned that if it hadn't been for Cora Bell's house and her girls bringing in customers, he'd have never made a penny. Right or wrong, that was the truth as he saw it.

Ma would say I deserved losing everything. I can just hear her now. "You lie down with dogs Theo, you're bound to get up with fleas." I got up with fleas, all right... It will be hard to face Ma and Pa. I promised I would be a success if they would just help me. I always aimed t' pay back everything they lent me, and I will just as soon as I get me another deal goin.' Just wish I didn't feel like an old hound dog coming home with his tail between his legs. They'll all be askin' questions ... and th' truth be known the whole valley will be talkin' about me before tomorrow comes.

I wouldn't want Pa and Ma to know about that gold mine. Wouldn't want them to know about Cora Bell's girls, either—or about Mandy Rose. Mercy, no! If they were to find out the truth about her and me it would kill them both. I can hear Ma now. "Wicked woman of the night," she'd say. I could never live that down. They'd never help me out again. It's better this way. I don't need to be upsettin' any of them.

It ain't really a lie—nah! If I spare their feelings.

Picnics and Kisses

The note fell on the floor. Vy grabbed it quickly, but her spontaneous laugh and consequent hiccups gave her away.

"Girls! Did you hear me ask you not to talk during this examination?"

Vy blushed, embarrassed. "Yes'm, I'm already finished, Mrs. Lucinda."

"What about you, Mary?"

"I am finished too, ma'am."

"Then I suggest you both retrieve your lunch pails from the cloak room and make your way outside to eat, and please refrain from talking as you leave."

"Yes, ma'am."

"Yes'm, Mrs. Lucinda"

Mindia looked up, frowned, and then turned her attention back to the test, trying to finish so she could be excused to eat lunch with Vy and Mary as well.

The girls found shade in a favorite oak tree at the corner of the school yard. They plopped down on the mossy ground and opened their pails. September had begun to color the leaves on the trees, and the cool breeze hinted of fall.

Mary took a big bite of an egg salad sandwich and watched as Vy munched on her ham and biscuit. She was in deep thought. "Oh m' gosh, I thought we were caught that time."

"Thank goodness she didn't see the note and take it up."

Vy started to unfold the piece of paper, but Mary grabbed it from her hands and started tearing it to shreds. Vy was startled.

"You know the only thing that my mother ever told me that really made sense was 'Don't ever write down on paper anything you want to keep secret.'"

"That does make sense, but what? What's the big secret, Mary?"

"It's me' n' Will, Vy. We are in love."

"Oh m' gosh, Mary. Will Graves? Are you sure, Mary? When did all this happen?"

"Oh yes, Vy, I'm very sure. We've been seeing each other for quite some time now—and we know we are made to be together. We can hardly stand being apart, Vy."

"Well, Mary, I guess that is great—I mean, I am happy for you. Just seems like you are awfully young, though. I don't know Will very well, but he seems like a very nice fellow."

Mary shook her head. "Oh Vy, we are not too young. Will and I think it's wonderful. We know we are right for each other, but my mother is so against us. We have to sneak around just to have a little time together, and it makes both of us feel so guilty and nervous."

"Why can't you just sit down with your mother and be truthful—explain to her how you feel?"

"Good mercy no, Vy! She would lock me in a room and throw away the key. I really don't know what her problem is, Vy, but I tell you the truth, if I ever get out of that house and away from her, I will never go back. Daddy is not like that. I actually think there are times he understands and sides with me, but he is afraid of Mother, too. I hate her, Vy. The only reason she lives is to rule my life. Or I should say, ruin my life!"

"Don't say you hate your mother, Mary. Hate will hurt you more than it does anybody else. You know the situation between me and my mama. I don't have any idea what's goin' on in her life at all and never see her anymore unless we accidentally happen to run into her in town. I always see her somewhere like the mercantile, Skene's Mill, or some place else like that. She will say hello to me, just like a stranger, and then run away as fast as she can. It hardly seems like she's my mama anymore, Mary. Seems like she would rather forget that I exist. I guess I will never understand, and it really hurts. I admit there was a time when I said I hated her, but I was the miserable one, Mary. I have always needed her love, but felt it very few times. So take it from one who knows. It will help you if you pray about this thing between you and Will—and pray for your Mother, too, Mary. Prayer can work wonders. You know that passage we studied in the book of Luke where Jesus tells us to pray for those who hurt us and despitefully use us? Remember?"

"Mmm hmm, I know."

"No doubt it is hard to accept, Mary. It's a hard thing for anyone to do. But you're a Christian, and y' must forgive. Be patient with your mother and let God take care of this. If God wants you and Will to be together, it will happen no matter what y' mother does."

Mary threw up her hands in a show of desperation. "Oh, Vy, I know everything you are telling me is right, but you don't know how my mother is. Sometimes I feel like she is stronger than God!"

Vy winced.

"Oh, Vy, you know I'm jesting about that, but in all seriousness it sounds like you have a lot more faith than I do. Do you know that Mrs. Lucinda and Mother are good friends and have been since they were young girls in school? Let me tell you right now, if that busybody teacher finds out I have been seeing Will Graves again, she will dash right over and tell my mother about it first thing."

There was a look of surprise on Vy's face. "Hmm. No, I didn't know the two of them were friends, Mary. It appears to me that Mrs. Lucinda has always favored you and doesn't like me. I can't imagine her wanting to hurt you, being a friend of your mother and all, but don't worry, dear. You know that Min and I won't tell anyone about you and Will."

"I know neither of you will, Vy."

Mary smiled mischievously. "There's something else I wanted to talk to you about. Just a little something' I want y' to do for me. Just one little favor to ask."

By the look on Mary's face, Vy dreaded hearing what the favor was.

What in the world is she going to ask me to do?

Mary smiled and went on. "Would you consider going on a blind date with me n' Will?"

"What y' mean, a blind date?"

"Well, it will work like this. I will have Will bring one of his friends as your date, and then we'll all meet for a picnic—the one Min and I have been planning for this Saturday. Mindia already has a date with Ross Seymour. Did you know that?"

Vy nodded. "I know they have been friends for some time now. He comes to the house to see Min a lot, but I don't know how she feels about him. She takes drives with him in the family's carriage, and he likes to hear her play the piano. He's a real funny guy and makes everybody at our house laugh with his jokes."

Mary leaned closer and began to whisper so no one would hear her plan.

"Well, I figure Ross and Min could come by and get me. If I tell Mother I'm just going on a picnic with the two of them, she will allow me to go. I have to figure some crazy way to get out of the house every time Will and I see each other, Vy. She caught us together in town once, and she slapped me in the face right there in public—in front of Will and everybody on Main Street. Then Mother proceeded with her horrible accusations and insults. She swore to the both of us she would call the sheriff and have Will put in jail if he ever tried to see me again. It was awful. I was embarrassed to death, and he was so upset. I can never let that happen again.

"Listen to me now, Vy. Here's the plan ... Will and his friend—whoever he brings for your date—will come pick you up. The three of you will head on over to Graveston Park where we will have our picnic. It's pretty secluded there and not likely that anyone will see us. Mindia and Ross will pick me up in their carriage a bit earlier, and we'll be waiting for you at the park. I'll fix us a lunch. You and Min could bring something if you like. Oh, Vy, we'll have so much fun."

Mary's face lit up as she talked about her young man. "Will is really a wonderful person, Vy. I know you have met him once before, but the more you know Will, the better you will like him. He is a great kidder like Ross Seymour is. He loves to laugh and joke around a lot. I have really been crazy about him for a long time. He left and went out to Arkansas for a little while, but he told me he couldn't stay away because of me. I thought I would die while he was gone. Will loves me, Vy. We're going to get married just as soon as he saves up enough money for a house."

"Good land sakes, Mary! How come you haven't told me about all this before now?"

"You would have been the first person I'd have told, Vy, but I haven't told anyone because I was afraid it would get back to her—to Mother." Mary's hands were shaking.

"You just don't know her, Vy, and tell y' the truth, it makes me scared and upset to even discuss it. She is determined to ruin everything I want. She has plans for me to marry one of those snobby boys from her country club in Whitesville. She and Father are talking about moving over there because it would be closer to his work, but the real reason she wants to move is to separate me and Will. I wish she and father would go on, just move and leave me here, because I'm not leaving Will no matter what they do to me."

"Mary, you know I would do anything for you, don't you?"

"Yes."

"And I guess I will do this thing for you, too, but tell me, who is this person, this blind date that Will is going to bring for me?"

"I don't know, Vy. But Will has a lot of handsome friends."

It was after church let out on Sunday morning. The pastor had cut his sermon short, and the parishioners were in animated conversation when Will Graves strolled up to Theo Taylor, slapping him on the back. "How about doin' y' old pal a big favor, Theo."

Theo rolled his eyes. "By all rights, I should skin you alive, Will Graves. You skipped out on me in Arkansas and you know it! I didn't know where the dickens you were or what happened to you until Ma wrote me and said you had come back here. I hardly think you're in a position to ask any favors of me. Don't you need to be thinkin' about paying me what y' owe me 'stead of askin' me to do you a favor?"

"Don't worry, Theo. I'll pay you what I owe you. I always meant to send the rest of that money to you and just never got around to it. I don't see how you stayed out there in Arkansas as long as you did. I hated that place, Theo, and besides, I had to get back home to my girl."

"What girl?"

"Mary, Mary Mynatt. I thought you knew her. Don't you remember, Theo? You met her. She was that beautiful brunette at Winfield and Sadie's wedding. I am smitten, Theo, and I'm not afraid to admit it, but there's only one fly in the ointment. Her mother hates my guts and, so much so, told me she'd have me tied to the jailhouse if I ever tried to see her again. We have to sneak around like a couple of idiots just to have a little time together. Mary's a great girl, Theo. She's the one for me, and I'm going to marry her just as soon as I save up enough money to get us a place."

Theo whistled a long low whistle with a distressed expression. "Y' really are smitten. Y' got to be kiddin' me, Gravesy! Surely you ain't getting married and leavin' ole Theo and bachelorhood behind!"

"No, I ain't kiddin,' Theo. I'm in love with Mary like a crazy person."

"Gravesy, man, I believe y' must have lost y' mind. Boy, I feel sorry for you!" Theo looked at Will's face, reconsidered his words, and patted his buddy on the back. "Naw, I'm just kiddin, Will. There's no offense meant. But marriage ain't for me! No, sir! I'm not thinkin' any such thing. You know you had me fooled, Will. I really thought you and me would end up out west runnin' some kind of business together." Theo chuckled. "Or a goldmine or somethin.'"

"A goldmine, Theo?"

"Didn't I tell you that old Mr. Page and Arnold Zayle talked me into investing in a gold mine? Had me believing the stock on it would soar—and to tell y' the truth, it did at first. Then just about the time I thought I'd made a huge profit on it, they told me the mine went bust. I had to turn around and let those shysters have my inn back to pay off that loan. I put up with a load of worry and hard work for nothing but a dud goldmine."

It was the first real shame Will had felt for abandoning his friend, and the shock on his face told Theo as much.

"Good grief, Theo! I'm really sorry for running out on y,' old pal. Y' know, the moment I first walked in and took a look at that Zayle fellow, I suspected he was a crook. To tell y' the' truth, that whole place out there gave me the shivers. That sleazy house of girls next door to the inn. Oh, they were pretty enough, but in such a cheap floozy sort of way." Will shook his head. "You know, Theo, those girls were nothing but—"

Theo interrupted his friend with a challenging look. "Don't talk about Mandy like that, Will."

Will's eyes widened in surprise, then he questioned in an apologetic tone, "Mandy Rose? You ... uh, got to know her pretty well, did y,' Theo?"

"You could say that."

Realizing he had said too much, Will started to express regret. "I-I'm sorry, Theo … I didn't know—"

"And no one else is to know either, Will. Y'understand?"

"Sure, Theo. It's forgotten."

Theo nodded. "Now, about this friend of Mary's she wants to fix me up with. Who in the world is she?"

"I don't know, Theo, but Mary has a lot of gorgeous friends."

Yelling over her shoulder, Mindia grabbed her shawl and ran excitedly out as Ross's coach pulled up. "I'm leaving now. Ross is here! See ya, Mom! Bye, Nanny. See y' later, Vy!"

The sun was shining, and the cool breezes kissed Min's cheek as she opened the front door and started out the door. What a picture perfect day for a picnic!

Not waiting for him to get down and help her, she scrambled up beside Ross in the driver's seat on her own. The couple was running late and realized they must hurry if their little plan was going to work. Min and Ross knew very well that Jessie May Mynatt would refuse to let Mary out of the house if they didn't call for her at the exact time agreed upon, so they were driving the horse drawn carriage hard. The plan was moving forward with no backing out now.

Mindia and Vy had hedged somewhat on Lotia's questions about the picnic, not desiring to explain the whole thing to her. Frankly, they were afraid she would object to their involvement if she or Nanny found out they were helping Mary to deceive her mother.

Vy seemed to have had a difficult time with everything all morning. Almost nothing had gone right, but she was almost ready—finally. Her auburn hair was at last, after many tries, wound and scooped up in a high bun on her head. She peered once more in Lotia's mirror and asked to borrow some rouge, which she carefully smeared on her lips, then delicately patted on some talcum. Vy wrinkled her nose, pinched her cheeks again, and looked dejectedly at her reflection. Your skin is pale as death, Vy Vittoye …

For the picnic she had chosen a new cream-colored waist with ivory lace edging the high collar. It was one she and Mindia had worked on together and had just gotten finished.

Lottie had taken the sad iron and pressed every tuck and ruffle on it to perfection. After much resolve, Vy had decided to wear the brown skirt with it, rejecting her new lighter beige one because today it refused to release wrinkles after she ironed and ironed it. Moreover, the party would undeniably be sitting on the ground, and a dark color would show less soil.

Vy pinned her cameo to the brown velvet ribbon tied at her throat, smoothed down her skirt one more time, and moved back away from the full-length mirror that stood in the corner of Lotia and Seth's bedroom. She viewed herself again from head to toe with a critical frown on her face and turned from side to side before she spoke to Nanny, who stood watching with interest.

"How does this outfit look, Nanny? Is my chemise tucked in the back? Is this tan belt right, or do you like Mindia's black one better?"

"The tan belt is right, you are tucked in, and you look stunning, Vy."

"I'm so tense, Nanny. Why did I ever let Mary talk me into doing this?"

"Just be your own sweet self, and everything will be just fine, honey. I imagine you will have a lovely time if you just give it a chance."

"But I don't even know this person Will is bringing for me, Nanny."

Nanny gave her a reassuring hug. "Remember, Vy, sometimes surprises can be a lot of fun, and besides, I know Will Graves would only bring someone nice."

Vy heard a horse whinny as Will's coach pulled up outside. Her heart began to beat faster, and her stomach churned.

Lotia appeared from the kitchen with a picnic basket full of goodies and thrust it onto the table in front of her. "Here's some snacks for you youngsters. I put in that chocolate cake you're so fond of, and, well, I did save a few slices for Seth since it's his favorite, too."

Vy threw one arm around Lotia's neck and hugged her tightly. "Oh, Lottie, thank you for going to so much trouble for us. I should have fixed the food myself instead of fooling around with my hair and clothes all morning."

"Now don't think another minute about it, dear. You just enjoy your date."

Vy put her hands up over her mouth. *Oh, m' gosh, I'm going on a date.*

Lotia stroked her hair, winked, and smiled jokingly. "I sincerely hope you like your mystery man, and it sounds like he has arrived! Come on, Nanny. We'll welcome the young fellows."

Vy could feel her heart pounding at the knock on the door. She grabbed a quilt and started looking for the wool tartan mackinaw she would need in case the weather turned cooler toward evening. Lotia and Nanny walked to the living room ahead of Vy, opened the door, and greeted the two smiling young men.

"Hello there, Will Graves. How are you this afternoon?"

"Hello there, Mrs. Seaton, Mrs. Selvidge. I'm fine, thank you, and how are you two ladies?"

"We are doing well. Thank you, Will." Will turned his attention to his friend who stood beside him.

"I would like you both to meet my companion here, Mr. Theo Taylor."

Theo extended his hand first to Lotia then to Nanny, greeting them charmingly as they offered theirs. "It's very nice to make your acquaintance, ladies."

"It's very nice to meet you, Theo. Please, both of you come on in."

As Theo stepped in, he took a look around the parlor, drawing in a sharp breath before he spoke. "Ohhhh, that old timepiece there is magnificent, Mrs. Seaton. Have you owned that very long?"

"Yes, we have, dear. Interested in clocks, are you?"

"Yes, ma'am. I surely am."

"That one there is very special, Theo. It's terribly old, was made in Germany, and has been in my husband's family for generations. I have to say it is one of my husband Seth's treasures. It took him and four other men to carry it in the house when we moved here."

Theo ambled boldly over to the giant grandfather clock, stood mesmerized by its ornate swinging pendulum for a moment, and spoke reverently. "I have always loved clocks, watches, any sort of time piece. And I also enjoy repairing—tinkering with them quite a bit as well."

"Well, maybe we can hire you to come over and check this one out for us since it seems to be losing time lately."

"It would be a joy, ma'am."

Nanny directed her attention to Will, inquiring of his family since she was a longtime acquaintance of the Graves's. "Nice to see you again, Will, dear. How's your Ma and Pa and the rest of your family?"

"They are just fine, ma'am. My mother sends her—"

At that precise moment, Vy appeared from around the corner with the picnic basket of food and her mackinaw in hand.

As Theo's eyes met hers, a complete look of enchantment spread across his face. Before Will could finish his sentence, Theo had hurried across the room to Vy, taking her hands in his.

He spoke, interrupting Will.

"Well, well, well, it's been quite awhile. Yes, indeed it has, but I believe I already know this young lady. Hello, Violet. You and I have met before, haven't we, dear? M—mmm. Yes, I would have known you anywhere. However, I can truthfully say that you have grown up and become only more charming since the day of Winfield and Sadie Campbell's wedding."

Vy hoped the elements of surprise and delight were not too revealing as she stood enthralled, looking into Theo's striking gray eyes. She could not keep a pleased smile from spreading across her face.

"Hello, Theo Taylor."

The picnic would be remembered as one of the most memorable days of Vy's life. The girls' plan came off without a hitch, and the parties enjoyed a lunch that was fit for a king. They munched on cold sliced ham sandwiches, batter fried chicken, potato salad, coleslaw, yeast rolls, cheddar and Swiss cheese wedges, Nanny's special pickles, chocolate cake, and fried apple and cherry pies. The young people ate and the girls laughed at the boys, who stuffed themselves first on the main course and then had to try some of each dessert.

Between Will's jokes and Ross's stories, everyone was doubled over in laughter. Theo's quick wit only added to the merriment, and Vy thought her stomach muscles would never be the same.

While the girls finished cleaning up, the boys found a perfect flat lawn and played a game of stickball.

Mary grinned and sighed with satisfaction. "I told you we'd have fun, Vy. Mother didn't have a clue either. Everything went as planned."

Vy did not answer.

Mary, picking up on Vy's hesitation, changed the subject quickly. "Do you really remember Theo from Sadie's wedding, Vy?"

Mindia looked up. "Of course she does. Who could forget Theo Taylor?"

Mary spoke with a warning in her voice. "Don't be upset now, Vy, if Mindia and Ross, Will and I disappear for a little while. You do realize this is the only time we get to have some privacy."

Vy looked at Mary accusingly as Mary laughed. "Don't look at me like that, Violet. We just want to be alone for a few minutes."

Vy looked first at Mary then at Mindia. "Great day, do you two plan to go off and leave me alone here with Theo all day?"

Mindia giggled. "Oh, Vy, it won't be all day."

When the boys returned from playing ball, Will kissed the top of Mary's head, put his arm around her shoulders, and the two of them disappeared on the path that led down toward the creek. It was evident they were so enamored with each other they hardly knew anyone else was present, and it was almost the same for Ross and Mindia, who ran hand in hand together up and over the hill, attempting to fly Ross's kite.

The situation did leave Vy and Theo alone practically all day, which could have been very uncomfortable had they not gotten along so well. Just the opposite was true. Theo was quite animated, just as Vy remembered him to be, easy to talk to, entertaining, and quite taken with Vy's beauty. Vy was surprised at the ease she felt in his presence.

Theo sat back and pondered the girl. "I declare, you are a very gorgeous lady, Violet Vittoye. Your name suits you perfectly."

Vy's thoughts flashed to Gran for an instant as she blushed with satisfaction. *I guess my clothes and hairdo are okay and my lip rouge has stayed put.*

"What goes on in your life now that you are quite grown up, Violet?"

"Most of my time is taken up with school studies and church."

"You attend church now?"

"Mmm hmm. Every Sunday I attend Rose Hill Church with the Seatons. I've become a Christian."

"That's wonderful, Violet. I was raised in church, as you know. Although I am the first to admit I have done some things for which I have had to beg forgiveness."

"None of us lives as well as they should, Theo."

"I bet you do."

"I couldn't do anything without Jesus. I have much to learn about being a follower of the Savior, but I have learned a lot since coming to live with the Seaton family."

"I've been wondering about that, Vy."

"Wondering about what?"

"Oh, just how, I guess, and for what reason did you come to live with the Seaton family?"

"Hmmm … I'm really not sure myself, Theo. I guess that probably sounds crazy to you, but it's true. It is really a very long story—and I may share it with you sometime, but I can tell you this much right now. Living with the Seatons has been a very positive experience for me. Their family has been a real blessing in so many ways, and I really care for all of them, although I still miss my mama very much."

"I can understand anyone gaining a lot by getting away from their home—away from their ma and pa. My going to Arkansas was a huge learning experience for me—was it ever!"

Relieved the conversation was not pertaining to her life anymore, Vy continued on. "Why did you decide to come back home?"

"I ran into two old gangsters who caused me to lose everything."

Vy's question had caught Theo off guard. *Good grief! What is it about this girl that makes me spill my guts to her?* Theo quickly directed the conversation away from his failures, steering them toward his expectations for the future.

"I have some awesome plans, Vy. I aim to get out of this one horse town again someday. I'm a born entrepreneur; it just comes natural to me. I ran a hotel like I had been born doing it, and I'm looking for another good business opportunity, and I will know it when I find it. What are your plans for the future, Vy?"

"Well, I don't rightly know what I will be or where I'll end up someday, but I will tell y' one thing. God knows and is there to direct me, for I pray to Him every day about my future. I literally cling to His beautiful promises—especially one in Proverbs. Do you know it, Theo?

> Trust in the Lord with all thine heart;
> and lean not unto thine own understanding.
> In all thy ways acknowledge him, and he shall direct thy paths.
> Proverbs 3:5–6

"Oh, yeah, I know the verse. Well, I wish I had the faith you do, Vy. When I get married someday—of course, way in the future—I would want a girl like that, like you, Vy—with faith."

"What a nice thing to say, Theo."

"Not just saying it, I mean it."

Theo had been relaxing on the blanket, staring up at the sky and chewing on a straw. He turned toward Vy, who was leaning back on her elbows, and suddenly reached over and touched her hair.

"You are so beautiful, Violet."

As Theo stroked Vy's hair, he let his hand linger near her face. She dared not move. At that point, he moved a little closer. He was so close now she could smell the spicy scent of his shaving elixir. She could feel her insides begin to tremble.

Dear Lord, don't let him know I'm shaking.

Theo lightly caressed Vy's temple and then her cheek with one finger.

Vy felt a rush of pure excitement run from the tip of her toes to the top of her head.

"You smell so lovely, pretty one. This has been a wonderful day for me." His face was now inches from hers. Theo's lips brushed against Vy's soft cheek and paused. She closed her eyes. He moved his body closer to hers, and his lips found her mouth. It was a delicious, delirious moment, that first kiss, and one she would never forget.

Theo nuzzled her neck and then kissed her again until she could not breathe. This Romeo was not going to stop, and she suddenly realized it. Vy quickly pushed him away and sat up.

After an awkward pause, Theo broke the silence. He took her face in his hands and turned it toward his. "I'm really glad I came on this picnic today, Violet Vittoye. May I see you again?"

Vy stood to her feet, straightened her skirt, and answered. "Y-yes, Theo. You may." She held out her hands for his with a laugh. "Come on, Theo. Let's see if we can find those other scalawags."

Dear Diary,
Today Mary, Will, Min, Ross, Theo, and I went on a picnic. My date was Theo Taylor. We got along so well. He liked me—at least he said he did. I spilled sarsaparilla on my waist but don't think he noticed it. Mary says she is in love. Isn't she too young?
I don't know what is going on with Mindia and Ross—they may be in love, too. What is happening to all my friends? Theo said he has plans to leave Maynard's Valley in the future. I don't want him to leave because I really like him a lot.
He asked if he could see me again, and I told him yes.
He kissed me—I never felt anything like that before, dear diary.

During lunch breaks at school, the girls couldn't stop whispering about their picnic date and the fact that their plan to outwit Mary's mother had worked. Mary was already at work planning another outing so she could spend a whole day with Will before the weather got too bad. It had been two weeks since the picnic, and a cold rain was falling outside. It was too wet to take the usual afternoon break outside, so the whole class had to lunch at their tables. The girls hated that because Mrs. Lucinda stayed in the room and they could not talk freely.

Their teacher had been quite snippy and sarcastic for the last few days and seemed as though she was trying her best to eavesdrop on the girls' conversations.

When she excused herself and went outside to the privy, Mary whispered quickly to Vy and Mindia. "I hope it's only my imagination that she suspects something is going on between Will and me. She has been so curt with me the last few days. What do you all think?"

Mindia shook her head. "I haven't noticed anything different. She's always rude to me."

Vy laughed and replied. "Me too, Min."

"I haven't told you girls, but Will is coming by in the carriage for me today. I told Mother that I was going home with you two."

"Oh, Mary, you didn't!"

"Oh, don't panic, Vy. It will be okay. I told her I was sleeping at your house tonight, that you and Min had invited me, and since there's no school tomorrow, she agreed to allow it. Will is going to bring me to your house later."

Vy shook her head. "Lottie is not going to like this, Mary."

Mindia agreed. "Ma doesn't like you lying to your mother, Mary. Whatever are we going to tell her when you come in?"

"Oh, I don't know. I know it's terrible, but how else am I going to see Will? Don't worry about your ma. When I show up tonight, she will just think Mother has brought me over."

Vy shook her head and countered with concern; "This makes me so nervous, Mary, lying to everyone. It isn't right."

Mrs. Lucinda entered the door, glared at the two girls, and for a moment appeared as though she was going to speak. Instead she turned, picked up the hand bell, and rang it. School was over for another week.

Seth was waiting outside for Mindia and Vy because it was much too far to walk in the bad weather. The girls ran through the cold mist to the carriage, huddled under the quilts Lottie had supplied for their ride home, and called out, "Bye, Mary. See you after while."

Mary answered, "Bye, girls. I'll be over as soon as I can get there."

Seth glanced back over his shoulder. "Is Mary coming over our house tonight?"

Min and Vy exchanged glances. "Yes she is, Dad. Directly."

Mary peered through the peephole in the outhouse door to see if Mrs. Lucinda was gone. When it looked safe, she braved the pouring rain, running without a pause down the hill and through the woods to Will, who was waiting patiently in his parked carriage. Will jumped out to help her inside.

"Get in here, Mary. Mercy, girl, you are soaked. I would die if being out in this rain makes you sick."

"It is the only time I could see you, Will—and I had to see you."

"I almost have enough to get that little house we looked at, Mary. Another paycheck or two plus my savings, and I'll have the sum to acquire it."

Will took a laborious look into Mary's troubled eyes then kissed her forehead before he spoke. "I don't want anyone or anything to hurt you, Mary. I need you with me all the time so I can take care of you. We will be married soon, and then there will be no sneaking around. She won't be able to keep us apart then—no one will. I promise you that, my sweet."

Mary fell into his arms. "Oh, Will, I do love you so. Please tell me it won't be much longer now."

Lottie grabbed her robe when she heard the soft knock and hurried to open the front door. "Mary! What in the world? Whatever is wrong, dear?"

"Uh—I'm so sorry. Did I wake you, Mrs. Seaton? No. No, nothing is wrong. I just came to spend the night with the girls. Are they, uh, Vy and Mindia, are they in bed? We—uh—I just now got away to come over here. I'm very sorry it's so late, Mrs. Seaton."

"It's okay, Mary. I'm just glad nothing's wrong. Just come on in here, dear. I don't think the girls are asleep. Maybe Mindia is. I know they are both are in bed. You may go on in Vy's room. I see her lamp is still burning."

Mary blushed and stammered. "Th-thank y,' Mrs. Seaton."

Lotia ushered Mary to Vy's door, knocked, and opened it. "You have company, Violet. I remind you girls that Seth has to open the store very early on Fridays and needs his rest, so please talk quietly."

"We will keep things quiet, Lotia."

"Yes, Mrs. Seaton, we will—and I apologize again for being so late."

"Goodnight, girls," Lotia softly replied and closed the door.

Mary whispered, "Vy, thank goodness you are still awake."

"Mary, good grief. I had given up on you coming tonight. What time is it?"

"I don't know. It's pretty late."

"Where have you all been, Mary? What have you been doing?" Before Mary could say anything, Vy held her hands up and turned her face away. "No, no! Don't even tell me. I don't want to know."

"Oh, great day, Vy. We have only been, well, talking—making plans. You won't let on to Lottie that I had Will bring me over here, will you? Please don't tell anyone, Vy. I am so afraid of my mother. She will break us up for sure if she finds out I have been seeing him again. I wish I could tell you everything, Vy, but it's best if you don't know some things. Believe me, if you think that you hate all the lying and sneaking around I have to do, just think how much I hate it. Things would be so different if my mother would let me date like a regular person. If she would just allow me to be courted by a young man like the other girls are. We are going to have to get married very soon in order to see each other. Great day, Vy! There now, I've already gone and told you."

"Mary! Surely you can't be serious! Are you sure you are ready for marriage? It's one of the most important decisions you'll ever make in your whole life. Do you even know Will Graves that well? And Will, is he ready for such responsibility? Does he have a secure position and earnings enough to provide for you? Oh, darling, please don't hasten into anything. I want to see you happy, but I would hate to see you make a terrible mistake."

"Vy, you don't understand. I can never be happy unless I am with Will. We are going to be married, with or without my parents, or anyone else's consent." Mary gave Vy a pleading look. "Please just be glad for me."

Vy could see the hurt and desperation in her friend's eyes. She gave Mary a reassuring hug as they settled down under the covers.

"Of course I'll be glad for you, Mary. I love you. You're my dearest friend."

The Invitation

It was a Saturday morning and the Seaton's day to shop for supplies. That meant a trip to the Maynard's Valley Mercantile to acquire the things Seth did not stock in his store.

Vy and Mindia had agreed to ride in town and purchase the needed items, and their arms were loaded down with piece goods and other objects when Vy caught sight of Theo in the back corner of the mercantile.

He was working intently on an item in his hand and had not noticed the girls coming in. His job repairing timepieces at the mercantile was keeping him fairly busy, paying a good wage, and in his mind was serving him well as an interim position until he could find another place of employment in the big city.

Vy ducked down behind the load of packages in her arms so Theo couldn't see her. It had been four weeks and one day since their distinguished picnic date together, and Vy had long since expected a call from the young man. In her mind, Theo had had sufficient time to call on her if he really had enjoyed her company as much as he avowed. She had all but given up on him ever getting in touch with her again.

Covering her mouth with one finger, Vy whispered to Min, "Shhhh. Don't look now, but Theo Taylor's right over there, Mindia. Let's get out of here before he sees—"

At that instant, Theo looked up and caught sight of the two girls. He sat up and called out excitedly across the store, "Hey there, Violet, Mindia!"

Mindia smiled, giving Vy a mischievous look, and immediately bounced over to Theo's little office desk in the corner of the mercantile.

"Hey there, Theo. What y' doin' here?" She peered over his desk at the scattered parts of a watch.

"I'm just workin' my job, Min. What are you and your beautiful companion over there doing in town this lovely Saturday morning?"

"Oh, we're just picking up a few things for Nanny and Ma. We had no idea you worked here."

"Mmm. Yeah, I have a little watch and clock repair business back in this here corner. I talked Mr. McVae into renting out some space to me. Figured I could get enough business to raise cash for my next venture, whatever that may be. Haven't decided that yet. And I'll say one thing," Theo made a gesture toward the time pieces that surrounded his desk, "I never expected this little watch repair venture of mine to be so profitable. As you can see here, I'm covered up with work."

From across the aisles of the store, Vy waved her hand, blushed, and hoped she was far enough away so that the red in her face didn't show.

Although he had been carrying on a conversation with Mindia, Theo had kept his eyes glued on Violet, who was now strolling indifferently across the room, trying hard to hide her excitement at seeing him again.

As she neared his desk, he reached out for her hand, causing several of her packages to tumble to the floor. Theo smiled, politely picked them up, and spoke with enthusiasm.

"Well, hello, pretty Miss Violet. Looks like you and Mindia have your hands full today. How have you been? Y' need a watch repaired or something?"

Vy could feel her neck burning. Dear Lord, don't let me be blushing like a fool! No thanks, Theo. I don't own a watch and I'm fine. How have you been?"

"Well, I'd be a lot finer, Violet, if you would let me take you for a ride this weekend in my new carriage. That is, if the weather is good. I came by your house the other day, and I guess you were out. Anyway, nobody was at home when I rode by there. I have been getting this little office set up here, and by the time I do a few repairs it's pretty late when

I get out. Here, let me help you load your carriage with these packages, won't y,' girls?"

Theo took as many packages from the girls as he could manage, and the three walked outside the mercantile.

Min's eyes were shining. "You said y' have a new carriage, Theo?"

"Well, it's pretty new. Mr. McVae had one for sale, and I took it. Walk down here with me and see what I've bought."

After depositing the parcels in the Seaton carriage, the girls followed Theo down the street to where his spirited horse and shiny new carriage waited.

Mindia's eyes widened with delight. "Oh, boy, that's some fancy carriage, Theo!"

Vy could agree to that. "Yes, it really is. It's beautiful, Theo."

After the two girls had oohed and aahed enough to satisfy Theo's ego, Mindia boldly asked, "When do we get to take a ride in it?"

Vy, embarrassed, gave Min a horrified look. "Mindia!"

Theo, pleased and amused, laughed aloud. "Any time we can agree on is fine with me, Min."

Quickly turning his attention back to Violet, he continued, "I been thinking, Vy, that you and I, we—well, maybe we could drive over to the Whitesville Fair that's due to begin in about three weeks. What y' think?"

"Drive to Whitesville? A fair? Oh, goodness, I don't think so. Dear me, Theo. That would never do. It's such a long way over there."

Mindia broke in. "Wouldn't it take the most of a day just to drive it?"

"Well, it would take an afternoon at least. I'll admit it is a good piece to Whitesville, and that's why we would have to leave on a Thursday. I remembered y' told me that y' don't have school on Fridays, isn't that right? Just think how much fun we'd have. I've wanted to visit that fair again ever since I attended it as a kid. I know you would love it, Vy. Theo studied the girl's troubled face, anticipating her hesitation, then was quick to add, "Oh, Vy, wait a minute here. Now, there would be nothing improper about it. I don't mean just the two of us. We would get Min, Ross, Will, and Mary—th' whole gang—to go."

Mindia perked up with anticipation. As soon as she heard Theo intended to include her and the others, she beamed.

"Oh, Vy, let's do it! I've never been to a fair. I will help talk Mom and Daddy into allowin' the trip."

"Oh, I'm so sure, Mindia. I can't believe y'! Can't y' just see us asking them to let us take off on a long fifteen-mile journey with three young men? Why, I can hear Lotia laughing at the thought of it, not t' mention what Seth would say!"

Theo took Vy by the shoulders and turned her to face him.

"Calm down, my pretty one. My invitation is not what you think. I repeat I have no improper intention here. We will have a chaperone waiting on us in Whitesville. My aunt Katie Faye, Ma's sister, lives right in the city, and she is forever beggin' me to come for a visit and bring my friends. Aunt Katie owns a big old boarding house in Whitesville with plenty of rooms. You girls would have your own full quarters. I tell you my aunt would absolutely adore having us come for a stay, and I'm sure she would attend the fair with us. She and her friends go every year. If you girls are agreeable, I will have Ma contact her well ahead of our trip for all the necessary papers with rooming arrangements and assurance of proper chaperones for you while we are there."

"Oh, Vy, let's do it! I do so want to go."

"Mercy me, I don't know…"

"You could have the Seatons talk to my parents, Violet."

Vy took a hard look at both Min and Theo in disbelief at such an idea. She was filled with excitement to think of it, but with more unbelief and apprehension than anything else. "We certainly would have to do that," she said.

Min tossed her head, placed her hands on her hips, and gave a grunt of disapproval.

"Oh, Vy, you really are such a prude! I shall have to be the one to explain everything to Ma and Daddy. Y' best just leave everything to me."

"That's exactly what I am going to do, Mindia."

The weeks simply dragged by as the girls waited anxiously for their trip to Whitesville. In the beginning, Lotia was extremely upset about the plan and Seth was dead set against the whole deal. There was much debate between husband and wife and some bending toward argument as to whether or not this could possibly be an appropriate event for the girls.

In the end, though, they agreed to allow it. However, if it had not been for an afternoon teatime visit between Lotia Seaton and Cordelia Taylor, the journey never would have happened. Lotia and Delia hit it off right away, and by the time Lotia had left the Taylors' house, she had viewed all correspondence between Lotia and her sister, Katie Faye, and was quite aware of every detail concerning the trip that Mindia and Vy were looking so forward to.

"My sister, Katie, will watch after your young girls, Lotia, and they will have a wonderful time there. Sis loves all young people and simply adores Theo. As a matter of fact, I've always suspected that he is the favorite of my children. She has always cherished and enjoyed visits from my babies, as she has never had any of her own. I can understand how you and Mr. Seaton would be reluctant to allow this trip, but don't you worry. Your girls will be in good hands with Katie."

Nanny's intervention on behalf of the two girls didn't hurt any either.

"The girls are seventeen and eighteen years old, Lotia. Remember, dear, you had been married two years by the time you were as old as Vy. We have to trust them and their good judgment. You have taught them well, and they do know right from wrong."

"I am perfectly aware the two of them know right from wrong, Nanny. However, temptation is strong when you are sure no one is looking over your shoulder."

"The Lord is always looking over our shoulder, Lottie, and Vy and Mindia know that."

Vy was determined she would have no input on the final decision, so she kept quiet. She was happy enough to leave that task to Mindia and Nanny. However, her fervent prayer was that the group would be able to enjoy a lovely journey to Whitesville.

There was no thought more delightful than several days of fun and travel with good friends, not to mention a trip with that one special person who was in her mind almost constantly now—Theo Taylor.

The verdict was announced at supper one night. The decision had been made. The girls would be permitted to go to the Whitesville Fair!

There was much laughing, celebration, jumping up and down, and giggling. The girls hugged and thanked Lotia, Nanny, and even Seth (who by the way relented, but still did not like the idea) for allowing their upcoming adventure. Vy and Min gleefully set about making a list of what all they would need to pack for the journey.

It seemed like things were working out perfectly. Mary simply asked permission to spend those particular days of the trip with the Seatons. Jessie Mae Mynatt and husband Burl were due in Whitesville themselves for a conference where Burl, himself, was going to be a featured speaker, so she agreed to allow Mary's request. Jessie May figured she would have a sullen daughter on her hands if she insisted that Mary attend the boring business convention with them.

The plan appeared to be a perfect solution to Jessie May, keeping Mary safe and out of her hair so she could relax and enjoy her own friends in Whitesville.

On that prearranged Thursday afternoon, Theo pulled his new carriage just over the hill, waiting for the girls, as per Mary's instructions. It was the exact spot where Will always parked—out of sight of the school and Mrs. Lucinda's inquiring eyes.

"Old Lucinda Ellis can't see us or our carriage because the grove between here and there is thick."

"Why the devil do you care if she sees anything, Will? I say we just drive right up to the door and say, 'Howdy, Mrs. Lucinda Ellis, did you know these girls have their parents' permission to go on this trip with us?'"

"Theo, man! Mary's parents think she is spending the next few days with the Seatons, and the only reason they've agreed to let her have that much pleasure is because they are taking a trip to Whitesville themselves and don't want her along. You don't realize how much trouble that flaunting this in that old teacher's face would make for Mary and me. Old Lucinda is a friend of Mary's mother, who is insane as an ape and sure to make it a living hades for Mary if she finds out we're going off somewhere together. She doesn't want us to see each other. Period. You should have seen her the last time she caught us together. She slapped poor Mary in the face and beaned me right then and there. Crazy old hag said she would have the sheriff on me if I tried seeing Mary again."

"What are you going to do about that, Will? Sneaking around dating Mary is not the thing to do. You just need to have it out with her old lady."

"Don't lecture me, Theo. I'm going to marry Mary is what I'm going to do, and then her mother can go to blazes for all I care. I just don't want to make it hard on Mary until I can save enough money to get us that little house." Will looked up and took a deep breath, trying to calm down. Just talking about the situation got him hot under the collar.

"Look. Here come the girls!"

"Glory be! Look, it's only—it's, it's only Vy and Mindia"

A wave of panic struck Will as he put his hand to his mouth and muttered. "Dear Holy heavens! That old woman is onto something—she's holding Mary back!"

Will stepped out of the coach to meet the girls as they approached, quite out of breath. "What is going on girls? Where is she? Where's Mary?"

Theo jumped down and helped Mindia up first. Then he offered help to Vy, guided her to the seat beside himself, and threw a warm coverlet over her. He then got in, took his seat close to Vy, and reached for her hands. Vy felt warm all over as she looked into Theo's eyes. *His eyes make me feel feeble. He is so beautiful. I can't believe this is happening to me.*

What is happening to me?

Will was about to panic. "Mindia, do you know where Mary is?"

"She was right there behind me, Will. At least, that's what I thought."

Vy spoke up. "No, Min, I heard Mrs. Lucinda call her back as we started out the door. Said she wanted to talk to her about something or other."

There was an anxious wait for about fifteen minutes before Will shouted, "Thank the Lord! Here she comes now."

Mary ran down the hill to where the carriage was waiting. Will helped her climb beside him in the driver's seat, noticing the young girl was near tears.

"Thank goodness you're here Mary! Whatever happened?"

"Old nosy Mrs. Lucinda started questioning me about who I was staying with while Mother and Father are in Whitesville. I told her the Seatons." Mary searched Will's face. "She's going to make trouble for us. I know it, Will."

"Don't you worry, Mary. We're not doing anything wrong and shouldn't have to worry about that old lady's meddling."

Vy wasn't about to say anything at this point but could not help but worry about the deceit Mary and Will were involved in. What will happen if Mrs. Mynatt runs into Lotia or Seth and finds out Mary went to Whitesville with us? I can't do a thing about it now, but I feel that Min and I are taking part in this deception, too. I just hope Mrs. Lucinda never becomes our enemy. I don't trust her.

Will gave Mary a reassuring hug and snapped the horse's reins as the carriage lunged forward with a gallop.

The young men had agreed to take turns driving, and Will volunteered to be first. Mary snuggled close beside him in the driver's seat, pulling a warm quilt tight around her shoulders. Ross and Mindia were already engrossed in chatter and amusement in the seat across from Vy and Theo. Excitement was sky high, and laughter was abundant.

"Whitesville, here we come!" the gents shouted to the top of their lungs, for the little band was on its way. There was a sense of anticipation such as the group had never felt. What a wonderful time they would have. What a fantastic trip this would be.

Ross told a silly joke and started everybody laughing. Then he began singing a comical song. The pleasure had begun.

School was forgotten and so was Mrs. Lucinda.

No one noticed the single figure that stood watching at the top of the hill.

Midnight Rites

Light from the moon was bright as she found her way outside. It was almost midnight, and they had to hurry.

The wagon wound its way around the dark road headed to the groves.

Sally took a long look at the disgusting man sitting beside her. What good is any thing? I am vile, you are vile. But I can't help myself. I am trapped. The monster will never let me go—never let go of me. Just look around the bend, and it will be all right—all right...

The fires of Bel were blazing—the sacrifices were ready. The rites, the ceremony could begin soon.

The circle was waiting anxiously as Sally and her escort exited their wagon, joined the group, and dropped their clothes next to the others. The air felt cold against her body but the fire felt warm.

Sally opened her mouth and partook of the ritual hemp stick, inhaling deeply as the ground spiraled around and that state of euphoria took hold.

Her mind whirled, relaxed, then soared as her body started to unfold.

Here it is. My answer—the pain, it all melts away...

Sooooo good. I see it now—the D divination, the omen, yes!

"I am the Divination..."

"Can you see, Sally? Can you see?"

"I can. I can see it all. Yes, I belong—I belong right here with the goddess. I am hers. My babies, my sacrifices are gone. I gave them up for her."

In perfect automation, Sally joined the chanting and began to wave her lithe body before the priest.

Calvin took her in his arms once more.

Whitesville

Vy had never laughed so much or had so great a time in her life. Theo's Aunt Katie was landlord of the Akers Rooming House and had exactly three charming full-time residents besides herself. They were Mr. Orville Monroe, his youthful son, whom everybody simply called Sonny, and Mr. Benjamin Williams.

Theo, Violet, Will, Mary, Ross, and Mindia attended the Whitesville Fair together with the delightful group for two whole days running.

They would all boast later of walking the whole of the fair's outlay many times, examining every exhibition, eating or at least tasting every new food, and even taking a thrilling ride in Henry Ford's brand new horseless carriage that was there on display.

Everyone was somewhat exhausted and worn out from their grand experience, but it was a star-studded Sunday night, so they had decided to enjoy the pleasure of conversation and relaxation outside on Katie's big front porch in the cool of that October evening.

Most of the amusement was enthusiastically provided by Ross Seymour, a natural born comedian and ghost story teller. Ross was truly quite animated and full of scary tales and other yarns. Some of them were believable enough to be true, and, well, some were not. He had been talking—rather, telling his tales for over an hour.

> "It's a fact, folks. They are still there to this very day,
> and y' can easily see the rope marks in the rafters
> of the barn where the old farmer
> and his lady of the night hung themselves.
> Some swear that y'can still hear 'em

walk that empty old barn,
wailing each night for their poor lost souls.
And I don't know if y've ever heard the one about
the poor boy that drowned at the mill…
Don't know if I ought t' tell that one, though.

"Please go on, Mister Ross!" Sonny pleaded. "Tell us another one. I don't git t' hear ghost stories much!"

"You pipe down, Sonny Boy, now, and let the man take a breath and rest a minute. I declare, you would wear anyone out with yr pleadin.'"

"Aw, Daddy, I don't never get to hear about ghosts and goblins and things. Please let the man tell one more, okay? I'm havin' so much fun. I like these people, 'specially the pretty girls." The skinny fourteen-year-old looked past Will and winked at Mary.

The group united in laughter at the red-headed freckled-faced youth that his father, Mr. Orville Monroe, simply called Sonny Boy.

Vy smiled and considered the lad. She realized that his playful personality had added to the group's pleasure all weekend. What a delightful boy. His wit and open honesty is too charming. Katie Fay interrupted Vy's thoughts as she pushed her chubby body out of the wicker lounge chair, adjusted her fringed shawl about her shoulders, and directed her apologies to Ross.

"I'm sorry, son. As much as I have enjoyed your entire rendition of ghost stories as well as this most pleasant chit-chat, I am just worn out and simply must retire." Waving a bejeweled hand toward her kitchen, the pretty matron declared, "You youngsters may stay up as late as you like; help yourself to any victuals you may fancy, but I do request that you re-cover any foods that you care to snack on, and, Theo dear, would you put out Miss Tabby for me, and make sure the screen door is latched so that little raccoon varmint won't open the door in the night and make himself at home!" Theo nodded.

Taking an exit cue from Katie, Orville Monroe got up as well, yawned, and tousled Sonny's red hair. "It really is time we two retire as well, m' boy. We've an early day and a roof to start working on tomorrow."

The lad's face revealed a pout of displeasure and dismay at having to leave the companionship and conversation, but he obediently followed his father.

"Aw, shucks, Pa. I was just gettin' interested in Mr. Ross's new ghost story."

"Maybe you can come to Maynard's Valley someday and visit us, Sonny. I've a lot more funny stories and ghost tales as well."

"Can we, Pa? Can we go to Maynard's Valley and visit Aunt Katie's kin someday?"

Orville Monroe, obviously irritated, ignored the boy's plea, waved, and disappeared through the door with one statement. "Enough talk, Sonny. Goodnight to y'all ... "

Mr. Williams excused himself as well, leaving the three couples to enjoy the balmy night air and a little privacy.

Ross and Mindia decided they were hungry and headed toward the kitchen, debating whether to attack the delicious chocolate cake or the bread pudding that Aunt Kate had so considerately prepared for her guests.

Mary and Will decided on a walk in the moonlit garden and disappeared arm in arm down the pathway. Theo and Vy sat rocking back and forth in the creaky porch swing. The air was cool and crisp with the scent of falling leaves. It was so quiet and peaceful. Theo slipped his arm around Vy's shoulders.

"Are you cold, pretty one?"

"No, Theo. I'm fine."

He's looking at me with those eyes again. Why do they make me melt?

Theo reached over and gently turned Vy's face toward him. "You are gorgeous, Violet."

He kissed her lips once, then twice. She couldn't breathe.

"Theo, we can't. Your aunt. Someone will see."

"We don't care, do we?" Theo kissed her again and Vy pulled away, breathless.

"That—that's enough, Theo."

"Hey, sweetie. What's wrong? You like me, don't you, pretty one?"

"Y-yes. Of course I do. Y' know I do."

"What's the matter then, Vy? We are only doing what comes natural to those who care about each other. Just loosen up. Wasn't the trip to the fair a great idea? Didn't you have a good time?"

"I had a lovely time, Theo. I-I'm having a wonderful time."

"Then relax, pretty!"

Vy spoke with apology in her voice. "Please don't be mad at me, Theo. It's just that I can't—we can't ... "

"It's okay, honey. I love you anyway. I love your conviction, your certainty, and I respect that. I respect you, Violet."

Vy stood up and walked down the porch steps, straightening her long skirt.

Oh, Lord Jesus, help me. I'm as tempted as Mary is when I'm with Theo. I can't think straight when he kisses me. Help me, Lord!

Theo followed Vy down into the yard, approached her from behind, and slipped his arms around her waist. He rested his chin on the top of her head, inhaling deeply the scent of jasmine coming from her hair. Theo looked out in the night, pointed Vy toward the lights of the fair shining up the yon hill, and spoke with a yearning she had never heard in his voice.

"Can you understand at all what I'm talking about, Vy, when I say a big town is where I want to be?"

Fear gripped Vy's heart. *Oh, Lord, he's going to go off and leave me someday.*

Please don't let him leave me. "Well, I can see that the city is a lot of fun to visit, and I've had such a great time on this trip, but I don't know that it could never compare to our Maynard's Valley."

"Great heavens, girl! Why the dickens not? What's Maynard's Valley got that a big city doesn't have ten of?

Vy paused, rubbing her forehead nervously and considering the significance of this question. She gave her answer deep thought for several moments, not wanting to anger Theo but realizing for certain that the truth was absolutely essential if they were to understand each other. She simply had to make him comprehend her point of view here.

"H-mm. Well, there's my church and my family, the Seatons, my friends—of course, Mama, too. Then there's the land, Theo. Acres and acres of beautiful land—Maynard's Valley land. Land to work in. The fruits of my own garden ... beautiful and wonderful rising mountains that surround Maynard's Valley."

"Oh, pooh. The devil with all that!"

Vy was startled that Theo's words had returned to her with such quick indignation. Her shocked and injured expression caused Theo to soften his voice.

"I'm sorry, Vy, but, I mean, I do love my family, and I have a feeling for the old stompin' grounds somewhat. However, I want a lot more than just those things in my life. You tell me, what good is a plot of land that will work me to death and make me old and gray before I am forty? That two-hundred acre farm Pa owns in Maynard's Valley has him nearly dead right now, and has made him and Ma both old before their time. No, sir, dearie! Hard land and hard farmin' is not for this old boy. I will find something special. I already have some ideas, some thoughts in the works. I know they say money won't make you happy, Violet, but it sure isn't going to make me sad." Theo was speaking now with dead resolve. "I will start my own business and have something someday, Vy. My dreams are much bigger than Maynard's Valley."

Theo took Vy by the shoulders and softly turned her to face him. She melted into his arms as Theo softly nuzzled her forehead, the tip of her nose, and then her lips.

He was captivated by the innocence in her uplifted face as the moonlight bathed her ivory skin. What a beautiful girl here in my arms. How pure, chaste, and dear this little one is.

Violet's eyes, bright and blue, searched Theo's face, seeking reassurance, trying hard to reconcile their differences or simply disregard, forget there was any at all.

"There is something big in my future Violet, I can feel it."

Let it be me, Theo, she thought. Let it be me.

Vy scooted her chair over toward the blonde headed little girl's high-chair as chubby arms stretched toward her.

Dale bounced up and down in her high chair. "Here ... here! Sit by me. By—wit—" It was obvious the child was a favorite of Vy's, and Vy was a favorite of Dale's. It felt good to be needed and wanted. Vy poked her fingers underneath Dale's upreached arms and goosed her gently, causing the little one to fall into hysterical giggles.

Seth spoke gently but sternly. "Settle down now, Dale, and let Daddy ask God's blessings on this table."

"Okee, Daddy. I say it!"

"Very well. Y' start our prayer, Dale."

"God is gweat … God is good
Wet us fank Him f'r our food …
Bwess dis fam'wy, and fank you f'r bwingin
Min an' By home safewy to me
In Jethus' name!
Aaaaaa … men!"

Dale kept her head bowed but smiled and opened her eyes a tiny peep, watching for Seth to continue. Seth cleared his throat and began.

"Lord, we thank y' for the blessings y' bestow upon us daily.
We want t' ask y' for y'r forgiveness if we offended y' in any way, Father.
Thank y' for bein' with our daughters, Lord, and protecting them on their trip.
We praise ye fer bringin' our family back together and ask y'r blessin' on this here food
and on my dear wife and mama, who prepared the whole table for us.
In Jesus Christ's name, we ask these things.
Amen!"

There was much merriment and talk about how the trip to Whitesville went, and both girls had fun telling about exhibitions at the fair and the trip over and back. Min and Vy had pooled their money while at the fair and purchased a china doll for Dale, pretty decorative hair combs for Nanny and Lotia, and a pocket knife for Seth.

Min passed the gifts all around as Vy helped Lotia and Nanny clear the table and wash dishes.

After supper, Mindia disappeared into her room, unpacking her grip, and Vy took Dale in her room and settled her on the bed with her new doll.

Picking up her diary, Violet began to write:

Dear Diary,

What a week. My friends and I had the most delightful time. I think I have never had that much enjoyment in my life, laughing like I never have before. Ross Seymour is a real clown. He is so funny and amusing. I can see why Mindia likes him.

It was good making friends with Theo's aunt, Katie Faye Akers, and her tenants. There was a young boy living there in her house who reminds me of someone, though I can't imagine who.

I hope Mary didn't get into trouble over the trip. Her parents were not there when we arrived at her house, so maybe they will never find out about it. I really hurt for Mary, and I pray for her. She is so in love with Will and he with her. I hope it all works out for them.

Another thing: Seth's prayer was quite surprising to me tonight. He thanked God for protecting his "daughters." What is he thinking? Was that a slip of the tongue, or does he think of me as his daughter? I wish I were his daughter. Mindia is very lucky. No, she is very blessed to have the father and mother that she has.

Seth is a wonderful man, and Lotia is a great woman. I admire them and owe them so much.

The most wonderful thing, though, dear diary, is I think Theo really likes me. I know I like him. No, it's more than that. I'm in love…

Vy snapped her diary shut and put it in the little table by her bed. She got down on her knees beside her bed and bowed her head and silently prayed:

> Dear Father,
> I praise y'our Holy Name. Ye are mighty and wonderful.
> Forgive me for the hateful wrongs I have done, and grant me the faith I need so badly.
> Thank y' for all your blessings. I am so happy here with the Seatons now, Lord.
> Thank y' for Seth, Lotia, Mindia, Dale, and Nanny;
> this dear family that has loved and cared for me for five years now,
> especially Nanny, who led me to you and y' savin' grace.
> Y' know I still miss Mama, Lord, and I always will.
> I wish I could be near her, and I want her to know that I still love her.
> I pray for her, dear Father, and I want to tell her about you.
> You know that I long to find, to know, my earthly father, too, but only if it is your will, Lord.
> Please forgive Mary for deceiving her parents. It's only because

she loves Will so much and her mother does not understand, Lord. Please let it work out for her—for her family.

And, of course y' already know, don't you, Lord—that I am in love with Theo.

And if it could possibly be your will, let him love me.

In Jesus' name I ask these things. Amen

Mrs. Lucinda

"Violet Vittoye and Mindia Seaton, please come on up to my desk after I ring the bell. I shall have a word with you."

Mindia shot a sharp look at Vy, and Vy shrugged her shoulders because she had no idea, although she had never been asked to stay after hours at school when it was a good thing that Mrs. Lucinda wanted.

As the class emptied, several classmates gave the girls looks of pity as they filed out the door.

Mindia followed Vy as the teacher motioned for them to come and stand in front of her desk. Lucinda Ellis held her wooden marker and kept tapping it on the desktop. Her menacing presence encapsulated the whole room. With folded arms and cold narrow eyes, she peered over her wire spectacles, horrifying the cowering girls.

Vy could feel Mindia shaking and took hold of the girl's hand as Lucinda's allegations began to hurl.

"I have discovered the abominations you girls are guilty of, and it will do you no good to deny it. With my very eyes, I witnessed the two of you, as well as Mary Mynatt, board a carriage. One, I might add, that you thought was well hidden from me, and ride away with three young men to traipse off somewhere for an unrestrained and scandalous tryst. I have suspected something disgusting and outrageous like this has been going on for some time now."

Her eyes focused on Vy, and her words froze the air.

"Although I hate to say this, Violet, I am convinced that you have had a very ill influence on Mary Mynatt and Mindia, here. I had hoped against hope that you would not bring trouble when you were brought here to live. However, it now appears that, in spite of the fact that you are a bright student, you are following after someone's depraved ways. I, for one, simply will not tolerate this unacceptable influence in my school and on the other girls!"

At the sound of the teacher's words, Vy began to feel numb. As the numbness turned to anger, she began to pray silently but fervently. Oh, dear God, help me! Help me in this situation, Lord. Help me do what You would want me to do. I need y,' Lord.

Mindia started to cry. Ignoring Mindia's tears and Vy's stunned expression, Mrs. Lucinda continued with her tirade.

"I have taken it upon myself to send a messenger to your house— well, to Mr. and Mrs. Seaton—and have requested a meeting with them here this afternoon to discuss your penalty. Since I suspect that you, Violet, have largely been the instigator in this whole episode, I feel they have a right to know what kind of person they have taken into their home. As for you, Mindia, I feel that you have been influenced by Violet and, although you don't share as much responsibility as she does in this, there is no way you should be excused from punishment. I am certain the three of you should bear severe consequences for your actions. I have already met and informed Jessie May Mynatt of this whole repugnant affair—and you will notice Mary has been kept home today. I suppose she is being punished at this very hour."

At that point Lucinda walked over, opened the door, and signaled Seth and Lotia Seaton to enter.

By now both girls were sobbing with thoughts and fears racing through both their heads. Vy reached over and handed Mindia a hand-kerchief then reached inside her pocket and pulled out one for her self.

Mindia wiped her eyes, blew her nose, glanced first at Vy, then at her mom and dad. She felt completely at fault for this terrible mess, as she recalled it had been she who had begged and eventually convinced Vy to take the trip to Whitesville. Feeling terribly at fault she wondered if there was anything at all she could do or say now to take the blame off poor Vy, whose face had drained of all color. She also wondered what was happening to Mary—poor Mary! She looked up at Miss Lucinda and silently told herself, This horrid old woman is a beast!

Vy looked at Seth and Lotia's troubled faces as they walked in the room. The embarrassing sight broke her heart, and Mindia's sobbing was devastating. She felt completely at fault since she had wanted to attend the fair so badly with Theo. She wondered what in the world was going to happen to all of them, especially Mary, knowing how strict her mother was. *I may never see my dear friend again. Dear Lord, I pray for Mary.*

Visibly upset at the girls' tears, Lotia and Seth walked over and stood on either side of the two. Lotia spoke first. "What in the world is going on here? What is this all about, Mrs. Ellis?"

"I will be more than happy to tell you, Mrs. Seaton. It is about the lies, deception, immorality, and the disgraceful conduct of these two girls standing here. As their teacher, it is my duty, so I have taken it upon myself to let you know the scandalous act they have been involved in." Mrs. Lucinda's eyes blazed as she pointed her finger at Vy. "I expect the whole episode was instigated by this girl right here—and, of course, her bad influence has caused Mindia and Mary Mynatt, who is not here today, to stray as well." With an evil look of satisfaction, Lucinda posed a question. "Do you, Mr. and Mrs. Seaton, have any idea where these girls have been for the past week?"

Seth was calm, but Lotia's hands started shaking and her face was becoming bright red.

"I believe we always know where our daughters are, Mrs. Ellis. Indeed, if you are going to tell us that they have been on a road trip to Whitesville to attend the fair there in the company of three young men—young men whom we approve of and trust totally, ma'am, yes, we are quite aware of a trip they took since we gave our permission for them to do so."

Mrs. Lucinda's surprise was evident, but, recovering, she put her hands on her hips, cocked her head, and with a sneer on her face, added, "Well, did you also know that they attended a certain fair with these so-called trusted men very much unchaperoned, as well as spending nights with them in some rooming house there. And were you aware, Mr. and Mrs. Seaton, that Mary Mynatt deceived her mother, telling her that she was spending that time with your family and then took off in a carriage to go and do God knows what with some worthless boy who is at least three, maybe four years her senior?"

"I believe we have heard enough, Mrs. Ellis. My husband and I beg to differ with your conclusions. It is true that at first we had some reservations about allowing the girls a trip to the Whitesville Fair. However, after a visit with Mrs. Cordelia Taylor, who wrote the necessary papers and secured proper chaperones for the event, and giving consideration that Mindia and Violet know right from wrong, that they have never given us one smidgen of trouble, that they are faithful in school work, excel in their studies, and are involved in many church and family responsibilities, we changed our minds and gave the trip our blessing. It might also benefit you to know that the young girls certainly did not slumber in the same room with their escorts to Whitesville, and, to put it bluntly, Mrs. Ellis, I do very much resent the fact of your most foul presumption. Furthermore, if you require proof of our girls' behavior, I can supply you the post of Mrs. Katie Faye Keller, Mrs. Delia Taylor's sister, who entertained the group and acted as chaperone for the party of young people."

Seth patted the girls shoulders gently and kept right on nodding his head in agreement with Lotia. When Lotia finished speaking, Seth spoke with finality.

"Seein's y' feel these two girls are a disgrace to your classroom, Mrs. Ellis, they won't be attendin' Rose Hill School anymore. They have had near about all the book learnin' they need, and what's left of it me or my wife will be glad t' be responsible for."

It was plain to see that Lucinda Ellis was frustrated and very dissatisfied at the reaction she had gotten from the Seatons. She had been sure she was going to inform them of something they were not aware of and have the satisfaction of watching them transfer their wrath onto Violet with a little left over for Mindia. It was not working out as the teacher had planned at all, and she was having a hard time letting it go.

Fairly screaming, the woman's voice took on a frenzied high pitch.

"D-do you deny allowing Mary Mynatt to deceive her mother this weekend? The shame of it is on the both of you two! No, no Mr. and Mrs. Seaton, you'll not dismiss this infraction I have discovered and shield these guilty girls. My concerns shall not be discharged by the likes of you. I am highly offended at your attitude, and I do not think that the citizens of Maynard's Valley will look at this matter as leniently as you do after they hear the truth. Let's just see what the parents of the three young men involved think of these three females after I confer with them—and I might add that this event shall be reported to every church in the valley as well. We will see what the good members make of it!"

Seth sighed and spoke with weariness in his voice.

"You just go on ahead and report anythin' you care to, Mrs. Ellis—and I might just have a report or two myself. Why, ma'am, don't y' know it ain't right to go around threatnin' people? Sure seems you oughta know that, bein' a teacher of children n' all." Seth continued, "You know, Lucinda, it's a fine and good thing to have your pupils and their morals at heart, but it's quite another to accuse them of something bad without knowing the facts! Why, I'd think that you would want to be sure of all y' information before you'd want t' go and charge a body with somethin.' Seems t' me that ought t' be the premise you'd be holdin' to, there again, bein' a teacher and all. What's more, Lucinda, what in th' world would your mother-in-law, Maudie Ellis, think of y' trying to hurt these girls like this? Especially Vy, here. Y' know how much Maudie always loved Sally and Violet. Why, they are like Maudie's own daughters."

Lucinda's face flushed a pinkish-purple color while the veins in her temples stood out like they were going to burst. She took on the countenance of a wild woman as she fairly screamed in Seth's face, "Don't you dare speak of my mother-in-law in the same sentence with that woman, Seth Seaton! Sally Vittoye is nothing but a ... a ... "

Vy had been staring at the floor trying to close her ears from the discourse between Seth and Mrs. Lucinda, but upon hearing the last sentence, she quickly looked up and questioned, "What about my mama? What has my mama got to do with this?"

At that point Seth's long arms encircled his family, signaling the girls and Lotia to take their leave. It was plain to see that the man was thoroughly appalled with the teacher and finishing this matter here and now. As he ushered his family to the door, he called back over his shoulder, "We will hear no more from you, woman!" Seth's loud words and deliberate tone startled even himself. As he continued to guide the three women toward the door, he cleared his throat, trying to gain control of his emotions. Then, in a quieter, more respectful manner, Seth Seaton tipped his hat and stated, "We'll be a takin' our leave now, Mrs. Ellis. Good day to y,'

ma'am."

Mindia entered Vy's bedroom, eyes red and swollen. She plopped down on Vy's bed, cross-legged and facing her. Vy was still in shock about the whole incident. She looked up.

"What is it, Min?"

"Oh, Vy, I want you to know I am so sorry. Can you forgive me? You love school, and now we can never go back, and it's my entire fault. You told Theo we shouldn't go to the fair, and I insisted. I am the one who begged for Nanny to talk Ma and Daddy into letting us go. I'm so sorry, Vy. I would never hurt you for the world."

Vy reached over, hugged Mindia, and sat up on the bed, facing her. She took Min's face between her hands, speaking sternly.

"You listen here, Mindia! I wanted to go on that trip even more than you did. Don't you know that I want to be with Theo all the time? Don't you think for one minute that this was your fault. It was not.

"The simple truth is that Lotia and Seth allowed us to go, and we did nothing wrong. The thing is, I can't figure out why Lucinda Ellis has it in so badly for us. I have always felt like she didn't like me. There is something there, but what in the world could it be? Have you any idea? She mentioned Mama—didn't you hear her say 'Sally Vittoye is a…' That's when Seth interrupted her and practically drug us out of there. What in the world does this have to do with my mama, Min?"

"I don't know, Vy, but I never saw Daddy quite so upset, else he wouldn't have told her we would not be coming back to school anymore."

"Oh well, since we are almost finished anyway, I guess it doesn't matter too much. I wonder if there is any way we could receive our certificates."

"If Mrs. Lucy has anything to do with it, I'd say we're out of luck. Yeah—there may be someone Daddy can see about it. We have worked hard for those certificates, Vy."

"I agree."

"Min, I think I'm going to ride to the mercantile tomorrow and tell Theo what's going on. Mrs. Lucinda said she was going to tell his parents some bad stuff. What in the world is she going to tell them? That my mama is crazy? That I'm crazy just like her and not to allow Theo to see me anymore? Theo's ma and pa seem to like me now, and I don't want them to hear a bunch of mean allegations from Mrs. Lucinda. Theo needs to talk to them first before she gets to them. Would you like to ride with me?"

"I have a piano lesson tomorrow at Mrs. Wells' house in the morning or I would. But don't worry, Vy. The Taylors did approve our trip. There's no way they will listen to Mrs. L's allegations—they will listen to Theo. And besides that, Ivy told me that the Taylor family loves you."

"I can't get over this, Min. Why does that woman hate us and want to hurt us so badly?"

"I wish I knew. I'm sure there's a reason, Vy, but what is it?"

Dear Diary,
This is a distressing day. I feel all worn out and upset. Mrs. Lucinda called Mindia and me up to her desk after school this afternoon. She accused Mary Mynatt and both Min and me of doing immoral things when we made a recent trip to Whitesville. She even called Seth and Lotia to come to the school today, confronting them with her charges against us. It is true that we attended the fair with three young men but were accompanied the whole time by Theo's aunt, Katie Faye, and the tenants who live there in her boarding house. The trip was all prearranged for us by Theo's ma, Mrs. Taylor.

After she made her allegations to the Seatons, Seth told Mrs. Lucinda we would not be coming back there because we were innocent of the terrible things she accused us of. He told her she should get her facts straight before accusing anyone of something bad. Mindia and I know we did nothing wrong—and so do Seth and Lotia.

This is not fair! I feel terribly disappointed because Mindia and I won't be going back to school anymore. That also could mean that I may never get to see Mary again. Her parents may be so upset that they move away from here and take her to Whitesville to live. I can't bear the thoughts of losing my dear friend. I just cannot.
I'm glad I have had the chance to attend Rose Hill the years I did, though, as it gave me a chance to read many books and stories.
Tomorrow I am going to ride up town and talk to Theo. I want to let him know what has happened.

Vy put her diary down, knelt on her knees beside her bed, and bowed her head:

> Lord,
> In your Word, you tell us:
> "Seek and ye shall find.
> Ask and it shall be given unto you.
> Knock and it shall be opened unto you."
> Well, I'm askin' y,' Lord,
> What happened today—and why?
> Why does Mrs. Lucinda hate me and Mama?
> What does Mama have to do with any of this?
> Help me to understand, Lord.
> I don't want Mindia or Mary
> hurt because of me.
> If there is anything I can do to make this better,
> help me to know what it is...
> I pray, in Jesus' name,
> Amen.

Truth and Lies

Nanny entered and shut the bedroom door behind her, sat down in the rocker, and directed her words to Seth, who was sitting at his desk. He turned his face away from her pleading eyes.

"Son, you need to go ahead and tell them the whole story. It is time. Did you hear poor little Violet today, asking all of us what that awful teacher has against her. She wants to know why that woman Lucinda Ellis brought up her mama's name. I think y'd better tell them both—before someone else does it, Son."

Lotia nodded her head in agreement with Nanny and urged on, "Nanny is right, Seth. Vy has had enough time to get know all of us, come to love us—and Mindia should have been told a long time ago. T' tell y' th' truth, I've been awfully close t' tellin' the both of them myself."

Seth buried his face in his hands and shook his head in anguish.

"They will be so upset with me—maybe even hate me. I should have attended to all of this well before now—way back when they were younger—in the beginning. I guess I'll just add this to the list of mistakes I've made in my life."

Lotia spoke with more than a hint of impatience in her voice.

"Oh, Seth, stop it! You have got to stop thinking of y'self now and realize ye always did what y' thought God wanted y' t' do concerning th' both of them. The girls are both old enough to understand that, and it ain't right to keep the truth from them any longer. Y' got t' try and remember what strong young women they are, Seth."

"Lottie is right, Son," Nanny interrupted. "Y' know both of those girls know and love the Lord and are perfectly capable of understanding all of this. They will be able to comprehend and forgive all of us. I have to believe that."

"I pray you are right. Violet has been through so much with her mama, not to mention what I have put her through bringin' her here. Y' both know why I've put off tellin' her, but th' more I avoid it, the more I dread it."

"Vy deserves to know the truth, Seth—so does Mindia—and y' know that!"

"I know y' are both right—it's got to be done."

Nanny rose and started out the door. "Goodnight, you two. Ask God's guidance once more and get some sleep. Things'll look a lot less complicated in the morning."

"Goodnight, Nanny." Seth walked to the door and gave his mother a hug. "Night, Mama."

Next morning, Vy got up, prepared her horse, and was riding to town long before the Seatons awoke.

When she arrived at the mercantile, she walked in, glancing this way and that, hoping to see Theo already working at his desk.

"Hello there, Miss Vittoye. May I help ya this mornin'?"

"I'm lookin' for Theo, Mr. McVae. Is he working this morning?"

"He was workin' on Winfield Campbell's watch real early, Miss Violet, but Bertha came by, and he left to go somewhere with her. They didn't tell me where they were goin,' though."

"Oh, really? Hmmm. Very well. Thank you, Mr. McVae, I think I'll ride on over to his house. They may be there. And if he should come back here, will you tell him that I need to see him?"

Bertha's pa smiled his usual friendly smile and nodded affirmatively. "Sure thing, Miss Violet. G' day t' y,' now. Be sure and tell y' folks I said howdy."

Cordelia Taylor and her daughter Neppia were sitting on the front porch in their favorite rocking chairs, stringing green beans for the noon meal.

"Yon cloud there looks like heavy rain comin,' doesn't it, Nep?"

"Yeah, Ma, it's sprinklin' some. Pa better hurry up and come on in or he's gonna get soaked."

"Look yonder, Neppia, is that him comin' there?"

"Don't look like Pa to me, Ma. That's somebody else. Looks like a girl, don't it?"

"Yeah, I believe y' right, dear. T'is a girl. It's Violet, I think—Violet Vittoye."

"Wonder what she's doing over here without Theo this early in the day, Ma?" Neppia asked. "Isn't he working at the mercantile today?"

Ivy opened the screen door and interrupted as she let it slam shut. "Theo is supposed to be at the mercantile today, but I bet he ain't there," she said.

"What do you mean, Ivy?"

"I saw him talking or planning something with Bertha last Sunday right after church. She had that pouty face of hers on real good—was all snuggled up to Theo, askin' him questions. I heard him agree to somethin,' but I don't know what."

"Hmmm. I bet Vy wouldn't like that one bit."

"No, I know she wouldn't, but you know Theo, don't you?"

Violet rode up and pulled on the reins but continued sitting on her horse.

"Howdy there, Violet! What brings you all the way over to Ailor Springs?

And how are you and the Seatons doing?"

"Hey, Mrs. Taylor. Hi, Ivy, Neppi. Oh, the Seatons are all just fine and I am, too, but I was just wondering if Theo is here. I really would like to talk to him.

Ma Taylor shook her head. "No, darlin,' I'm sorry, he's not here. And I declare, I'm not sure where th' boy is, Vy. Did you try the mercantile?"

"Mmm, I sure did, Mrs. Taylor, and Mr. McVae said he had just left with Bertha. I thought he might have come on back here for something."

"Oh, goodness, Vy, I hate you had a long ride all the way over here for nothing—and it lookin t' pour th' rain. Won't you come in and sit awhile with us, dear—have a cold drink or some refreshment? Theo's bound t' be back here after while."

"Hmm. No, thanks. I'd love t' stay and talk, but I think I'll ride on back and see if he's returned to the mercantile. I'd really like to see him about something before I have to go on back home." Vy's mind began to spin, and she made a sudden decision to discuss this matter with Mrs. Taylor. "On second thought, Mrs. Taylor, I'd just like to ask you—to make sure, really—that you and Mr. Taylor approved the recent trip my girlfriends and I took to Whitesville with Theo, Will Graves, and Ross Seymour. You and Mr. Taylor did agree to it, didn't you?"

"Of course we did, dear. Why, I'm the very one who wrote my sister about your visit and received assurance from her of your proper supervision. I'm lookin' to hear from her any day now about all the fun y' young ones had. Why, dear … is anything wrong?"

Vy nodded affirmatively. "I'm afraid so, Mrs. Taylor. Our school teacher, Mrs. Lucinda Ellis, has another idea about our trip. She has gone so far as to charge that all of us were unchaperoned in Whitesville and that we carried on in a wicked way. She intends to report to the whole community some hideous falsehoods about our conduct."

Delia waved her hands in a show of disgust. "Oh, pooh! Violet, I sure hope you pay no attention to that old lady's yapping! Everybody in Maynard's Valley knows about Lucinda Ellis and her imagination. There's always someone ready to believe the worst about people and start a line of rumors brewing." Cordelia smiled, trying to give some assurance to Vy, for she could see the girl was really troubled. "Don't worry, dear, about any of our family a listenin' t' such gossip. I'd say that woman needs to keep her nose out of other folks' business, and that's exactly what we will tell 'er if she comes round here with her lies!"

Vy managed to force a weak smile. "Thanks for y' kind understandin,' Mrs. Taylor. That's exactly how the Seatons feel, though we have heard Mary Mynatt's mother is in agreement with Mrs. Lucinda and is going to punish Mary to the maximum."

Ivy stopped chewing on her apple and broke in. "That is awful, Vy! I'm so sorry to hear that. I think so much of sweet little Mary."

"So do I, Ivy. Mary is my dear friend. I need to go over her house and see how she is managing all this. It even appears that I won't get a chance to see Mary much at all now that Seth has removed Mindia and me from school."

"Well, don't you worry your pretty head one minute about anything that Lucinda reports to any of us, m'dear. We know you, Violet, and that is enough for the Taylors."

Vy was touched by this kind and understanding woman. How blessed Theo is to have this woman for his mother.

"Oh, thank you so much, Mrs. Taylor. Y' don't know how relieved I am to hear it. That's what I wanted to talk to Theo about. I didn't want y'all to hear a bunch of lies about our trip. Would you just tell him that I came by here and what I wanted to talk to him about in case I don't catch up with him today?"

"Of course we will, darlin.'"

Neppia broke in and took on a pleading tone. "Sure wish you could come inside for a while and chat, Vy. I'd like you to teach me how to make that pretty lace you do."

"And we need to get all of us together and have a girl party—an overnight one," Ivy added. "Wouldn't that be fun, Vy? You know, invite Mindia and Mary and Sadie. I want to tell you all about my new beau. He's—"

"Oh, pooh. He's not your beau, Ivy," Cordelia said with a look of displeasure.

"Oh, yes he is, Ma!" Ivy retorted.

Violet turned the horse around, not desiring any part of a mother/daughter disagreement.

"Sounds great, Ivy. I know everyone would love a girl party!" Vy tried to offer a laugh, but it sounded shallow, insincere. "Maybe next time I won't be in such a hurry and we can visit more—and we'll plan our girlie gala. Right now I think I'd better head on—it does look like rain f' sure. And thanks again for everything, ladies. Sure was good to see y'all again. See you, Neppi. I will show you how to do that lace soon. I promise."

"Okay, Vy. Bye now!"

"Good day t' y,' Violet!"

Vy snapped the reins and disappeared out of sight as her horse galloped down the dusty road.

"Why didn't you tell her where you think he is?" Ivy questioned Neppia.

"I wouldn't hurt her for the world. She is such a lovely girl."

"Theo should settle down and latch onto that one as quickly as he can."

"Wouldn't you love to have Vy in our family someday, Ma? She's so sweet."

"Yeah, I really think the world of her—a fine Christian girl—and so talented. Exactly what my boy needs!"

"We'll all just have to pray for that, Ma."

The clouds were gathering thicker, and thunder rumbled in the distance. *Where is he?*

It's going to pour the rain on me, but before I go home I have to find out. I think this is the road leading to the McVae's farm. I wonder... he wouldn't... would he?

Vy turned down the road, topped a hill, and rode at least a mile before the McVae farmhouse came into sight. Sure enough, there was a carriage sitting in front of the picket fence at the gate. Vy's spirits fell as fear gripped her heart. A carriage—someone is there! Oh, good heavens, it is Theo's!

Vy pulled on the reins and guided the horse off the path behind the thick trees across from Bertha's house. She was having a hard time believing what her eyes beheld and on top of it all, feeling very guilty, much like a spy.

There was a sharp bolt of lightning and huge crash of thunder as the rain commenced to pour. Vy reached for the woolen mackinaw kept inside her saddle bag and threw it over her head. Her eyes were so focused on the McVae's porch that she hardly felt the pounding raindrops. I should not be here, she thought. But I can't leave until I know.

The cloud burst let up after a few moments, and two figures appeared in the doorway. As Vy suspected, it was Theo, followed by Bertha, and the two of them were deep in conversation. From Violet's angle the girl appeared to be wiping her eyes. Is she crying?

Theo embraced the girl, patted her on the cheek, then kissed her goodbye.

Vy was not prepared for that. A flash of hot anger shot through her body like the lightning bolt she had just witnessed.

Whaat? That devilish two-timer! I won't put up with that—no, I won't!

Bertha waved her handkerchief goodbye to Theo then turned and went back inside her house, shutting the door behind her.

Theo hurriedly made his way down the path through the picket gate, shielding his eyes with his hands against the rain, which had finally slackened into a fine mist.

Vy bolted out of the woods into the clearing, almost knocking Theo over as he started to mount his carriage. He was startled.

"Hey! Wha-what the devil? What you doing here, pretty one?"

"Hmph! I could ask you the same thing."

"I'm here to see my friend Bertha, Violet."

"Do you kiss all your friends goodbye?"

"Just what are you accusing me of?"

"Just what are you guilty of, Theo?"

"You don't deserve an answer to that—and I will tell you something else. Nobody spies on me, Violet—and nobody tells me who I can have for a friend."

"Well, Theo, I will tell you something. Nobody cheats on me! Do you hear that?"

"I didn't know we were betrothed, Violet."

"And, Theo dear, we will never be! Y' can count on it!"

Vy jerked her horse's reins so hard he whinnied. She took off like a streak of lightning, splattering mud from the horse's hooves all over Theo's trousers. The downpour had now subsided, but it had soaked the mackinaw Vy was using for shelter. She balled the wet blanket up and crammed it back inside the saddle bag. Her cheeks were wet from both rain and tears. Her eyes were clouded, and her mind was boggled. She could not reconcile what had just happened. *Was Theo wrong— or was she wrong?* She knew the kiss between Theo and Bertha could have been only a friendly kiss, but why did he have to kiss Bertha at all? *Did all his words of love for me mean nothing? He said we are not betrothed! Oh Father, Jesus, please let him care for me. Don't let my* angry words and actions separate us forever. Don't let jealousy ruin my life. I love him so, Lord.

Vy needed to talk to someone. She needed her best friend Mary.

If only I could talk to Mary, Lord, she might help me figure this out.

Vy tossed the idea around in her head, pondering whether to go or not, realizing for sure that she would not be welcome at the Mynatt's house.

In spite of knowing how much Mary's mother despised her, Vy ultimately headed on over to see Mary. She made a decision to stay on her horse when she arrived and would call Mary outside to talk for a few minutes. Surely Mrs. Mynatt could not be so cruel as to prevent two dear friends from seeing each other for such a little while.

Lost and Found

The rain had completely stopped, but the clouds hung low on that dark day. Through a window Vy could see a lantern burning in the back of the Mynatt's home. Guardedly, she rode up to the front porch, just sitting on her horse for some time, trying to work up nerve to dismount and knock on the door. She could detect no light or movement in the front of the house, though the loud and angry voices coming from the open windows were clear and distinct. This was the second experience in a few hours where Vy had felt like a cheap spy, causing her to consider turning around and just getting out of there. However, as she started to pull on the horse's reins, the words she heard made her stop and freeze in place.

A female voice Vy recognized as Mary's mother screamed out, "How dare you humiliate me like this, you stupid and unappreciative girl! Pregnant! This is the last straw! William Graves is a know-nothing loser! Leave this house, Mary! Go on, get out of my sight. I don't even want to look at your face—and you don't bother wagging your fat and swollen body home when you have nothing to eat! Do you hear me?"

Vy could tell Mary was crying when she heard her friend's devastated and broken voice crack as she countered, "Y-you can call me names if you want, Mother, but don't you dare call the man I love degrading names! Will Graves is my husband now, whether you like it or not. He is a wonderful man, and I love him with all my heart. I had anticipated you were a better person than this, Mother—had hoped you would at least try to understand when I told you that we were married. I can't imagine you being so cold and uncaring that you would turn y' back on me—your only daughter—as well as my baby—your own grandchild that I carry."

"Your filthy deeds and rebellion is what has dissolved our relationship, Mary—not me," Jessie Mae screamed at the top of her voice. "You are the one that has chosen to have a child by trash like Will Graves—disgracing your family—and it is you who have been running around town with that bastard Violet Vittoye! Why, y' are no better than her or her devil worshipping mama, Sally. Are you aware that Lucinda Ellis is divorcing her husband, Calvin, because he has been sleeping with your friend's mama—that whore? Do you know that she is mixed up in a cult—some sort of Satan worship? Did you know that, Mary? Your illegitimate friend, Violet, and her mama are evil, Mary."

"Violet and her mama were not too evil to make the dresses we wear, were they, Mother?"

The words came at Vy like a sharp dagger piercing her heart and soul. The abusive language being flung at her dear friend Mary was hard enough to bear, but she certainly had not expected to hear her own name brought into this terrible brawl between a mother and her daughter. Fear and anger caused a rush of adrenaline to push her heartbeat so fast that she began heaving as though she were going to throw up. She sat there for a moment just holding her stomach—wanting to wake up—or die. As the realization of Mrs. Mynatt's accusations soaked in, she became extremely weak. She could not possibly face Mary now. She could stand to hear no more. Vy's hands flew to cover her ears, nearly causing her to lose balance and fall off the horse. The words were still circling round and round in her brain. That bastard, Violet Vittoye—did I hear her right? She called me a bastard. Was that what she said? "That bastard, Violet Vittoye?" She called Mama a whore—my mama? Oh dear God—if it's true—that I am illegitimate and my mama is a whore, and a devil worshipper—it is no wonder people hate me.

Pangs of fear clutched at Vy's stomach as longed-for answers started summing up in her brain. Oh dear God, help me. This can't be the answers I have prayed for, can it? What have you done to me, Mama?

It is no wonder you ain't told me who my daddy is—you probably don't even know!

Cordelia Taylor shook her head.

"I'm sorry, Mr. Seaton. I don't know where Vy is. She was here and she seemed to be real upset about the recent turn of events. You know, all that nonsense with Lucinda Ellis. The girl said she was looking for Theo, that's for sure—to talk to him about it. I tried my best to calm her down—and it worried me, too, because right after she left the house th' rain started to pour. Seems like I recollect she said something about goin' over t' a friend's house, but I don't remember exactly. I'll tell y,' sir, if she rode around much today she's wet and cold f'r sure. Wish I could be o' more help to ya."

"Thank y,' Mrs. Taylor. If Theo comes on back over here with her— or if she turns up again by herself, ma'am—would you put up her horse fer me and have Theo return Violet to us in his carriage? I'd be more than appreciative if y' could do that fer me, Mrs. Taylor. I'm right concerned about her now, and I'm gonna be out a lookin everywhere till I find her."

Seth turned his buggy around and headed back across the county. He had no idea where in the world to start looking.

The horse was galloping—heading somewhere, but Vy hardly realized she was riding. The animal seemed to have a mind of its own, just following the road. Where was it going? How long she had been riding? She only knew she needed to talk to somebody.

Then suddenly she knew. There it was in the distance—home.

My cabin. Mama…

The sun had finally broken through the dark clouds but was hanging low in the western sky. It looked dark inside the cabin as she approached.

Vy dismounted the horse and tried the front door. She was not surprised that it was bolted shut. She ambled on around back, pushing hard on the window she had used to climb through once before, but it would not budge. Pushing once more as hard as she could, the window gave way with a sudden jerk, jabbing a sharp piece of wood into the side of her hand.

"Ow! That hurt!" Blood spurted and ran down her arm from the deep cut, but she climbed on in the window and stumbled around, looking this way and that for some matches. Vy lit a match then shook her head in disbelief at the filthy, disheveled cabin.

How did I ever call this place my home? How long has it been since I cooked and played and laughed and lived here so happily together with Mama and Gran? What has happened to Mama since I left? Has she always been the county prostitute? I know what she was doing at night time with the stranger now. She made me a bastard.

What in the world do I do when the Seatons find out? They will hate me—get rid of me. What a fool I was to think I had a home with them. They say they love me. They won't love me now. Did you hear that, Jesus? Do you save bastards, too? Can I still go to heaven with you? I hope so—because I feel like I'm in hell now.

Vy sank down on her old bed. I have no place to go. I can't go to the Seatons—can't let them find all this out. I will tell them I have decided to come back here and live with Mama, the whore.

Blood was dripping all over. The cut on Vy's hand was deep, and until now she had paid it little attention, but it was getting sloppy. She needed to take care of it. She found an old bottle, stiffened her arm, and winced as she poured some liniment over the cut. Maudie's salve or ointment should be in this cabinet. There was nothing.

Vy found a rag beside the dry sink and wound it around the cut, but blood saturated it quickly, soaking right through. Suddenly Vy had a wonderful thought. Of course! Maudie! She will fix my hand. Vy could literally hear Gran saying, "Maudie can fix anything—let's go and get Maudie!"

She knew she had to rush, for the sun was setting. Vy mounted the horse once more, sprinting down the hill toward the valley and up and over the winding mountain road to the Ellises' house, unconsciously prodding the horse into a faster and faster gallop. Her mind was darting this way and that—trying to digest the day's events—to cope with the awful facts now confronting her.

I need to talk to Mama—ask her—make her give me some answers. Maudie, she always loved me, but will she hate me now? How can I tell her that her son and daughter-in-law are getting a divorce because of my mama? No wonder Mrs. Lucinda hated me. Maybe Maudie already knows—has some answers—but what if she doesn't? I will tell her everything—everything I heard. She will understand. That's the kind of person Maudie is. I remember that wonderful Christmas at her house. How we all prayed together. The snowstorm. Mama saving us. I was only twelve then. Made all those gowns for Sadie's wedding. Seems like it was only yesterday—that wedding. The wedding was where I first met Theo. Theo, oh, Theo, what is to become of us? Have I lost you forever?

What a wonderful Christmas we had at Maudie's house that year—except for Mama leaving me early. Left me there alone on my thirteenth birthday. Calvin Ellis left, too! I remember now—how it made Mrs. Lucinda upset and Maudie tried to stop him from leaving. Mama and Calvin, they both left at the same time. Even then? The stranger! Oh, dear mercy me! Calvin Ellis is the stranger! No wonder he always came to pick Mama up after dark. No wonder he didn't want me or' Gran to know who he was. One of the Ellis boys! That dirty slime! He carried my Gran's casket right up that hill. Oh, dear God, please give me strength to bear all of this. My own mama—and Calvin Ellis! Maudie probably already knows. I won't have to tell her anything. I bet she can tell me.

She approached the farm and was glad to see lanterns ablaze in the Ellis cabin as if someone was expecting her, but when Vy came closer, the fear crept in ever so stealthily, causing her to have second thoughts about telling anything to anybody. Feeling terribly weary and upset, she had no idea what she was going to say, so she stopped a piece short of the house and pondered turning back. Maybe telling Maudie wasn't such a good idea after all.

"Oh, Lord, I don't know what t' do," she prayed aloud. "Please help me. I need you. I need faith, direction. Your Word says:

> Trust in the Lord with all thine heart; and lean not unto thine
> own understanding. In all thy ways acknowledge him, and he shall
> direct thy paths.

"I do acknowledge you, Lord, and I sure can't lean on my own understanding. Help me to lean on yours, Lord. Show me what to do."

A lantern flashed as the door opened and Maudie peered out into the dusk. "Who's there? Is that you, Sadie?"

The last time Vy had seen Maudie, her hair was jet black, and now there were more than a few streaks of gray. Deep wrinkles lined her face as well, but it was still the kind and gentle face that Vy remembered.

"No, Maudie. It's not Sadie. It's, uh, Vy—Violet Vittoye. How you doin,' Maudie?"

"Violet! Mercy me, darlin! I'm fine, Vy. Is anything wrong? What in the world brings you all the way cross th' county from the Seatons' house this late in th' day, child?"

Vy dismounted and walked toward Maudie, who rushed outside, throwing her arms around the girl for a hug. She let go of Vy then drew back, studying the girl's face, which was clearly tearstained and troubled. "Git on in here 'n sit y'self down now, Vy."

Maudie adjusted her glasses a bit, trying to assess what problem lay before her.

"Well, I'll say one thing—you have grown into a beautiful woman, Vy. That much I can tell, but you're going to have to tell Maudie what's wrong now."

Giving Vy a moment to gather herself, Maudie went into the next room to put on a kettle for tea. When Maudie returned with a tray of steaming tea and some hot soup and biscuits, she realized Vy was trembling.

"Lord knows it looks like y'er wet plumb t' th' skin, child."

As Maudie removed Vy's topcoat, her arm came out of the sleeve, revealing an ugly wound half covered by a blood-soaked rag.

"My gracious child, what's this? What in th' world happened t' your hand?"

"Oh, it's nothing. Just got cut as I was tryin' to get in the window at Mama's cabin."

"You let me see that, honey. That needs a tendin' to right now!" Maudie pulled out a suitcase full of doctoring elixirs and utensils, and after first washing the wound with a sterile cleansing agent, she squeezed on some sticky yellow ointment. She then unrolled a wide swath of sterile cotton cloth, tore it to the right length, and wrapped Vy's hand professionally. The painful hand started feeling better immediately, and in the care and nursing of this wise and adept woman, Vy began to calm and relax.

Maudie brought out some dry under things and a chenille robe that Sadie had left there awhile back on a visit, as well as a blanket for Vy to wrap up in. She helped the girl out of her damp things and strung them up to dry, then settled her by the fireplace, urging her to sip the hot tea. Maudie then went in the next room to check on Clyve, who was in bed ailing.

When Maudie appeared back in the room, Vy questioned her.

"Is something wrong with Mr. Ellis, Maudie?"

"Well, he isn't feeling very well tonight, Vy. Tell y' th' truth, Clyve don't have many good days anymore. Don't seem like my doctorin' does much good to my own.

"As fer you, girl, eat some of this here soup before it gets cold, and then you fill old Maudie in on what y' are a doin' here, m'darlin.'"

Vy took a sip of tea and dropped her eyes. "Oh, Maudie, I probably shouldn't even be here, be a puttin'—unloadin' my troubles on you. I didn't—don't have anybody that I can talk to about the awful things I heard today. I just thought that you might know if they are true or not."

"You just go right on and tell me what happened, Vy, and I'll be glad t' help y' if there's any way I can, child. There ain't much in this world I ain't already dealt with in some way 'nother."

"Well, it happened today when I came by my friend Mary Mynatt's house. I only wanted to talk to her about Theo. That's all I wanted."

"Theodore Taylor, dear?"

"Yes, he's my ... he was my ... well, we have been courting, but when I went to see him today, this morning, he was with another girl. He was over at her house, Maudie. I saw him kiss her. I was so upset, and I didn't know what to do. I just thought if I could talk to Mary—you know, Mary Mynatt, my good friend ... "

Maudie was listening intently, her curiosity peaking as to what could have caused this girl to be in the terrible disposition she was in. She had a suspicion of her own but hoped she was wrong.

"I rode over to Mary's house, Maudie, and then I heard the most hideous things."

Maudie took on a worried look. "Is something wrong with Mary or Jessie May?"

"Well, yes, you could say that for sure. They're not sick nor nothin,' but the two of them were having a terrible fight when I rode up and stopped there at their porch. I was so stunned I couldn't get off my horse. They were screaming at each other so loud—and it was all right there in the open window for me to hear. I was getting ready to turn around and get out of there, but when I heard my own name mentioned, Maudie, I stopped short and listened. I know I shouldn't have been eavesdropping, but I couldn't help but hear what they said. That's when Mary told her mother that she was already married to Will Graves."

"Oh, my."

"It surprised me, too, Maudie, but then ..." Vy took the back of her hand and swiped angrily as the tears started to roll down her face again. Maudie rose and handed her a folded handkerchief she retrieved from a bureau drawer.

"Go on, darlin.'"

"Well, Mrs. Mynatt started telling Mary some very repulsive things. She made some dreadful accusations—said awful things, Maudie—and they were about me and Mama."

Maudie's heart started to race, for she knew what was coming.

Vy continued. "Mrs. Mynatt said Mama was a devil worshipper or something like that and that she was having, uh, an affair with ... with ... "

Maudie knew she needed to make it easier for this upset child and finished the sentence for her.

"With Calvin Ellis," she said.

"So it is Calvin! Oh, I'm so sorry, Maudie. You already know about all this. I shouldn't be speakin' of it—upsettin' you."

Maudie's face fell as tears sprang up in her eyes. The woman moved closer to Vy and patted her arm tenderly.

"Oh, Violet, I am so sorry, honey. I always hoped you would never have to find out. What an awful way for y' to find out."

"You ... you know about Mama and Calvin?"

"Of course I have known, dear—and, oh, how I've prayed for it to end. I have talked and begged and prayed that Calvin would leave your mama alone—or for her to get over her fascination with him. I have always hoped that it would end before you had to find out about their shameful relationship—that you could just have a wonderful life with the Seatons and not be hurt by your troubled mama and my troubled son."

Maudie bent over to hug Vy then got up and strolled slowly across the room to the window, gazing out at the night sky. High winds were breaking up the clouds. The moon and stars were now shining brightly. She could tell just by looking outside that it had turned colder.

Breathing a deep and heavy sigh, she rubbed her head as though a painful headache was starting.

"It isn't going to be easy, Vy, but you are old enough to hear this—and I guess you were bound to find out someday, though I wish you could have been spared knowin' of the abomination your mama and my family have been involved in . . . "

"Involved in? What are you talkin' about, Maudie? Y' are one of the best women me and my mama have ever known. Y' family has always been wonderful—always helped us. When Gran died, and when Mama was so sick after Baby got stolen . . . " Giant tears burst to the front of Vy's eyes and rolled down her cheeks. "How could my mama being—uh—what she is have anything to do with you? It ain't nobody's fault but my mama's that I'm . . . I'm illegitimate."

Maudie moved close and put her arms around Vy. "Let me tell you, first of all, that there is never a precious baby born who is 'illegitimate.' There are only evil and irresponsible ma's and pa's. Don't y' ever go referring to y'self in that degrading way, Vy. You are a precious child that God created and He loves. You are a Christian now, Vy. Ain't that true?"

"I am."

"Well then, don't ever forget that y'are God's pleasure and His treasure."

"If you listen very carefully to the things I'm about to tell you, it might help you understand some of the things that have upset y' so much today—might help you understand some of what you are going through right now, and what you have to face with your mama. Now I'm only goin' t' tell you these things in the hope that you will get on with your life—forget the madness—the sadness of today and go back to being y' joyful self serving the Lord. The whole thing started many years ago—a way back before I was even born. My own mama and daddy hadn't even been in this here country very long, and they belonged—or was part of—a group of people right out of the old country who refused to give up a pagan Celtic worship. There's not a lot of members in that old Druid cult no more, but my son Calvin got mixed up in it a long time ago, and he's the one who got y' mama involved in it as well."

"What y' mean, a cult, Maudie? What is it? I ain't never heard of one—and what's it got to do with my mama?"

"Well, honey, a cult is a pagan religion—a group of people who do strange and sometimes very evil things undercover, in secret, Vy. In Maynard's Valley, the cult I speak of celebrates their rituals deep in the woods. Their members are forbidden to speak freely of their beliefs and practices. The leader, most of the time, gains a mind control over the whole group and forces them away from family and friends.

"That old cult group of Calvin's actually worships one or any number of false gods, such as the green earth, as they call it. They worship the ancient gods of pleasure such as Dionysus or Bacchus, as well as the mating forces of mother earth, Vy, and their entire purpose is so the members will deny the truth of God's Holy Word. Since God's Word calls all mankind to accountability, a cult will always reject God's Word as well as His Son, Jesus.

"The Bible teaches what is right and what is wrong, but cult members refuse to believe there's any such thing as wrong. They simply choose to be their own god. The members carry on their celebrations by taking drugs and alcohol. They practice fornication, incest, and all kinds of immorality, and it has been said they drink blood and other disgusting body fluids. Mind-altering plant use is common at their midnight rituals. At times, they sacrifice animals, and it's even been said that they have sacrificed human beings to their false gods. Can y' imagine they still hold that all the things they do are for good?

"Now, if you were to go and ask your mama or Calvin about any of this, you can be sure they'll be a denyin' every bit of what I'm a tellin' ya. That's why their evil is done under the cover of night and deep into the woods where no one bears witness to their shame." Maudie took a deep breath and shook her head. "Those awful orgies are what holds Calvin to that old cult—and the dope is what holds your mama, Vy,—the dope as well as some terrible grasp my son has on her.

"My very own pa was raised by his folks to be part of that horrible abomination. 'The ways of the old country,' is how he always excused it. What's more, I hate to tell it, but at one time he actually was one of the cult's high priests. It was my mama's love for him that caused her to become part of that pitiful abhorrence.

"When I was a youngster, I was witness to that fiendish cult because they actually took me to their meetin's. That's how I know these things are true. It's also where I learned a great deal about the plants and doctorin' remedies I now use t' help others.

"A great change came when I was about nine or ten years old and beginnin' to develop into a young woman. Can you believe that my own pa, as one of their priests, told my ma that I might be the next sacrifice at their All Hallow's Eve fest?"

Maudie hesitated and swallowed hard, for the story was hard to tell. "God forbid it, Vy—the ceremony I'm talking about is an abomination where all the men have their way with a girl-child before she is tied down and sacrificed on their altar. Can you imagine a father wantin' anything like that to happen to his own little girl? Well, Ma had always gone along with the horrid things he had asked her to do before that, but she wasn't about to let him do anything to me. She don't like to talk about it none now, honey, but my ma will tell you that God gave her the strength to wait till that old man, my pa, was asleep one night and then make her escape with me. I remember it like it was yesterday, Vy. Me and Ma fled to the little mountain church right here in the valley where they gave us protection and a place to live until we could get on our own. Old pastor James and his good wife led me and my mama to Jesus that very night. We never lived with Pa after that."

Maudie raised her hands and looked up to heaven. Her voice broke as she cried out, "Oh, how I praise Jesus and thank Him for my mama and the people of that little mountain church!" Wiping her eyes and clearing her throat, she tried to continue.

"Eventually, after Pa got old, he tried to get out of that old cult, but someone killed him for it, Vy. And people around here knew exactly what happened t' him. There was some sure as heaven knew who did it, but nobody spoke up. They were too afraid."

"Y' would think that old pagan religion—the epitome of Satan worship—would have died out by now, but somehow a part of it has survived through the years. There are folks around here that would laugh at y' if you'd mention anything about all this. They would tell you no such thing ever existed here in Maynard's Valley, but believe you me it has, and does.

"I know it does, for my son is still a part of it—God help him. Years ago, when I was in the woods searching for some special specimens of plants I needed, I stumbled across one of the cult's meeting places. There were stones piled up for an altar and some symbols and signs scratched out there in the dirt. I recognized them because I'd seen them as a young girl. It was soon after that we found evidence that Calvin was involved."

"Oh, Maudie, I can't believe this. It's so awful—your own son—m-my own mama ... and me wanting to tell her about Jesus ... "

"There is nothing wrong with that, Violet. You just go on ahead and tell her, but she ain't gonna listen t' nothin' about Jesus if she's on drugs."

"No wonder she's always stayed out all night, Maudie. No wonder she was so sad and cried all the time. I found some kind of stuff by her bed—stuff I guess she had been drinking. I thought it was some kind of medicine. Our cabin is not fit to live in. It is filthy, Maudie. Mary's mother was right. My mama ain't nothin' but a—"

"Don't, Vy! Y' mama is a troubled and sin-sick woman who needs the Lord. We both love her and have to pray for her."

Vy looked at Maudie's face hesitantly. "I need you to ask you something else, Maudie."

"What is it, darlin'?"

"Is Calvin, m-my daddy, Maudie?"

The aging woman shook her gray head and smiled as a look of sadness came across Maudie's face. "No, darlin,' he's not."

At that point she moved closer to Vy, hugged her closely, looked straight into her eyes, and declared, "You sweet girl, I surely wish you were my very own granddaughter, but I know Calvin is not your father because he spent the year before you were born with his uncle in Whitesville. He was not around when your mother became pregnant with you. We knew something was wrong with him, Vy—with Cal. Me n' Clyve found out he had been smoking some kind of dope. He had been acting real crazy, so we thought a year in the city with my brother would help him—get him away from that bad influence. Well, it didn't help a' tall. He came right back and started it all up again. The drugs and that devil's cult had gotten hold of our boy's mind before we knew it. Lord help us all, I've heard that Calvin is th' high priest in that cult right now. If he is, then that explains why he's got mind control over Sally—and why she can't stay away from him.

"I pray and pray about it, Vy. All th' time, I do. Our son has broke mine and Clyve's hearts. To tell y' th' truth, I think that's why Clyve is so sick. He's just brokenhearted, that's all."

"Why don't somebody stop it, Maudie?"

"Over the years different things that the cult has done have been reported to the law, but nothin' ain't ever been done. Most people just deny it exists, and the ones that know it does are afraid to come up again' the evil of it.

"You know Alan Graves, don't y'? Will's grand daddy? Well, he accidentally ran upon the group during one of their rituals and reported right then and there what all was going on. His report finally got brought before a judge, but all those called to give evidence denied the charges and testified fr each other. Swore an oath they were having an innocent birthday celebration—that some got out of hand and drank a little too much whisky. There was not a single arrest made.

"Violet, darlin,' I'm a telling y' all this so y'll return home to the Seatons and leave that old cabin and your mama's troubles behind y.' Prayers are the only thing you and I can give her. A change has to come from her heart, not yours. Y' are not accountable for her actions no more than I am for my pitiful son's, and it's a situation a Christian has to give over to the Lord. There are some things that are simply out of our hands."

Suddenly both Maudie and Vy were overtired and weary. They sat side by side for a good while there in the firelight, staring into the glowing embers as if all had been said—as if all had been done.

The long day's events had sapped every ounce of strength from Vy, and the recalling of so many unpleasant facts had pretty much taken its toll on Maudie as well.

Maudie rose and held out her hand.

"Won't you come on up the stairs and lie down in Sadie's old bed? We can talk some more about this in the morning, dear. I'll not have you a startin' out anywhere this time o night, you hear?"

"Uh, no thanks. I don't want to go to bed. I couldn't sleep. Do you mind if I just stay here in this chair by the fire, Maudie? I am warm now, and thank you so much for telling me—helping me understand. You…you please just go on in there with Mr. Clyve and take care of him. I am fine, and I have taken too much of your time—have upset you by dragging all this up, making you remember. I can see how it hurts you to talk about it, Maudie."

"Now don't you worry none about that, darlin.' I'm okay. I'm just sorry you had to hear all this. You just try to get a little rest now. We will figure it all out in the morning. You may ask more questions if you want. Then I will drive you back home to the Seatons. Y' just try to rest. Promise me?"

"I will. Thank you again, Maudie. Thank you."

Maudie kissed Vy lightly on the cheek and turned to go. She purposely left a candle burning low for the little girl who sat quietly now in the firelight. She had an ache deep within her heart for this dear one. Maudie knew Vy was suffering, but there was no more to be done this night. She shook her head, sighed, and then disappeared into the room where Clyve lay sleeping.

Vy was trying to shut it all out—to turn her mind completely off. The events of the day were simply too much to comprehend, and she was exhausted.

Stretching her legs out on the soft ottoman, she adjusted her head in Maudie's feather pillows and tried to relax, but her hand was aching again, and her temples throbbed in pain. There was something that felt like a chain around her, causing a terrible pressure on her chest, and her stomach was churning. Vy pulled the soft quilts up under her chin and stared into the flickering flames of the fire as fearful and sinful thoughts once more began to torment her tired and weary soul.

It's easy for Maudie to say, "Just go on back to Seaton's and have a wonderful life. Just tell them the truth." Yeah, sure I will. "Well, hello there, everyone. Seth, Lotia, Nanny, Mindia, and everyone else in Maynard's Valley. Do you know what I found out today? Just a little snippet about me, Violet Vittoye. Well, my mama…well, she's in a devil worshipping cult, and that's not all. I am illegitimate. Do you hear that, everyone? I am a bastard. My mama has made me one. She is the valley whore." You know what? I once said I hated my mama—and now I hate her again!

Oh, dear God, help me! The devil has me in his clutches—exactly where he wants a Christian! What's that Scripture again?

> Thou art my hiding place; Thou shalt preserve me from trouble; thou shalt compass me about with songs of deliverance.
>
> Psalm 32:7–8

> Many sorrows shall be to the wicked: but he that trusteth in the Lord mercy shall compass him about.
>
> Psalm 32:10

Vy threw off the quilts, rose from chair, and fell to the floor on her face, calling out to God through tears.

"Oh, Jesus, my Heavenly Father. I cannot bear this alone. I need you now. You promised you would not allow more to bear on me than I could stand. I can't stand hating my mama, no matter what she has done or what she is. Forgive me and help me, oh Lord."

> Rejoice in the Lord always: and again I say Rejoice! Let your moderation be known unto all men. The Lord is at hand. Be careful for nothing; but in everything by prayer and supplication, with thanksgiving let your requests be made known unto God. And the peace of God, which passeth all understanding, shall keep your hearts and minds—through Christ Jesus.
>
> Philippians 4:4–7

Words from the Bible, God's holy words that were hidden in the heart of a young girl suddenly appeared like a miracle speaking to Violet's troubled soul. The Holy Spirit reached down with love, covering His child with peace like a soft warm blanket—beautiful peace, the kind that passes all understanding...

Vy didn't know how long she had been there on the floor—praying, then falling into a weary sleep. She thought it was the wind at first—that soft knock on the door. Vy raised her head. There it was again—a knock, soft but distinct. Someone is there.

Raising herself up, Vy found her way across the dimly lit room to the door. The old grandfather clock in the corner chimed, its hands pointing to three thirty a.m.

Who in the world could be coming here at this hour? Must be a neighbor in trouble or something—someone probably needing Maudie's help.

Vy picked up the table lamp, struck a match, and lit it, carried it over, and opened the door. It was terribly dark outside, so she held the light up higher. As her eyes adjusted, soft lamplight fell on a man's tall figure. Vy rubbed her blurry eyes and positioned the lamp to shine directly on the man. 's face. It was then she recognized his kind and familiar face.

"Seth!"

"Thank God! Thank God I found y,' Vy! Are you okay? I been looking fer you all day and night, girl. Y' bout had us worried t' death, honey. What y'a doin' way over here, near 'bout cross th' world at th' Ellises'?"

Seth Seaton fairly picked up the young girl, her blankets and all, as he hugged her tightly and kissed her head. Relief was written all over his face.

It suddenly dawned on Vy how much worry and heartache she had caused the Seatons by riding off and not coming home. Vy felt a wave of remorse for worrying everyone she cared about, but was so exhausted she could not gather energy enough to make her apology sound sincere. All she could muster was, "I'm so sorry fr' worryin' you all, Seth. Will y' please forgive me. There's been so much happened to me today. Time just got away, and I forgot about letting you all know where I was—what I was a doin.' I am so sorry..."

She then motioned Seth inside to a chair by the fire and offered to take his coat.

He refused.

"No, I'll not shed m' coat, Vy. I've come t' get you. Get y' things, and let's go on. We need to get on home and let Lottie know you're okay. You cn' write Mrs. Ellis a note and tell her why you left, honey—that you went on home with me. She's a nice lady. Maudie'll understand.

"Lord knows we've been s' worried about y.' What in th' world hap-pened to y' t' make y' run off like this today? Was it all that garbage Lucinda Ellis got started? Is it that that's got y' so upset y' run plumb away from home? I thought we got all that settled. Why, there's nothin' t' all that. Lucinda's just a trouble maker. Nobody's a goin' t' believe anything bad 'bout you girls."

Vy shook her head and looked at Seth. Such a wonderful man who's done so much for me. Traveled all the way over here in the middle of th' night just t find me. He's gonna think I'm awful when I tell him where I come from—who I am. I should have let them know where I was.

I have been ungrateful and uncaring, but I have to tell him.

"It ain't just what Ms Lucinda said, Seth, that's a botherin' me so bad, though I guess that is what started it all. It's a long story—what I'm a doin' here—but you all need to know the truth of it. It may just change your attitude about me livin' with you and your family.

"Today I got the shock of m' life about my mama ... and about myself. Mama's a carryin' on an affair with Maudie's oldest boy, Calvin—Calvin Ellis. And Mrs. Lucinda knows about it. She's gonna get a divorce from him over my mama. I guess that's why she hates me—why she accused Min and me and my friends of those horrible things ..."

Vy sank down on the chair and put her head in her hands. She breathed a weary sigh, tried to straighten herself up, and continued. "I went over to Mary's this morning, Seth, to talk to her about Theo ... " She paused, her eyes clouding over again. "Theo—that's another story too, Seth. I saw him with another girl, uh, Bertha McVae. It upset me so badly. I should have come on back home right then—to your house—but I wanted to talk to Mary—to tell her and to see how she was.

"Well, I rode on over to the Mynatt's house, and when I got there Mary was having an awful fight with her mother. "Mary's gone and got married to Will Graves, Seth. She had just informed her mother of it when I rode up. Mrs. Mynatt was furious; fit t' be tied. I was startin' t' leave and get out of there, but then I heard them yell out my name."

The tears started pooling in Vy's red and worn out eyes once more. She rubbed them away with the now soggy handkerchief Maudie had given her and tried to go on. "Mrs. Mynatt said Mary had ruined herself by running with trash like me. She called me and Mama some awful things, some terrible names. She said my mama is in a cult—that she is a devil worshipper, or something like that. Maudie tried to tell me somethin' about it. She knows all about it, Seth. It is true, and it is horrible. They do terrible things, this group of people. My own mama. Can you believe that? And there's something else that I must tell you, Seth.

"I'm...well...Mama wasn't married when she gave birth to me." The tears were rolling down Vy's cheeks freely now. "I-I'm illegitimate, Seth, and that is a mild word compared to what Mary's mama called me. Truth is, I don't have no pa. I can't live with you good people—you Seatons—and disgrace you now. No, I won't."

Seth took a fresh white handkerchief out of his coat pocket, walked over, and wiped Vy's tears with tenderness. He put the white cotton square that Lottie had embroidered with the initials SS in Vy's hand. He had never witnessed a more heartbreaking sight than this little girl. So desperate. Feeling totally lost and alone. How he had dreaded this moment.

He looked into Vy's tortured eyes, and his heart felt heavier than it ever had in his life—heavy as though it would break in two. How he wished he could take her in his arms and erase it all—take this innocent girl's pain away—the pain he was responsible for.

Seth brushed back the damp curly auburn hair falling down into her face, kissed her forehead, and prayed a silent prayer before he found her searching eyes.

Oh, God, forgive me for the hurt I have brought on this child. I promise y, Lord, I will make it up to her and to you ... if it takes the rest of my life, Lord—I will ...

Seth's voice broke as he began to speak. "Vy, you could never be a disgrace to anyone. You are a wonderful child who's loved and cherished by all of yore family. Y' don't know it, but y' ain't a tellin' me a thing bout your mama I don't already know. You may be upset about all th' things she's done and is a doin,' but she's y' mama, and you got t' love and pray fer her.

"And there's somethin' else too, Violet. Somethin' I should have told y' a long time ago, darlin.' Ya ain't without a daddy. Y' have one who loves you very much. He's come t' take y' home. You're a lookin' at him."

Escape

It was early morning, and the woods were dark as pitch, but she sprinted on, pushing her body to its limit. She had been running for some time now—dodging and leaping over brush and trees. At first she ran with the speed of a gazelle after managing to pull free from his crashing blows. Luckily, that one hard smack to his temple from a rock she had been able to seize as she lay pinned beneath him gave her an instant to wriggle free from his stout hold and break away.

The right side of her body was beginning to feel strangely numb, except for the splintering pain in the bottom part of her leg. She surmised his blows had broken it, along with some of her ribs because of the stabbing pain and burning she was now enduring with each breath. It was extremely difficult to see, for one of her eyes was swollen and bloody, making her completely blind in one eye, but she ran desperately on even though there was no path to follow, no plan of escape. She was simply fleeing, making a getaway—if it were possible. I have to make it this time. I will not take it anymore. It did not matter in what direction she ran or where she ended up. Anywhere would do—anywhere away from the monster.

She was acutely aware that her broken body would not be able to run at this pace much longer. She was also aware that she would not be able to withstand this pain for any length of time—and now she was starting to feel faint. Her head had begun to spin.

As she raised one throbbing arm in an effort to swipe back the bloody matted hair now falling into her good eye, she touched her cheek and jaw where the swelling was worsening.

Her legs started to buckle beneath her body; they were growing weak, refusing to run. One breath. I must have some air. In a desperate effort to inhale, Sally fell for one instant up against the trunk of an old oak tree.

She could hear the thuds from his giant boots coming closer. As the sound of those dreaded footprints sounded louder, closing in, she looked up at the beautiful stars in the autumn sky and felt the earth start to swirl. Sally's legs finally gave way as her body slid down the tree trunk onto the damp earth.

I knew this would happen wh—whenever I tried to leave him. The monster is going to kill me now—and I don't even care.

Sally heard the gunshot, then everything went black.

Understanding and Acceptance

Mary rose from in her kitchen rocker, grabbed another pillow for her back, and sat down at the table in a straight back chair.

"Y' don't have to finish hangin' those curtains today, Vy. It's enough you made them for me, and I do love them so much. They're so fresh. I really like th' pretty lace you trimmed them with. It matches my new willowware dishes perfectly."

Mary took on a pleading tone as she watched Vy string another rod through a curtain panel.

"Please, Violet darlin. I wish you would just come here now and talk to me awhile. We hardly get to spend any time together now, and after this baby is born we'll have even less.

"I never got to tell you how sorry I am for all the terrible things mother said the day you came over and heard us in that dreadful fight." Mary glanced out the window, recalling the distress that she, herself, had suffered that day. She sighed deeply, feeling some responsibility or guilt for her friend having heard those awful remarks Jessie Mae had screamed out about Violet and her mama. She had wished a million times she could explain it all away—take it all away!

"I knew mother would be upset when she found out that Will and I were married. Maybe if I had just left there as soon as I told her and not allowed her to pull me into that awful argument, you wouldn't have had to hear the horrible things she said. Can you believe she has forbidden me to ever come back home again? I just hope and pray she will reconsider and change her mind someday. I would hate for my baby not to have a maternal grandmother, and wouldn't it be terrible for her to miss getting to know her first grandchild?"

Vy laid down the curtains and poured two cups of tea into which she stirred lemon and sugar. After handing Mary one of the steaming cups, she pulled out a chair and sat down across the table facing her friend. She rubbed the freshly ironed tablecloth unconsciously considering her words carefully. "Your mother was upset because she learned you were married, Mary. I don't ever want you to feel bad about the things I heard her say that afternoon. It took some time for me to see, but God created a wonderful blessing out of it all. Because of all the things that happened that night, I finally found my father."

"Oh, Vy, that is the most amazing thing, isn't it? I still can't believe that Seth Seaton is your father. What a wonderful man to have for a dad."

"Did I mention to you that my own father has come to see me several times—and even drove me to Maudie's to let her check on the baby a couple of weeks ago. He has become very fond of Will and is so excited about being a grandfather. If only Mother wouldn't take the joy out of it for him. She would have a terrible spasm if she knew he had been coming over to visit me."

"Well, dear, I am glad to hear your dad is being supportive of you, and you must keep praying for your mother. Y' have to leave the situation between you and her in God's hands. That's what I have had to do concerning my mama. Both of us need to concentrate and thank God for the amazing blessings we do have—and try not to be concerned with things that have hurt us. Just look how God has blessed you, Mary. You have a dear husband, Will, who fairly worships the ground you walk on. You are members of a sweet church where you serve the Lord together. You have your dad, an adorable little home, and a wonderful child coming soon. You have many friends, and one sitting right here who loves you very much."

Mary took a sip of tea and reached over and found Vy's hand. "I love you too, and I do realize all those things. I wake up in the morning, pray, and leave it at Jesus' feet. Then, a bit later, I get to mulling it over about how miserable Mother has acted—is acting, and I get mad and upset once more. Don't you ever do that—ask God to forgive you for something and then turn right around and get angry and worked up again?"

Vy smiled and nodded affirmatively, squeezing Mary's outreached hand. "Oh, of course I do. I'm sure we all do that at times. It's for sure we're all sinful humans!"

Mary was not sure how her friend would feel discussing the harsh way she had learned about her father, and although curious to discuss it, she wanted to approach the topic with care. "I imagine it was natural for you to feel very upset and disappointed that Seth had never revealed to you that he was your own father." She searched Vy's face for any sign of discontentment with the subject, but seeing none she continued, "I know I haven't asked you about it before, but I've wondered about it a lot. We haven't had a real chance to talk about that horrible day and night, Vy, and if it makes you uncomfortable we won't discuss it any further. I think because of all that has happened to me—getting married to Will, the argument with Mother and consequent separation from my parents, moving away and trying to get settled, finding out I am going to have a baby, I failed to give you and Mindia the care and concern that my two best friends deserved in their time of trouble."

Vy shook her head. "You didn't fail anyone, Mary. I guess I did avoid the subject for a long time there, but I don't mind talking about the events of that day anymore. I was terribly bitter and angry about so many things. Not at you, of course—mostly Mama, and well, I have to admit just about everybody else in my family as well. I can't tell you I can understand all the why's and wherefore's or have everything that happened all reconciled in my mind perfectly, but I am able to talk about that night, Mary. However, I don't know if I ever would have been had it not been for Nanny."

Now more than ever Mary was interested. She was wondering how in the world Nanny could have helped Vy to accept what had happened to her since Nanny, too, was one who had kept silent for so many years.

"Tell me, dear—tell me how you have come to terms with everything," Mary begged.

"Well, you know, I was there on Maudie Ellis's floor praying, and God had just given me some peace when Seth knocked on the door. When he told me right then and there that he was my daddy, well, at first I didn't believe it. Then I was joyful—elated—just so happy to think that Seth Seaton, the man I admired most in the whole world—and had even come to love—was my father. It was a wonderful feeling to know that my daddy had been lookin' for me all day and had found me, and I did so need someone to care for me right then and there, Mary.

"All the way home, I had some sort of a feeling of happiness to learn that I had finally found my daddy—a home, a family, and two sisters besides—but I could hardly comprehend it all. It was simply too much for my mind to take in. It was more like a dream than anything, and it didn't seem true because my mind was still reeling from all that horrid stuff about mama."

"Besides that, you know all that Seth told Mindia and me the next day was that he was our natural father and that Sally Vittoye was our mother. It was as though he didn't want to talk about it—answer our many questions. I'm sure it was as embarrassing and awkward for him as it was for us. And to tell y' the truth, I didn't even know where to begin or what questions to ask.

"Actually, the whole thing just sent Min into a stage of depression, and I think I was in one as well. I think we both just stayed kind of numb for a period of time there.

"Then, after a few days, it started to register with me—hit me cold. I got to thinking about everything, and it was then the anger set in. The more I pondered on how Mindia had received so many material benefits from Seth and Nanny ever since she was a baby and I had not, the more resentful I became. I felt a lot of anger toward Nanny and Lottie for hiding the truth of everything. I begrudged the fact that I had felt like an outsider all that time in my own daddy's house and shouldn't have had to. I could not understand their motives for keeping my father's identity a secret, and sometimes I still don't.

"Mindia had really changed a lot since she found out the truth of it all as well. She kept to herself a lot and acted as though she hated me and everyone else in the family. You must understand how she felt, Mary. Even though he thought it was for her own good, Seth had kept Mindia from knowing her own mother. Actually, she has never met Mama to this day. A terrible change took place between Min and me

for a good while, and I was furious at everybody for losing her friendship, as well as for everything else that had happened.

"It was Seth that Mindia and I blamed the most. We both reasoned
that everything was his fault. Even things mama suffered and things
she was, I blamed Seth with. The anger began to consume me—to eat
me alive, Mary—and I could see it destroying Mindia as well. My attitude even came between the Lord and me as well. I found excuses for
skipping church, and it almost got to the point where I couldn't pray. I
would try to remember that night at Maudie's—when I was on my face
praying and how God had answered my prayer and given me peace.

"I tried to focus on how God had revealed the identity of my own
father; how He had caused Seth to come looking for me—answered a
prayer I had prayed all my born days for—but my pride and self pity
would not let me forgive. I was bitter toward my family for hiding the
truth from me."

Vy paused in her story, pondering all that had happened, rose, and
placed her empty teacup in the dishpan. She walked over and looked
in wonder out the kitchen window at acres of pasture the season was
greening up so magically. Bright yellow jonquils, red tulips, and lacy
candytuft blossoming beside smooth marble stepping stones revealed
the patience and talents of Mary and Will. Her eyes pondered the blue
mountain range in the distance then scanned down to Will's newly
plowed plot of ground with its rich dark soil. Memories of her own
garden from years ago flashed by her crowded mind. She could see
herself and Mama hoeing the weeds in the hot sun. Those were precious memories now, though at the time it only seemed like hard work.
Wildflowers blooming under the big oak tree. Maynard's Valley in the
spring—so beautiful. Violets! Granny!

Engrossed in Vy's story, Mary shifted her cumbersome body once
more and interrupted Vy's daydream. "Go on, Vy," she urged, "tell me
the rest."

Vy sighed deeply and walked over and sat back down in the chair
next to her friend.

"Well, one day Nanny called Mindia and I into her room—said she
needed to talk to us about something—said she was concerned about
both of us and our bitter spirits.

"You should have been there, Mary. She couldn't have said anything that would have made us angrier. Mindia turned and walked right out of the room, but Nanny got up, took her by the hand, and led her right back. I was just as perturbed as Min was. I looked at Nanny and thought to myself, *Who do you think you are to call my spirit or anyone else's bitter? What do you know about anything Mindia and me are going through?* But I didn't say anything.

"Nanny simply ignored my hateful manner as well as our insolent attitudes and said she had a story to tell both of us—one that we desperately needed to hear.

"I had a notion to run right out of that room just like Mindia did, but I just sat there."

"'Girls,' Nanny started, 'there was once a beautiful young girl who played and grew up with two fine and handsome young boys. The three children were the best of friends. In fact, their families enjoyed friendship together, attending the same valley church. As she grew into her teen years, both boys came to adore the beautiful young girl. She loved both of the boys as well, but she only loved a certain one of them in that special romantic way.

"'The certain young boy that the beautiful girl loved became involved with some dark and shady characters, and he fell into something way out of his control. The young man's whole personality changed as he took his eyes off the Lord. He was constantly getting into all kinds of trouble with the law, using damaging and addictive spirits, lying to his parents, stealing things, and disappearing for long periods of time.

"'The people he got mixed up with had certain old-world supernatural beliefs that seemed to intrigue or charm the young man. After getting in trouble with the law a few times, the sheriff advised his ma and pa to send him away from the valley for a time, hoping that if he was separated from those who had such a bad influence on him, it might help the boy to see reason and get his life straight.

"'Well, his parents did end up sendin' their son to stay with his aunt and uncle in Kingston, hoping and praying it would help.

"'Instead of helping things, the separation of that young boy from the young girl caused her to sink into a deep depression and run straight to the other young boy, her other best friend, for comfort. She hid the fact as long as she could, but before too long it was evident to all that the young girl was expecting a baby, though she was able to keep the father of her child a secret, refusing to reveal his name even to her own ma and pa.

"'Then there came an unholy uproar about the girl's condition at the church where the two families attended. When it became apparent the girl was with child, it caused enough bitterness and discord in the little church t' split it right in two. Eventually, enough members got their heads together and voted to expel that little girl from the church. That single act caused her parents to withdraw and stop going to church anywhere.

"'Well, it wasn't long after that happened that the beautiful girl's very own pa passed away. It has always been said that th' poor soul died of a broken heart.'"

"By this time, I was beginning to get interested, and I could tell Mindia was as well. We were both growing curious as to why Nanny was telling us this story."

"'What happened then, Nanny?' I questioned, and she continued on.

"'The other family's hopes were high when the disturbed boy finally returned home from Kingston, but it turned out he had not changed much a' tall. That child continued right on a meetin' with that degenerate and misguided crowd who found their pleasure in the old-country Druid rituals and such. The boy even tried pressing the beautiful young girl to involve that little baby of hers in their wicked midnight meetings in th' woods, but she had sense enough to refuse. When the boy's pressure became too much for her, she went runnin' right back to her little girl's own pa, cryin' on his shoulder once again for comfort. Loving her and his own daughter like he did, that young man welcomed her right back into his arms and begged her to marry him.'

"It was right about that time the story took on a similarity to the story Maudie had told me, and suddenly it occurred to me who Nanny's story was about. I stopped her right then and there and asked her if the story was about mine and Mindia's mama, and she admitted it was.

"'That's right, girls,' Nanny said. 'I'm tellin' y' a true story about Seth Seaton, Sally Vittoye, Calvin Ellis, Violet Vittoye, and Mindia Seaton. That's who this story is all about.

"'Sally soon found out she was going to have her second baby by Seth, but she refused to marry him. She simply could not bring herself to stop seein' Calvin Ellis and attendin' those shameful rituals with him. Calvin simply had some strange control over your mama's mind then, and I guess he still does.'

"'It was about eight months after, that I myself helped Sally Vittoye deliver her second baby—another precious little girl. That baby was you, Mindia. I helped birth you right there in our back room. Sally, y' mama, wanted desperately to keep you—take y' home with her, but y' daddy would not hear to it. He had some awful powerful arguments with Sally about her takin' y' home, because he knew she was still under Calvin's influence. As y' know, Seth finally won out, and when Sally got able to leave here, old Calvin came by and picked her up. She went on back home and told her ma that she had a miscarriage and lost the baby. I want y' both to know this. I am certain that your mother, Sally, loves the both of you girls. She has had a lot of tragedy and hurt in her life, and it has caused her to be a lost and troubled soul. Instead of judging her, y' should pray for her every day. Seth Seaton loved her with all his heart and more than one time begged her to marry him, and I cannot count th' times he pled with her to let him bring you, Violet, here t' raise—bring you here to live with us—but your ma would not give in.'

"Oh, Mary, when Nanny said that, you should have heard how Min cried. She started those heart wrenching sobs that really got to me and kept saying, 'But she gave me up, Nanny! My real mama, Sally, gave me up. She wanted Vy, but she didn't want me.'

"Nanny then tried to explain that Seth gave Sally no choice in that matter. She said, 'Mindia, Seth refused to let her take you, and then, right after that, y' daddy practically set out t' find a perfect mama for you. Oh, I know he loves her now, but the real reason he married Lotia was to give y' a good mama, and neither of y' girls could have found a better mother than Lottie. That's a plain and simple fact. Y'll not find a better woman anywhere than Lotia Seaton.

"'As for you, Violet, you may resent the early childhood years Mindia had with this family. Ones y' did not have, but y need t' think about this. Y' were able to grow up knowing and lovin' your ma and having a relationship with your Gran, who shared with y,' taught y' how to read, write, sew, grow a garden, to cook, and a host of other things. That's something Mindia did not get to experience and never will.

"'Y' pa wanted you to live with him, but he knew you were safe as long as your Granny was takin' care of y',' Violet. It was only after hearing of her death that he informed Sally he was going to come for you no matter what she did. He told her right there in the Ailor Springs Church at Sadie Ellis's wedding. Oh, honey, it broke his heart and mine as well to bring you here against your will, t' see you so brokenhearted like you were that first few months, but y' daddy knew he had to do it because you were being left alone at night while Sally was out with Calvin. He couldn't put it off any longer.

"'All of us wanted to tell both of y' the truth—th' story of how y' came t' be—but we were afraid—afraid of how y' would react. So we kept on puttin' it off, and it just got worse and worse. I believe we made a mistake in not tellin' y' sooner, but we are human. Y' just have to find it in y' hearts to forgive us and get on with your happy lives.

"'Y' daddy prayed day and night. He prayed long and hard to seek God's will about both you girls, and finally felt he had God's answer when he came to Lotia and me and said, "If I can just make my daughters understand how much they are loved before they hear the whole story, then maybe they will understand the mess I made and forgive me for waiting so long to tell them everything."'

"Nanny was almost finished but went on with her story. 'I'm telling you girls all this now because I want y' both to know that in spite of making some grave mistakes in his life—mistakes concerning both of you—Seth Seaton has always loved y' both and tried to do what was best, whether it was to give y' up to your mama or raise ye right here, and he deserves your respect and honor fer that, girls—as well as y' love'

"Mindia and I just sat there sort of speechless, spellbound, then Nanny said: 'There is only one more thing I have to say to y' girls. Violet, you were loved by a wonderful grandmother who has gone on to glory now. You are loved by your daddy and by Lotia. You are practically worshipped by little sister Dale. Remember how you told me that all during your lifetime you prayed God would lead you to your daddy—to let y' know who th' other part of y' family was? Don't you realize what has happened? God has answered y' prayer, Vy! He gave y' your daddy and another whole family besides. God answered and gave y' a double blessin'!

"And listen to me, Mindia Seaton. Y've been raised by two of the most wonderful parents a girl could have. They have given y' your heart's desire and loved y' with all their mind and strength. Do y' recall just how many times y' prayed for a sister or a best friend? Well, dear, God has answered your prayer and blessed y' with not one sister, but two. God gave you a double blessin' as well. He gave you a best friend in Vy here.

"'I want to see that sweet Violet spirit again—the one you have always had.

"'I want to hear that happy Mindia laughter—like I haven't heard in a long time. You are two beautiful Christian girls, and in y' heart y' know what you need to do. Y' need to get over your pity party, throw off this petty anger, and thank God for all your wonderful blessings!

"'And I might not be such a great blessin,' but right here sittin' beside y' is another grandmother who loves you and prays for y' every day.'

"Then Nanny got up, kissed and hugged us both, and left us sitting right there in the room staring at each other."

Mary wiped her eyes and swallowed hard.

"Oh, Vy. What did you and Min think about all that? What did you do?"

"Well, some of it was hard to take," she said, "but the story answered our questions. It's amazing how the truth sets everything in place. We both knew Nanny was right about forgiving everyone and getting past our anger.

"I have tried hard to do that very thing, Mary—and Min has, too. She's been her old sweet self since then. She still has lots of questions about Sally and Gran that make me feel, well, uncomfortable at times. I guess that's because I enjoyed a special relationship with both of them and she did not. I try to tell her stories of my childhood, those early days, but I admit it is hard—and it is almost overwhelming to try. I can never tell if it makes her feel better or worse.

"I want Min to meet her—Mama, that is. Maybe someday they can meet—if Mama ever breaks free of the terrible curse that controls her.

"Nanny encouraged us to talk to each other about our feelings of resentment and then to bow together and ask God to help us with forgiveness. This has worked miracles for us, Mary, and we are really both enjoying the wonderful bond of sisterhood."

"Did you ever ask Nanny or Seth about who kidnapped y' baby

brother?" Mary asked. "Did y' ever question anyone about who the boy's papa was?"

"Mmm hmm. Nanny told me that Baby was not Seth's child, and that mama would not tell Seth or anyone else who his father was. Maudie told me he was not Calvin's child either. It's so sad, Mary. Somewhere I have a dear brother, and I don't have any idea where he is. I wouldn't know him if I passed him on the street. He must be about...about fifteen years old now. I think he was about two-and-a-half years old when that horseman rode past our well and snatched him right out of my mama's hands."

"I was only six, but that's a night I will never forget—and the way my mama suffered afterward. I don't believe she has ever had her right mind since then."

"Who do you think took the boy?"

"Many's the time I heard Granny say, 'I hope Baby's Pa is good to th' little feller,' so I always believed that it was his pa that did it, whoever he is."

Violet breathed an exhausted sigh and smiled at her dear friend. "Enough about me and my family. Tell me about you. What's it like to be married to the man you love and wanted so badly and have your own little house?"

"Oh, it's so wonderful, Vy—a dream come true, actually. Will and I cherish our time together, though he is at work a whole lot, and since I been expecting and so hard to get around now, he helps me do things when he gets home from work.

"Will actually likes his work over at the Meat Packing Company. You know, Theo's brother is his boss. Did I tell you that?"

Vy rolled her eyes and nodded slowly and deliberately. "Yes, Mary dear, you did tell me that—only about a hundred times."

Mary laughed. "You know, dear, it's none of my business, but I don't believe there was anything improper—I mean, Theo being at Bertha McVae's the day you saw him over there. The two of them have always been, well, sort of just pals."

Vy shifted in her chair uncomfortably and looked out the window. "Don't do this to me, Mary, I really am trying to forget."

Mary continued. "And there's something else I heard, Vy. Now listen to me. I know this to be the truth. Bertha always had a thing for Will, not Theo. And that's a fact. Sadie just told me last week that Bertha almost had a breakdown when she learned Will and I were married, and that came right straight from her father, who owns the mercantile."

Vy couldn't believe what she was hearing and tried hard not to act too interested. "Hmmm … really, Mary … I'm not so sure I'd believe that."

Mary laughed with self satisfaction. From the look on Vy's face, she could tell that she had just passed on some valuable news to her friend even though she might not admit it right away.

"You know, Theo is working in Whitesville now—running some store."

"I heard." Vy refrained from questioning Mary but couldn't keep her mind from racing. Could it be true that Theo didn't really have feelings for Bertha after all—that the kiss between them didn't mean anything? Have I lost him forever because of my suspicions, my jealousy?

Mary interrupted Vy's thoughts, changing the subject. "Well, I'm glad you and the other girls are going to stay with me for a couple of days while Will is in Whitesville with the Graves family for his uncle's funeral. Do y' think his family will understand, realize I couldn't possibly have made that long trip in my condition?"

"I'm sure they will, honey, and a fine condition you are in, too." Vy reached over and touched Mary's tummy. "I declare, it looks like you've two watermelons in that belly. Are you sure it's not gonna be twins?"

"Oh, I'm not sure of anything, but wouldn't that be something—two babies at once. I wonder if Maudie has ever delivered twins."

"As a matter of fact, she has," Vy said.

Mary looked down, hugged her abdomen lovingly, and then suddenly, hearing the carriages, pushed her swollen body up from the table. "Listen, Vy, somebody's here." Running toward the door, she shouted excitedly, "Yes, there is Winfield with Sadie and Ivy. An' here comes Seth with Min right behind them. Everybody's here, Vy. All at once!"

Violet and Mary ran excitedly out the front door into abundant laughter, plentiful hugs, kisses, and profuse chatter on the lawn—with everyone talking at once, of course.

Ivy was the first to hop out of the carriage. Vy threw her arms around the petite girl, took a good look, and said, "Give me a hug, dear Ivy! You are simply beautiful with your hair up like that."

Pleased as punch with the compliment, Ivy smiled broadly. "Oh, I couldn't do a thing with it this morning," she said. "It isn't naturally curly like your lovely hair, but thank you, darling! It is so wonderful to see you! Can you believe we are finally having our girl party? We have tried to do this for such a long time."

Taking a good look at the bevy of friends surrounding her, Ivy sighed with pleasure and remarked as if to herself, "I still can't believe we really are here—all of us together at Mary's very own house!"

Mary, having to walk a little slower behind Vy, made her way out into the yard, and called out to Mindia, "Hey there, sweet girlfriend! Did you make that pretty bonnet or buy it?"

"I bought it, of course!" Mindia replied between giggles. "I think y' must have me mixed up with Vy. Y' know I can't sew a lick!" Mindia, plainly fascinated with Mary's condition, tried to hug her friend, but it was plain that Mary's abdomen was interfering. Rubbing a gloved hand over Mary's swollen middle and motioning with the other, she called, "Come over here everyone. Look at our Mary! Isn't she perfectly radiant? Can anybody believe our Mary is married?"

Sadie laughed heartily as Winfield helped her dismount the coach and quickly quipped, "Of course Mary's married. She'd better be to be in the shape she's in!" Everyone broke out in laughter.

Sadie's little joke made Vy's mind race backward to another young girl in the same shape years ago, who was not married. She pondered for a moment the terrible disgrace, humiliation, and fear her mama must have felt. Why couldn't Mama have loved and married Seth, our father? Things could have been so different…

Sadie's voice interrupted her thoughts. "I declare, don't you always look so darling, Violet Vittoye. No one looks as pretty as you do in yellow."

Vy quickly looked down at her apron, checking for any soiled spots. "Oh my goodness, Sadie, I've been cooking all morning and somewhat of a mess. You are the beautiful one in that lilac organdy."

Sadie touched a ruffle running over Vy's shoulder and whispered slyly, "Both of us have perfect taste, darlin' because I have a pinafore just like your yellow one, but mine is blue."

"Do y' really?" Vy asked. "Did y' get it at the mercantile?"

Sadie nodded her head affirmatively. "Mmm-hmm, I did, and it was on sale!"

Vy threw her hand over her mouth in mock horror. "Well, doggone it! I had to pay full price for mine—just my luck!"

Vy turned around to open arms and Mindia's familiar voice. "Hello again, dear sis! Would you help me carry some of these bags? I think I've brought everything but the kitchen stove!" The two girls shared a warm embrace as Vy gave silent thanks that she and Mindia had adapted, accepted, and finally become appreciative of their relationship. She was so relieved they had actually begun to enjoy being friends again—along with the bonus of sisterhood.

After toting in enough bags, grips, and paraphernalia that would allow the bevy of females to stay for a month, Winfield kissed Sadie for the umpteenth time, telling her he would return for her and Ivy in a few days.

Seth hugged his two girls and said, "Goodbye, daughters. I will be here on Sunday afternoon to fetch you. Now have a good time and don't gossip too much about everyone in the valley. Have some mercy!"

Mindia and Vy laughed, both giving Seth a goodbye kiss, then bounced back in Mary's house together, arm in arm and so excited to have a long-awaited girlie get-together with nothing to do but eat, laugh, and talk!

Everyone surveyed the delicious looking provisions that Vy and Mary had prepared for their noon banquet. Sadie and Vy walked outside, chatting the whole way, to cover the little outdoor table Will had made with a pretty linen cloth and set it with Mary's new dishes. After they laid all the places with napkins and silverware, they decided on gathering a bouquet of jonquils and daisies for the centerpiece.

"Oohhh, it looks so pretty now!" Sadie cooed.

"Mm hmm!" Vy straightened a napkin and answered, "Let's go help the others carry out the trays."

"Yum, yum. Everything looks so good, Mary! And I'm about starved after that long ride."

"I'm glad you're hungry, Ivy. Somebody needs to eat all this food. Vy has about killed herself cooking! Here, darlin,' would y' like to carry out this tray of glass tumblers for me? Let's see, I think we have everything now. Sliced ham and chicken for biscuits, potato salad, yellow slaw, dills, cheddar wedges, tea cakes, and fried pies."

Mary carefully picked up a big platter of ham and gave directions expertly. "Fetch that big crock of cold tea from the spring house, will you, Mindia? And Ivy, could you carry an extra chair out here, please? Hmmm, I believe we've about got everything."

Vy showed up about that time, taking the platter of ham from Mary's hands. "Goodness, darlin,' let me have that heavy thing. You go on outside and sit y'self down now. You've done quite enough for today."

Mindia took Mary's arm, helped her down the steps, and remarked, "This is enough food for an army, girl. Did you do all this?"

"Well, to tell you the truth, Violet has been here for over a week, and she deserves the credit. I did make up some biscuits, sliced the ham, and did a few other simple things, but it's for sure Vy is responsible for the most of this delicious feast."

Ivy carried two covered dishes to the table as Min retrieved the crock of sweet tea from the spring house. The party had begun!

Mary was so excited she could hardly stand it. After all, it was her first effort at hospitality since moving into her new cottage. She kept chattering as she sat down at the table, speaking first to one friend and then the other.

"I hope you girls are in no hurry t' go t' bed t'night; I been waitin' all this time to' have y' over to my house."

Ivy made room for the last dish of food and spoke. "Y' know, we have talked about doing this for so long but never could find the right time. Now here we are with three whole nights and four days to ourselves. Heavens! We might just catch up on everyone and everything. I'm so happy to be here with all of you I don't think I can stand it!"

The girls joined Mary and sat down at the little table that Will had made. Vy gazed at the pretty girls all around her. The spring sunshine shone in all its glory, but the sun seemed pale in comparison to the cheerful smiles on the beautiful faces at that table. What a lovely moment was burned into Vy's brain that day. What a lovely memory to cherish forever. Best friends bowed together as Mary asked Violet to pray.

"Dear Heavenly Father,
I ask your blessing on this food before us. Thank you for your tender mercy and grace that gives us eternal life through Jesus. I especially want to thank you for each one of these precious girls sitting here today and the blessing each one is to me. We are more like family than friends, Lord. I beg you to keep us close always—best friends forever. I ask your protection for Mary and Will, their home, and their precious baby Mary now carries. Keep each of us in your holy will and help us do whatever it is you call us to daily. In Jesus' sweet and precious name I pray, amen."

Forgiveness

It was on the twin's dedication day it happened. Mary's precious babies—a boy and a girl—were to be dedicated at Ailor Springs Church. The little ones, William Vandiver Graves and Mae Violet Graves, were two months old, and it seemed like everyone in Maynard's Valley had turned out for this, their special morning.

Babies were usually dedicated long before two-and-a-half months, but Mary had been recuperating herself. She had suffered a hard delivery with the twins—one of them being breach. Had it not been for Maudie Ellis's expertise in child birthing, mother and children might have all perished.

Violet knew that Mary and Will had requested that she stand during the dedication with them since they had chosen her to be their baby's godmother, but she was not aware in the least that Mary had purposely failed to tell her who had been chosen to be the twins' godfather. She shifted uneasily, sitting alone in the front church pew on that cool and sunny September morning, waiting for the service to begin.

Seth, Lotia, Nanny, and Mindia had taken their places several rows back. It didn't look as though Mary and Will had arrived yet, but Ailor Springs Church was filling up, and soon there would be no place to sit.

Vy stared down at her feet for the umpteenth time. Her new fall leather boots were handsome enough but were terribly uncomfortable, depending on how tight they were laced. Apparently she had tied them up far too tightly this morning, especially the left one, which was causing her toes to cramp. If only I could let out these laces a bit it would help. Maybe if I excuse myself quickly, I might be able to run outside to the privy and adjust them—that is, if I can stand up! Her toes were starting to go numb by now.

Glancing out the window and starting to rise from her seat, she decided against her plan and sat down quickly. Too late now. Here comes the parson with Mary and Will right behind him. In desperation, Vy hurriedly bent forward, reaching below her skirts and down to the floor where she began adjusting the laces on her left boot—the one that was pinching her toes. Ohhh, that's better. She was still bent over and had begun to untie the right boot when she felt someone jar the pew slightly. Vy froze. Someone had sat down beside her, placing a hand on her back!

With gray eyes sparkling and winking with mischief, he peeped over her shoulder and queried, "Hello, beautiful. What's going on with you and your tootsies down there?"

Vy jerked up quickly, and she was sure the stunned look on her face showed. She was not prepared for this, not ready for it. Her heart started to pound, and she could feel her face getting hot. *My face is turning red. What is he doing here? He moved away, out of town.*

Vy managed to gather her wits and open her mouth without a single thought as to what she would say.

"What are you doing? Here, I mean. What are you doing here? How are you? Uh, I was just adjusting my boots. They are all right now—a little tight."

"I'm fine, pretty one, now that I am right here looking at you."

Vy spoke to herself. Calm down, Violet. He can hear your heart beating. Oh, Lord, you must help me! I am over this person. It's been a whole year now. I am fine. I am okay.

Just then Mary and Will, complete with squirming twins, came out the side door with the parson, who spotted Vy and Theo sitting on the front pew.

"Theodore, Miss Violet, if you two will please come to the front and take your places, we are about ready to start now."

Theo offered to help Vy get up and walk to the front, but she deliberately ignored his hand and went on ahead.

"Miss Vittoye, I'll ask you stand on that side, right over by Mary there. Theodore, if you will take your place over here by William, please, we will be ready to start."

With a nod from the parson, the pump organ boomed out. The music director announced, "Everyone turn to page 144, stand with me, and sing 'A Mighty Fortress.'"

The organ played, and the little congregation joined in singing:

> A mighty fortress is our God
> A bulwark never failing…
> Our helper, He amid the flood…
> Of mortal ills prevailing…

Vy was talking to the Lord and to herself at the same time.

Our helper amid the flood, please help me with this flood today. This flood is Mary's doing, and I'm up to my neck in it. Why did she want to do this to me? She knows what Theo did.

I ought to turn and walk out of here right now—not take part in this dedication at all! Get a grip on yourself, Vy. Mary would never hurt me on purpose.

Forgive me, Jesus, and help me. I just have to get through this day, and with your help, I will.

The parson had started the ceremony, and Vy tried hard to concentrate on what he was saying.

"Dearly Beloved, forasmuch as God desires that all should come to Him, and that Christ our Savior did say, 'Suffer the little children to come unto Me, and forbid them not, for of such is the kingdom of God,' I beseech you now to call upon our Heavenly Father, that in His bounteous goodness He will bless these two children both physically and spiritually. We know that they are in His grace and care until that time when they are old enough to make the choice to follow Him. Each of you here today shares a responsibility for that spiritual growth." Then the parson took both the babies and held them, one in each arm. Little Van started to whimper, and Mae Violet squirmed. Mary reached out to help the parson with her twins, but he held to them tightly and continued posing his questions to the congregation.

"Do you, God's Church, promise to pray for these little ones and live a godly life before them, teaching them Jesus' love in all you say and do, so in time they will come to love Him and invite Him to be their Savior?"

The congregation in unison answered, "We will."

The church bowed their heads as the parson led the benediction prayer:

"We beseech Thee, Our Father,
that You may aid each and every witness gathered here today
to live a life exemplary to these, y' children.
Such that would lead them to know you.
We thank y' for your sacrifice,
Your free gift of grace that y" offer to all who will accept it.
We pray that these precious babies
You have put in Mary and William's care
will grow in wisdom, stature, and favor with God and man
as your Son Jesus did when He walked this earth.
And we pray that these two children will bring glory to you, Lord,
forever and ever,
At this time, we, your church, do hereby dedicate
William Vandiver Graves and Mae Violet Graves
to you, Lord.
In Jesus' holy name,
Amen."

When the parson dismissed the congregation, Mary and Will each took a wiggling, squirming, two-month-old and turned to receive the church family's handshakes, hugs, and good wishes.

There was a pile of presents waiting outside for Mary and Will to open as well as a big cake, platters of sandwiches, and crocks of sweet tea and hot coffee for the whole assemblage.

Vy could not see Theo anywhere in the crowd and couldn't decide if she was relieved or upset.

Just then a familiar voice rang out.

"Hey, Violet! Hey there! Come here. I want you to meet someone."

"Oh, hello, Ivy! How are you, dear?"

"I'm fine, Vy. This here's my, uh ... "

The big hulk of a young man offered his hand to Vy.

"Ed Murray's the name, ma'am, and it is nice to meet you."

"It's very nice t' meet you, as well. From around here, are you, sir?"

"Oh, no. I'm from Florida—Ocoee, Florida. Heard of it? It's right smack in the middle of the state. I'm here visitin.' I have kinfolk right here in Maynard's Valley."

When the Taylor family suddenly appeared and struck up a conversation with Ed, Ivy quickly whispered to Vy.

"Isn't he darling, Violet? I'm simply crazy about him, and I think he's quite taken with me. You remember me telling you about Ed, don't y,' Vy?"

"Mmm hmm, I remember y' talked about him quite a lot at our party a few months back. You—you're not real serious about this man, are y'? Not thinking of moving off to Florida and leaving Maynard's Valley or any such as that?"

Ivy laughed. "Oh, Violet, you sound like Ma! Y' know I would never do anything like that. I'm the baby, the home body, my pa's girl. How could I, or anyone, that is, ever leave Maynard's Valley?"

Vy bade Ivy goodbye as she took Mae Violet from Mary, heading into the church's aside room. Min took little Van from Will and followed so the proud parents could have a little time to fellowship with friends.

Mindia rocked a baby in one chair, and Vy took another. The twins settled down, falling asleep in that quiet place and were tucked down in two little handmade cribs side by side, sleeping soundly by the time their mother came in. She walked over, re-covered Mae Violet, who had wiggled totally out from under her blanket, and looked at her children with awe and wonder.

"Thanks, girls, for tending my little lambs. Wasn't that a sweet ceremony the reverend planned for us, and neither baby cried. I was so glad."

"They are just frightfully beautiful, Mary," Vy alleged. "Simply precious, and turns out you are just a natural mama—so at ease with them. Twins, too. Do you realize that?"

"I guess you're right, and to think I was so afraid. But when a body gives birth, God must just fill your brain up with what to do. Everybody told me it would just come naturally, you know, caring for them, and it really has."

The three girls stood in the little room together, quietly looking down at the sleeping babes.

Vy finally looked up, scanning the little room. "This is the room where Ivy, Bertha, and I got dressed for Sadie's wedding. Remember?"

"I remember that day. Imagine, Sadie's wedding was the very first time we met." Min smiled and looked at her newfound sibling. "Neither of us knew we were sisters, then."

Violet squeezed Min's hand and nodded as memories flooded her mind: Sadie's wedding. It was the day I saw Seth and Mama talking in the back of the church. My daddy was telling my mama that he had decided to come and take me home to live with him and his family. I thought he was with another woman, cheating on his sick wife. I didn't for once dream I was watching my daddy talk to my mama, telling her that he was going to take me from her—to live with him. And that day was the day, when I was decorating the church, that I met—

Mindia interrupted Vy's thoughts, nudging her friend. "Didn't you meet Will that day, Mary?"

"Mmm hmm, it was that very day, Min."

"And wasn't Theo Taylor with Will that day, too?"

Mary seized the perfect opening, smiled, looked at her friend, and asked, "By the way, dear, didn't I see you talking to Theo right before the ceremony?"

Violet looked at Mary with playful irritation, tapping her cheek with a finger.

"Didn't forget or anything, did you, my dear Mary, to tell me that he was the chosen godfather, who would be standing up with us during the ceremony."

Mary smiled a big smile and looked straight at Vy as she put on her best look of childlike innocence, answering, "Oh, no. Did I do that?" Then, with a look of complete gratification, she asked, "Were you surprised?"

"Mary, I cannot believe what you did. We were both terribly uncomfortable. At least I was! I was just going to forget about it, but now that you bring it up, I have to admit I was more than a bit perturbed with you. And furthermore, I hope I don't see him again."

Mary rolled her eyes, shaking her finger from side to side. "Are you sure of what you are saying, Violet? You really do not convince me."

"Yes, my friend, I'm sure."

Min glanced out the side window at the throngs walking up the hill, crowding around the tables laden with food.

"Hey, I'm kind of hungry," she said. "I think I'm going on to the picnic grounds and have a sandwich. Besides, I want to catch up with Ivy and meet that young fellow she's so proudly been introducing around. Want to come with me, Sis?"

Little Van started to whimper as Mary diapered her son with expert ability. Vy was caught up in fascination at the maternal skill her friend had amassed in such a short while.

Time flies so quickly. Where does it go? Mary is a mother now and this room a nursery for her babies. I saw her mother and father here in the congregation today. Her mother must have had a change of heart. That's a good sign, an answered prayer. I'm glad for Mary. Thank you, God.

"Violet! Where is your mind, girl? Are you coming with me to get something to eat?"

"Oh, I'm sorry, Min. I didn't hear you. No, dear. You go on. I'm not hungry at all and sure don't want to walk all the way up that hill. To tell you the truth, I think I would die if I had to. These new boots are killing me. I think I'll go on outside and wait for the rest of you in the coach. Will you please tell Seth and Lotia for me that I said not to rush. I'm really just fine, a little tired."

It would be a long ride home, and the last thing Vy wanted was food. *I want to get home and forget him, forget those eyes that make me weak. How can I be over him if he affects me like that? How? Shake it off, Vy. Just get out of here and find the family carriage.*

After hugs and kisses for the twins and bidding Mary a fond goodbye with promises to get together again soon, Vy walked out into the crisp cool fall day, holding up a hand to shield her eyes from the bright sun streaming through the trees. Those beautiful trees of autumn were already releasing their red, yellow, and brown leaves with every gust of wind. Winter was on the season's heels, pushing as fast as it could. Vy shivered a little as she looked up and down the row of carriages.

Where did Seth park? The coaches look the same. Is it that one? Oh, there are our horses. Vy walked down the row of carriages and found the one she was looking for.

I hope the family doesn't stay too long. I know they are having a good time visiting with everyone, though, and Seth does love his coffee and cake. I'm going to take off these hateful boots and rest in here. I'll be okay if I can just take off—

Vy opened the door of the carriage and was so startled she almost fell backwards.

"Theo! Wha—what are you doing in here?"

"Waiting for you."

"This is Seth's carriage."

"Well, I knew you wouldn't be coming to mine!"

"The family will be here any minute now. You'd better leave."

"I just want to talk to you, and what I have to say won't take long. Come over to my carriage. Let me see you home."

"No, Theo. We don't have ... I mean, there's nothing to say."

"I have something to say to you, Vy."

Their eyes met, but Vy looked away. *I can't think straight when he looks at me that way. What is he doing—going to say? Make some lame excuse for wooing and kissing Bertha—for leaving me—moving away without a word.*

Theo reached out, took her hands in his, and simply said, "I love you, Vy."

She could feel her shoulders start to shake and her knees grow weak. She tried to pull her hands out of his, but he would not release her. Totally mute and at a loss for words, Violet's mind raced a mile a minute. I thought I had forgotten you. I have tried for a whole year to forget you were the person I loved with all my heart, my whole world, then you hurt me so deeply. Now, here you are stirring up all those old feelings again. This is not fair!

Vy cleared her throat, trying to regain her composure, but as she searched Theo's face, the tears were starting.

He was talking faster than usual because he wanted to get it said, tell her quickly, before she could run away.

"Just listen to me, Violet. You have to listen to me now. Bertha McVae is a friend, a very dear friend, but only a friend. I have never felt anything romantically for her, and all that was going on the day you found me at her house and got so angry at me, was a hug and kiss from a brother to a sister. In fact, Bertha has been in love with Will Graves, not me! It was only the Sunday before that day that Bertha found out about

Will and Mary being married. She was terribly distressed, devastated. For some time, Bertha thought she had a chance with Will, but he only cared for her as a friend.

"You know, from the first moment Will saw Mary at Sadie and Winfield's wedding, he fell madly in love with her. I was at Bertha's house trying to help her deal with it. That is the truth of the whole incident, Vy. The plain unvarnished truth."

Vy, who had regained a little composure by this time, looked straight into Theo's face, speaking very slowly and deliberately.

"And it's taken you a whole year to tell me this? To tell me that you lo-love me—that you care about me? You could have written, or come—"

Theo reached out and took her face in his hands. He kissed her lips gently, tenderly. Vy felt weak all over, trying not to respond and pulled away. *I will not let him do this to me again.*

Theo knew he had not convinced her, but he was determined to do it here and now.

"Listen to me. I tried to see you. You know I did. I came by your house more than once, but you would not come out to see me. You were so mad you wouldn't even listen to what I had to say. Then that opportunity in Whitesville came up. That's also what I wanted to explain to you—about leaving here, going to the city.

"You see, I found out about this little refreshment stand in a prime location, right by the L&N station in Whitesville, that needed a manager. I applied for it, got the position, and went to work there last October. After I got settled there, I wrote letters to you explaining everything but always tore them up. The words only sounded like empty excuses—sounded silly and without meaning on paper.

"I missed you, Vy, but I didn't know what I could do. I needed a plan. Something to show you I was serious—to show you how much—"

There was the sudden sound of voices and laughter as someone neared the carriage. Theo stopped mid sentence.

Seth appeared with food and water for the horse and swung open the coach's door. It was evident that he was surprised. "Well, great day! Hey there, Theo. How are you doin, young fellow? You want us to drive you home?"

"I'm fine, Mr. Seaton. No. I … we … I just wanted to talk to Violet here.

"I haven't seen her in some time now and have a lot to say to her. Would y' mind if I drive her home in my carriage?"

"That's fine by me, Theo. We all thought you had moved Whitesville. And no, of course I don't mind, son. It's okay by me if that's Violet's wish."

Theo took Vy by the hand and helped her out of the carriage.

Seth reached down, spoke to Vy, and hugged her as she kissed his cheek.

"Bye, honey. We'll see you this evening."

"Bye, Seth." Vy smiled and corrected herself. "See y,' Daddy."

Seth smiled from ear to ear as he took a good look at his pretty daughter. He had waited years to hear her call him that.

Mindia bounced up, punched Theo in the arm, and tossed her head playfully at him.

"What's goin' on here with you two? Anything you want to share with me and the family, Mr. Taylor?"

Lottie grabbed Mindia's arm, fairly pushing her up the steps and into the carriage, whispering, "Shhh, Mindia! Let's mind our own business, now!"

Min giggled. "I'm only kiddin' them, Ma."

The couple rode in silence, but Vy's mind was racing. He actually said he loved me. Did I hear him right? This is what I prayed for, but is it really true? Can I trust him? You know I want to, Lord. More than anything I want to believe him, forgive him. Let it be possible, Lord. Help me here. Mary did tell me that Bertha and Theo were only friends, that there was never anything between them. I didn't dare believe her, though. Oh, Lord, is this an answered prayer? Where is my faith? Give me faith, Jesus, to want your will, whatever it may be.

The carriage bumped up and down as the horse lumbered on down the dusty road. Vy recognized the terrain, suddenly felt a wave of panic, and sat up. Where are we? This road looks strange. Where are we going?

This is not… I hope he's not taking me in to see his family. I don't look like or feel like small talk and pleasantries right now.

Confused and shaken, Vy jabbed Theo's arm with her elbow.

"Theo! This is not the way to my house."

"I know it isn't, pretty one. There's something I want to show you."

"This is the way to your house, Theo."

"Yes."

"I'm in no shape to see or talk to your family."

"You won't have to. They're all still back at the church."

"You said you have something to show me?"

"Yes."

"What—what is it?"

"You'll see."

Vy wiped her eyes as the horse rounded a curve. Theo pulled on the reins and brought the carriage to a stop.

The site was about a hundred feet from Theo's parent's house. Where before there had only been an open pasture, there now stood the frame of a brand new bungalow. The house itself did not have windows or doors yet. No roof tiles, either, but Vy could tell that a lot of work had already been done on it and that it showed great potential of being a lovely home.

"What is that? I mean, who lives there?"

Theo laughed. "Nobody, Vy. It's not finished yet."

"I know that. I can see that. I mean, what are we doing here? Whose house is it?"

"It's yours."

"What are you talking about, Theo?"

"It's our house, Vy. Yours and mine. That is, if you will marry me."

Nanny held up the dress, bit off a thread, and sighed deeply. "How long y' reckon we been workin' on these dresses, Lottie?" she asked.

"All winter, I suppose, Nanny." Lotia held up an aqua voile gown that was near finished except for some trims. She turned it side to side, admiring the delicate handwork of her own hands. "Min will look pretty in this color, won't she?"

"Oh, yes. I love th' pastels Vy chose for th' girls."

"Has Mindia tried that on since you set the sleeves in?" Lotia queried.

"No, indeed she has not and must do that after supper so I can pin up the hem. Then, thank heavens, this one will be finished!"

Nanny's remark had a tone of weariness. It was evident she was tired of sewing wedding dresses. She thought for a moment then said absently, "I remember that Sadie Ellis, or rather, Sadie Campbell, had pastels in her weddin' dresses."

Lotia paused, trying to remember being at Sadie's wedding, but she could not. "Was that the wedding where Vy made most of the gowns?" she asked.

Nanny looked up, smiling. "Sure was, and she was only a child then. You should have seen them, Lottie. The gowns were beautiful. I examined them closely that very day. She has always been so talented, that one."

Lotia took off her thimble and rubbed her head thoughtfully. "It's no wonder I don't recall that wedding. I didn't get to go to it, remember? I was still in bed from childbirth with Dale. She had just been born."

"What in the world are we going to do about Vy and Theo's weddin'? Our little church is not going to hold everybody, Nanny. It's just that simple. I guess we'll just announce the time and allow the first come first serve rule concernin' the seating."

"I sure can't give you th' answer, Lotia. All of Ailor Springs will be a comin' out for Theo, and all of Rose Hill Church will be there for Vy. I guess we could just limit the invitations t' special friends and not ask th' whole of both church memberships to attend."

"Oh, Nanny, we could do that, but if we do, it will hurt so many people's feelin's."

Seth stuck his head in Vy's little room where Lotia and Nanny were working and queried, "What's goin' on in here, Lottie, Ma? You-uns gettin' lots o' stitches in?"

"The job is comin' along, Son. Just wonderin' to ourselves how t' get th' members of two churches inside of one."

"Don't worry y'selves about th' weddin.' Th' good Lord will take care of it."

Nanny put one final stitch on the little ribbon rose she had finished making and laid it carefully in the box with the other beautiful trims and laces that would be added to the girls' dresses last thing. She looked at Seth and nodded. "You are right, Son. I guess we're just gettin' nervous about the whole affair."

Just then a perky curly top stuck her head in around Seth's legs and yelled in her familiar lisping five year old way, "Mommy and Daddy and Nanny… Come on, now! Min and Viwet thay thupper is weady, an gueth what it is?"

"Smells like fried chicken and biscuits to me, Dale."

"You guesst it, Nanny!"

"Well, we're a comin' right now 'cause we are very hungry. Aren't you, sweetie?"

"I'm weally hungwy, too!" Dale Seaton's lisp was very pronounced now that she had lost her front two teeth. Her black curls bounced as she jumped up and down, and her big green eyes sparkled. "You makin' my weddin' dweth yet, Mama?"

"Not yet, darlin,' but we will for sure make it soon. The big day is getting nearer."

Dale was looking forward to being Vy's little flower girl and spreading the "wose petals" all down the aisle of the church. She was having quite a time understanding why her big sister needed to walk on them, though.

"More mashed potatoes, Daddy?"

"No, Vy. I'm full to the brim."

"Well, save room for the cherry cobbler."

"Did you add onions or what to this fried squash, Mindia? It's delicious."

"It did turn out good didn't it, Daddy? It's Mary's recipe, and Vy helped with it."

"Vy is going to make a cook out of you yet, Min."

"No she's not. She's going to get married, leave me, and make me the old maid sister!"

While everyone held their sides laughing at Mindia, Vy scooped out dishes of pie and passed them around to her family.

Violet looked around her, surveyed the happiness, the fellowship, the beloved image surrounding her and breathed a silent prayer of thanks:

> Thank y,' Lord, for hearing my prayers. Thank you for the beautiful blessing of this dear family and making ma a part of their lives. Your blessings are great and wonderful. You are great and wonderful. Thank you for Theo. I thank y' that he does love me. I pray for my mama and my lost brother, Lord—wherever they may be. Please let my mama turn to you.
> I thank you for answered prayers, Lord, no matter what they may be.
> In Jesus name, amen.

After the dishes were washed and the kitchen wiped down, Vy retired to her room and read a chapter of the Psalms. The days were getting longer now, and there was more daylight to read or sew by after the evening meal. She glanced at the table beside her bed, picked up her diary, and dusted it off. I haven't written in it for such a long time. How long has it been? More than a year, I guess.

> Tuesday, May 13, 1890
> Dear Diary, where do I start?
> So much has happened since my last entry. It would take a year to write down everything that has happened. But for those who come after me, who are interested at all, I will record these things.
> I asked God for the answers—all the whys and wherefores of my life—and He has answered.
> He has blessed me so that my cup runneth over. I asked Him to let me find my daddy, and Seth Seaton, my daddy, found me. I did not dream of asking for two dear sisters and a loving step-mother, but Lotia, Mindia, and Dale are mine. I did not dare to ask for another precious grandmother, a dear Christian lady—one who would lead me to Jesus—but God saw and blessed me with Nanny. I asked God for my lost love to return, and Theo came back to me.
> Soon I will be a part of his dear family as well—the Taylors. Ma and Pa Taylor are picking me up here tomorrow for a visit with them so I can be of help to Theo.
> I will start painting the rooms of what is to be my new home. Ma and Pa will be our chaperone. I will share a room with Ivy, Theo's

sister. I feel as though I am a part of their family already. I don't
deserve to ask God for anything else because He has blessed me so
mightily. But I will approach His throne boldly just like the Bible
tells me to do and ask for the healing of my mama and to find my
brother. I will also ask God for faith, so that I might glorify His
holy and wonderful name.

Love Songs
and Miracles

"Here is another watch to be repaired, Theo. Mrs. Davis left it yesterday. When can I tell her you'll have it done?" Theo took the watch, turned the stem, and studied it closely with an expert eye.

"I'll get to it as fast as I can, Mr. McVae. Hmmm ... could you give me at least a week, sir? Y' know I'm spending a lot of time trying to get the house done."

"I understand perfectly, Theo. How about I tell her two weeks, okay?"

"That would be just fine, sir. I really appreciate y' understanding."

Theo wrapped the time piece carefully and returned it to the box as Mr. McVae walked behind the counter, smiled, and asked, "Now can I get you anything else today, Theo?"

"Mmmm ... I think the nails and roofing tiles are all I need today, and I want to pick up and pay for that last load of lumber I ordered yesterday. That is if you will get that total for me. And, oh yes, Vy wanted me to ask about the piece goods she has on order. Did they come in?"

Mr. McVae scratched his head, put on his little spectacles, pulled out a large cash book, and turned the pages.

"The total you owe me for the building supplies is fourteen dollars and eighty-five cents—and no, son, I'm awfully sorry, but that dress material didn't come in with today's order either, but that does remind me here is something you need to take to Violet. I was out back putting up stock yesterday morning, and when I came in here, I found this silver box lying right here on th' counter. Don't have any idea who left it, but it has a note addressed to Violet on it."

"Hmmm … Yep, I see. To: Violet Vittoye." Theo took a money clip out of his pocket and counted. "Twelve, thirteen, fourteen dollars and eighty-five cents. There y' are, sir, and thank y' kindly, Mr. McVae. I'll see that Vy gets this here box."

Theo motioned for the youth standing by the door to help him with the large package of roofing tiles and carefully placed the silver box in the trunk of the carriage.

"Come on, Sonny Boy. We got to get that pack of roof tiles to my coach."

Cordelia Taylor sniffed at the new wood and fresh paint smell as she poked her head inside the empty house, stepping gingerly to avoid the wood scraps and bent nails. "That room will get painted after you and Theo are married, Violet. Come have some of these oatmeal raisin cakes I made. They're still warm. Is Theo back yet, and did he pick up the piece goods for your dress?"

Vy wiped her hands and brow on an old rag, put the paint brush aside, and sat down beside Cordelia Taylor. Breathing a frustrated sigh, she answered, "Nope, Ma, he ain't back yet, and I honestly don't know what t' do if that silk material doesn't come in soon. I was up there at the mercantile yesterday, and all they got in was the same old gingham and calico. I'm baffled. Mr. McVae and I, we ordered that bolt of cloth over three months ago, and there's still no sign of it. He told me it's the first thing he looks for when he opens the parcels every day. If it doesn't arrive soon, Ma, I may have to get married in flour or potato sack material."

Ma Taylor gave up a hearty laugh, and then a look of concern shadowed her soft wrinkled face. She pushed a wisp of silver hair that was threatening her eyes off her forehead.

"Y' know, your wedding is in three weeks, child. I declare, it's gonna take all of you girls a sewin' day and night to make you a weddin' dress, even if th' piece goods arrive by this time tomorrow! Ain't you a'tall worried about it?"

"To tell y' th' truth, I haven't had much of a chance to worry about the wedding with all the work we been doing on the house, but I admit it's gettin' me a little concerned now."

Vy shook her head again in exasperation, gave a weak laugh, and bit into a warm oatmeal cake. "Mmmm, these are delicious, Ma. Didn't you tell me they were Theo's favorites? You'll have to let me know how you make these things!"

"He loves them, all right, and so do all my other youngins. Y' bet, honey. We're gonna have plenty of time t' be out in th' kitchen cookin' together. I'll be glad to show you lots of preparations, and I've heard you know your way around the kitchen, too! Bet you could teach this ole girl a thing or two!"

Vy laughed. "I don't know that I could teach you a thing that you don't already know, Ma. You havin' raised a family. It's going to be so great, though. God is so good—Theo and me living right here beside you and the rest of your wonderful family. How could I worry about anything, Ma? I'm just too blessed and happy to worry!"

Delia reached over and gave the girl a spontaneous hug. "You don't know how we prayed for this, Violet. You are the girl this whole family wanted Theo to marry.

"Y' know, when the boy took a job in Whitesville a year ago, we thought it was no use. But then he came on back, and I just knew it was 'cause he was missin' you, Violet. That's exactly what Asbury said, too, and everybody right there at the supper table agreed with us. They said that the only thing that would have brought Theo back to Maynard's Valley was Violet Vittoye. I declare, that's just what they all said."

Vy laughed out loud as she picked up her paint brush, started back into the next room, looked back over her shoulder, and mused, "I just hope it was me he came back for, Ma Taylor, and not this new house he's so involved in."

Cordelia chuckled, rose to take leave, and then jumped back, nearly dropping the platter of oatmeal cakes because of a sudden deafening bang outside. Theo and Sonny had just unloaded a pile of lumber off the parked wagon and were back and ready to work.

His mama watched as the tall and handsome young Theodore Taylor unhitched the horses from his carriage, led them to drink, wiped his brow with a handkerchief, and took determined strides toward the house. She also curiously eyed the young boy walking slightly behind her eldest child and smiled as she addressed them both.

"And who is this young man you bring with you, Son?"

"I'm sorry, Ma. This here's Sonny Monroe. Don't y' recognize this boy? You've met him before over at aunt Katie Faye's. This here's th' lad I told you was a comin' t' help me with th' house."

Sonny Monroe removed his hat and bowed his head slightly. "Howdy do there, Mrs. Taylor. It's nice t' see y' again."

"And it's good t' see you, Sonny Monroe. Been a long time since I took any trips toward Whitesville, and you've surely done a lot of growin' since I last visited my sister. I remember you, all right, but as a wee lad. Not as a fine young man that I see standin' before me now. When did you get here, dear?"

"I Just arrived on th' train this morning, Mrs. Taylor."

"Sonny just came on ahead of Aunt Katie like I asked him to, Ma, and he has agreed to help me on th' house until we get it finished. His last job in Whitesville was complete less than a week ago."

"Well, we're real glad t' have you with us, Sonny, and I'm much obliged to y' for helpin' my boy out."

"I thank y,' ma'am, and really appreciate Theo letting me help out and earn some cash. I know about buildin' houses. That's what my Pa did 'fore he died."

Delia shook her head in an anxious manner. "I'm so sorry, Sonny. That has to be awful hard to lose your dad, and you so young. Have any other family, do you?"

"Nope, ma'am. Just me and, of course, Aunt Katie. She's just like a mama to me. Only one I've ever known."

"Don't have any other family, son? Nary 'nother kinfolk anywhere?"

"Never knew none 'cept my Pa and Aunt Katie." The boy looked uncomfortable, and Delia thought she had probed his mind long enough, so she motioned with her hand all around her. "Well, just look around you, Sonny, Theo and Vy here can use a whole lot of help on this here house. H'it's not nearly finished, and these youngins' weddin' is only about three weeks away." Delia stopped short, walking near the youth to examine his face more closely.

"I declare, Sonny, you look awfully familiar t' me. Lookie there, Theo. I swear, the features on this youngin are remarkably familiar, ain't they? Is it Violet he looks like?"

"Hmmm ... I don't know, Ma. I ain't good at features."

Cordelia laughed out loud.

Having returned to her painting in the other room, Vy had not been paying any attention to the conversation, but at the mention of her name—the statement made by Ma—her curiosity peaked, and she walked back into the room.

"Mr. McVae said to tell y' that no parcel came in for you today, pretty one, and that we would just have to check up there tomorrow," Theo said.

Vy's eyes dropped in disappointment as the pang of anxiety mounted in her stomach.

"Good grief! Theo, I am really going to be in a mess if it doesn't come in by this weekend."

Theo grabbed his betrothed around the waist, pulled her close playfully, gave her a kiss on the nose, talking to her, and at the same time winked his eye at his Ma.

"Hey, beautiful, why don't ya just wear a potato sack? We could still say our I dos and save a lot of money, too."

Vy laughed, playfully shaking her head at his foolishness.

"It's good to know you love me that much, Theo, but I really think you might change your mind if you really saw me in a burlap sack. And have you felt of one lately? They are awfully dirty and scratchy."

She gently pulled away from Theo, slightly embarrassed by the affection he was giving her so freely in the presence of this young boy.

Turning her attention to the visiting lad, Vy queried, "Well, now, and how are you, Sonny Monroe? Do you remember me? We met a few years back at Aunt Katie's when I visited Whitesville. I think you must have been about thirteen or fourteen years old." Vy searched the boy's face, assessing all the remarks she had heard Theo's ma make. *Ma Taylor said he resembled me. His hair, it's like mine—auburn and curly, and I can see a resemblance around the nose, the nostrils. He has deep-set hazel eyes and has no memory of his mama? Where did he come from?*

"I don't think I would have known you since y' have gone and grown up so big and tall." Violet came closer, smiled warmly, and chided the boy. "Are you sure you are the same boy I met when we all went to the fair together?"

Sonny turned to face Vy and gave her a big toothy grin. "Shore am, Miss Violet. I'm one and th' same, and you ain't changed a'tall. You're still pretty as ever and I'd a known you anywhere."

Theo slapped the boy on the back playfully. "Hold on there, Sonny, that's my girl you're talkin' to now!"

Vy ignored Theo's kidding and continued talking. "I am very sorry to hear the bad news of your pa."

"Thank y,' Miss Violet. I do miss him something fierce ... something fierce."

Tears welled up in Sonny's eyes, but he took a big hand and swiped them away, trying to speak bravely. "Orville Monroe, my dad, Miss Violet, was a fine man. He was that all right, but he's gone on home t' th' Lord, and I got to make it on my own. If there was anything my pa taught me, it was t' be dependable in whatever I do and work hard.

"That's why I'm so thankful for Mr. Theo here, and this job, because I aim to continue right on workin' th' construction of houses. Did you know, Miss Vy, that I've worked on some real fine projects in Whitesville? One was a really big house just around the block from Aunt Katie, and then there was another out toward East Whitesville—out close to where we attended that fair. The one next t' Aunt Katie was a big ole, new style. I think they call it the Victorian. Had three stories or more. I guess I love the building trade. Must be in my blood like it was my daddy's. Y' know, he wasn't afraid of heights, and I ain't either. Why, I nearly framed and roofed that one big old house all by myself. Is that where you want me to start now, Theo? Up on the roof?"

"Ummm, no, Sonny. I think I want you to start on the porch right out here. I want y' to use that new tongue in groove lumber we just unloaded." Theo squatted down to examine the big pile of boards more closely. "Look here, Sonny. See this? Looks a little warped to me. Don't use a piece if it's substandard. Mr. McVae will replace all these for me."

Sonny turned back to Vy and Ma Taylor as Theo kept inspecting the lumber piece by piece.

"As I said, I'm real proud to be a helpin' out here while I'm waiting for somethin' another—a big project, y' know—to get started back up in Whitesville, and it's so nice of you people to welcome me and put me up in your home."

Cordelia smiled her best welcoming smile and patted Sonny's back. "Just like I said before, Sonny. We're just awful glad to have y' here. Now ain't you awful hungry, son, after such a long ride out here t' th' country?"

"Not really, ma'am. I ate on the train, so I ain't hungry right now, but I shore am lookin' forward to sample those fine vittles I heard you can cook."

Cordelia let go with her big hearty laugh once more before she answered the boy.

"Seems like that's all I've ever done, dear. Been in th' kitchen cookin' near every day of the fifty years I lived."

Speaking further instructions authoritatively, Cordelia then turned to her son.

"Now, listen here, Theo. You take this boy's grip and all his things on in the house. He will be a sleepin' on that spare cot right there in th' room with you.

"When Aunt Katie gets here, I'm puttin' her up in Ivy's room where she can have her privacy and th' best bed, of course, since she suffers so with the rheumatism. Ivy will go in and sleep in the bed with Neppia, and we've moved Violet's bed in there with the two of them."

As Cordelia started to take leave, she remembered she needed a bit more information from this lad. "Now, when exactly did my sis say she would arrive, Sonny?"

"Aunt Katie Faye will be here on Friday, Mrs. Taylor. She was still packing her things when I left. Matter of fact, she gave me this here let-ter for y.'" At that point, Sonny reached inside his jacket and produced a well-worn envelope addressed to Cordelia, whose eyes lit up with pleasure as she accepted it.

"Oh, I surely thank you, son, for a bringin' this to me, and, well, children, I guess I'd better be getting' on in and tendin' to th' things I've put on t' cook before they burn up. Az will be comin in fore long, n' he'll be hungry.

"You young folks just go on about y' work, but we're gonna eat supper in a couple hours or so. Around five, I'd say." Delia shoved the covered plate of fresh oatmeal cakes into the youth's hands before she disappeared into her house next door. "There's a crock of fresh milk t' go with these here cakes down at the spring house. Theo will show you where 'tis."

Violet had continued to study their visitor closely, curiously. She questioned him once again.

"Now, where did you say y' are from again, Sonny? Your pa and you?"

I reckon we'uns is from Whitesville, miss. If Pa was from somers else, he ne'r mentioned it t' me."

Vy smiled, dismissing her striking resemblance to this teenaged boy as coincidence, and returned to finish painting what was to be her bedroom in a bright sunny yellow color.

Cordelia entered her house. The delicious aroma of fresh field peas and cabbage wafted from the kitchen through the screen door. She quickly checked the field peas, adding more water, then took the cabbage off the fire to cool. After cooling the green leaves, Ma would pack each leaf with her famous ground pork stuffing and then roll the whole thing up, ready to bake.

Grabbing a sack of potatoes, sharp knife, and mixing bowl, Ma Taylor peeled about fifteen and washed, rinsed, and chopped them in cubes before she poured them into scalding fat already heating in her big iron skillet. After greasing another big black frying pan with lard, she stirred up the corn bread batter, poured it in the pan, and stuck it in the oven of the black wood stove to bake into a golden pone.

Cordelia poked the fire, added more wood, wiped the perspiration from her brow, sighed a deep breath, took up the letter from Katie Faye, tore it open carefully, and sat down at her kitchen table.

As she opened it, another folded and sealed envelope fell out. It was addressed:

To: Mr. Theo Taylor and Miss Violet Vittoye
In Care Of/ Mrs. Cordelia Taylor
Maynard's Valley, Tennessee

Mmmmm, must be a wedding present. Most likely a good sum, knowing Katie. Delia turned her attention to the letter addressed to herself and started reading the familiar handwriting of her sibling.

Tuesday, May 12, 1890
Dearest Delia,

I hope you can read this letter. I hardly can myself. My whole body is in mortal pain from this rheumatism, and at times it seems my hands suffer the worst, and at others I can hardly walk.

My knees crack and pop like dry sticks when I get up out of a chair. I was wondering if you suffer with the same ailment as well, since we are sisters. You never did mention it if you do, but then Cordie, you never did complain about anything. I hope this letter finds you fairing much better than me and that the rest of your dear family is well and having a fine time preparing for Theo and Violet's wedding.

By now, the boy, Sonny Monroe, will have arrived ahead of me, and I am so thankful to Theo that he is giving him a position of employment while we are there for a stay. As you know, this young man has been with me for many years and has become very close to me. He is the son I never had, though he has never been much of a baby. He was always extremely intelligent, talking at a very young age, and has been exceptional in all of his school assigns. He is graduated now, but has not yet found a place of employ.

That was when I reasoned on bringing him along to your house as we visit there to be a part of Theo's wedding on Saturday, June seventh, eighteen hundred and ninety.

It was very soon thereafter that Theo wrote and asked if Sonny could come a bit early and help on the house. I deemed it a very excellent idea and agreed since his father, Mr. Monroe, was always in the building business himself. I hope us being there doesn't put you out too much, dear. I realize you don't have the rooms in your house that I do, so I hate to come visit in some way, but in another way I would never want to miss Theo's wedding. I really did grow to love Violet when she was visiting here. We had a marvelous time attending the fair together.

I must admit, I do envy you acquiring another daughter, Cordie, because you already have two very special ones, my own dear nieces, Penelope and Ivy. I am convinced that Violet will simply enhance the lovely family you already have and that is good.

Well, I will catch the train next Friday and will expect someone to pick me up at the station promptly on Saturday morning. Please have Asbury or Theo to check the train's schedule as to when the morning arrival from Whitesville will be, as I don't look forward to a long wait because of the situation with my troubled legs. If need be, you may wish to send Sonny to the station to meet me. Any one of the three men will be satisfactory with me.

I am looking forward to a wonderful stay with you and your dear family, Cordelia, and I will be seeing you on Saturday morning if all goes as planned.

I am your loving sister,

Katie Faye

Since Sonny was engrossed in building what was to be the front porch of their house, Vy hated to interrupt his good progress and train of thought.

The best way to get these nails on the roof to Theo is simply to carry them up myself. Although a ladder would be no ordinary feat to accomplish for a girl with a dress on, Vy decided not to be outdone, wrapped her dress tightly around her, and determinedly tackled the task. Filling her pockets to the brim with the nails Theo needed, she stepped up on the first step of the rickety old ladder. It popped and creaked with her every movement. One, two—up and up she climbed until she reached the top step. Oh, how lovely the view is from up here.

Vy gingerly stepped off the ladder and onto the roof as she took in the beautiful scenery of Maynard's Valley.

Wow! I'm on the roof of our house—mine and Theo's. Right down there is where we will sit on the porch together. There in the yard is where our children will play—in the shade of that old tree. We will hang a swing from the tree over on that side. There will be rocking chairs and a big porch swing on our porch. You will be able to smell the wonderful aroma of whatever I am cooking for our supper. We will be so happy. I will be so happy in our house, this blessed beautiful house—Theo's and mine. "Violet Louise Taylor. I love the sound of it."

Suddenly Theo's loud voice rang out. "Good heavens above, Violet! What th' dickens? How in the world did you get up here? My goodness, girl, don't you know you might have fallen and killed yourself on that ladder?"

"Calm down, Theo. I'm fine, dear. I brought these nails to you."

"I wanted Sonny to climb up that rickety old ladder and bring these to me.

Not you! Not someone with a dress on." Theo reached out put his arms around her waist and pulled Vy close. "But since you're here, how about a sweet kiss for a working man? I'll admit you are a lot nicer than Sonny Boy, my very pretty one."

Theo kissed Vy's mouth, her temples, her nose and forehead.

"Do you know how much I love you? How much I want you, my beautiful Violet?"

Vy smiled and happily laid her head against her betrothed's chest, enjoying the caress of his love. "I know how much I love you, Theo."

"It won't be long now, Vy."

"I know. We'll just live here in this beautiful house forever."

Theo drew back slightly. "Well, now, I wouldn't say forever."

"Wha-what do you m-mean?"

"Well, you never know where we'll end up, dear. Forever is a long time. We might just end up selling this house, making a huge profit, maybe moving to the city. You know how I love the city, Vy."

"Oh...I...well, I thought you had forgotten about all that! I thought you wanted to live here, in our house. I thought this was my house, our house."

"And it is, my darling. It is. It's just that I don't like to think in terms of forever in one silly old place. Just try to think of it this way, Vy. There's a big world out there. We don't want to limit ourselves, do we, to one little old backward place? Not when there is so much to see and do, so many progressive places to go—so much to explore and try."

"I don't know what to think now, Theo. You're confusing me."

"It will be okay, my pretty one. With you and me together, wherever we go, it will be okay. I promise. Do you believe me?"

Vy looked into Theo's eyes, and then he kissed her once again until she could not breathe. "I believe you, my love. Of course I do."

Theo held out his hand and helped Violet back down off of the ladder. Now that she was safely on solid ground again, he could climb back up on the roof and finish nailing the rest of the tiles that were waiting.

Vy's head was spinning round and round with a myriad of questions about their future. The man she adored had managed to mix her up once more.

He's still talking about the city and all its wonders. Why would he want to leave his family and friends? Why would anyone want to leave Maynard's Valley? Where in the world will we end up? Why are we working so hard on this house?

Deep in thought, Vy was about to pick up her paint brush and get back to work once more when she heard a distant but familiar lilting sound.

What is that song? Where is it coming from?

Vy stopped and strained to hear a little better, for someone was singing a tune she had not heard in years.

The tune was hypnotic. It picked her up and carried her—carried her all the way back to a little cabin in the woods. For an instant she was a child again, dancing and prancing out of doors. Granny was humming, and mama was singing and strumming a mandolin.

Tiptoeing closer around to where she could see and hear even better, Vy beheld a fascinating sight. For there, working on the porch with his measuring tape in hand, was Sonny Monroe, lost in singing that beautiful Scottish ballad Vy had heard sung by another person so many times in her life.

> Ohh. ... .ye'll tak' the high road, and I'll tak' the low road
> And I'll be in Scotland a' fore yeeeee
> But me and me true love will never meet aa-ginn
> On—th' bonnie, bonnie banks o' Loch Lomond...

Could it be? Is it possible? Vy crept closer, stretched her neck, and turned her head, straining to hear every single word. She stood motionless, mesmerized, waiting for the next verse as Sonny began to sing.

> Where little violets do spring—and th' wee birdies sing—
> and in sunshine th' waters are a sleepin'—but th——

Upon hearing the first line of the second verse of that familiar old ballad, Vy thought her heart was going to burst right out of her body. She could hold her excitement no more. Tears ran down her face, and her stomach turned over in anticipation as she rushed up to the young boy, grabbing his shoulders, shaking him like a limp rag doll, and nearly scaring him to death.

The youth dropped his measuring rod.

"Whoa, there, Miss Violet! What gives?"

"Who taught you that ballad, Sonny," Vy demanded. "Tell me! Who?"

"I-I reckon I always known that song, Miss Violet. I-I'm sorry if it offended ... I didn't think you'd mind, miss. It is just that I work better when I'm a singin.'"

"Great day, I don't mind your singin,' Sonny, but I have to know how y' came by that song—those particular words!"

"Came by what, ma'am? What words, Miss Violet?"

"The song! That verse. Think now! Who taught it to y'? Did y' learn it in school? From a music teacher? Or was it y' pa, y' father? Oh, please think, Sonny! This is very important. You must try to remember and tell me!"

Sonny Monroe was truly bewildered and looked as though he might cry.

"Miss Vy, I-I'm really truly sorry, but I can't tell y' who taught that song t' me a'tall. N' that's th' honest truth, ma'am. I have just always known that song. Known it far back as I can remember."

Vy took a deep breath and tried to calm a little—to talk more slowly and deliberately. "Do you have any remembrance of your mama at all, Sonny, or riding on a white horse at night?"

"N-no. I don't think so. Well, now come t' think of it, I—I mean, my daddy and me, we did have a white horse when I was a wee youngin, and I do have maybe a remembrance of a lady when I was awfully little. But that may be just a dream I have always had. Th' memory of it—if it is a memory—is awful fuzzy, and in my mind I can't really see what she, I mean, the lady in my dream looks like. I've always wondered if it was a memory of my mama. Pa wouldn't talk about her, y' know. Just said she died when I was a baby." Sonny was more than curious by this time. "What is it, Miss Vy? You tell me what is so important about that song."

Vy was trying desperately to get hold of her emotions—calm down—not daring to hope—but her heart was beating so fast it was hard to do. Oh, God, help me here. Could it be, Lord? Is it possible?

Nearly choking, she managed to spit out the words. "Sonny—you know in the last verse of that song, there? The one you sang just now. 'Where little violets do spring... and th' wee birdies sing'?

"Well, I only heard one person who ever sang the song that way. I mean, sang the song and substituted those particular words. 'Little Violets' instead of the correct words—'wild flowers.' It was my mama, Sonny. It was my very own mama, and she sang it that way—changed the real words and put my name in the song. She did it because my name is Violet."

"Then how'n the world do I know the verse that way, Miss Vy—the verse with y' name in it?"

Vy impulsively grabbed the youth and hugged him.

"Oh, Sonny, that's just what I'd like to know. That's what I have to know."

Hanging low and golden, the moon shone through the tender new leaves of the old oak trees, and the sweet perfume of Ma Taylor's jonquils, baby's breath, and lilac wafted around the Taylor's house, filling the lovely May night. Supper had been eaten, and the family had settled into their respective rooms where most were already asleep and dreaming.

That is, all except Violet Vittoye and Theo Taylor, who sat together in the darkness on the front porch. The porch swing creaked back and forth with every move, but Vy was neither aware of sound, moon, or the soft fragrant breeze. Her thoughts centered around one thing this beautiful dark and velvet night, and only one thing.

Nervously but unconsciously rubbing her hands together, she stared pensively into the darkness while directing her words to the man sitting beside her.

"I have to know, Theo. I have to talk to Mama. I am going to her tomorrow. Do you understand? I must find out what she knows, if anything, about Sonny Monroe's father. And if she doesn't know, well, then we... I may never find out. He has no family. There's no one else to ask.

"And just to think, I was right there in his presence when we were there at the Whitesville Fair. He's the man who could have told me if he took him, if he snatched him right away from my mama that night—and from me. But he's dead now, and I'll never be able to ask him anything."

Theo reached over and took Vy's small, damp hands in his in an effort to try and calm her. "You know, dear, supposing your suspicions are true, even if you had questioned Sonny's father about the past, Sonny's past, you surely know he wouldn't have admitted anything—especially a kidnapping.

"Whoever kidnapped y' baby brother went to a whole lot of trouble to keep him hidden away from Maynard's Valley and from your family all these years, Violet. Names can be changed—things done, covered up."

Vy turned, looking into Theo's eyes, and declared with firm resolve, "If I had looked right square into that man's eyes and asked him if he was the one who caused that horrible night, I believe with all my heart that I could have told if he was telling the truth or lying about it, Theo. I would have known."

"Did you tell Sonny your suspicions?"

"No. I didn't want to upset him. I think he thought I was crazy, going on so about a song he was singing."

Theo breathed deeply and patted her hand with tenderness. "Well, I hope your mama agrees to talk to you about this, pretty one, but she might not want to you know. You do realize that, don't you?"

"Yes. I'm prepared for that, too. I don't even know what shape I'll find her in tomorrow, but I have to go and try. I've told you, Theo, Mama had a breakdown. She went to pieces, right over the edge after Baby was taken from her, and she ain't ever been the same since."

"I know. I know all that and I completely understand your concern, Violet, but you have got to take it easy. I cannot stand seeing you this upset and anxious."

"Don't worry about me becoming anxious, Theo. You just pray I get some answers. I'm going to ride over to Mama's cabin first thing in the morning. On the way back home tomorrow evening, I aim t' go by and see how Nanny and Lottie are coming along with the wedding dresses. You and Sonny can keep right on working on the house."

Theo interrupted and held up his hand to halt any disagreement.

"No, Violet. I'll leave the boy instructions to go ahead and work on the porch tomorrow while we're gone. You are not riding all that way by yourself. Mmm hmm, I'm aware you've done it many times, but tomorrow I will drive you over there in the carriage because you are not in any state of mind to go off on that long trip by yourself. Coming home could be even worse. Don't you realize it'll be dark if you spend any time at all with your mama? You need me, pretty one, and I'm going to go with you if you must go."

Theo put his arm about Vy's shoulders and turned her face up to his. "Anyway, we have both worked hard every day for a month now. I think we deserve a day of rest. Don't you? We will only be gone one day—two at the most, if we decide to spend the night with the Seatons.

"Now if you think you could promise me you'll try to calm down a bit, we'll make it special. We will ask Ma to pack a picnic basket for us and enjoy being together for a day. Stop and eat by that little creek with the lovely clearing you're so fond of. How's that sound?"

"Oh, Theo, I love you so much! Thank you! Thank you! We'll leave early. I'll get up and help Ma Taylor pack a beautiful lunch. We'll have the whole day together—just the two of us, and on the way home we could have supper and stay the night with Daddy and Lotia. That will give me a chance to see all of them and find out how they are coming along with the wedding plans—and if they need me to do anything. Speaking of th' wedding, I must see if they have any ideas about where we are going to get a dress for me. I was thinking of asking Sadie to let me borrow hers."

"That's a possibility, I guess, but you did want one of your own."

"I did—I do, but other things are more important, Theo. And you're right—I do need you with me when I go to see Mama. This is going to be hard for me."

"Do you think she will tell you anything? Do you think she knows anything?"

Vy stared out into the darkness and shook her head. "I don't have any idea. None a'tall."

By the time Theo and Violet got on their way to Sally Vittoye's cabin, the sun was high in the sky. They had intended to get a very early start on their trip, but things had come up. Theo had to make a run to the mercantile to pick up another load of building materials because Sonny had run out of certain trims for the porch. While he was there, Theo remembered he needed to buy extra nails and some more tiles for the roof. He examined his bank book thoughtfully.

This house is going to take every penny of my savings before it's done. I just hope I don't have to borrow money from Pa.

Theo returned in the wagon, and Sonny ran out to start unloading the supplies.

Vy had put up her hair, dressed, helped Ma pack the picnic basket, hitched the horse up to the carriage so Theo would not have to bother with it, and was waiting impatiently for her fiancé to arrive.

Ma Taylor handed her son a freshly ironed shirt as he scrubbed his hands and face and re-combed his hair. Theo was fastidious in personal cleanliness and would not go anywhere unless he was perfectly groomed. He changed his clothes as quickly as possible, then hurried outside and hoisted Vy up on the driver's seat beside him and they were off. Exhausted already, the two rode for a long while without saying a word.

Blossoms filled the trees. The spring air was sweet and warm and the breeze quite heavenly. Theo breathed in the pleasant fragrance and broke the silence. "We picked a glorious day for a trip—that's right, pretty one. May, the beautiful month of new life—flowers, birds, butterflies—mmm—a wedding."

Vy didn't answer.

I am trying to deal with these butterflies flipping around in my stomach. Here I am again, Lord. I promised Theo I would calm down. You will have to help me do that. I always get anxious when I go to Mama's. That's why I don't go—why I don't try to see her—because I never know what I may find—what to expect. She could be out of it or acting all crazy. Does she know anything about Sonny Monroe's daddy? And if she does will she tell me? She never would answer any of my questions before. Why should anything be different now? Theo doesn't even know my Mama, Lord. He won't understand her. I shouldn't have let him come with me, should I? She is going to embarrass me. He will probably think I'm crazy with a mama like her. Lord, help me. Please let all this go well.

> Trust in the Lord with all your heart; and lean not unto thine own understanding.
> In all thy ways acknowledge him, and he shall direct thy paths
>
> Proverbs 3:5–6

The verses of God's Word rang clear and true once more—with a sweet peace attached. The butterflies in Vy's tummy subsided, died down.

Theo studied her face.

"What's going on in that head of yours, pretty? Are you worrying again?"

"I'm sorry. I'm afraid I was."

Theo reached over with a free hand and held hers. He looked at her face and chided her gently. "Okay, there, miss Bible quoter, what's it say in the Good Book about worry?"

"Says not to do it."

"Then let's just do that—give it all to the Good Lord and let Him take care of it."

"You're right, Theo." Vy squeezed his arm and looked at his handsome face lovingly. "Thank you, dearest."

The bumpy road and warm sun began to get tiring after about two hours.

Traveling across Maynard's Valley to Mama's cabin from Ailor Springs on the winding dirt road and in a horse-drawn coach took a lot longer than riding fast on horseback straight through the woods like Vy was used to doing. She decided to remove her over jacket and fanned her face for a little breeze.

"Seems like this trip is taking forever today, Theo. Aren't you getting awfully warm?"

"Yeah, I am. It can't be much farther, though. That little spot—the one with a nice clearing by the creek—remember, I mentioned it to you last night. I think it's right up ahead. Yep, I'm sure of it, and, boy, I'm famished! Aren't you hungry?"

"Uh, sure. I sure am." Vy was not exactly being truthful. She felt the last thing on earth she needed in her stomach was food.

Sure enough, Theo remembered where the long awaited picnic spot was located. After about a half mile, he pulled the carriage off the road and into the little open space and helped Vy dismount.

The clear creek was rushing, and cold and the beautiful clearing was dappled with sunshine and welcoming. There were day lilies, Queen Anne's lace, and other wildflowers in bloom.

The thirsty horse lumbered over to the stream, glad to rest and drink.

Theo bent down, cupped his hands, and slurped up the cool, clear water as well.

Vy surveyed the picturesque grove all around her.

This looks like my little stream—the little brook close to my cabin— where I used to play.

She started to spread out the blanket on some soft green moss but stopped when she spotted the bluish-purple and white mounds of blooms.

Violets! Granny, oh, how I miss you!

Lovingly brushing her hands over the little flowers, Violet moved the blanket over a bit, being careful not to disturb the delicate blossoms.

Ham biscuits, jam, cold fried chicken, baked beans, and apple cake all laid out on the little checkered cloth made Theo's mouth water. After asking the blessing on their picnic, Theo immediately started to eat. He ate hungrily for a few minutes then suddenly looked up at Violet.

"Wha—what's the matter, pretty?"

"Nothing. I'm fine, dear."

"Why aren't you eating? This food is delicious."

"I'm just waiting a minute." Vy's face started to turn red, anticipating pressure.

Theo picked up on her discomfort. Giving a laugh, he reached for another biscuit.

"It's okay, honey. You don't have to eat if you don't want to. I'll eat mine and yours, too."

Vy did not smile.

"You're still very upset. Nervous, aren't you?"

"I'm trying to turn it over to the Lord."

Theo moved closer and put his arms about her. "I'm here, Vy. God has put me here for you, and it's going to be all right."

"I know. I'm sorry."

The cabin was shut and bolted tightly, but Vy remembered her little window with the broken bolt and showed Theo how she always crawled in.

"Good grief, Vy! I hope we don't get caught breaking in your mama's cabin, here."

Vy snapped back, "This is—was—my home, and my mama lives here. I'll go in it anytime I please, Theo."

After a few hard shoves, the window came open, and Theo hoisted her up. She climbed over the sill and jumped inside, knocking over a little table sitting beneath the opening.

Vy looked around and slowly walked over to unbolt the front door for Theo, who stepped inside with her.

The couple turned, looking around.

All was silent except for the chirping of a mockingbird somewhere outside. There was a slight damp aroma to the cabin as if it had been shut up for a while, but it was immaculately clean. The old iron cook stove glistened in the rays of sun dancing on its chrome trim. Dishes and pans had been washed, wiped, and stacked neatly in rows on the shelf. The beds were neat and made up with pretty patchwork quilts. Floors were swept clean, and there was no clutter, but Sally Vittoye was nowhere to be seen.

Vy caught her breath at all the familiar sights around her and all of a sudden she was eight years old again.

Theo's presence vanished from her mind. She could hear Granny's laughter, feel her touch, hear her calling...

"...I declare, Sally. Look at the lace this child has tatted. Why h'it's beautiful, ain't it? What a talented child you are, Violet! And you're Gran's little flower—my little Vy—my angel."

She could see Mama sitting right there on the bed, plaiting her long brown mane of hair—smell the delicious aroma of her biscuits and coffee she has just put on... Beautiful memories... Here is my own little bed. I sleep here with Granny...

Mama. Where are you, Mama? My mama, she's gone. You ain't

coming home tonight, are you? He has come and got y.' I can't sleep 'till y' get home, Mama.

There's that awful smell. Mama brought it in the house. I hate it. What is it?

A chill ran up and down Vy's back, causing her to shudder. Her mood had changed. As quickly as the good memories had come, the bad memories had overtaken them.

In the distance, Theo was calling.

"Vy!"

"I'm sorry, dear. Wha-what?"

"I been thinking. I don't know how long we ought to stay and wait on your mama t' come back, for she may not return here a'tall.

"There's been no fire in the stove or the fireplace in a good while, Vy.

"There are almost no canned goods down in the celler—only a few jars of pickles. And by the looks of things around here, the house has been empty awhile.

"I walked down there to the spring house, and there's nothing—no food of any kind. It's totally empty. Matter of fact, looks as though no animals have been in the barn out there for a good while either. It's clean as a pin."

"There's no food in the cupboards either, Theo. Are you saying Mama ain't living here no more? Then where in the world could she be?"

"You are asking the wrong person, pretty one. I don't have any idea. You ought t' know more about that than me."

"Well, I don't know, unless she's somewhere with that awful Calvin Ellis."

"Well, what do y' want to do? We'll do whatever you say, but we can't wait too long because we want to get back to the Seaton's before dark."

"I will leave her a letter. That's all I know to do. I'll tell her that we came to see her and why. If she wants me to know anything about Sonny Monroe, she'll answer me." Vy shook her head. "If she knows nothing or refuses to help me, then I guess I will have to forget all about it. I just don't know what else to do. There is a pen and some ink in this desk, but I can't find anything to write on."

After scanning the room, Theo remarked thoughtfully, "Wait here, dear. I have a tally book out in the carriage. I'll go tear out a blank page for your letter."

Vy sat down at the little desk and started to plan just what she would say in the note to her mama while Theo went to fetch the paper. When he returned, he not only had the paper, he also carried a big silver box. Vy's eyes widened in surprise when she saw the familiar box under Theo's arm.

"What are you doing with that, Theo? Have you been up in our attic? Where did you get that box? Give it here now!"

"I got it at the mercantile—from Mr. McVae. It's yours—I forgot it was in the coach's trunk."

Violet irritably snatched the box and sat down at the table, still snapping impatiently at Theo. "Well I don't see how that's possible! This here is Granny's silver box, and it's been right upstairs there in that cabin loft forever."

At this point Theo was totally dismayed and getting fed up with the hateful tone her words carried. He replied flatly, "I know nothing of the box being Granny's or anybody else's, Vy. All I know is that Mr. McVae instructed me to give it to you. I may be guilty of forgetting that I put it in the carriage box for you, but nothing else, dear."

"I just can't see how my Granny's silver box got to Mr. McVae at the mercantile."

Theo, trying to calm the situation, proceeded to turn the container over and pointed to the attached note. "I'm sorry I forgot to give it to you, Vy. I've just had so much on my mind. This here note will probably explain everything. It was on the box."

Suddenly Vy realized that she had been unkind, short spoken, and demanding—that Theo was telling her the truth no matter how far-fetched it sounded. Taking one look at his face, she knew she should apologize for her rude and abrupt behavior.

Forcing a little smile she spoke. "I'm sorry, Theo. I should not have spoken to you that way. Will you forgive me?"

Theo smiled and said, "Forget it. Let's open this thing—see what it is and who left it at the mercantile."

"I know what's in it. It's Granny's silver box—the one I was always forbidden to touch. It has letters, her hair trinkets, pictures, and a lacy shawl or something that Mama spanked me for trying to look at. She told me the contents of this box were hers and dared me to ever open it again—and after the walloping she gave me that day, I never did.

"To tell y' the truth, I'm almost afraid to now."

Theo was somewhat amused and urged her on.

"Open it. Y' have my permission, and I won't let y' mama spank you!"

Vy ignored Theo's joking words and slowly sat down, still with the feeling that something terrible could happen if she dared open the forbidden box. Her trembling hands grasped and raised the silver lid.

There were no letters, trinkets, pictures, or any other thing that she had expected to find inside; there was only the most beautiful antique wedding dress she had ever beheld. She gave an involuntary gasp and held her breath. When her composure calmed somewhat, she reached out to feel of the garment, still not believing her eyes. Carefully, tenderly, she grasped the fine gown with both hands, holding it up to the light to examine this thing of beauty.

The dress was more than lovely; it was exquisite. Not one ribbon was frazzled. Not a single pearl button was missing. Right here in her hands was a gorgeous wedding gown, complete with veil—both perfectly intact—in absolute flawless condition.

"Ohhhhh, Theo! It must not have been a shawl that I saw in Gran's silver box when I was little. It must have been this wedding dress. Oh, my! Oh, heavenly days!"

Theo poked the letter at Vy. "Open this. See what it says, who it's from."

With hands still shaking, Vy tore open the envelope and started to read.

> Dear Violet,
> This here is the weddin' dress Rebecca Vittoye got married in. You know 'course that was my momma, your granny and paw. Me and Maudie has fixed it up and tried t' size it just right to fit you. We both hope you can get some use from it on your wedding day. That is if you want to wear it.
> It was not made for me like I always thought it was, Vy. It was made for you.
> With love, Mama

The tears burst forth, and Vy's head slumped to the table as she cried like a little child, cradling the beautiful dress and rocking back and forth. "Mama, Mama, Mama, you do love me. You do."

Theo sat down beside the weeping girl and held her in his arms, allowing her to cry for a time. After a while, he got up, picked up a towel, and wiped her tears away. Taking her chin in his hand, he lifted her face to his.

"I think something very wonderful has happened to you today, hasn't it, dearest."

"Oh, yes, Theo." Vy hugged the dress to her breast. "God has answered my prayer. My mama loves me."

Dear Mama,
Thank you for the beautiful dress of Granny's that you sent me in the silver box.
You could not have given me anything more precious, and I will cherish it forever.
Theo and me came here and waited and waited on you to come back to the cabin.
It doesn't look like you have been living here for a while. Where are you, Mama? I need to talk to you about something. It may be something wonderful. I need to ask you some questions, Mama, and I hope you get this note.
Please come to mine and Theo's wedding. We really want you there.
I love you, Mama.
Vy

United and Reunited

The sun peeped over the mountains on a perfect June day as wedding bells rang out over Maynard's Valley. Since Ailor Springs Church was larger than Rose Hill Church, both families agreed it was best to hold the ceremony there. Guests had started arriving a full two hours before the service was to begin, and by now, people were standing in the back and around the sides. There was even a gathering outside the church and people at every open door and window hoping to get a view. It appeared that everyone in Maynard's Valley had turned out for this happy event.

The ushers that Theo had chosen were his brother, E.E., Will Graves, Winfield Campbell, and Ross Seymour. Asbury Taylor would serve as his son's Best Man. The young men were handsome in their midnight blue tuxedos but had their work cut out for them today seating the packed church full of family and friends.

It was only moments now before Violet would walk the aisle and meet Theodore at the altar where they would each pledge their troth to love and cherish each other forever.

The little side room where the bride and her maids had gotten dressed was still fairly abuzz with last minute details.

"I can't get this flower to stay in my hair, Vy. What am I going to do?"

"I will fiss it, Min!" said Dale, who put down her basket of rose petals and climbed up on a chair, fully intent on helping Mindia fix her hairpiece. Vy quickly lifted her young sister off the chair and placed the basket back in her chubby hands as flurries of diminishing rose petals scattered across the floor.

"Thank you, Dale, but you better hold on to this basket, honey, and try not to spill anymore cause you will need to save a few rose petals to scatter down the aisle in just a little while."

Dale scurried around, trying to retrieve the fleeing petals strewn all over the floor.

"Okay, Vi-let. I try not spill no more my woses."

"Here, Min. Let me help you with your hair."

Mary took Vy's hand, pulling her away.

"Violet, you don't need to do that. Get y'self over there while I help Mindia. That's what a Maid of Honor is for, you know."

Vy drew back two damp, trembling hands and blotted them with her lace handkerchief. She was grateful and simply replied, "Thank you, Mary."

Sadie looked in the little mirror Lotia had placed inside the room and pushed a tendril of her hair back in place. Turning around, she looked Vy up and down, placing her hand over her mouth. "Oh, Violet, you are simply the most beautiful bride I have ever seen."

Vy protested. "No, Sadie, you were the most beautiful bride. I remember distinctly."

"Not me. No, Vy. Oh, no, darlin,' it's plainly you now, today."

Ivy stared at Vy once more. "What about that gown everyone? Have you ever seen a dress fit anyone as perfectly? It's the most beautiful one I've ever laid eyes on."

"I know it, Ivy, and it's even more special because it was her Granny's."

Neppia Taylor knocked on the door and then poked her head in the door with a warning. "It's almost time, young ladies."

"Just a minute more, Neppia. Mary's fixing my hair piece."

"There you go!" Mary laughed. "That should hold it now. I just hope I didn't poke that hair pin into your head, Min."

"I'm so nervous, I wouldn't have felt it if you did," said Mindia.

"Come girls!" Neppia announced. "We need to gather at the back of the church right now. In the order we practiced. Do you remember? Dale first, Ivy second, Sadie third, Mindia fourth, and then Mary right before Violet and Mr. Seaton walks. The pastor and groom have already come out to the altar, girls. Let's go!"

The organist pumped the old organ, and the wedding march rang out.

Dale's pink cheeks dimpled with a bright smile as she bounced down the aisle, happily strewing the basket of rose petals for her sister to walk on.

Vy gazed down the aisle at the beautiful array of her friends. The girls in their pastel dresses looked like a beautiful rainbow swaying in motion as they and their escorts walked down the aisle one by one and took their places at the front of the church.

Vy closed her eyes for one second and silently gave thanks. *This is the day, Lord. Thank you, God. Thank You for answered prayers.*

The organ boomed louder, announcing the bride.

Parishioners stood to their feet, turned, and faced Violet and her father.

There was a gasp from the congregation at first, and then a hush fell on the crowd as Vy slowly began the walk down the aisle on her father's arm.

Theo could not take his eyes off her, for she was truly a vision of loveliness in Granny's antique gown. The delicate silk skirt was covered with hand-done embroidery and filled with insets of lace. The bodice had an overlay of silk chiffon that accentuated her delicate shoulders and the high collar was made of lace crochet and satin ribbons. A satin cummerbund set off Violet's tiny waist. The dress's antique French lace train had to be a good six feet trailing.

Theo smiled with wonder and awe as he watched Vy stroll down the aisle and marveled that a bride as beautiful and sweet as she could be coming to meet him. He silently promised himself that he would make her happy—give her things—be a great success—someday.

Seth Seaton looked down at his daughter and squeezed her hand on his arm. The antique veil that covered her could scarcely hide Vy's radiant face. She smiled back at Seth, then turned her gaze to Theo as they continued down the aisle.

Daddy, you are delivering me to the most wonderful man in the world. There he is—the one I love—and have loved from the first day we met. I will always be able to look into his beautiful eyes—the ones that make me dissolve. I will lie in his arms tonight and forever.

Sitting in a pew near the back, Sally elbowed her friend gently. "Look! She has it on, Maudie! They got it to her. Oh, how beautiful! It fits her perfect. We got it just right. I was almost sure it would. Ain't she th' purtiest bride y' ever saw, Maudie? Ain't she?"

"She is that for sure," Maudie replied. "Yep, she shore is, honey. Do y' think she saw y' when she walked by us?"

"No, I don't. She was lookin' straight at Theo and didn't look this way. I'm sure she didn't. They's such a crowd here t'day, I don't see how she could make out a soul anyway, do you?"

"You know, y' ought t' be sittin' right up there on th' front row, Sally, instead of way back here. You're her mama."

"I ain't gonna do that t' her, Maudie. I'll not embarrass Violet today. No, this here's her day, and it ought t' be perfect."

"If she knew y' was here, Sally, she would have y' right up there in th' front."

"I don't know about that. She probably hates me for all I've put her through."

"No she doesn't, Sally. I'm sure of that."

"Look at her. She really seems taken with that good lookin' young feller waitin' up there at th' altar. Looks at him like she really loves him, don't she, Maudie?"

"She sure does, honey. I just hope he loves her."

"Shhh. Listen. Th' parson is a talkin' now.

Dearly Beloved,
We are gathered here today in the sight of God, and in the presence of this company to join this dear couple in holy matrimony. Marriage signifies the union between Jesus Christ and His church and is not to be entered into without consideration. No other vows are more sacred than those these two are about to take. Who in the company gives this woman to be married to this man?

"I do."
Seth smiled again at Vy, took her hand, placed it in Theo's, and sat down beside Lotia as the couple pledged their vows.

The old church organ boomed out the music immediately after the parson completed his prayer and proudly presented the brand new Mr. and Mrs. Theodore Taylor to the congregation.

The crowd, rising to its feet, cheered and clapped as the happy couple turned, faced the back of the church, and walked down the aisle smiling broadly, arm in arm, at a fast pace.

Theo, radiant, looked down at his bride. "We're married, eh, pretty one? Or I should say, beautiful one."

"Oh Yes we are, Theo."

"You are all mine now, Violet Taylor. I love you."

"And I love you."

Theo impulsively kissed Vy near the back of the church as a familiar face flashed into her mind.

"Mama! I think that was my mama, Theo!"

"Where?"

"I think we walked by her."

"Are you sure? I didn't see."

The crowds were pouring out of the church and by now were surrounding the couple so that Vy could neither see nor hear.

Congratulations fell into a jumble of laughter and conversation as the family lined up to accept gifts and good wishes from friends.

I must try to smile and thank everyone. Be gracious. So many people. Good friends everywhere. I'm sure I saw my mama, though. Maybe she really is here, but then again maybe it was only wishful thinking.

Congratulations and best wishes came from all sides.

"How beautiful the ceremony was, Vy."

"You two were meant for each other, Theo."

"What a handsome couple you make."

"Let me give you a hug. Where did you get that beautiful dress?"

"Are you leaving for y' honeymoon today?"

"How do you rate a beauty like Violet, Theo, old boy?"

"Here, you two. It's only a small gift, but we want you to have it."

"I simply must kiss this beautiful bride."

Vy found a break, whispering to her new husband, "I have to excuse myself, Theo. I mean it, dear. I have to go outside now."

Theo grinned, looking down at his bride mischievously, and asked, "Would you like me to walk you to the outhouse, dearest?"

Vy laughed. "I think not, darling!"

As she started making her way to the outhouse, Violet tried hard to hold up her skirts, walk fast, and still graciously greet friends as they stopped her, still showering her with a multitude of congratulations and kisses. Weaving this way and that, on and on she pressed down the hill, turning her eyes from the crowd and their curious looks, finally reaching her destination. *How embarrassing! How am I going to manage with this dress? I will die if I soil it. I must be careful with Gran's beautiful dress.*

Do you see me, Granny, in your dress. I feel like an angel wearing it—your angel, Granny. Were you as happy as I am on your wedding day, Gran?

Vy finally finished, adjusted her skirts, opened the rough squeaky door, and stepped outside as a familiar voice spoke to her.

"Tell me you're happy, darlin.'"

Violet whirled around. "Oh, Mama! It is you! I wasn't sure, but I thought I saw you in the church. You did come!"

"Of course I did! Now y' think I'd miss my beautiful daughter's wedding?"

Sally walked closer, held out her arms, and embraced her child for the longest time.

Through damp and misty eyes, Vy searched her mama's face and ran her fingers over the skirts of her cherished gown.

"You sent this dress to me. Gran's dress, Mama. Y' gave it to me. Thank you, Mama! Thank y' so much. You'll never know how much it has meant t' me. I—we, Theo and me, we came to th' cabin t' see y,' but you wasn't there."

"No. I haven't lived in our cabin in a good while now."

"I'm living over at Maudie's. It's only the two of us. That is, since Clyve passed on, and we are real good for each other. I help Maudie out. She's got arthritis real bad, y' know. And she's good for me, too."

"Wh—what about Calvin?"

Vy couldn't decide whether the look on her mama's face was regret, apology, or shame, but Sally only replied, "Calvin Ellis disappeared last year, Vy. Some say he is dead."

"Oh, my! I don't wish him any harm, but I do hope he stays away from you, Mama."

Sally looked in her daughter's face and spoke with finality. "He is gone from me, Vy."

❦

The reception tables lined up in rows were magnificently adorned with cloths of wedding white. Their centerpieces were tall mauve vases holding greenery, pink roses, and lilac blossoms, which had been skillfully entwined with hundreds of violets. Each bouquet was woven and tied in lavender, periwinkle, and white satin ribbons that ran all the way down each table.

Lottia, Nanny, and the church's ladies had worked on the beautiful wedding decorations for weeks and had practically outdone all the previous wedding celebrations.

Besides the decorations on the sit-down tables, the food and wedding cake tables were laden with enough food to feed any army.

Violet glanced up the hill, marveling at the lovely scene she beheld. I would never have dreamed it—this beautiful wedding—beautiful friends—this beautiful day. She knew where all good things came from, and she had to thank him once more.

It was all made possible by you, Lord. You are beyond wonderful. You are great and mighty. You have granted my heart's desire. Y' have caused Theo, my true love, to love me. Standing right up there beside him is my lovely family: Daddy, Lotia, Nanny, Mindia, and Dale. Y' made them mine, Lord, even when I didn't understand. Y' have given me another family, too—Theo's family—the Taylors, and now, oh, dear God, now my mama is here beside me. These are all direct answers to prayer, Father. Your love is too much to comprehend.

You have even helped me to forgive those who have hurt me, Lord, and I can only do that with your Holy Spirit to help me. You know who they are, Lord, and I lift their lives to you; Mrs. Lucinda, Mrs. Mynatt. Even Calvin Ellis.

I don't deserve anything you have given to me—any of it, but I want you t' know I love you and thank you. Help me never to forget this wonderful day and all of your countless blessings.

The assembly was now gathering, walking up the hill, lining up, all of them ready to shower well-wishes on the happy couple as well as meet and greet the whole wedding party before they began to feast on the myriad of delicious goodies.

Violet held her mama's hand, looking toward the crowd until she spotted a familiar face.

Right out in front, waving his hands anxiously in a motion for her to hurry up and come stand in the receiving line beside him, was Theo—and right beside that brand-new handsome husband, munching a pastry and talking to Mindia Seaton, stood Sonny Monroe.

Vy put her arm around Sally, smiling at her as they started up the hill together.

"Come right up here with me, Mama. There are some people I want you to meet."

Epilogue

September 15, 1890

Dear Mama,

How are you and Maudie? I hope this letter finds you both fairing well and through with the harvesting that has taken so much of your time.

Ma Taylor, Neppia, Ivy, and I have put up enough food ourselves to feed an army. I thought we were going to kill ourselves on the corn, but the okra was even worse, and I don't care if I ever see a green bean again. Maybe we will have enough to see us through wintertime. I bet there are a thousand jars of food in the cellar down there. I hope so, as Theo, E.E., and Pa are hearty eaters. I am glad we have most of it finished because I have been feeling somewhat weak and tired, which you know isn't like me.

I just spend most every day down at the creek beating the dirt out of Theo's clothes. His work clothes are not bad (though I spend a lot of time ironing his shirts, as he is quite particular about them), but when he helps Pa Taylor out yonder in the field, I can hardly get the mud out of his overalls. Of course, I don't mind it, but I try to wait until the sun has warmed the creek water a little before I take my basket and head down there. That lye soap just won't dissolve in the cold.

Pa is depending on Theo and E.E. more and more, Mama. He has been having some terrible pain in his arms here lately, and it makes it real difficult for him to use the plow horse. I can tell that it is worrying Ma Taylor. She hasn't as yet been able to talk him into seeing Doc Haun, though.

Today the rain is coming down hard, and Ma Taylor is making bread for the week. I admit I usually love to smell it baking, but it is making me feel sick again this morning. I have been thinking of asking Theo to bring me over to see you all on the first pretty day so Maudie could give me something for my stomach. There are still two more rooms that I need to paint, but every morning when I try to get started, a wave of nausea hits me and I just have to stop. I slept past eight o'clock this morning. That never happens to me.

Ma Taylor said she bets that I'm in the family way and will have a little baby in about eight months or so. You know I would love that, but I don't know how Theo would feel about it.

I guess Theo just went on to the mercantile and had coffee with Mr. McVae. It sure made me feel silly when I woke up and the clock said eight twenty-three. I hope he doesn't think he has a lazy wife. Maybe I'm just suffering from the change of seasons, as another beautiful fall is upon us.

I am so happy, Mama. I love Theo so much. I can't believe how good God has been to me. It seems I have everything I ever wanted. I want to thank you and Maudie again for redoing Granny's wedding gown for me. It's a miracle how it fit me perfectly. I still don't know why that silk I ordered did not come. I think it was just meant for me to wear that dress of Gran's. I have it carefully put away, Mama, and someday (if I ever have one) maybe my own little girl can wear it in her wedding.

Please write me soon, Mama. I miss you so much, and tell Maudie that Vy says hello and that I hope I can see you both soon.

I am your loving daughter.

Violet

P.S. What did you mean, Mama, in your last letter when you said the sheriff came out Maudie's to question you about Calvin Ellis? Didn't you tell me he was dead?

Write and explain. Vy